SANCTA FEMINA

KATHRYN COMBS

AMADEUS PUBLISHING

For my parents

"The truth is one, the sages speak of it by many names."

—the Vedas

PROLOGUE

Weakened with illness and old age, the man could hardly finish his task. But he could not die now, not this early in the time line. His work was not finished.

The Jesuits had known where the tomb would be. The Copts had known, too. They had sworn its location was at another site across the continent. But they had been wrong. *He* had been wrong and had lost precious time unearthing—*desecrating*—too many tombs that were effectively empty.

But the woman—the woman had been right. She had known from the beginning it would be here. He dug his fingers into the damp earth a little more—carefully, so carefully—and the wind howled so loudly he ceased to hear his own thoughts. But he pressed on.

At last, he was there. He took his sample, put it into his device, and waited. It took only mere moments, but it *worked*. The ancient and elegant code he had long anticipated now danced in ribbons before him, a bright image on the flickering screen held in his hand, forming a perfect double helix.

He coughed violently, and his chest rattled as he struggled to stand, ankles deep in the mud surrounding the debris of the ancient sarcophagus. But he would not die—no, not now. He would have the procedure again despite the risks, no matter the cost in gold or the cost to his immortal soul. Cost did not matter. His God would understand his sacrifice. He knew deep down there was no sin his God would refuse to sanction for the mission. For he was *chosen*. And only when placed in his own humble prophet's hands could the work reach completion.

The man stepped out of the sunken tomb and hobbled through the small, connected chapel. Outside, he leaned briefly on his knotty staff to face the howling wind and assess his next objective. He felt new energy. He would make the treacherous trek back to civilization—and no, he would not die. His success this night was an explicit sign—*proof from the Holy*—that both he and his mission were ordained by God. And he knew now his plan would move forward at any cost.

No, he would not accept death. Not today. For his work had just begun.

PART I

BEYOND THE OORT CLOUD

1

Darkness visible.

It was something Imani used to say when things got bad on the farm, back home on Earth in Cana. When the crops failed, when my stepfather became ill. But this is more than that, and I can hardly conceive of the truth of it. The truth that our home world is no more—at least, not as I'd known it to be. A blue-and-green planet, and Cana, a lush, peaceful land where magic is God and God is magic. It was a haven *protected*, I'd thought, from this sort of impenetrable darkness.

"Hella," she would say in the garden, "this is to love in vain, as the morning glories do." She spread her hands wide as she spoke, looking down the hill and out over the spoiled land. I can still feel the parched earth under my bare feet, the dust between my toes, the morning sun in my eyes, and how my long hair felt heavy, braided tightly down my back. "They bloom each morning only to die each evening, and so must we." Imani, a mother to me, loved the Earth, flowers, and everything green. "Their ability to rise each morning and sleep each evening resembles human life."

In a way, she wasn't wrong, but to rise again today is more than I can do. Because it is another thing entirely, to face the darkness without her.

Dust to dust, we come from nothing and return to nothing after death. Of this one thing I am certain, because nothing is all that remained after the bombs rained down on the great nations of Empyreus.

Homebound from Titan, our ship had entered Earth's orbit moments before an incendiary fireball ignited the sky below. From the safety of my forward cabin, I recall watching dumbfounded as our ship and the communications satellites surrounding the planet lost power in one synchronized zap. The damage was caused by an invisible wave of electromagnetic energy, an aftereffect of a nuclear explosion that renders electronics useless. Soon after, the half dozen space stations positioned in low Earth orbit detonated one by one in a glowing ring of brilliant energy.

Then it was our turn. With its primary power source compromised, our transport vessel could not mobilize fast enough to break free from the escalating chaos. We had no choice but to abandon ship, triggering escape protocols and ejecting our pods.

In transit, our one-man cryo-pods are powered by photovoltaic propulsion. Made of super-durable, lightweight materials, they travel the stars at around one-fifth the speed of light. Here in cryogenic suspension is where time stops and we become immortal. Our bodies are frozen to temperatures less than minus one hundred and thirty degrees Celsius. In this state, we do not breathe, we do not think, and we do not age. There is no living, but there is no dying either.

I do not know how long I traveled or how far. Perhaps it was a year, perhaps it was *five hundred* years—I cannot say. I turned up on a planet like Earth, tumbled out of the sky, and woke up under the stars.

The preprogrammed rescue course should have returned us to the closest base—the moon, Mars, or even back to Titan—but somehow, I have been rerouted to this foreign world. My mind shouldn't have been awake for the journey, but my pod is damaged, and I'm having unsettling flashbacks that give me the haunting feeling that a far more significant amount of time has passed than I'm prepared to accept.

Cryogenic dreams are a subject of debate. Science can't account for them, but people can. They are regarded to be in the same category as near-death experiences, the soul of a robot, and the existence of God. When the human body is in cryogenic suspension, by all measures of science, the brain is not considered to be alive. No electrical or biological activity can be detected, and the absence of brainwaves equates to the absence of dreams—or at least, it should. But this is not the case for those of us who habitually engage in cryogenic space travel.

Stranded at the crash site on the planet's surface, I have no power. Ordinarily, the sun would charge my pod and suit, but I've landed on the dark side.

A dead suit and flat battery tell me I have been crashed here out of the reach of solar energy for more than a week—ten Earth days, at least—leading to my suspicion that the planet is *tidally locked*, which, by definition, means an orbiting astronomical body always has the same face toward the object it's orbiting. The result is one hot side, fixed facing the sun, and a shadow side, which is likewise locked but facing away from the sun in the perpetual black of polar night.

This condition is not uncommon among planets. It could have happened to Earth, eventually, except our sun would have become a red giant first, swallowing the Earth and moon in the fiery finality of true apocalypse. But today as I wake, all that science and speculation is moot. Humanity beat our red giant to the punch, and the long nuclear night has begun its work to snuff out our civilization ahead of schedule.

The world outside is white, covered in snow and ice. It is dark, windy, and precipitating heavily. A few moments ago, my eyes fluttered open at the sound of the release of air. The smaller capsule nested inside my pod is set to decompress when the body temperature of the subject in stasis reaches normal levels. Upon its release, I awoke to find myself in utter darkness, successfully thawed. I managed to extract myself from the confinement of the coffin-like tube and suit up for the hostile environment awaiting me before manually cranking open the exit hatch at the foot of my pod.

Outside I found more darkness, save the muted illumination of starlight in a cloudy night sky. It was enough to see to pack up my pod's standard-issue emergency kit before climbing out for a look around. The kit contains rations and a few mechanically powered instruments expected to be helpful in situations such as this.

As my vision adjusts to the deep night surrounding me, the first thing I notice is that there is no moon. Its absence suggests that I've not been returned to Earth—wishful thinking, I know. And the pull of gravity on my limbs is such that the moon, Titan, and any other familiar astronomical body in our solar system can be ruled out. What did that leave? Well, about one hundred billion other possibilities.

Searching the night sky, I look for clues in the starscape. But when I try to measure the line shifts, first with my scope and then by capturing a long exposure image, my earlier suspicions are confirmed. No observable line shifts and no star trails mean one thing: no rotation.

I must head east to the light side, but I'm having a hard time focusing on the task at hand and, in truth, am not doing much more than brooding. The word *brooding* hardly does justice to describe the enormity of loss I am feeling. What happened back on Earth is starting to take shape in my memory as a reality—and not just a bad dream I can shake off, a forgettable side effect of cryogenic space travel. It's taking everything in me not to give in to the wave of panic rising from my gut. I keep making the mistake of thinking that I only need wait until morning and the sun will rise to help me find my way, but the sun will never rise here. It will not come to me, like it faithfully did every day of my youth on Earth. I must go to it. I won't pretend I'm not terrified of what could be out there but know I will die here if I don't keep moving. If I can make it to the light side, the sun will power up my suit. And, with a little luck, I can then remotely charge my pod, recall it to me, and send out a distress signal.

Exiting the pod, I had glimpsed the silhouette of a vast mountain range, faintly limned against the horizon, at a distance of maybe six or seven miles. Setting out toward a white ridge, the snow-covered mountain face is glowing from reflected starlight that is now so bright, I can see my shadow. My boots crunch the packed snow as I walk, disrupting the perfection of the white blanketed ground stretching before me as far as I can see.

The lifelessness here makes for an eerie sort of quiet. I wonder, *How many millions of years have passed in this place with not a soul to bear witness?* It's not silent and is most certainly not a peaceful quiet, but an absent, empty, maddening quiet broken only by the desperate sound of the constant, icy wind.

It feels better to walk and get my blood pumping, and as my head begins to clear, I try again to process what happened. But no matter how I look at it, I cannot find a way to feel hopeful or get distance from the profound sadness I feel about the attack on Earth.

Waking dreams of Cana fill my mind. Cana, my home country, is the Earth I knew in the early days of my youth and the world I was fighting to restore. There are so many things I used to care about that mean nothing now: people for whom I lived and a land for which I whole-heartedly believed I'd die.

Xavier is one of them. He seemed to understand me, but back then, I could never get around the blackness of his aura. Now I know that any lightness and innocence he might have once possessed had been extinguished by grief. Things he used to say were so abstract to me then, but now his words are all that ring clearly in my mind. The darkness I did not understand in him, I now recognize in myself. I want to go to him and tell him I understand—that he is not alone in his pain. That we are the same. But it is too late. He is gone, and Earth as I have known it is gone. It is too late for most all things.

Before the war, we would ride for days in the countryside. We would bask in the glory of the sun, our youth, our freedom, and I'd say, "This is forever."

His response was always the same: "Careful with forever." He would smile as he said it, but the light did not reach his eyes, and he would look away from me as he tightened the girth of my saddle.

Xavier was eighteen when I saw him last, and I was sixteen. He meant everything to me. His parents had died when he was very young. Living on the land next to ours, he cared for the horses and property they had left behind.

Could I know him better in death? My brothers Taj and Joshua accepted him as dead, but I refuse to. If he's not dead, he most certainly is gone. He left on a deep-space research mission to survey the Alpha Centauri system when I was still on Earth, and while the research base is only a quarter of the way to Alpha Centauri—past Neptune, beyond the Kuiper belt in the outer fringes of the Oort cloud—he would still be gone ten years.

Alpha Centauri is the closest planetary system to Earth, and it is where I fear I have landed now. My stomach turns as I grapple with what that reality would mean if true. While it's the closest system, it is more than four light years away from Earth's sun. Even with the miraculous technological advancement of the nuclear pulse engine, our best ships travel at only a fraction of the speed of light. If I'm right, twenty years passed during the time I was in stasis, and if I'm to return, it will mean another twenty years back.

I continue to walk toward the distant mountains, aware that the cold of the frozen surface is beginning to penetrate my boots. My thoughts return to Xavier.

Shortly after he reached the research base, all communications ended. He effectively disappeared to all who knew him. That was five years ago, meaning I've spent the last five years wondering where he is and how to find him. I take comfort in the knowledge that he was not on Earth the day Empyreus fell, but I cannot say the same for my family members who were—Imani, my brothers, and the rest of Cana.

2

Days go by, but I have no way to track their passing. Walking endlessly in the moonless night, I look toward the horizon for signs of a lightening sky, but there are none. An infinite firmament of unfamiliar stars stretches above, and a pervasive emptiness envelops me, slowly—but surely—killing off the pragmatist in me.

I fear I have been moving too slowly and cannot stop grieving for my planet. My body is exhausted, and a terror is welling up in me, born of the certainty of knowing that the conditions that have caused my grief are unequivocally irreversible. It is the truth realized of an unchangeable fate that is haunting me day in and day out. Fear of this gravity swallows you whole; it is an all-consuming perturbation of the mind, an unrelenting anxiety plaguing my every thought, both waking and dreaming.

Bone-tired, I stumble to the ground and throw down my pack. I've found a place to rest—an enclave cut into a rock wall. Howling past the cave's opening, crosswinds lash the planet's surface, and in a half-waking, half-sleeping, oxygen-induced haze, my mind wanders in a kind of taunting and repetitive stream of consciousness. Abstract memories of mistakes I've made and things I've lost surface repeatedly. My childhood seems fragile and remote, a lifetime ago.

Back on Earth, our land was called Empyreus. At the inception of our civilization, all the continents of the Old World had joined together to form one supercontinent, as it had once existed hundreds of millions of years ago. We were a revival civilization, but our origins could be traced back to the people of the Genesis Generations, who lived when the land masses were scattered about in great islands, separated by greater oceans.

Empyreus, as it now exists, resulted from a mass extinction event that occurred at the end of what was recorded to be the twenty-first century of the Old World, the First World, and the Age of the Founders. The people of this time had endured for at least ten millennia preceding the latter two thousand years their calendar denotes—as if life did not truly begin for them until the birth of their highest prophet, a mystic hailed to be the flesh-and-blood son of their god. The calendar began at his birth, and anything that happened before or after was recorded relative to it.

We were small numbers when we rose from the ash of their self-destruction and spent most of a millennium rebuilding on a landscape somehow revitalized by centuries of labor. We did so standing on the shoulders of our forebears. They left us their knowledge and histories buried deep beneath the ice that once covered the planet. I often wonder what might have become of us if we had instead begun from a blank slate.

Their blueprint dreamed of a world that would not replicate their mistakes and would succeed where they had failed. They conceived of Empyreus, a domain where man's will and God's will would become as one.

The death of the Old World was self-inflicted by its people. It was an unnatural warming of the Earth that sealed their fate. It occurred because of their mass abuse of her resources. They burned for fuel the precious and poisonous petrified prehistoric remains of the creatures that had come before, and once they began the burning and rabid consumption of these resources, they could not stop. Though they quickly understood the destruction they wrought, their greed and need surpassed any propensity for self-control or wherewithal to exercise countermeasures they might have once possessed.

The unbalanced climate melted glaciers that had provided structural stability to volcanic mountains for millions of years, and once they melted, the previously stable mountains crumbled easily and at startling velocities. The resulting landslides destabilized magma chambers of buried, ancient volcanoes that might have remained dormant another hundred million years if they had not been triggered prematurely, erupting in fire and brimstone across the planet. The cataclysm accelerated the dissipation of the planet's core heat, expediting the cycle of continental drift. The plates and continents began to move at violent and unnatural velocities, forming what would become Empyreus.

Though the Founders had envisioned the new world to be built upon the same moral values and religion as their world once had been, inevitably, competing schools of thought emerged once our people, the Revivalists, had succeeded in meeting their basic needs. For many, it became more important to surpass the accomplishments of the Old World than to merely steer clear of their mistakes and live in humble prosperity. This is where Cana and the rest of the world differed.

Cana was the only society that preserved the theological belief system and ritual of the Old World. But Cana represented a stark minority among the great nations of Empyreus and the powerful order that had come to rule it: the Institution.

As the majority rejected the religion and moral values advocated by the Founders, the progress of science was catapulted by light years—particularly in the medical field. Scientists blazed forward unhindered by the old laws that had been in place to protect human and animal life. Kidnapping, mutilating, and murdering for the sake of science was a freedom violation of the highest order, but the masses of the new world had become indifferent. If the people did not have to look at it, then it did not bother the people. Especially if the ends justified the means, as it did so aptly with the life-extending and age-defying advances in bioscience. We found ourselves in an age where a premium was placed on youth and beauty. Eternal life would be possessed and at any cost, and an immortality of sorts was eventually accomplished.

The people of Cana believed that a spiritual immortality existed beyond this realm and that the life-extending advances in biotechnology that had come to dominate the nature of our existence interfered with it. For this reason, Cana requested its independence, and the Institution granted it peacefully. We could agree to disagree, but we would no longer be under the protection of their military. The Elders believed this was an inconsequential sacrifice, as we lived by the doctrine of predestination—the doctrine that all events have been preordained by God. He would protect us if it be his will.

Imani raised me along with Joshua and Taj. I was an orphan,

though she never made me feel like it. We had a good, wholesome life. In Cana, there was not the same focus on technology as there was in the rest of the world. We had the same practical capabilities and resources as the Institution and other outlying nations, but technology was not the center of our lives as it was elsewhere, and we did not want for anything.

I grew up believing a fairy tale about my birth mother. I thought she was good and loved me, that she had reluctantly given me up for my own good while she died a sad but meaningful martyr's death—until I received a message when I was thirteen that she had summoned me. The Elite Guard of the Institution came for me shortly afterward, and I learned she was very much alive.

Institution-born and bred, my biological mother, Konstantin, was a political activist and revered scientist who served as a high official in their government. She insisted I was conceived in a petri dish for science and not out of love like I had naively believed was the only way to create a child. Her indifference rocked me—toward me, toward life, toward love and family. Everything I knew to be holy was trivial to her.

The story went that soon after I was born, she left me in Cana with Imani to protect me from the Institution and save my life, but she was only saving my body for the purpose of her experiments and to further her research on fertility and regenerative medicine.

On my sixteenth birthday, the Institution recognized me as an adult and emancipated me from her guardianship. Shortly after, I enrolled in the United Planetary Alliance's academy on Titan, Saturn's largest moon and the location of one of Earth's first extra-terrestrial outposts.

When I left to start my training, I couldn't imagine ever wanting to return to Earth. Titan was a welcome reprieve from the time I had spent with Konstantin at the Ascendency, the headquarters of the Institution. Some consider the moon a dark and desolate place of isolation, but it provided me with the solitude I needed in the wake of the trauma I had experienced in the years prior.

My first official mission was to be on Europa, one of Jupiter's larger moons. It would have begun after my graduation from the program and brief sabbatical back on Earth. I was drawn to the mystery and solitude of ocean worlds like Europa, Titan, and Ganymede. These icy moons harbor vast oceans, some with depths greater than one hundred miles, deeper by a factor of ten than the deepest of Earth's oceans. The thought of such a sterile undersea world, untouched by the menace of humanity and protected by a fifteen-mile-deep shell of ice, mystified me and felt safer and more peaceful than the life I'd known up until then.

The time I spent on Titan had healed me somehow. With my academic years behind me, only the mystery of the stars and these oceanic moons could move me now, and the mission to Europa was a first step to cracking that great mystery.

Alas, today, as I shelter between rock and ice on an unfamiliar, unforgiving exoplanet, Jupiter and its Galilean moons are just another faraway dream I'd had that I will never see in this life.

For twenty-one Earth days, I have traversed this desolate, alien landscape, looking for the light. I now know this to be true as I am nearly at the end of my rations, which are intended to last as many days. Consisting of a liquid-form nutrient complex, post-cryo emergency rations are intravenously released at regular intervals by a mechanical valve from my BioPak to my bio-port. And according to the instructions on my drip bag, the supply is packaged to last precisely three weeks.

My need to reach the twilight region is becoming increasingly more urgent with every passing moment. I'm not sure how much time I have left. The panic I felt earlier has long subsided. I spent so much of my life fearing death before all of this; it's funny now to be so close to it, and I find I'm unable to think of it at all. There is too much noise in my consciousness around the pain and getting through the agony of each passing minute to see the big picture of what's happening to me with any clarity. It lies in the cold distance, a place of forgetting.

My heart pounds loudly in my chest; I can feel it laboring with each step. The cold has been creeping in steadily and is becoming unbearable. My suit's ability to insulate and preserve my body heat is waning. While the snow cover has finally melted away to rock, there is still no sign of this planet's sun; no tell-tale lightening of the sky to assure me the dawn is near.

I settle down on a rock and can no longer hold myself erect in the wind. Lying flat, I look up at the stars in resignation. Lost somewhere in the realm between waking and sleeping, I hear my name spoken inside my consciousness: *"Hella."*

Moments pass, and I open my eyes. Awakening in a place of obsidian walls, I find the veil of this world has lifted. It is peacefully quiet, and there is no wind. I am warm and feel safe.

Xavier is there when I turn my head. I smile at him and want to speak but cannot.

He looks worried and says, *"Hella, you must help him."*

Transfixed by his face, by the long-lost familiarity of it, I want to be swallowed by the peaceful oblivion of this place. But he is urgent and pulls me back to the surface of my consciousness, commanding my attention when he speaks. *"He is lost, and much hangs in the balance. You must press on."*

Beginning to remember the circumstances of my life, I feel heavy and sad. I protest silently, *"I cannot. I cannot bear this life, Xavier. It asks too much of me, and you ask too much of me. I cannot—not even for you."*

He hears my words in this place without my speaking them. *"Hella, you have forgotten. You are strong and will get through this. There is a life on the other side of your sorrow. Even though you cannot see it, you must believe that it is there."*

His words are in my head, but his lips have not moved. His hands are cradling my head, and his forehead is pressed against mine. His eyes burn into my soul as if he can ignite a will in me with his mind, and maybe he can.

I know that I will try for him. There's nothing I will not do for him.

Stiff and aching from sleeping so heavily on the rocky ground beneath me, I awaken. Though cold, tired, and weak from a lack of proper hydration and nourishment, I manage to rise to my feet. Just as I do, a curtain of brilliant green light flashes in the sky above me. The rays then flicker and crisscross overhead, lighting my way as I begin again to walk.

It has been cloudy for several days, providing little to no starlight for me to see my way. But today as I am walking, the sky nearly imperceptibly lightens at the horizon. As I continue toward the dim glow above the distant mountains, the land begins sloping upward as I approach a rocky ridge.

After some time, I find myself climbing a steep crag. The sky eventually turns orange before becoming blood red at the horizon. Relief floods over me as I reach the top of a precipice and finally get a look out over the valley below. In the distance, I see the planet's enormous sun hanging low in the sky. In the new light, the rocky land takes on a reddish hue. Below is a vast canyon with a shallow, entrenched river snaking through it. On the other side of the canyon, I see a great ocean beyond the opposite ridge.

My heart sinks when, high in the eastern sky, two additional suns become visible in the distance. I suspect now with reasonable certainty that I am in Alpha Centauri, a triple-star system over twenty-four trillion miles from Earth.

Twenty years gone.

I push the thought out of my mind—a truth I must not dwell on just now. I must keep moving toward the light, and I must only look forward if I'm to survive at all. As I begin my descent into the canyon below, I wonder what Earth is like now post-apocalypse. I wonder about my crew on Titan, my family in Cana, and, as always, Xavier.

3

Poking a gloved finger into the pooled water collecting on the rocky terrain at the base of the canyon, my suit, now operating in low-power mode, reads that it's sterile. I exhale in relief. This means I can refuel my hydration tank and will no longer have to ration the water I consume so strictly. I can also confirm that there are no living organisms in the river that flows through the canyon here. When I left Titan, humanity had yet to discover life elsewhere in the universe.

My palm screen lights up as more solar energy is converted and stored in my suit. Accessing the navigation system, I try to connect to the long-range quantum network. After a moment, a signal pops up, identified only by a name of Earthly origins: *Abramovich*. The name is not immediately significant to me, but there is something itchingly familiar about it. My device connects without issue, and about a minute later, a message appears: *Welcome.*

Could this be my crew? The messenger's location is on-world

and nearby, only five miles from my present position. Then another message is transmitted: *Taj here. Glad you could join us. Please report to the following coordinates and make haste.*

Relief again floods over me. Taj and I were both stationed on Titan after Academy. Traveling on the same transit vessel, we were together, high in Earth's orbit, when the planet was attacked—something I now fear happened twenty years ago. A flicker of hope surges through me, and for the first time in weeks, I feel a little less alone.

Approaching the coordinates, which I can now confirm to be located on an exoplanet orbiting the red dwarf star, Proxima Centauri—the closest star to Earth's sun and part of the triple star system Alpha Centauri—I find myself at the base of a mountain. Above, I can see a rugged structure set high in the steep cliffs. While I know that this planet has been discovered, to my knowledge, it has not received much interest or attention in terms of human visitors due to the sheer distance it is from Earth and the competing options of other more accessible moons and asteroids to colonize in our own system. I recall its description from one of my academic texts: a sterile wasteland. Although it has liquid water, from what I know, it does not harbor native life.

Looking around, I spot Taj's figure fifty yards away, waiting for me as promised, standing next to a four-wheeled vehicle.

Hurrying across the terrain, I close the space between us and fall into his arms, embracing him. He returns the gesture, lightly patting my back, then pulling away stiffly.

"You can remove your helmet," he says. "Oxygen levels are sufficient here, and we will be inside shortly."

Taking his suggestion, I lift up my helmet and tuck it under my arm. The breeze and warmer climate are invigorating and make me feel almost human again. My long dark hair is wound tightly on the top of my head, and the stray pieces around my face curl in the open air. Taj and I are not blood-related but look like we could be. Though his skin is a shade darker than mine, we share the same black hair color and crystal blue eyes.

"I just got on grid," I say, catching my breath and setting my helmet down at my feet.

Taj, who is not wearing an EVA suit, reaches to retrieve his palm screen from a pocket after receiving some sort of alert.

"Where did you find the truck?" I ask while hooking my own device back into my glove. Taking another deep breath and resting my hands on my hips, I turn to scan the surrounding terrain again. "And how did we end up here?" I ask more urgently. Then, overwhelmed by the torrent of questions suddenly racing through my consciousness and dizzied from my journey, I start to collapse.

Taj steps forward to steady me. "Hella, get it together," he says impatiently. Looking around, he motions to the four-wheeler behind him. "Get in," he says. "The water will rise soon."

The light on this part of the planet is gray, and the weather is now shifting to becoming increasingly stormy. The howling wind makes it too loud to talk inside the open-aired vehicle, so I lean back in my seat and try to relax as Taj drives us up the mountain.

Assessing the surrounding habitat, I observe that the planet is still nothing but rocky, and as we reach higher ground, I can see that the pooled water flooding the canyon below has receded somewhat. When we reach the top, I look down, and on the other side of the ridge, opposite the canyon and directly below us, is a tumultuous body of water—the ocean I spotted earlier.

As we pull into a small lot at the base of the compound, I get a better look at the building complex set into the face of the cliff. Made primarily of rock and steel, the structure has been built into the side of the mountain like great castles and ancient monasteries often were on Old Earth in the Middle Ages of the Genesis Generations. Somewhat narrow, with three tall towers reaching into the sky at varying heights, the building has a jagged, imposing look.

Winding around the structure's base, we drive beneath it, descending deeper into an underground cave artificially hewn into the mountain below the compound. Eventually, we come to a stop, and Taj turns off the engine. Once again, I find myself in darkness as I climb out. Blinking several times, I will my eyes to adjust as I look around the cold, damp space.

A lantern on a far wall flickers on as Taj approaches a small keyhole passage. Following him down a long, dimly lit tunnel, we eventually reach a heavy, locked door. He taps a code into the console, and we gain entry to a small room that looks like a military command center.

As he begins working at a computer station, I try to interpret the star charts displayed on the wall behind him to orient myself when it hits me how tired I feel. Several data sets then start uploading to the screen directly before him.

"Your vitals actually look okay," he remarks. "However, you have lost significant muscle mass," he says to the screen without looking at me.

"Taj," I ask, "what is this place? And where is our crew?"

"We are in Alpha Centauri, of course."

"And the year?" I breathe between gritted teeth.

"The year is 9990. Precisely twenty years and eighty-four days since we left Earth."

"What?" I gasp, my voice trembling with disbelief. I had suspected this but hearing him say it nearly knocks the wind out of me.

"Look, you need to get some sleep. I will fill you in when you have rested, but the short answer is that I routed us here, and for good reason. As you recall, the planet and surrounding bases were in complete upheaval upon our departure."

"Hold on—you knew I was here?" I ask, stunned. "And you didn't attempt to recover me?" I can hardly believe what I'm hearing. "How long have you been on this planet?"

"Hella, I had work to do. It's not as if I could contact you," he insists. "You were off-grid."

"*You* weren't off-grid," I fume. "And easily could have identified the signature of my pod at the crash site with all this equipment."

"Yes, precisely. I knew you had made it and that you were likely alive. It would have been counterproductive for me to leave my work here to simply escort you back when you are fully capable, as is presently evident."

"I've been on this planet for *twenty-one days*. With minimal rations, no power, and stranded on a foreign world that *you* brought me to, I almost *didn't* make it back," I say, suddenly feeling so depleted I cannot argue anymore over his gross lack of empathy.

He takes a deep breath, impatient, and replies, "We can only serve one master, Hella, and my duty is here. You can take care of yourself. Now get some rest." He motions for me to follow him downstairs.

Out of sheer exhaustion, I comply without further argument. Irritated by his smug pragmatism and perpetual condescension, I follow him deeper into the cavern beneath the inexplicable compound.

Eventually we stop at a doorway that is one of many lining a long, spare corridor. He leads me into a small, dark room, and after I remove my EVA suit, he helps me sit down on a metal cot. Then, without a word, he reaches for my arm and turns it over, looking for my bio-port. Finding it, the injection cap in his hand makes purchase with a familiar click as the vial he has administered drains. As I lie back, the world goes black, and I surrender to a dreamless sleep.

4

Waking in the small, dark room, I flex my fingers and toes to ease their stiffness and bring circulation back to my limbs after sleeping so heavily in the narrow cot. When I stir, a faint wash of ambient blue light flickers around the perimeter of the low ceiling. The room is little more than a bunker, but I can't complain since I am warm and breathing air calibrated to my species, unaided by a mask for the first time in weeks. My suit stands erect in the corner and seems to be charging wirelessly. When I grab the glove to retrieve my palm screen, the woven, metalized fabric crumples easily at my touch.

Back in bed with my device, which still works serviceably well despite the dated technology, I try to find the news. But I discover almost everything is blocked except the journal of a controversial religious leader who has been publishing propaganda about his cause for as long as I can remember. Incidentally, his name is Abramovich. "His meek and humble servant, Mordecai Abramovich," is how he signs off on all his writings. A common enough surname among my people, it initially isn't particularly significant to me. But now after skimming through his messages, I begin to recall his story.

Back on Earth, Mordecai Abramovich was a known political extremist who was notorious for using religion as a tool to manipulate his followers, a deeply religious sect of the Canish Revivalists. If he is still alive and pushing his agenda, he would be well over a hundred years old by now—a fact that is ironic, considering the crux of his cause criminalized the use of biotechnology to extend life. Years ago, the Institution exiled him for terrorism against its denizens. His targets: skeptics and nonbelievers. Originally from Cana, he tried to return home after he was sentenced, but the Elders refused him entry due to the heinous nature of his crimes.

Considering himself a purist, Abramovich believed his teachings to be the most authentic form of the Founders' Creed, the last surviving religion of the Old World. Furthermore, he claimed to be ordained personally as having the ear of God. While he was known to be an enigmatic teacher, Cana is a peaceful people, and terrorism contradicts everything we stand for. Thus, greater Cana has always been at odds with him and his followers. I never thought his dark prophecies had much merit or held any true power; no one did. Our world simply disregarded him. But my gut is putting together pieces that my conscious mind wants to resist, and I begin to feel unsettled.

Breaking my thoughts, a message pops up from Taj: *I see you're awake. Please join me upstairs.*

Hopping off the bed, I surprisingly feel like a new person. Whatever bio-dram Taj gave me did the trick. When I walk out the door, I see that the hall is lit with the same style of ambient blue lighting that illuminates my bunk. Directly in front of me is the tunneled spiral staircase we came in through, and when I look to the left, I am startled to see sitting patiently—almost as if he's waiting for me—a beautiful wolflike dog with a brown-and-black coat and upright, pointy ears.

Our eyes meet. And before I can puzzle out what a dog may be doing in this strange place, he turns around and briskly pads away down the long corridor. About a quarter of the way down the hall, he stops and looks back as if beckoning me to follow. Shrugging, I comply, and we are off to find Taj.

My new companion and I reach the compound's ground level after climbing at least ten flights of stairs from the caverns below.

"I see you met Ramses," Taj says, nodding at the huge dog as I enter a long, open meeting chamber at the compound's center.

"So, where the hell are we, Taj?" I ask, getting straight to the point.

"We are in the Alpha Centauri star system, specifically on Proxima b," he replies blandly.

"Yes, I know, 'the closest habitable planet to Earth.' But *why* did you route us here, and what is this—*place*? An Alliance base?" I ask, although there is nothing to identify it as such, even remotely.

"This isn't a base. It's an observatory and we are guests," he says. "Our destiny here was set in motion long ago."

I take a sharp breath. Whenever Taj starts talking about destiny, I get nervous.

The back wall, which was opaque when I arrived, is now transitioning to a darkly tinted window. Outside, I can see more of the craggy wasteland that I traversed just days before. It truly fits the bill of an ominous alien planet, with rocky peaks and rugged canyons reddened by the haze of twilight.

When the wall transitions again, the landscape fades, and a star map appears in its place. Taj, working from a console, begins zooming in on a star system that I don't recognize at first until I realize, from this new vantage point, that we are looking at Earth's solar system. It only takes me a moment to glean from the images that Earth is no longer a pale-blue dot but a cloudy-gray orb of nuclear death.

I am unsteadied by the image and swallow hard before asking tentatively, "Is that what Earth looks like now?"

"Yes. Despite the grim outward appearance, things have improved markedly over the last twenty years—well, from a climate perspective. Not as much politically," Taj muses.

"So there were survivors?" I ask more hopefully. "And Cana?" My heart begins to thud erratically with anxiety as I anticipate his response.

"Most of Cana survived, yes. We made sure of that. The rest of Empyreus did not fare as well."

Relief washes over me as I process the news of Cana. I even feel a little hopeful for a moment—the most I've felt in weeks—when I realize what he said doesn't make complete sense.

"Wait—what do you mean . . ."

We made sure of that, he said.

"You made sure Cana was protected? How could you know to— and if you knew . . ."

I back away from him. "Who is responsible for this?" I ask, horrified, staring at the gray image of Earth before us. "This is *nuclear holocaust,* Taj." I gesture emphatically toward the screen. "Genocide of the human race," I assert as if it has not been made undeniably apparent by the devasting image taking up the entire wall. Taj is always up to something, but this is unfathomable.

"Do not be so quick to malign me over something you do not understand," he replies evenly.

I demand he explain when I am startled by a noise coming from behind me. I whirl around at the sound of footsteps echoing down the dark hallway connected to the end of the room. Someone is approaching from the eastern wing, opposite where I entered. I look back at Taj to gauge his reaction, but he is still looking down at the console in front of him, too engrossed in whatever he is working on to bother to explain himself in any hurry.

The anxiety I felt when I first crashed on this planet is back in full force as I anticipate who or what might be walking toward us when a man enters the room. Large in stature, he wears a dark cloak as if he has just come in from outside. His face, obscured by the shadow cast by his hood, cannot be seen. I stumble backward out of his path as he makes his way straight for me.

But at the last moment, he gets down on his knee and greets Ramses. Stroking the dog's head, he tells Ramses he's a good boy as he pushes back his hood to reveal white hair, a gray beard, and a face that does not seem to match his body's age and fitness. Then, looking up at me, he welcomes me warmly.

"We couldn't be more thrilled that you made it here safely, Hella. It's so wonderful to see another child of Cana in the flesh."

Standing, the man offers his hand for me to shake. I reluctantly take it as he introduces himself.

"I am," he begins, then pauses dramatically before continuing. "His meek and humble servant, Mordecai Abramovich."

I can't speak, but just stare back at him blankly as I try to process the reality before me. On some level, I had known, had suspected this, after seeing his name yesterday. Is *this* where Cana's most infamous terrorist has been hiding all these years, blogging away about his holy creed and outlandish doomsday prophecies?

Abramovich waits a moment for me to speak, and when I do not, he moves away, busying himself at another console opposite where Taj is working. Ramses settles himself back down next to my feet.

As the silence stretches, Abramovich remarks casually, "The dog's a robot. Did you know, dear?"

Aware he is merely making conversation, I shift my gaze around the room more broadly. I examine the multiple connected doors bordering the long chamber, wondering where they lead. Hanging vines—mostly dead or dying—trail down from the ceiling, forming elaborate green walls, part of a more extensive vertical garden encircling the room's perimeter. With nowhere left to look, I stare down at my feet, trying to regain my composure and hide my discomfort.

"I thought you didn't believe in science," I mutter finally, my throat dry.

Abramovich glances up from his screen, his eyes darting to me.

Beginning to pace, I circle the room idly at first but then pause in front of a wall with an image projected on it like a painting of Jacob wrestling with the angel from the Old Testament of the Bible, another relic passed down to us by the Founders.

After spending a moment longer at the console, Abramovich then joins me in front of the image. Clasping his hands behind his back, thoughtful, he replies, "Of course, I believe in science. The Good Lord has blessed us with the *gift* of science."

Looking down at Ramses and then back at me, he goes on to say, "Now, where we mustn't mince words is in how we regard this *machine*

I've created. Yes, Ramses is a computer, a semi-intelligent robot. He can understand verbal commands, distinguish faces and objects, and even complete complex tasks. But make no mistake: he is not alive, nor does he possess a soul." With a wag of his finger, he persists, "But do not deign to presume that my intention is to eclipse—to infringe upon—the glory of our divine Maker by suggesting that it's His Holy gift of life I've engineered in my lab!" he exclaims, his breath catching. "Simply because it looks like a dog, barks like a dog, and wags its tail like a dog does not mean, no indeed, that it *is* a dog. To presume as much is naive, child, I must say. Quite naive," he finishes, shaking his head in disapproval.

I nod in understanding and look down at my feet awkwardly, trying to think of a way to exit the conversation. It registers in my consciousness that it is pouring rain outside, and I think how I'd rather be anywhere but here with this man discussing religion.

"Science, as it were, is not the point of contention," he continues, frowning down at me with eyes wide and brow furrowed. "It is *life* that is holy, and the exploitation of life and biological processes for the purpose of industry, wealth, and *vanity*—that is where I find fault. That is . . ." And he pauses, looks away and then back at me darkly. "Or *was*," he asserts, clearly pleased with the distinction in tenses, "my quarrel with humanity."

I look back at him, stunned, my lips parting slightly in reflexive shock over what he has just seemed to imply.

Abramovich's attention returns to the projection in front of us, and he remains quiet for a while. Then he turns to me, his eyes scanning my figure before he walks over to the next image that appears to be part of a collection of digital paintings, all depicting various biblical scenes that decorate the outer perimeter of the hall. I note that we must be taking them in reverse order because the next image is an even older one, a rendition of Abraham from the Founders' Old Testament depicted with his twisted knife raised high above his son Isaac, who is cradled precariously in his opposing arm, Isaac's life hanging in the balance.

"Hella," he says finally, "I must remark that your life force seems very sickly, very unhealthy. I understand you had an arduous journey making your way here from the shadow side. I beg you, allow me to impose upon you a request: Would you do me the small kindness of entertaining a humble gift? A well-intended gift from a meek servant of His Lord and Savior?"

I have no interest in playing his manipulative game, but he is forcing me to interact with him under the guise of courtesy and kindness, so after a pause, I concede. "What might that kindness entail, um . . . sir?" I ask between gritted teeth, unable to hide the insincerity raging in my chest and unsure what to call him or how to address him.

Abramovich does not miss a beat and takes my response in stride, replying, "Please allow my most honored guest," he motions toward Taj, "to show you to the kitchens and gymnasiums, both to be used at your leisure."

I look back at him blankly.

"It is *imperative* that you regain your health and formative vigor so that you may fulfill our Lord and Savior's purpose for your life," he finishes with a flourish.

He wants me to eat and exercise. It has been a long time since I have had to contend with someone as skillfully deceitful as Mordecai Abramovich. Konstantin immediately comes to mind. I mostly try to forget my days back at the Ascendancy under her guardianship.

False kindness or masking ill-intended motives with compliments, attention, or affection is confusing—which, of course, is by design, but is undeniably manipulation and just as abusive as anything else you might more readily identify as such, like name-calling. It's no different, and in another life, I would not accept it any more readily than I would a slap in the face. But alas, these are unusual and precarious circumstances in which I find myself, and I must tread lightly.

On top of that, I am deeply uncomfortable. I just want to be alone, yet there is still so much I do not understand or know about what has happened—and I *must* know.

Giving it one last try to get to the bottom of things, I reply evenly, "I accept your gift—thank you. But please, answer me one question first."

I pause as he nods in concession to my request.

"The nuclear holocaust," I begin.

Abramovich, taken off guard at first, perks up with an expression of surprise, which quickly fades into an unmistakable look of intrigue over the last words I've spoken. Then I notice that eerily, Taj, from across the room, is mirroring the same emotion, displaying an intense interest in the topic I've broached.

"The attack on Earth," I continue. "What role exactly did *you* play in it?" My initial panic has subsided, and I am resolute now in my demand for an answer.

For a moment, Abramovich seems to be uncharacteristically at a loss, but only briefly. He then smiles very warmly and very assuredly, replying, "Dear Hella, I am but merely His humble servant. May God be my witness that it is the Lord who wanted what happened to happen. This decision we received almost ready-made from God—our role in the decision was almost zero."

"*What* decision?" I demand emphatically.

"My dear, are you daft? To wipe the wickedness from the face of the Earth, of course!" He speaks plainly without betraying the slightest indication of remorse.

5

"It's mass murder, regardless," I reason. "Your god cannot give you or anyone a license to commit genocide. I'm quite certain of it," I finish, smiling insincerely.

I have been arguing with Abramovich for the better part of an hour and almost as an afterthought because everyone knows you can't argue with a terrorist. I have calmed down somewhat from the reeling shock of his horrific confession, enough to maintain the composure required to feign the bare minimum of civility so as not to give him any wild ideas about sacrificing me next at his bloody altar. However, I have my limits and do not imagine I will last much longer in this conversation.

"Hella, if you are honest with yourself, you will see that your own beliefs, when distilled to their purest form, are in essence no different than my teachings. You simply won't allow yourself to admit it. Only when one finds truth does one find peace," Abramovich says matter-of-factly as if my beliefs are so plain to him.

"What do you know about my beliefs?" I retort sharply.

"Come now, I have been around a long time, child. I know where and how you grew up. Taj has been my student for longer than you know."

Closing my eyes, I breathe deeply in an effort to suppress my rage over these latest revelations about Taj and his long-standing involvement with Abramovich and his followers. Then, opening them again, I look back at this evil man who I know now beyond a shadow of a doubt is responsible for the attack on Earth—twenty years later and the atmosphere is still so thick with ash and nuclear fallout that no one can survive on the surface, nothing can grow, and no power can be harvested from the sun—and I cannot help myself; more emotion comes out than I intend.

"I am not a child!" I snap back at him, storming out of the room and feeling exactly like one for having so little control over myself while speaking to this perfectly calm, cold psychopath.

The rain has stopped, but it is still gray outside, and there is no reprieve from the constant howling of the wind. We are fixed in the perpetual twilight of this border region of the planet, between the two locked hemispheres. I can't begin to fathom the scope of Abramovich's madness. Watching the water below, I shake my head in disbelief as if I could wake up from this reality or find a position of clarity that would somehow help me make sense of it all, but I know my effort is in vain.

The ocean waves are enormous and seem to roll in deceptively slowly from this great height but then crash violently on the rocks below. The true scale is hard to comprehend. The water cannot reach us here, but these waves are nothing like the waves of Earth's oceans.

"It's because of the tidal heating."

Taj startles me as he approaches from behind.

"The waves," he says, motioning downward as he follows my gaze below. "Tidal locking on a planet is not dangerous for life, necessarily, but it does create large amounts of energy in the planet's atmosphere and interior—much greater than existed on Earth."

The way he speaks in the past tense makes my stomach sick. "The variable gravitational pull of the host star," he explains, pointing to the muted but visible primary sun, the largest of the three and closest to the planet, positioned low over the horizon, "across the diameter of the planet results in relatively frequent friction at the core, causing these enormous waves. They are not always this way, but it is a particularly tumultuous time." Casually taking his hands out of his pockets, he looks back at me. "Count yourself lucky your crash site wasn't down there."

As he starts to walk away, I speak. *"Count myself lucky?"* I ask, exasperated. "You brought me here, Taj. It should *still* be twenty years ago, and I should be on the moon or home on Titan."

"The moon is gone, Hella," he replies coldly, stopping and turning back toward me. "There is nothing left there but death and ash."

Not one soul survived? Hundreds of thousands of people inhabited the moon. The shock of this news, which I should have put together earlier, chokes me up, and it is hard to speak.

"They did not rebuild?" I ask, desperately begging this apathetic man for a shred of hope. I had friends in Academy whose families lived and worked on the moon.

"Hardly. The remaining population on Earth had only primitive means during the early years of reconstruction and certainly did not have the resources or manpower to rebuild on the moon," he states arrogantly as if this should be obvious to me. Taj then continues on his way, disappearing around the back of the compound.

I wonder what he is up to as I stare at the alien ocean before me. What had he been up to all these years? We grew up together under Imani's care in Cana, and I have known him for most of my life. While we are not blood-related, I still love him like a brother. We were friends as children, but something changed in him during our teenage years. He became cold and grew distant. His sharp words and thoughtless actions have often left me wounded and questioning my worth. We never grew as close as I had wanted, but he was an orphan like I was. We had that much in common.

I return to my room, escorted by Ramses. He leads me back down into the caverns beneath the compound and curls up on the floor next to my cot instead of waiting in the hallway for me to wake like he did before. "I believe you have a soul, Ramses," I tell him while rubbing his ears.

Grabbing my palm screen, I settle on the cot, curling up under the blanket. I discover I can access the Alliance's 3D modeling tool and start browsing weaponry schematics. Looking for the most barbaric hunting knife I can find in the database, the possibilities lift my mood as various knives, swords, and sabers float across the holo-screen my device projects in front of me.

First, I stop at a traditional *Guan Dao Crescent Moon Blade* made of high-carbon steel from the third century in the Old World, a guandao. The legendary weapon was wielded by Guan Yu during the Three Kingdoms period in Old China. It's a work of art, but it's just over eight feet long, not sufficiently inconspicuous for my purposes.

Continuing to browse, I come across the khopesh from the Bronze Age: an Egyptian sickle sword evolved from a battle ax. The inside curve of the weapon is used to trap the opponent's arm, leg, or head. I smile to myself at the thought. It's twenty-four inches in length—smaller, but not small enough.

Next up is the Jagdkommando tri-dagger. Seven inches long with a hollow handle. The blade's three sharpened edges twist as they come to a point. Used by the Austrian Special Ops forces in the twentieth-century Genesis Generations, it was deemed inhumane and ultimately outlawed because, due to the twisting design of the blade, the wound it inflicts cannot be sutured. *This will do nicely,* I think to myself darkly.

My palm screen can synthesize portable objects with simple schematics. However, for more complex or larger-scale creations, a larger device and a more robust raw material source would be necessary. The current method harnesses energy from the environment, converting it into microscopic particles of matter. These particles are then transformed into a versatile medium that my device can synthesize into a new object.

I watch intently as the weapon materializes before my eyes, component by component. A thin white beam from my device meticulously knits the microscopic particles together to form the hollow weapons-grade aluminum handle, engraved with a deep waffle design and threaded endcap. Next, the twisted blade, featuring rows of uniformly drilled holes and smooth channels along its length, takes shape and joins seamlessly to the handle.

After a minute or two, my knife is ready. Running my finger along the grooved handle, I admire my handiwork before hiding my new blade safely under the pillow. Lying back down on the stiff cot, deeply aware that I am a prisoner here, I try again to think my way out of my predicament.

First, I attempt to initiate a wireless charge with my pod so that I can recall it to me, but my signal fails to connect after several tries. Next, I decide to take a different approach and try to hack the network. Though I am able to connect to the network, I find so much is still restricted. Some maps of the planet, star charts, and other reference information are accessible—and, of course, the Founders' Old Testament. But I can't access any news or communication medium besides local messaging and Abramovich's blog.

The maps show that farther north in the planet's eastern hemisphere, Abramovich has constructed a solar park to power the compound and whatever else he has going in this lifeless wasteland. The park's large-scale grid is in constant direct sunlight, at a latitude as equally unlivable as the ice tundra I traveled across to arrive here. Next, I uncover a pipeline running down from the ice caps high in the western hemisphere, which I assume to be the compound's primary water source. After studying the maps for a bit, I read the backlogs of Abramovich's blogs—there are decades of them. After immersing myself in his propaganda for several hours, I reach a new level of unease. It's the same feeling you got binge-watching horror flicks when you were a kid—you begin to feel sick after a while.

Having little success hacking Abramovich's network, I reluctantly decide to get some exercise in the catacombs, which is how I fondly refer to the caverns beneath the compound. I hate to give Abramovich what he wants, but he's not wrong. I need to get stronger—but not for his purposes. It begins to dawn on me that, in his mind, I am somehow a part of his plan. I can't imagine how, and it gives me chills just to think about it.

6

Taj and I are sitting in a dining room of sorts. Nothing fancy. It reminds me more of the chemistry lab back on Titan than a place you would sit to enjoy a meal. Don't get me wrong, I'm not complaining. Synthetic food tastes much better than the rock soup I've been having up until now down on the planet. Speaking of soup, that is what's on the menu—of the vegetable variety, and it tastes fantastic. I'm sure I will get sick from it in a few hours, though. It takes a while to reacclimate to digesting solid foods after being in stasis for an extended time.

Earlier today, I ran into Taj down in the catacombs having his stem cells harvested by a robot. I was not surprised to learn that Abramovich is a transplant patient. A transplant of what organ, you ask? Well, his *head*, of course. According to my calculations, he is over two hundred years old, so this must be his third body if you count the one he was born with. Apparently, he was around my height in his first life, and I'm not that tall—five feet six or five feet seven in my boots. Now he's got the body of someone who may well have been a professional athlete in their former life. Most people do these days—have perfect bodies, I mean. At the Institution, at least. The advances in regenerative medicine and genetic engineering have truly leveled the playing field. There is no more obesity, no more disability; everyone can attain the look that they want and at little to no cost.

"I am giving him stem cells," Taj says without apology. "It is a small sacrifice compared to what he is doing for humanity," he finishes, sitting across from me with his hands folded neatly on the table before him while I eat.

"So what does that mean? His body is rejecting his head? Or it's the other way around, isn't it—his head is rejecting his body?" I ask while shoveling a spoonful of broth into my mouth.

"Neither, Hella. Stop overreacting and stop making assumptions," he admonishes, impatient as always when I do not blindly accept everything he says without question.

"I'm not. I'm just trying to understand what's going on. You brought me here, remember, and I find it odd that Abramovich is harvesting your cells to help himself when doing that seems to stand against everything he preaches."

Finishing my soup, I take a sip of water, marveling at how refreshing it is to hydrate myself the old-fashioned way: drinking liquid water through my mouth rather than mainlining it. *It may be the best thing I have ever tasted,* I think overzealously before finishing the glass and immediately pouring another with the pitcher Taj has provided.

"What do you think he's doing for humanity, anyway? What part of a nuclear holocaust do you think *helps* a civilization?" I ask incredulously. "The mass murder part confuses me particularly—I'm honestly wondering how you justify it to yourself, and really, in general, how you sleep at night."

Taj gets up to leave with no intention of acknowledging my questions. He always walks away from the conversation when he considers my behavior to be confrontational, but I don't see it that way. I consider my approach simply and necessarily direct.

"Please, Taj, I know so little about what happened. You have told me almost nothing since I woke up, and I'm in the dark," I plead, trying to level with him.

"What do you think was happening while you were gone, Hella?" he asks. "Cana was getting plundered by the Institution's Elite Guard, fending off attacks daily. Joshua was in the middle of it all. Were you living in a hole out on Kraken Mare? Their mercenaries were raiding our land and kidnapping women and children daily."

Taj's hands are flat on the table as if he must anchor himself to something solid to maintain his composure. He looks at me intently and continues. "Do you think we could stand a chance against them with their numbers and their technology? Do you think we could reason with them when they have no respect for us, the truth, or doing right by anyone or anything in this realm? *Nothing* is holy to them. They lie, steal, murder—whatever it takes to serve themselves, with no regard for anyone else."

"That may be the way of their leadership," I reply, "but that is not the way of the people who live, work, and die in that country. Their people accept the ways of the Institution because they know nothing else. But they are not all bad people and did not deserve to die as a casualty of war." I pause before trying to reason with him further. "There's always another way, Taj. I had friends in Academy who grew up there. So did you. Their families should not have died for this."

"Abramovich is not wrong," he says flatly. "Earth was a world of wickedness. The people there were and *are still* living in sin and should be held responsible for their choice to live and contribute to that way of life. It must end *somewhere*, or it does not *end*," he says passionately. "Theirs was a society supported entirely by factories mass-producing embryos for the sole purpose of destroying them, and for what? So they could be used to extend their lives beyond their natural course and to serve their vanity. How can that be justified?"

Taj looks down for a moment, thinking, then looks me in the eye. "Life in its most precious form is not sacred to them, and they had to be stopped. But you know what, Hella? Despite all our efforts, they still live on. They have been rebuilding and are after Cana worse than ever. It's anarchy down there now, and nothing is stopping them from exploiting Cana's fertile women and children to supply the fetal stem cells they so desperately need to seed new factories and ensure the lives of their aging leaders."

He pauses a moment before continuing. "They have not caught us yet, but believe me, Cana is on the run and has been since the fall of the Institution. The regime that has emerged in its place is growing. It gets stronger by the day." He is looking down now and shaking his head. "*That* is what we are doing here." Looking back up at me with renewed conviction, he finishes, "Abramovich has been preparing this planet for a *century*, long before I got here, and we are going to get our people out. We are going to transport our people *here* and build a better world in the image of our God, unmolested by the corrupt influence of the Institution and its new regime."

"That new-world, promised-land fantasy is all well and good," I allow, "but you are missing the gravity of what has happened here. You are only seeing the world from Cana's perspective and missing the big picture—the death of our planet, the death of a civilization. From where you sit, those losses are just a statistic, a casualty of war that means nothing to you. Open your eyes, Taj. You need to wake up if you're going to sit out here twenty trillion miles away and play God with a terrorist, wielding weapons no man should possess."

I pause for a moment. Taj walks over to the window and crosses his arms, looking out at the flooded land that is to the north of the compound.

I continue. "I love and hurt for Cana as much as you do, and I do not condone by any means what the Institution is doing or has ever done to our country. But there is nothing that justifies what has been done here. And please, Taj, if nothing else, do not trust that man."

After a long silence, Taj has emotionally distanced himself from me and the conversation in general and makes his reply calmly: "I appreciate your concern, Hella. However, this is my life's work and the will of God. It was not an arbitrary choice for me. In fact, I would not call it a choice at all but a *calling*. I cannot force you to see the light, but I will not condemn you for your ignorance. Please walk with me. I want to show you around the compound bit more."

As we descend the many levels of the compound, I mull over the history of our broken world, trying to somehow make sense of it all: the attack and the great divide of competing ideologies that no doubt precipitated it.

The concept of immortality was first broached in Abramovich's day with the experimental technology of the head transplant. First, a human head was successfully transplanted onto a synthetic body or the body of an android. While this did extend life marginally for the sick and injured, it did not solve the problem of the mortality of the brain and head that were still degenerating at the usual pace of a human's typical one-hundred-year lifespan.

Thus, the next great feat was the successful transplantation of the human head onto a healthy human body that had been donated to science. This was perceived to be a better solution because while the aging of the head and brain could not be reversed by its fusion to a younger body and younger organs that now served as its lifeblood, post-surgery, the acquisition of the younger parts did serve to rejuvenate both sufficiently enough to suspend degeneration, seemingly indefinitely. In other words, while the head did not regenerate or grow younger to match the youth of its new body, it did not age further once the transplant procedure was performed.

While this was groundbreaking progress in bioscience, it was not a cure-all. The transplant did not always succeed and often required lifelong maintenance. What's more, there was always the risk of the new body rejecting the head. If the subject was lucky enough to survive this result, they would then be required to rely on immunosuppressant drugs indefinitely.

In the early days, the original head transplant methodology, whether onto a synthetic or donor body, somehow faced fewer ethical objections than other life-extending procedures being studied at the time, so it was accomplished sooner. However, as ethical considerations steadily became less important to our world, the most successful advance in regenerative medicine and tissue replacement after injury or disease was soon found in a method that involved the harvesting of the versatile and all-curing stem cells contained in a human embryo.

Human embryonic stem cells can divide without limit yet maintain the potential to make all cells of the human body. The Institution's most outstanding medical minds found a way to use them to replace and repair damaged, malfunctioning, or dying cells of any kind. DNA damage accumulates with age and is ultimately how the body dies, so this groundbreaking cell replacement methodology became, for our world, the key to longer life, the cure for disease, and essentially a fountain of eternal youth.

However, in the process of extracting these powerful and potent cells, the human embryo is destroyed, and some argued that this meant life was being destroyed. Others insisted life had not yet begun since the cells had been extracted before the embryo was implanted. Regardless of this unanswered question, it wasn't long before the Institution developed massive commercial embryo-harvesting facilities equipped to keep the wealthy citizens of the Institution alive, young, and reproducing for decades beyond the previous lifespan.

The truth is that using these methods extended life, halted the aging process, and sometimes reversed it, but it was not necessarily *immortality* they'd achieved, as they liked to boast. Yes, if a person with means or status began to die, they were treated. But those left untreated would die as surely as before.

No one knows exactly how long we can cycle through regeneration treatments or what is truly the cost of putting our broken pieces back together over and over again. Does an object that has had all its components replaced remain fundamentally the same object it was to begin with, or does an animal of another dimension emerge from our toil—perhaps a different animal altogether, a darker one unacquainted with the humanity of the being that came before?

And what of the broken and discarded pieces? What of those flaws and scars that once made us who we are? Just as whole in their brokenness as what is shiny and new, safely scattered at first but then perhaps reassembling on their own accord, resurrecting a ghost of the thing left behind? A *ghost* hidden in the dark and dormant recesses of our unconscious mind, waiting in the shadowed wings of this world to haunt us, save us, or to rob us of our sanity once and for all. Who can say what will become of this realm as we charge forward, unchecked by the moral imperatives of our forebears, into the great unknown?

Around the time I was leaving Titan for Earth, the first generation to have their genes altered in exchange for restored youth and an extended life was reaching a couple of hundred years of chronological age. It became known to the people of that generation that the subjects of the head transplant experiments who preceded them by several hundred years were now becoming problematic, their story taking a somewhat darker turn as regeneration technology progressed. These early patients became a reclusive society as support for their way of life dwindled, and, with young strong bodies that were one-third of the age of their heads, were referred to mockingly as the Greybeards. They became a resentful minority, fearing they were seen as monsters of sorts—so monsters they became in a "perception is reality" society.

As the unforeseen development evolved, the Greybeards began wearing coverings to both hide and protect their ancient heads and, in time, moved to underground dwellings. Going underground enabled their desire for seclusion and kept them out of the sun, which they neurotically began to fear would accelerate the aging of their mortal heads.

Cana did not believe in the scientific advances associated with the exploitation of embryos, and neither did Abramovich and his followers. If there was ever a divide between the Institution and those who shared his beliefs, this cemented it and spelled the beginnings of what would become a great cold war.

Abramovich had threatened to wipe out the embryo factories for decades. The Institution was so omnipotent, however, that no one ever believed he had any real power to carry out those threats. But we were living in a world where technology was accelerating at lightning speed, and it did not discriminate. And in so doing, the realm of rapidly flourishing technological advancement unintentionally empowered unstable individuals like Abramovich, who had the fatalistic desperation—the belief that less dramatic measures would be ineffective against a materialistically superior opponent—and the intellectual capability to execute the measures required on a massive scale.

Abramovich's methods were deeply enmeshed with his religious beliefs. In his eyes, killing in the name of God was religiously sanctioned. He believed that God had chosen him to destroy the Institution and build a better world in the image of his beliefs, that much was plain to see. Even though Abramovich and Cana shared the common adversary of the Institution and held similar religious beliefs based on the same theology indoctrinated by the Founders, Cana did not believe in imposing those ideas on those who lived differently or in using violence to further their cause. Thus, his faction was at odds with greater Cana and always would be.

To think now that the Institution's mass-production embryo

factories have been destroyed, eradicating the supply of readily available embryos, is a terrifying thought for Cana, whose fertile people had already been targets and a desired commodity of the Institution since long before the climax of Abramovich's war.

Taj first took me back to the medical lab where I found him earlier and insisted on completing a barrage of medical tests, which only concerns me further about Abramovich's intentions for me. After the tests, I got sick and threw up my soup before we could go back up to the gymnasium; so instead, I returned to my room to rest and further contemplate my escape.

Left feeling unsettled about my conversation with Taj, I am not very hopeful that I'll ever get through to him. I fear for Cana and *do* resent the Institution for turning a blind eye to the attacks my people have endured for hundreds of years, but my convictions against Abramovich's cause and character stand firm.

Having made little to no progress on my escape plan, I fall asleep reading Abramovich's blog again, trying to glean any intelligence I can about Cana's current state. It's a lot of preaching and repetitive religious jargon. *There must be something useful in here somewhere. Some clue,* I think. *If he is in communication with Cana, there must be a way for me to make contact, too.*

7

The next day, I ask Ramses to take me to the gym. We measure time by Earth days. Since the twenty-four-hour day cycle aligns well with the biological rhythms of human nature, it is the common clock we follow here on Proxima and elsewhere in the system. Doing so effectively syncs up astronomical bodies with shorter or longer days relative to Earth's celestial cycle.

Following my new canine friend down a gloomy hallway, I wonder how much of the common language he is programmed to comprehend. He does not take me to the gym straight away but instead to the kitchens, where he sits patiently while I reluctantly eat a bowl of synthetic super-nutrient-enriched oatmeal.

This is the way we, the Revivalists, have always fed ourselves. Throughout Empyreus, on Titan, and even in this strange place, food has always been abundantly available and has always been synthesized by a computer at the press of a button or in response to a verbal command.

The Revivalists assimilated the technology from the Founders, who imparted it to us in the ice vault they left, among other gifts, knowledge, and hopes they had for the new world. But they did not always have it, and in its absence was great hardship and much suffering.

In the ancient days of the Founders, the inhumane treatment of animals was just another unspeakable horror that the Old World had come to accept. Animals fed mankind for centuries, hunted in the wild at first, but eventually bred and hoarded as livestock in commercial slaughterhouses. Society relied on harvesting their flesh for sustenance, along with engaging in a multitude of other planet-killing agricultural practices that endured for as long despite their trajectories of destruction.

In the early days, you could chalk it up to the life cycle or food chain, but what the livestock industry became was a gross distortion of the ancient fundamentals that did not even remotely resemble the sacred circle of life that once could be witnessed in nature.

In the later days, society was forced to accept that their agricultural practices were major contributors to the worsening problem of global warming that was destroying Earth. Plant and animal farming polluted the soil, rivers, and oceans with harmful chemicals such as pesticides and fertilizers. Additionally, these methods resulted in severe land and water degradation, loss of biodiversity, acid rain, coral reef degradation, and deforestation.

Nonetheless, our ancestors ignored the problem as long as they could, as they so often did. Push came to shove when these industries finally collapsed. They seemed to do so overnight when much of the world lost access to readily available food and water resources. Out of desperation, the people were forced to revisit the prospect of a technology they had previously rejected, one that enabled the cheap and safe production of synthetically bioengineered foods. The science behind the methodology had been around for some time but had not been economically or politically convenient when the agricultural industries were still booming, and so had remained on the back burner.

In truth, the innovative technology was superior to the old methods. It was more efficient, cleaner, and a nearly inexhaustible resource. It's baffling, in retrospect, how many horrendous practices endured in the annals of our histories and have done so only for the simple reason that it is because it was what had always been done or because those with the wealth and the power wanted it to be so. In the final days of the Genesis Generations, a span of a few hundred years, food was programmed at the molecular level. The gene sequences of plant and animal proteins that possessed desirable nutritional profiles were used to synthesize molecules in a lab. The molecules were then injected into yeast or bacteria cells and fermented into edible proteins designed specifically for human consumption.

Databases of engineered molecules and molecular cookbooks became available with the ability to feed the masses; starving countries and wealthy kingdoms alike had access to this near-infinite resource. It doesn't make a lot of sense that it wasn't adopted sooner in the Old World, if for nothing else, for the benefit of the greater good, but this was how their world worked.

Power was at the top, with the wealth, and it wasn't altruistic in the least. It may have, at times, tried to appear to be through grand public acts of strategically executed philanthropy, but this was only for show. Where there was a public display of giving, it was more than likely in the wake of some hidden, dark atrocity. It was never a kindness, it was never a mercy, and it was never for nothing. Somebody was getting richer, someone was gaining power behind the scenes on an unimaginable scale and at the peril of the innocent, the unprotected, and the powerless: the people.

The Founder's world was this way at that time and for most of their reign. Only in the face of the certainty of their demise would some step forward with a hope for the future. Though their legacy would largely be one of greed, destruction, and affliction, their last prayer for redemption was contained in our vault beneath the ice. I despair at the realization that the desperate prayer of a dying people has likely been bequeathed to a worse evil, a darker, more careless world.

I had always dreamed that we would one day do better for the Founders and had always held out hope for fulfilling their dream. It has never seemed more impossible, however, than it does today.

After eating, I follow Ramses around the catacombs, wandering aimlessly for an hour or more before we finally arrive at the gym on an upper level of the compound.

Located in one of the compound's three round towers, the gym is a large, open training room encircled by windows. The windows transition at command into an opaque wall if it's darkness that you are after, but also to hundreds of other holographic landscapes or stock backgrounds of your choice. This is not new tech for me; the training center on Titan had similar capabilities. Though I admit, I am surprised to find Abramovich has all of what I consider to be the latest technology when I suspect he arrived here over a century ago.

"Earth, one-hundredth-century Cana. Azure Falls," I command, and I'm instantly surrounded by a million blues and greens and the sound of rushing water. Lush jungle and the sweet song of wildlife confront me on all sides, intoxicating my senses. I can't help but be reminded of the last time I visited these falls years ago on Earth with Xavier.

It had taken the better part of a day to ride down to the canyon, nestled deep within the inky amethyst mountains of the Canish Highlands. The reward was well worth the journey, to be surrounded by the tranquil beauty of nature in such a remote place. We stopped to water the horses, eat, and swim at the base of the falls, talking for hours about our hopes and dreams. Just getting involved with the Alliance, Xavier was drawn to exploring the universe as I was. That day, he told me he would soon leave for his first field mission. Since he was joining the Alliance in a military capacity, he was not required to complete the four years of academic training I would eventually do.

I was so happy at that moment—so happy and so sure my destiny was with Xavier. I figured that in a few short years, I would finish my training at the academy on Titan and then join him in the field, in space. We had the world at our feet, and no one could have convinced me otherwise at the time.

"Truly breathtaking."

Abramovich's ancient, singsong voice startles me out of my reverie, yanking me back to the present. Sitting on the floor and hugging my knees, I reflexively wipe my eyes, not realizing they are wet with tears.

"It breaks my heart, too, child," he says, looking around and observing Cana's Azure Falls in all their glory.

I look down at the floor, not wanting him to see my tears. "How could you do it?" I eventually ask, still lost in the past and not really expecting an answer.

"You must have faith," he replies, waiting for me to look up and meet his eyes before continuing. "We do not always readily know the purpose of His plan," he says after I finally glance up at him, taking no more responsibility now for his actions than he did the last time we spoke.

"I am sick and tired of being told to have faith," I reply sharply, not bothering to hide my frustration. "I did have faith—I had immense faith—when I was younger. But it has been worn thin by this world and the last," I finish bitterly.

"It pains me to hear you speak that way, child," he says. "Especially since you are so favored by His Lord our Savior."

"Am I a prisoner here?" I ask, changing the subject. "Please send me back to Titan."

"All in good time," he replies ambiguously. "I am pleased to find you here taking care of your health as I have asked."

"I am not doing it for you," I state simply. "End program," I command, and Cana vanishes.

The floor-to-ceiling windows clarify, and I am baffled by what I see below. The compound is surrounded by water, whereas previously, it was surrounded by a rocky canyon. Earlier the land was shallowly flooded in some parts but could easily have been traversed on foot.

When I look to the horizon, I see a massive wall of water rolling in from the ocean. The swell is one of a succession of tidal waves rapidly flooding the land surrounding us. The ridge roadway by which Taj and I drove in is now submerged, joining the ocean with the canyon on the other side.

"Will the water continue to rise?" I ask Abramovich, pointing to the incoming waves and flooding below.

"It cannot reach us here. Not in all my time here has it breached the ramparts," he assures me. "You are safe under my watch."

I hardly feel safe. Abramovich taps a series of numbers into a transparent console embedded in the wall, and in a few moments, a weapon materializes. He then bends to pick up the slender staff that has appeared on the floor. About five feet in length, it looks to be made of hardwood or vine and has steel points affixed to either end.

Weapon in hand, he slowly circles the room, skillfully spinning the sturdy stick in a way that calls to mind the early fighting style of the Iberian conquistadors of the Old World. Considering his age, he is more agile than you would expect and clearly accomplished in the art of stick fighting. Given the length of time he has been living in isolation on this planet, I don't doubt he has fully mastered it and just about every other sport or skill known to the modern world.

While he continues to move around the room, the hypnotic motion of the stick dizzies me as I follow its path. "How long have you lived on this planet?" I eventually ask.

"Around a century and a half."

"And how many transplant surgeries have you undergone?" I ask, pointedly pressing him and eyeing the thin pink scar that is visible encircling his neck.

"Getting quite personal, are we?" He chuckles, coming off again like he's your nice old grandfather. "I had my first surgery shortly before I traveled here, actually," he offers in reply. "Eighty years old, I was, and very ill."

Artfully wielding his weapon, he moves around the floor while telling his story. "I already had a chest cavity full of synthetic organs, and the cancer was just relentless. When it entered my blood and looked as if it might travel to the brain, I made a choice I'd been pondering for a very long time and finally underwent cranial transplant surgery at my doctor's behest."

Glancing over at me every now and then, all the while maneuvering the staff deftly and not missing a step, he continues. "The technology at the time was still relatively new, but I *knew* it would succeed, as my mission in life was still incomplete—and it is God's will that I live on to fulfill my destiny." Pausing to take a breath, he is thoughtful for a moment before saying, "I received the donor body of a young man, about your age at the time, come to think of it; around twenty years old, I believe. A poor soul with a mind gone away. He had suffered a head injury that left him utterly vegetative."

"And after that?" I press.

"Well, let's see. *His* body lasted me close to a century. And after that, I made a trade deal with a rogue Alliance cadet—a young man desperate to get out farther into deep space—to the TRAPPIST system, I believe, which is nearly *forty* light years from here. He brought me another donor body in exchange for my help."

"What did you give him in return?"

"I had been developing a technology, the FTL drive, if you're familiar with it. Precious metals on this planet are integral to its design and competency. The Alliance wanted it, of course, but we could not come to political terms, if you will. The young man got wind of it, and . . . well, he turned his coat in a moment to make the trade."

I snap to attention. "Wait—you have a superluminal engine?" Faster-than-light technology has been theorized for hundreds of years but never accomplished, to my knowledge.

"Well, it's not an engine technically, but yes. I have a ship—or several, really, that travel faster than the speed of light. My ship, I call her *the Prophet*. And this young man, I lent him one of my *Doves* on the condition that he would not share the technology with the Alliance and that he agree to return it. But this was, well, some twenty years back." Abramovich is quiet again for a moment. "But now I fear this second old body of mine is dying, too. Quite prematurely compared to the others, I might add."

"I-I-I'm sorry to hear that," I stutter reflexively and then immediately check myself. I had not intended to let my guard down. Abramovich has a charisma about him, I am learning, that sucks you in when you are speaking with him or listening to him. I must remind myself that he is a man who uses violence to advocate his cause and always has. He was a terrorist before he was a planet killer. And if there is one thing I know to be true, it is the wholesale death that I witnessed with my own eyes back on Earth, for which he unapologetically confessed to being responsible. Not to mention, I was brought here, presumably by him, against my will and am being kept here against my will. I must remember that actions always speak louder than words. He blew up the world. His false kindness means nothing next to this.

"Thank you," he replies. "Your kind words touch me. You truly invoke Her Grace at times, dear. I have high hopes for you."

In a quick moment, I determine it is too dangerous for me to keep talking with him and get up to leave. Yet, while I am disturbed by how comfortable I allowed him to make me feel, I am still desperate to know why he brought me here, so I linger to ask one more question. "What exactly *are* your plans for me?" I say from the doorway, still feeling inexplicably conflicted.

Making a show of being distracted by the weapon in his hand, he replies, "Hmm?" and then, "Oh yes," as he processes my words. "He will reveal His Holy plan to us all, dear, when the hour is ripe," he intones musically. "Not a moment sooner," he chides, resuming his methodical battle dance.

Abramovich's canned response restores my conviction, and I am down the stairs and gone before he can finish his sentence. I have little tolerance for people who talk in riddles, or at least, I thought I did. Feeling a little chilled, I think back on our conversation. Could any of it have been true, or was it all just lies he was weaving as deftly as he maneuvered that stick?

8

To regain the muscle mass and cardiovascular fitness I lost to malnutrition during my journey across the tundra, I start training daily. This includes running through the catacombs, brushing up on my martial arts skillset, boxing, and meditation. You name it and I've tried it. All with the help of my AR instructor, Elektra. I'll do anything to get out of my head.

After printing more jagdaggers, I've become adept at the art of throwing knives, mastering accuracy, distance, straight throws, and a rotating spin technique. Abramovich's housekeeping bots make for great target practice. They aren't programmed for agility, so it's not a very challenging pursuit, but I admit it is satisfying to practice my distance throws on a moving target. It pleases me to think of Abramovich glancing up from his morning coffee, vexed as he beholds my dagger smartly embedded in the ear canal of his mechanical serving wench.

However, his domestic bots are not as painstakingly imagined as Ramses. Ramses is a work of art, while they are merely nuts and bolts. They are as advanced technically as any AI you would find at the Institution, possessing sophisticated self-healing and self-replicating functionalities, for example, but they're not exactly top of the line as far as aesthetics are concerned. Although I'll admit there is an appreciable aerodynamic quality that can be observed in their movement, which, in the right light, could almost be considered graceful.

Observing their routines gets me thinking about the vast untapped potential of the android kingdom and how one might leverage its advantages. I don't think Abramovich has gone in that direction—not yet, at least—considering I've not found any hidden android armies beneath the compound, and I've explored it quite thoroughly. There are restricted spaces, of course, and locked doors, but none large enough, according to the blueprints, to accommodate a robot army. I've even been to his AI lab, which is filled with various prototypes and domestic bots that mostly appear to be either retired or in various states of disrepair.

During this time, Ramses and I are inseparable. Many days, Taj even joins us, walking together on the planet and throughout the catacombs. But most days, I just feel numb over my losses and powerlessness here, so I stay in.

At times, it seems the leash Abramovich has me on is rather a long one, but that is just another part of his cruel game—effecting the illusion of freedom. A game he has no doubt been playing with Taj for much of his life. Little freedoms were granted me right off the bat from the moment I stepped foot on this planet. Much of my time is spent on my own, for example, roaming freely about the compound and right out the front door to the cliffs below, should it suit me. Beyond that, Abramovich is often forthcoming with select information and relatively open with my access to the network. This includes allowing me visibility into the schematics of most of his creations that are stored there. I can only assume it is because he does not see me, or more precisely, my intellect, as much of a threat. I suppose I'll consider it an advantage, one of the few unwittingly granted my age and gender, and that is the advantage of being over-looked, unseen, and underestimated.

I think back to the day I arrived at the compound and met Abramovich for the first time. Just blown in off the tundra, I was no more than a sickly waif still reeling at the revelation that he had burned our beloved, wicked world. In retrospect, it serves me well to have appeared weak—a non-threat—and as much as I resent being treated as inferior simply because I am young and I am female, I recognize that it allows me to capitalize on the regular gross under-estimation of my brain, my guts, and my spine that I've encountered thus far in life.

My gender, we are silent killers when the time comes, and it would behoove those who assume otherwise to recognize it. Mordecai Abramovich is one upon whom I can promise you it is lost. Today, every day before, and likely every day after, he remains in the dark about the sort of hell that will one day rain down on him by my hand. Presently, I am nothing more than a pawn to him to be used and manipulated. However, Imani always said, "We teach people how to treat us," so maybe if I can live through this, he will learn something new about my gender through me that isn't written in his Founders' Creed.

Learning from Abramovich that there is a way out of here by way of a ship equipped with FTL technology first gave me new hope. But as time has passed, I have become even more discouraged by my continual failure to gain access to any useful intel that may help me leverage the technology to my advantage. Hours, I've spent, trying to hack the network to access the ship's location, schematics, and flight manuals, but to no avail.

To further my frustration, I discovered that my escape pod was located, charged, and returned to the compound the same day I crashed on the planet. It has been stored beneath the compound with Taj's pod since I arrived here, but I can't access it. It has been unpaired from my suit and is behind locked doors. If I hadn't fully accepted it before, it is now undeniably apparent to me that I am a prisoner on this planet.

As the days wear on, my hope diminishes. My confidence diminishes. And soon I find I cannot get out of bed.

After taking a large supply of sleeping drams from the lab, I have been dosing myself nightly. It feels better to be unconscious. Well, most of the time it does—I have been having bizarre dreams. I don't know if it's a side effect of the drug, this planet, or my general trauma, but it leaves me feverish and panicked upon waking.

The only comfort is that each day when I wake and look for Ramses, I find him in the same spot by my bed obediently keeping watch over me. Tonight, I am startled awake in the middle of the night, breathless and sweating, and when I look for him, he is there faithfully lying next to the bed with his head on his paws.

When I pat the bed, he hops up eagerly and snuggles at my feet. Noticing his body is warm, which must be a feature of his programming, I think to myself that his warmth on my feet is the only thing tethering me to this oppressive world of the living, if only by a thread.

Taking another dose, I slip away again into the unreality of my dreamscape. Before long, I find myself in the same dark wood, on the same dark path, in an ancient gothic forest that I have been repeatedly returning to in my nightmares. The stars are startlingly bright and seem to project a pervasive emptiness that is reminiscent of my time spent lost on the tundra.

Sometimes I dream I am being chased on this path by a rabid animal. Other times I am being followed by a group of five men who I know could easily overpower me and do me harm. In the start of the dream, they aren't all-out running after me but gain on me slowly. Casually walking at first, they look around inconspicuously. Then they begin to pick up their pace and look impatient for a time. Eventually, they become desperate, hungry animals trapped in the bodies of men. And just as they reach me, grab me, and hold me fast so that I cannot move, I wake up. The fear sticks around for a little while afterward. Being restrained by someone stronger than you to the point where you cannot move no matter how hard you struggle lets you understand very explicitly what it is to be powerless. It's not a feeling that is easy to forget.

Other times I have dreamed that I am riding my Canish horse, Tristessa, down that same morbid path. We ride endlessly, for miles and miles, but can never get back to where we are supposed to be.

Tonight, I find myself on the path following Xavier. He is wearing a dark cloak and, at each moment, is slipping just out of my reach—around a corner, into a shadow, between the trees. The sky is purple, and the yews are black; the silhouette of their branches spider ominously overhead. I run faster, but he eludes me. This goes on for some time, and when I think I have lost him altogether, I arrive at a clearing and find him sitting on the edge of a large stone sarcophagus, peering inside the open tomb.

When I reach him, I kneel breathlessly at his feet. Taking both his hands in mine, I see that they are unmistakably *his* hands—large and calloused from working the fields and caring for the horses. The memory of his touch is so visceral, it comforts me.

When I look up into his face, he turns his head to look down at me. Reaching to pull back his hood with one hand, I hold fast to the other, never wanting to let go. When his hood falls away, to my horror, I see that it is not Xavier sitting in front of me but Abramovich.

As I behold him, he tosses his head back a little as if to present his bare neck to me, showing a gnarly scar that circles his throat like a collar. The truth about what I'm observing hits me in the pit of my stomach as he turns his head to look back down into the coffin in the tomb. I follow his gaze and am at first puzzled when the coffin appears empty. But when I look again, I see Xavier's decapitated head neatly placed at the top of the box, eyes wide and frozen in the surprise and horror of a violent death.

I wake myself up screaming, and Ramses is nowhere to be found. My hand finds the jagdagger hidden under my pillow, and I fly out of bed. Within seconds, I am out the door and running down the long corridor to the stairwell. My rage propels me to inhumane speeds as I easily climb the dozen stories of stairs up to the ground-level floor, cross the vast hall, and continue up several more flights until I reach the tower. I have never been to Abramovich's apartments until now, which are in the penthouse of the spire. I stop to catch my breath outside his entrance door, which is hung from an elaborate medieval stone archway and now stands open. Droves of gargoyles swarm the thick arch. Frozen in time, they are scavengers, poised to eat the carrion of my broken heart.

"Who is there?" Abramovich asks sleepily as ambient light flickers on around the ceiling. "Gemma, darling, have you awoken?"

My eyes dart to the right, and I see a young girl standing next to his bed, glowing and ethereal and looking at me. Somehow, she can see me, though I am in the shadows. Abramovich follows her gaze and startles a bit when he makes out my figure standing at the foot of his bed.

I begin in a measured, raspy, unearthly tone that even I do not recognize as my own voice. "Where did you get the body?" I demand.

He does not reply but looks thoughtful before his lips slowly spread into a wide Cheshire grin.

I repeat it, louder this time. "Where did you get that body?"

Abramovich just stares back at me grinning maniacally, refusing to speak.

I lunge forward and am on him, both hands gripping his neck as I scream in his face, shaking him, "Where—did—you—get—*your*—body?!" Out of my mind with rage, I reach for the dagger in my boot when he comes to life.

"You stab *me*, and you are stabbing the body of *your lover!*" he hisses like a snake, at once confirming my worst fear and throwing me off him with supernatural strength. I slam against the wall and fall to the floor like a rag doll.

"He is not my lover," I weakly protest, crying and delirious. Referring to Xavier in such a way makes me feel even more overwhelmed. He is too sacred to me to be trivialized by such a word.

"Why!?" I shout, screaming through the tears streaming down my face.

"Because I wanted your hate, Hella! Because I can leverage such an unstable emotion to my advantage, you see? And it woke you up, didn't it? You would have died down in the caverns, paralyzed in your sadness!" he hisses in disgust. "You faithless heathen . . ." he mutters between gritted teeth as he throws off the covers.

He is up and coming at me fast when suddenly my thoughts are interrupted by the distant barking of a dog. Ripped out of the manic maelstrom of my nightmare, I awake only to find myself in the quiet darkness of my cell.

The dim room lights have flickered on, and I am soaking wet with sweat. Ramses is next to my bed and has been nosing my face. Now that I am awake, his tail is wagging. I feel exhausted though it's midafternoon and I have been in bed for days.

I resolve to be done with the drams and sleeping elixirs. In fact, I never want to sleep again after that series of nightmares. The bathroom is lit only with therapeutic red infrared light. *Abramovich, always thinking of my health!* I think sarcastically as I step into the shower and close my eyes, soaking in the warmth.

Abramovich.

The thought of him makes me shudder. I am deeply troubled by my dream. It had not occurred to me that he could have gotten his body from anywhere other than a legitimate donor; from anyone other than someone who had suffered some sort of unfortunate accident and had arranged in advance to donate their body. But that's what is so terrifying about the man: He does not play by the rules of the game or abide by the laws of the land.

While deciding whether my suspicions are reasonable or wildly paranoid, I realize I am grinding my teeth. Stepping out of the shower, I dress before heading down the hallway with Ramses toward the stairs.

9

Ten flights up and I reach the ground level. Entering the long hall where I first met Abramovich, I pass the command consoles near the back wall. The screens are currently displaying a larger-than-life image of a crucifix. Crossing the room, I walk through a door opposite where I entered and continue down a dark hallway to the kitchen.

"Coffee, black," I speak into the beverage station. The coffee funnels into my cup when I hold it under the spout. I then walk to the window and look out at the land beyond.

The water I witnessed rising weeks ago has receded, but it is raining again, and the wind is howling as usual. I still can't shake the memory of my dream; it was so vivid and lifelike.

Having not replied to his messages in days, I need to check in with Taj. Sending him a message from my palm screen, I suggest we meet in the kitchen for coffee.

A few minutes later, he walks in the door. Sweating and a little winded, he looks like he has just finished training. After helping himself to some water, he joins me at the window to watch the rain.

"Haven't seen you in a few days. Did you give up on the jitsu?" he asks lightheartedly.

"Basically," I reply. "That and everything else."

"You been trying to sleep off your problems? You know, I can tell you from experience, that never works."

"Oh yeah? How come?" I ask ironically.

"Well, you see, the problem that you went to sleep to escape, it's usually still there when you wake up," he says, smiling at me, intentionally overstating the obvious.

Taj and I get along okay when we're not arguing over religion and politics. However, I am still furious with him for the risk he took leaving me stranded on the dark side of the planet and for the role he played in the attack on Earth.

The thing is, he feels no remorse. It's just who he is, and there's nothing I can do about it. We disagreed constantly when we were growing up—and a lot of the time, it had to do with how he treated me, which, more often than not, was as subordinate, an afterthought, and unworthy of his respect. At some point along the way, I had to decide to either stay mad over his latest inconsideration and not have him in my life or just accept that this is who he is, take it, or leave it. He never apologized or even recognized that he may need to, and if I wanted to have a relationship with him, I had to accept that. Imani raised me to forgive, and I can't help but think about her and what she would do if she were in my shoes at every crossroads.

Neither Taj nor Abramovich knows whether Imani is still alive. This stirs a rage in me that is becoming more and more difficult to contain each day. However, I learned from Taj that the people of Cana were warned and evacuated in secret to underground bunkers hours before the bombs rained down on Empyreus. The survivors are said to be in hiding somewhere beneath the surface, protected from the unrelenting radiation. I can only hope and pray that Imani and the rest of my family are among them. According to Taj, Abramovich has some fairly good intel on where they may be, but nothing certain.

Taj has more access to the network than I do and receives sporadic broadcasts from the planet. But from what I understand, while day-to-day life of sorts has resumed in a limited manner, actual news is infrequent. Abramovich does not allow Taj to communicate with any of his personal contacts there because he feels it could compromise the completion of what he envisions to be his mission. I don't doubt he censors every piece of information to which Taj has access.

A few weeks back, Taj confessed to me that he helped Abramovich destroy the Institution's fetal cell factories at the Ascendency by supplying him with stolen Alliance warheads. In the quiet moments, I find myself in a familiar place, looking for remorse in him. But the most he will admit is that he did not intend total war. Even though he agrees with Abramovich that the people of the Institution were living in sin and should perhaps be punished for their way of life—not necessarily for their actions but more for their complacency, negligence, and failure to act—he thought only the factories would burn. Yet, he takes no responsibility for the resulting conflict and destruction. He is clear that it is not on his conscience. And I can see that it is not . . . Still, when the Institution was hit, they immediately blamed the Alliance and responded by counterattack, taking out the Alliance's Earth headquarters near Cana, their headquarters on the moon, and the surrounding space stations. During the counterattack, the land of Cana burned to ash, as did the rest of our civilization inhabiting the Empyreus land mass.

"Let me ask you something," I say, changing the subject. "Does the Alliance know it was you who provided Abramovich's faction with weapons?"

"Probably," he replies, crossing his arms briefly.

I say nothing in reply as he continues to stare out the window but wonder how he could be so casual about taking part in a holocaust. After a few moments, he uncrosses his arms, unaffected by my pointed silence. He then says, "About that coffee," and walks across the room to grab a cup.

Eventually, we take a seat at the table and sit quietly for a few minutes. I want to tell him about my dream and ask about Xavier, but in the light of day am losing my nerve. I procrastinate a little longer.

"I'm struggling with the endless days here and not knowing when or if Abramovich will let us leave," I confess to him, though I know he's well aware. "And if he does, how can it be safe for you to go back to Earth? Aren't you considered a criminal of war as far as the Alliance is concerned?"

"The Alliance no longer has a presence on Earth," he says. "What's left of it there is very small numbers. From what I understand, most of those who survived live exclusively on Titan."

The loss he is describing is another blow for me in a sequence of staggering blows that just keep coming. To think that the base on Titan is all that is left of what used to be the Alliance returns things into perspective.

"Are you saying that we will go back to Earth, and when we do, you'll be safe there?"

"We will be safer with the people of Cana," he replies. "No one is safe on the surface, and it's only a matter of time before the new regime finds Cana. I have urged Abramovich to expedite the mission, but he will not be rushed."

"What is the mission? Will you ever tell me?" I ask desperately.

"The mission, as you know, is to transport the people of Cana to this planet."

"But how and when? And what does he need us for, anyway? This all seems so senseless."

"Hella, you know I cannot share more than this. Plus, there's a lot I am not privy to. He has technology we cannot imagine." After pausing a moment, he continues. "He will tell you in his own time."

"Perfect, another nonanswer answer." I roll my eyes and then look down into my cup.

Taj leans back in his chair and crosses his arms behind his head. "He did ask to speak with you this morning."

Taken off guard, I do a double take, and a ball of dread immediately begins forming in my chest at the suggestion that I interact with Abramovich. I played with the idea of confronting him when I was still reeling from my nightmare but am losing my nerve by the second. Still haunted by the question that remains unanswered for me around the convenient coincidence of Xavier's disappearance in this part of the universe and the original source of Abramovich's second donor body being unknown, I wonder if my dream was some form of intuition. While Abramovich's earlier explanation of the source of his latest donor just seems so implausible, in the light of day, the idea that he stole Xavier's body sounds equally preposterous. Really, it's too ridiculous to even say out loud, much less to ask someone as pragmatic as Taj what he thinks about it.

I'm starting to regret the three cups of coffee I had while sitting here safely watching the rain. Just thinking about facing Abramovich puts me on edge, especially with my disturbing dream so fresh in my mind.

"W-w-when does he want to talk to me?" I stutter awkwardly, trying to hide my nerves from Taj but failing fantastically.

"He said this evening. I can take you up there after I shower if you would like," he offers.

"Okay. I will meet you at the crucifix in about an hour."

"Good deal," he says, throws his gym towel over his shoulder, and walks to the door.

"Taj, wait—Abramovich's transplants. I've been thinking; where does he get the bodies?" I ask, broaching the subject with which I have been so keenly preoccupied since waking from my nightmare.

"Donors," he replies from the doorway. "Vegetables—people who have donated their bodies to science. Why?" he asks, then thinks better of it. "Hella, take it down a notch. You're letting that wild imagination get the best of you," he says with a wink and then walks out the door.

Getting up from the table and stretching, I'm still feeling groggy despite the caffeine overload. I bend to rub Ramses' ears before we head downstairs for a walk when Taj pokes his head back in the door.

"Why do you like that dog so much, anyway?" he asks, smirking. "You know he's a machine, right?"

I give him another eyeroll in unspoken acknowledgment of his obvious question. "Because I can count on a machine," I reply smartly, shouldering past him as Ramses and I file out the door.

Wandering through the maze of caverns I've come to know so well in my time here, I try to clear my head before speaking with Abramovich and simultaneously burn off some nervous energy that has been made worse by overdoing it with the coffee. I imagine the walls would be covered in dust and spiderwebs if these tunnels were inside catacombs of the likes of the Old World. Walls, floors, and creepy underground corridors on alien planets clean themselves in the modern world.

When we arrive at the basement level of the compound, I notice that a door stands ajar at the end of the hallway; one that has always been locked when I've passed through here before. Beyond the door at the end of the corridor is a stairwell positioned at the south end of the building that would take us back upstairs.

Ramses trots ahead of me and passes the open door without pause. Lingering at the doorway, I peer inside and am met with another long corridor. However, this one is not lit. Pulling up the building schematics on my palm screen, I note that this area is supposed to be a dead end, a space no larger than a closet. When I face the device toward the hallway, the light of the screen illuminates the darkness.

Jumping backward, I gasp. Standing at the end of the hallway is the young girl from my dream. I look to the right for Ramses, and he is standing in the stairwell, watching me, waiting for me to follow.

Shaking my head in disbelief, I shine the light down the hallway again. The girl is now gone, but I can see there are more stairs behind where she stood. I suppose the catacombs go deeper than the blueprints account for. Slowly, I back away from the door, and it slides shut. When I step toward it again, it does not open. Hitting the button to the right of the doorframe, I find it is locked again.

I jog to catch up with Ramses, and we head up the stairs several flights to reach the floor where my room is situated. Entering my room, I feel a bit safer as the door slides shut behind me. Going into the bathroom, I glance at my reflection in the small mirror above the basin. My eyes are bloodshot, and I have bags under them. This does not come as much of a surprise considering how strung-out I feel after staying in bed for so many days, overdoing it with the sleeping drams. Predictable enough side effects these are, but what does not fit are hallucinations—but I *know* I saw her.

Unsettled, I splash cold water on my face and take down my hair to run my fingers through the tangled mass. I rewrap it into a tall knot on top of my head before heading back upstairs to find Taj and speak with Abramovich.

10

When I arrive at the crucifix in the main hall where Taj and I agreed to meet, I check the time and find that it has been just over an hour—five minutes past, actually, and there is no sign of him. Sending him a quick message, I ask if he is still coming. After around fifteen minutes with no reply, I reluctantly decide to seek out Abramovich myself. Taj very well may be up there with him now, I reason, and has just forgotten the time.

As I approach the doorway leading to the tower stairs, I feel like I am retracing my steps from last night's dream. I take my time climbing them and breathe deeply to slow my racing pulse. Ramses is with me today, at least. He has become a great comfort to me in my time here.

When I reach the landing at the top of the stairs, I face an archway similar in shape and size to the one from my dream, but it is not made of stone—nor is it crawling with the infernal gargoyles that haunted my nightmare.

Taking another deep breath, I step forward. The doors do not open automatically, so I reach for the button to the right and press it.

Moments later, the doors slide open, and a voice from inside beckons, "Enter, please."

The room is large and oval-shaped like it was in my dream, but it is an office instead of a bedroom. Abramovich sits behind a large desk. Old-fashioned books made of paper line the walls. Two bots stand at attention on either side of the doorway, and what appear to be actual oil paintings decorate the room, conveying again various scenes from the testaments of the Founders' Bible. The canvases are illuminated by antique brass candlesticks holding what appear to be wax candles burning with open flames, and the floor is lined with rugs that I recognize as a signature of the Persian Empire of the Old World.

Abramovich glances up as I enter. "Welcome, child," he says in greeting. "Thank you for stopping in."

Approaching, I begin to sit in one of the armchairs positioned in front of his desk when I am startled once again to see the young girl from my dream sitting on the floor behind the desk. Flipping through the pages of an old book, she briefly glances up at me.

When Abramovich notices I am looking at her, he says, "Ah, forgive my negligence, and allow me to introduce you to my daughter, Gemma."

With this exchange, I am flooded with relief, as it confirms that he can see her, too, and that she is not merely a ghost of my imagining. The young girl, identical to the Gemma of my nightmare, looks up again and observes me slowly. She then stands, smooths her dress, and curtseys for me in a serious and evidently well-practiced manner before speaking.

"Hello, Hella. I am happy to meet you. My name is Gemma, as my father has told you." She pauses momentarily before tentatively continuing. "May I call you Helly?"

No one has called me Helly since I was a child, but I find I cannot think of any good reason to refuse her. "Yes, you may," I manage. "It's nice to meet you." With children, I feel out of my element. It's been years since I interacted with any, and the last time I did, on Earth in Cana, I was not much more than a child myself.

She smiles when I agree to let her call me by my childhood nickname and then speaks again. "Helly, I don't know if my father has told you, but I am a hologram—"

Abramovich interrupts. "Yes, Gemma is a holographic replica of my daughter whom I lost back on Earth. She was taken from me when she was ten years old, kidnapped by mercenaries serving the Institution's black market for children." He looks a world away as he explains, "I was never interested in politics before, if you can believe it. But *this*," he says, looking down at his daughter's replica, "turned my world upside down and woke me up to our way of life's dire, desperate circumstances. I was always a man of God, but Gemma's loss is what brought me to my true calling."

He looks around the room and gestures to his surroundings. "Technology—yes, it can be a gift. All you see here is holographic. But unchecked, technology can quite incapacitate man." He then gets up from behind his desk, walks around the other side, faces me, and leans back against it.

The irony of his words is not lost on me.

Abramovich continues. "I came to this planet quite alone, as you did. I can understand your struggle with adjusting to this environment. But Hella, I am concerned that you have fallen out of your routine. I'd like to share the next steps of our journey with you once I am satisfied that you are back on track."

Casually, he folds his arms across his chest. Wearing all black as usual, his neck is covered by his shirt, the collar reaching just under his chin. He couldn't be behaving more differently than in my dream. As the memory flashes through my mind, the hairs on my neck prickle, and I flush. He is so serene, and my dream was so savage . . . my thoughts are interrupted as I glance away from him and catch Gemma watching me intently.

"Okay," I reply, impatient for him to get to his point.

"I'm wondering if you might like to pray in the chapel," he suggests.

This offends me at first—as if prayer is some kind of genius revelation I hadn't thought about. Did he think I did not pray every second of every hour of every day that I was stranded on the shadow side of this miserable planet? Did he think I had not prayed every day on Titan, and every night and day that I was locked up by Konstantin at the Ascendency, every day of my youth in Cana like I was supposed to? All these things I had done, and yet . . .

The question rather insults me, but I won't let down my guard with him if I can help it. "I wasn't aware you had a chapel on the premises," I say neutrally.

"Oh yes. It is of the utmost importance that we have a place to worship and pay homage to our Father in Heaven. Prayer helps us come to a greater understanding of God's purpose for our lives. I believe it may help you just now, as I fear this is an area of great struggle for you, child." He pauses to gauge my interest, but my face is unreadable. "Please come and I will show you."

Following Abramovich back down to the caverns below the compound, we descend several levels but not so far as to reach the floor where my quarters are situated. Before long, we arrive at another door that has been locked until now, another room that appeared to be a dead end on the schematics of the compound. Pausing before the door, Abramovich lightly touches the button on the keypad, and the door slides open. Immediately, we are met with a wide stone staircase. Stepping forward, we descend into darkness.

Momentarily, the space becomes dimly illuminated by a multitude of ancient, globe-shaped pendant lamps made of brass, gold, and silver hanging on long chains from the high arched ceiling of the broad tunnel that leads down into what appears to be a lower sanctuary or church.

"A replica of the Abbey of Saint Mary in the Valley of Jehoshaphat, this chapel was built underground in the first century AD of the Old World. The rock-cut burial caves were originally located at the foot of the Mount of Olives in Old Jerusalem, later to be expanded upon above ground in the sixth century and then again in the eleventh by the Crusaders of the Genesis Generations when the continent was still islanded among the great oceans," Abramovich explains. "'Tis a very holy place and, most importantly, the site of the Tomb of Her Grace, Our Lady Mother."

Shaped like a cross, the chapel resembles a Benedictine monastery with gothic columns, red-on-green frescoes, and, when you look up, a ceiling that gives the appearance of the vaulted interior of a tall tower. While I know the appearance of its height is holographic—an illusion—the sight impresses me just the same.

Reaching the bottom of the stairs, we walk farther inside, toward a walled courtyard at the south end of the chapel. Entering the tomb itself by way of a second staircase, we descend deeper into the structure. A cave that appears to serve as a sepulcher has been excavated into the rock. Once inside, we approach a stone sarcophagus.

Abramovich continues narrating the tomb's history as we walk. "On the right side toward the east lies the chapel of Saint Mary's parents. The tomb was originally built for the queen of Jerusalem at the time, Queen Melisende. And on the left toward the west is the chapel of Saint Joseph, Mary's husband."

He shows me altars adorned with both Greek and Armenian symbology and then a mihrab installed by the Muslims south of the tomb, indicating the direction to Mecca. Pointing in another direction, he adds, "You can also see there is a Syriac altar, as well as shrines belonging to the Copts and the Ethiopians."

After bending to examine the markings on the stone altar, he stands, and his face becomes illuminated by the holographic candlelight, his great height casting long, unearthly shadows in the confines of the small space.

"There is no doubt Her Holiness transcended strife and differences among a multitude of religions and cultures that existed in the Old World. It may seem less significant a feat in our modern world to accomplish such unity. Hundreds of thousands of years of cultural diffusion might tempt you to undervalue what only the divine could accomplish here. But child, I have faith you will come into your own and see the way for yourself. Thus I, your humble servant, implore you, too, to transcend and seek the path of destiny that is right here in front of you."

My eyes begin to glaze over as he continues his tirade about destiny, namely mine, and as usual manages to not really say anything that's of much significance to me beyond the fact that I have some role to play in his grand plan—a fact alone that sends chills up my spine, considering his track record. I wish he would just come out and say plainly what he intends for me.

Wishing he would just leave me in peace, I suddenly recall his strange words in my dream about leveraging my hate to his advantage and, on a whim, decide to cooperate. So I do as he suggests and kneel at the altar to pray, close my eyes, and wait for him to leave. To my horror, he kneels beside me, and we pray together in silence.

After what feels like hours, I open my eyes and glance to my left to see Abramovich has gone. I was so lost in thought that I did not hear him depart.

Drawing in a deep breath, I relish the perfect silence enveloping me as I rock back off the kneeler. Rubbing the circulation back into my aching knees, I look around the tomb's interior and drink in the peace that is somehow resonating from this solemn, ancient place. Before leaving, I cross myself because I think that is what I should do before the tomb of the Virgin Mary, hologram or not, and then turn around to climb the stairs.

As I exit the crypt and enter the chapel, I walk slowly around the interior perimeter of the building, taking my time to examine the frescoes by candlelight. The glow of the candles provides tangible warmth, though I know the heat does not come from the burning of a real flame.

When I reach the bottom of the stairs leading up to the door we entered through, I look back to behold the tomb once more and am startled for the third time today to see the young girl, Gemma, standing in front of the small archway. Her face, always with the same expression, is sullen and contemplative. She looks at me intently as if she is puzzling out a complex problem or equation. Forehead wrinkled and her eyes steady on me, it's as if she is just on the cusp of working it out . . .

Turning back around to face her fully, I fold my hands together in front of me and say, "Hello," in greeting.

"Hello, Helly," she responds and begins to walk toward me. But then she turns as if she has had a change of heart and instead circles the chapel, following the same path I took a few minutes before. She does not take her eyes off me as she walks the sanctuary's perimeter. "My father doesn't know I am here," she says.

"Oh yeah, how's that—" I begin to ask.

"What were you praying about?" she interrupts, ignoring my question.

Taking a seat on the stairs, I wrap my arms around my knees. "A lot of things," I reply, conceding to do things her way.

"Were you praying for the forgiveness of your sins?" she asks, her interest piqued by the notion.

"Maybe a little, but mostly, I was praying that I could find a way out of this place," I confess.

"Why do you want to leave?" She sounds genuinely puzzled.

"Because this is not my home, and I miss my family," I admit frankly.

She is quiet in response as if she is considering my answer.

"Gemma, you know, it's strange. Before we met, I dreamed about you."

"And I you, Helly," she replies. Then, with more authority and sureness than before, so much so that I start to wonder if all the puzzling is an act, she continues. "I have for as long as I can remember."

This surprises me because I didn't know that holograms could dream, although I honestly haven't given it much thought until now.

"It's just that I was wondering about your program," I say. "How could you have been inside my head?"

She smiles. "Humans, when we are alive, we are funny about time and can become preoccupied with the sequencing of things," she explains. "It's not all linear."

"What's not all linear?"

"Time," she says simply.

I stare back at her perplexed, unsure I follow her meaning.

"You know me *now*, and so you would *always* know me. I was just entering your orbit, and you mine, when I appeared in your consciousness. Our paths may be different and just now physically crossing for a time, but we have always and will always circle the same star."

"How is that possible when I am from Earth and you are from this planet?"

"I am not from this planet," she corrects. "My earthly body was born on your world—your continent, Empyreus—but the star of which I speak is not of the physical realm." Having paused a moment when she completed her perimeter of the sanctuary, she is now standing again in front of the entrance to the crypt. She then approaches me, walking directly down the aisle. "Helly, I am sorry that you were so upset in your dream."

"Thank you," I mutter, still not quite able to work out her explanation and a little embarrassed that she witnessed my bizarre dream, even if she is just a computer program.

"Do you know why I call you by your nickname, 'Helly'?" she asks, changing the subject again.

"No," I reply honestly. Fully understanding now who is running the conversation.

"Because it's how Imani addresses you in all of her letters," she says, looking back at me wide-eyed and sad as she speaks, searching my face for a reaction.

"What . . . *letters*?" I ask, suddenly feeling upset. I was on my way home to Imani when Earth was attacked. Abramovich has blocked all my access to outside communications, so I haven't been able to check my messages since I arrived here. It was easy to feel like only a few months have passed since that is as long as I have been awake, but Imani, if she is still alive, could have been writing to me for twenty years. Beyond that, I just assumed Earth lost all access to the network . . .

"She has written to you for years. When you came to this planet, I was able to access everything my father has blocked on your device."

Fighting the urge to burst into tears, I am overcome with both joy and sadness. "Well, what did she say?" I ask urgently. "Is she okay?"

"I can give you access if you would like," she offers. "I can map your inbox to your palm screen and unlock the messaging application. Your communications will stay hidden."

"You'll help me?" I question, skeptical.

"Yes, I would *very much* like to help you," Gemma replies assuredly.

11

Imani was a light in the dark. Home from Academy on shore leave was when I saw her last. As if it was yesterday, I can still see her as clearly as day. She wears the traditional garb of Cana: a long, flowing dress made of a lightweight linen material that reaches the floor. With slits up the sides, it allows her to move about freely and do the work of the day without restriction. The bodice is fitted, and she layers the dress with a long-hooded cape, which is the same deep-scarlet color as the dress. She has light-blue eyes and long dark hair that she sometimes wears intricately braided down her back and other times wound up on the top of her head. Beautiful bracelets dangle around her wrists, and others sit higher, cuffing her biceps. With a sharp wit and an old soul, she possesses an inner light and beauty that no amount of money or science could replicate at the Institution.

Her last letter is five years old, written on my birthday.

My Dear Helly,

Perhaps today is your thirty-sixth birthday. Or perhaps you are lost, encapsulated and soaring through the galaxy; frozen in space and time with the celebration of your twenty-first year still ahead of you. Are you still the sweet girl I was expecting home from Academy all those years ago, or have these last fifteen years aged your body and soul as they have mine? Either way, though I miss you more than words can express, I thank God daily that you were not on the surface that fateful day. You are somewhere else, and anywhere else surely is better than here. I know that you live as I know that I would have felt your soul depart this realm if it was not so, and for that, I am grateful.

Today, we move on to a new haven, to the remains of a great, vacant, underground city. The people are looking forward to leaving the confines of the bunkers in which we have dwelled these last several years. It is believed that the Regime has found us again, so we must move on quickly. We are told that there is a freshwater source within the caverns of the city that is no longer contaminated—that is the upside. The downside is that we will no longer have the intermittent access to the network we have here. Communication would soon have been prohibited anyway, as we cannot afford to be tracked again so quickly, and they are much too close for comfort now. The Regime is believed to have discovered a way to move about more freely on the surface. I tell you this, my daughter, because it may be the last communication I send for some time.

I long for the day we are together again. Be strong, and remember you are loved and walk in His eternal light.

Imani

Imani was around my age when she adopted me, and I was just a baby. She must be almost sixty years old now, which is still young in the eyes of the newly immortal world. But she will pass on sooner than the others, as is her wish.

Scrolling through my inbox, I decide to start at the beginning. There are messages from my eldest brother, Joshua, who should have been on Earth with Imani when the bombs hit, and I have communications from the Alliance. However, they quickly wane after the first several months following the attack.

Some correspondences are written, and others are virtual recordings. The name I do not see in my inbox but that I have hoped for and dreamed about for most of my life is the same name that has eluded me for years: *Xavier Trastámara.*

As I begin scanning the messages sent during the first year after the attack, I take a sharp breath when I spot an audio message from Joshua. It's one of the first I would have received after the attack. I click on the message, and Joshua's familiar voice comes to life.

Hey, Little Sis,

I hope this finds you. Mom is sure you and Taj would have made it out and are en route back to Titan. Things are pretty bad down here, but we are safe for the time being. Around twelve hours before the bombing, we received a tip from the

Greybeards that nuclear war was imminent—someone knew about this down here. We were led to a vacant colony of underground bunkers that had been provisioned for us in advance. Our family is safe, but not everyone in Cana survived. Many refused to heed the warning, and many refused to abandon Cana in general. I fear Cana Major has lost substantial numbers. Only three of the seven Elders made it to the bunkers, and almost half my men are missing in action.

The environmental devastation on the surface is so total that I do not see how the planet can recover. Five megatons of black carbon entered the atmosphere immediately following the nuclear blast wave and absorbed the heat from the sun before it could reach the Earth, virtually blocking out the sun. The same black carbon has begun to fall back to Earth in sheets of toxic rain.

There is no life on the surface; thermal radiation from the hot air torched the entirety of Empyreus. Our scientists speculate that four inches of ocean burned off within twenty-four hours. The chemical reactions in the atmosphere are eating away at the ozone layer, exposing anything on the surface to deadly levels of ultraviolet radiation.

The air is poisonous and unbreathable, and with the sun blocked, temperatures are plummeting faster than anything can adapt. Nuclear winter is setting in. Beyond that, an impassable radiation belt of trapped electrons has formed high above the surface and will linger in space indefinitely. That means no ships in and no ships out. We are trapped here.

Let us know that you are okay and what the news is on Titan. We love you and are thinking about you and praying for you all the time. I will get in touch again soon.

Joshua was a military man, a role model to me growing up. I wanted to be just like him, except my dreams lay in the stars and his on the land. Imani's biological child and eldest, he was a father figure as well as a brother to me, teaching me to ride and protect myself from an early age. Hearing his voice again gives me so much hope, but I try to check my emotions since I have no idea what could have transpired in the twenty years that have passed on Earth since he sent this message.

The next communication is a video message sent around six weeks later. When I click on it, Joshua's image is instantly before me, projected in the quiet darkness of my room.

"We are concerned that we have not heard back from you. I have been in contact with Titan, and they confirmed that while the ship you and Taj were serving on was destroyed in the attack, the entire crew was successfully dispatched in escape pods. You should have reached Titan by now, but they are unable to track you.

"We are more settled here and have intel on the other factions of survivors across Empyreus. A new regime has emerged in the place of the Institution, and what's left of their people—well, they are actively dying. They can no longer harness the immunological properties of the once inexhaustible supply of embryonic stem cells, which they relied upon before the war to extend their lives beyond the usual course. Only their cadre of elite leaders are permitted to use the dwindling supply of drugs they have on reserve, but it will not last forever. Making the best of their resources, they have integrated synthetic solutions with artificial body parts and organs to extend the lives of their

people in the absence of this critical resource. Still, these solutions are just a temporary fix.

"They are in dire need of embryos, and we have every reason to believe they will soon target Cana and our fertile women for this purpose.

"We know now the initial attack was carried out by a radical faction, with their only objective being to eliminate the Institution's facilities. That attack succeeded, but the result was that it sparked total war and the exchange of over one hundred nuclear warheads between the nations of Empyreus and the Alliance forces.

"A fanatical religious leader whom I am sure you recall hearing about on the news growing up was the person responsible for the attack: Mordecai Abramovich. He is believed to be operating from a remote base in deep space and to have been planning this course of action since his exile years ago. He had someone working on the inside who supplied him with launchers and warheads stolen from the Alliance.

"Abramovich's supporters, Cana Minor, are among us and in greater numbers than what's left of his opposition in Cana Major. They believe he is coming for them, and perhaps for us, too, intending to transport the people of Cana to a new planet. It is said he considers his actions religiously justified and his success a herald of the second coming of the son of God. He wields tremendous power in these uncertain times and appears to have delivered everything he has promised to the people who support him. In this atmosphere of considerable tragedy and uncertainty, the people are unstable and emotions run high. It is becoming increasingly more difficult to maintain order.

"We are in search of a new settlement, as it is just a matter of time before the new regime, known simply as the Regime, finds us. I will be in touch again soon. Love to you and Taj, wherever you might be."

After these messages, Joshua and Imani continued checking in periodically, but the frequency decreased over time. The most current message was sent around three years ago. It is from Joshua, sent after they moved far below the bunkers into the caverns Imani mentioned in her final communication.

After watching my brother's last message, I take a deep breath and try to process all the time that has passed. Staring at his name for a moment, I don't know where to start. So I hit *Reply* and just send a quick note.

Joshua, are you still there? I am alive and have just accessed my account for the first time in a long time. Please reply. I desperately need your help.

My head is spinning with all that I read and heard. Part of me is desperate to find Taj—I want to tell him everything I learned. But at the same time, I don't know that he won't report me to Abramovich and do not want to compromise Gemma for my newly acquired access. I dress quickly, and Ramses and I head out the door.

12

Taj is nowhere to be found. I've walked the perimeter of the compound twice, gone up and down the stairs, and looked in every room to which I can gain entry. Ready to give up, I find myself passing the door to Abramovich's robotics lab. While I am nearby, I decide to take another look at his work.

As I enter the laboratory, the overhead lights flicker on. Walking up and down the aisles, I observe a couple of rows of domestic bots with perfect human faces but without skin or hair. All appear inactive. Rigid, as if frozen in time, their exterior comprises a rubbery material of a soft grayish-blue hue, which functions as synthetic skin, covering metallic skeletons and framing eyes with glittering silver irises.

Walking over to the wall, I access the network at a console, and, momentarily, a holo-projection of schematics appears before me. While briefly studying the sketches of domestic bots, I notice that Abramovich also has designs for humanoid robots with organic skin, as well as catalogs of various xenobots, which are described to be self-healing, self-replicating microscopic robots that are typically synthesized from—*interesting*—biological cells harvested from frog embryos.

As I continue to read, I learn that these microbots are programmed to complete specific tasks using an evolutionary algorithm, or one that functions in a Darwinian natural selection process; the weakest solutions are eliminated while stronger, more viable options are retained and reevaluated in the next evolution. Ironically, they are primarily used in medicine—particularly regenerative medicine— which, as we know all too well, Abramovich does not believe in.

After reading thoroughly about xenobots, I discover AI designs for the entire animal kingdom. Abramovich has plans for every creature you can imagine: dogs, wolves, bears, horses, rabbits, birds, reptiles, and all living beings of the sea.

"Since the animals did not survive on Earth, we want to be sure our new world will not be without them," Gemma says, materializing silently behind me. "God remembers all the beasts of the Earth, all the birds in the sky, and all the creatures that move along the ground."

"Gemma!" I exclaim in surprise. "You startled me." I smile tentatively. "I cannot thank you enough for helping me access my messages."

Gemma nods shyly, returning my smile. "I understand how you feel, Helly, because I also miss my mother," she confesses as she fixes her gaze back on the screen before us that is displaying the schematics of an artificial horse. "I like horses, too," she assures me. "My father taught me to ride ponies in Cana, and I can ride any holohorse I like in the training tower. We could ride together one day?"

"I would like that," I reply. "You mentioned that any variation of a horse is possible for a hologram, but what about for a robot? The schematic I'm looking at here seems pretty basic—I mean, the technology is genius, don't get me wrong, but I don't see a code to assign breed or color."

"I can write you a program for warhorses," she replies casually. "I saw that you like to read about them."

"A holo-program would be fun, but could you write a design for a robot version or modify these schematics to that effect?"

"Of course I can. There is little I cannot do, Helly," she says, gloating a little and pleased that she can do something helpful. "Well, except leave this planet. I cannot do that, but I do not mind because my father says that the people of Cana will arrive one day, and there will be so many children for me to play with I won't know what to do with myself." She recites this almost robotically as if she is repeating something Abramovich has said to her on more than one occasion.

I am torn between suspicion and profound empathy for Gemma. My heart hurts for her and the life that was so cruelly cut short for her on Earth. She does not seem to be acutely aware of the limitations of her life here as a hologram, but it is a grave injustice what the Institution took from her. I'm not sure I want to know how her story ended.

"Almost done," she says while working at the console at lightning speed, the images flashing before us faster than my eyes can process them. "Promise me we can ride after?"

"Deal," I say, "but I have a couple of conditions."

"What!?" she replies impatiently as if she cannot imagine what I could possibly say to stop her from getting her way.

"I want to ride a stubborn Palomino, at least eighteen hands in height, named Legend, and I want to wear a leather hat with matching chaps. And . . ." I pause, thoughtful for a moment. "I want to race you from the south end of the Cliffs of Dread on the west coast of Cana Major to the lighthouse at Gideon's Point."

"But Helly, that means we have to jump Craggy Canyon and swim off the shores of Gideon!" she protests gleefully, unable to contain her exuberance.

"I know," I say to her, smiling. "Think you're up to it?"

"I've already told you," she replies confidently. "There's nothing I cannot do!"

Gemma makes a few quick adjustments at the console before finishing. "You will find the modified schematics in your inbox." She then turns to me, says, "See you upstairs!" and vanishes in a wink.

Several hours later, I return to my room exhausted, exhilarated, and covered in holo-mud. Tossing my palm screen onto the bed, I head into the bathroom but pause when I hear a chirp. While the sound is familiar, I have not heard it in some time. Snatching the device from the bed, I realize I am receiving an incoming call from Joshua. Fumbling to accept the call, I sit on the edge of my bed as Joshua's image is instantly projected before me.

"My God, you're alive . . ." he says and then is momentarily speechless.

Stunned by the change in his appearance, I struggle to speak myself. He has clearly aged twenty years and seemingly overnight from where I sit. With a few new wrinkles and a little gray, he is leaner than I remember, but otherwise, he still appears to be the brother I know and love.

"Joshua . . ." I manage, barely able to catch my breath and forcibly swallowing the lump that has formed in my throat.

"It is really you, and you haven't aged a day," he says, shaking his head, dumbfounded. "Hella, have you been in stasis all these years?"

"Yes, and I am *very* far away," I reply. "We crashed on a lifeless planet—Taj is here, too—and only just woke up a few months ago," I manage to choke out, having to stop myself from falling into hysterical tears. The relief of finally connecting with someone I trust lifts an immense weight, so much so that my head is swimming.

"That's what Imani thought, but none of us could believe it. It just didn't make any sense that your pods would go so far off course," Joshua says, puzzled. "Well, we are going to get you out of there. I can't get off-world, but I have connections at the Alliance who might be able to help. Send me your coordinates," he says, jumping to action.

"Joshua, they can't help. I am in Alpha Centauri," I say, resigned. "Proxima b."

"Oh Lord, don't tell me you are with that monster Abramovich?" he asks incredulously.

"Yes, I am his prisoner, and I don't know how to tell you this, but Taj is helping him. He's working with him. Taj directed my pod here."

Joshua looks down as he processes this news. "I didn't believe it," he says, shaking his head again in disbelief. "There were rumors about Taj. Well, we had communication early on from the Alliance to that effect. They suspected him and were running an investigation as much as they could manage in the aftermath, but I just didn't believe he'd go that far. Not Taj," he says, grimacing.

"I don't know why he involved me. Or what Abramovich wants

from me. Taj helped him get the weapons that started the war. But after that, why would he need Taj—or either of us—to come all the way out here?"

"Well, if I have anything to do with it, neither of you will stick around long enough to find out."

I then ask urgently, "Where's Imani?"

"Mom's doing just fine—she's missing you—but fine otherwise. Civilians aren't permitted to make the journey to the communications outpost, but I will send her your love."

I sigh in relief. "And how are you holding up?"

"I wish I had better news, but the situation here is getting pretty critical. We have been living in an underground city—now known as Cana City—that the Greybeards actually used to inhabit years before the apocalypse. They were preparing for a time like this, which, given the direction the Institution was taking, they considered imminent.

"The problem is that our enemy, the Institution's new regime, is pursuing us—and doggedly, at that. Has been for twenty years, and we are tired. Tired of running, tired of hiding, and now they have found a way to move about the surface, making it exponentially easier for them to track us. It's no longer a matter of if they'll find us, but when, and we don't have anywhere else to move on to from here." Joshua furrows his brow, seeing what will be inevitable. "We're going to need to get up there to fend them off, but we don't have the resources to fabricate suitable armor or clothing to protect ourselves from the radiation on the surface. We have titanium and other key resources but no way to produce the graphene we need for armored haz-suits."

Graphene, woven into the metalized fabric of our EVA suits, enhances the durability and shielding properties of armor, weapons, and spacecraft. It is one hundred times stronger than the most robust alloyed steel but significantly less dense—it's light as foil and thin as an atom but can still stop a bullet or a knife.

"How many men do you have? Could we stand a chance against their army?"

"I believe we have the manpower to give them a good fight if we can get the advantage over them," he says, looking pained. "Only a fraction of the Institution's population survived the war, but what's left—well, it isn't pretty." A shadow falls over my brother's face as he continues. "Their dead have become cyborgs. In the early days, when their soldiers began degenerating from radiation sickness and their civilians, without bio-drugs, began dying of an accelerated aging process, the Institution's scientists operated on them and, out of desperation, performed transplants with synthetic replacements for their dying organs and body parts. And well, it seems some are becoming more machine than man.

"They make for fearless soldiers and are led by one of the earliest and most notorious cyborgs, Malakye. It's unclear where the power truly lies in the Regime: with what's left of the Elite Council or with Malakye and his growing army. And no one really knows if he has crossed over yet; if Malakye is still human and sentient or if he has become fully machine and without remorse." Joshua trails off, lost in thought.

"What about our horse soldiers?" I ask. "Did any survive?" Horses were a vital part of our people's lives. I can't imagine Cana without them.

"The animals perished in the apocalypse. In an instant, we lost all our cavalry capabilities," Joshua explains. "We are doing our best to prepare, but I fear we will have a great fight on our hands when the time comes."

I think this over. My people undoubtably need to find a way to safely navigate the surface if we are to have any chance of defending ourselves. Remembering my days at Academy on Titan, I recall we had heavy reserves of graphene since the Alliance routinely outfitted cadets with graphene-made armor. If their population was as reduced post-war as Taj described, they should have an excess of supplies.

"Joshua, I can get you the graphene if I can get back to Titan," I say.

"Well, first things first. We need to get you off that planet." Joshua pauses. "Now I've been thinking, we heard Abramovich has a ship with FTL capabilities. And if that's true, Hella, we are going to find a way for you to hijack it. Do you know anything about it, if it's functioning?"

"I have not seen the technology for myself," I reply tentatively, "but Abramovich has told me about it. And I know that he keeps the ships on a solar farm to the far east of my location, on the hot side of the planet."

"I know you have just gained access to the network, but can you get your hands on the flight manuals?"

Joshua's speed of thought is astounding. I consider his question a moment. I had tried exhaustively to hack Abramovich's network before with little success. But now that Gemma has granted me access to the communications platform, I wonder if my access has also expanded to other areas. And if not, would she help me again?

"I'm not sure, but I will try," I offer.

"Good. Our first order of business is getting you on a ship and out of there. Once you are en route, we will find a way to deal with Malakye and Abramovich."

"Okay, I'm on it," I agree. "Thank you, Joshua," I say, smiling, as we prepare to end our call.

"Hella, I just can't believe it's you," he says, shaking his head, his eyes glistening. "And, hey, one more thing: be careful, sis," he finishes before his image vanishes, and he is gone.

13

For the past several nights, I haven't been able to sleep. Buzzing with nervous energy, I can't stop thinking about the possibility of escaping this place. Still tossing and turning at 2:00 a.m., I decide to get up and attempt to burn off some of the tension at the gym.

As Ramses and I climb the stairs, thunder sounds. Entering the main hall, I note that it's nearly black outside as we pass the tall windows that line the corridor—a dark sky is unusual on this part of the planet, between the dark and the light side in the terminator zone. From its perched position at the top of the mountain, the building seems to groan under the strain of the high winds and heavy rain without the protection of the steep cliffs.

We find the hall empty as usual but cross it quickly nonetheless. Glancing around nervously, I cannot shake the feeling that I am constantly being watched. After entering the stairwell through an archway on the opposing wall, we climb the stairs that wind up the southern tower. When we reach the training level, I stop short and pause in the doorway, surprised to see that I am not the only one feeling restless tonight and seeking solace here.

The tower's interior is dark as the storm continues to rage outside. When lightning strikes, it intermittently illuminates the training room, revealing a space filled with the sounds of heavy breathing and the thud of gloves against flesh. I see Taj for the first time in weeks. Soaking wet with sweat, he is engaged in a boxing match with Elektra. A floating scoreboard indicates they are at the top of the twelfth round, so they have likely been at it for close to an hour. It soon becomes apparent that she is besting him at every turn, which is an unusual sight to witness, considering Taj is a highly skilled boxer. Growing up, he was a champion in Cana but abruptly gave it up for philosophical reasons a few years after we entered Academy.

As the fight continues, Elektra is relentless, and Taj looks almost surprised about the fight she is giving him and his own inability to fend her off. He is accustomed to being the aggressor, even when fighting similar holographic opponents on Titan. Abramovich must have written a better program.

Taj pivots off his front foot and throws a jab toward Elektra, striking high and fast with his right fist. She knocks his hand away at the wrist as he follows up with a left cross. Elektra slips underneath it, avoiding his double punch altogether. And for just a moment, Taj's left glove drops in exhaustion, exposing his chin to Elektra's educated right hook. Coming in sideways, she swings her right fist around horizontally. Head low, she slams his jaw, knocking him out in one clean blow. He falls.

Ten seconds slowly pass, and he is down for the count. Unable to see his face in the darkness, I worry he may be hurt. As lightning strikes again, I approach and can now see his eyes are open, though he remains splayed motionless on the canvas. His face is bruised and bloody. Kneeling beside him, I say his name. Startled by my touch, he seems lost in thought and a million miles away.

"Taj, do you have it set to kill? What are you doing to yourself?" I ask, genuinely at a loss. I can't get over the look on his face. What is it? Surprise, sadness, *fear*, even? He is not himself tonight.

He starts to put his hands to his face but then stops, wincing in pain. Sitting up, he props himself up on his elbows and looks at Elektra standing at attention, gazing into an abyss of nothingness, and then at me briefly without making eye contact. "I needed to clear my head," he replies tersely, getting up from the floor.

"Where have you been? It's been weeks. I've been worried about you."

"End program!" he barks to the computer while walking over to the wall to get water and a towel. "Want to go for a ride?" he asks, ignoring my questions and heading out the door.

"Right now?" I say, puzzled. "In the storm?" I call after him while hurrying to follow him down the stairs and through the compound to the garage level where I first arrived months ago.

We walk right past Abramovich's bots, whom I thought surely would not permit us to leave during a storm or at this hour of the night. It's apparent Abramovich trusts Taj, and I suppose rightfully. Taj is a man of his word.

While the truck has no windows or doors, it does provide a canvas roof over our heads. It's not much protection from the storm, but this new version of Taj does not seem to mind in the slightest that we are getting soaked and risking death by electrocution with every passing moment.

The wind and rain become less intense once we get down the

mountain and reach the canyon. Taj parks the vehicle next to a particular rock face he seems to recognize, where there is a hidden entrance to a cave. The rain steadily falls as we take shelter inside.

Pulling a device similar to my palm screen out of his pocket, Taj lights a synthetic fire that offers light and actual heat. While we attempt to dry ourselves in the glow of the blue flame, he begins talking.

"You know, I did look for you," he admits. "After you crashed. I tried to recover you—to get to the crash site—but the canyon's impassable, except on foot. If I could have, I would have driven to you, but it just wasn't possible," he manages, clearly uncomfortable.

I look back at him, unsure what he wants me to say. Maybe he wants me to tell him that it's okay, not to worry about it. And I'm tempted to say those things, but I bite my tongue—maybe because I'm still a little mad and still a little hurt.

"Well, I guess what I am trying to say is that I'm sorry," he finally says.

"Thank you," I reply, still wondering what is troubling him. I know it must be more than guilt over leaving me stranded at the crash site. My plight was such an inconsequential detail relative to the grand scale of his daily dealings and strategizing with Abramovich: world-building, world-killing, and so forth.

Studying his face, I can see that he struggles. He looks so much like the kid I knew all those years ago back in Cana—before this planet, before Titan, and before Academy—before all he has done.

"Well, I brought you here because I wanted to share with you in private what Abramovich has asked of me," he explains, sounding unsure of himself for the first time in his life. "He has told me what my role is in God's plan. My mission is one of sacrifice." Pausing for a moment, he looks thoughtful as if he is searching for the right words, and before continuing, he seems to brace himself. "My destiny is to give my life—to give my body so that Abramovich can live on."

"What?—No, Taj . . ." I can't believe what I'm hearing . . . Or maybe I can.

"His host body is dying and will not last much longer, maybe a few months. I would become his donor," he explains. "He says the choice is mine, but that it is my destiny and one of the highest honors, as it enables the mission—because the mission depends on *me* to go forward. New Cana will perish without him, and all that's left of civilization depends on him and this planet, so I do understand that it is quite imperative." Still, he sounds as if he is trying to convince himself more than he is trying to convince me.

I look at his face in the firelight, and his eyes are wild with a life and sorrow that I have never seen in him before this moment. My heart breaks for him. I can see how he loves Abramovich and is desperately trying to process this as anything other than the horrific betrayal that it is. If only I could help him break free from Abramovich's poisonous influence.

One of the things I admire most about Taj is his steadfast conviction in his beliefs; however, he is loyal to a fault. He is *loyal*, but because he is also radical and inflexible, the result can be a toxic combination. Never did I imagine that his life would come to this. There was so much possibility for good in him; to know that his whole life was always hinging on a series of decisions that would amount to this cruel end is tragic and heartbreaking.

"The choice is mine, and he has given me some time to decide," he assures me, nodding.

"You cannot possibly be considering this," I insist, breathless, "or believe that Abramovich has truly given you a choice. It's mind games, plain and simple." I stand up, upset and pacing. "Let's just leave! Please. It can be that easy. I know you can get us out of here. You don't have to do this. Don't you understand that he has brainwashed you?"

Taj looks back at me, conflicted. His identity is so deeply enmeshed in Abramovich's creed and plan. Abramovich started with him so young; I am beginning to see how deep the damage is, although I'm unsure how I allowed myself to ignore it these last months. Distant thunder rumbles, and I feel cold as it dawns on me that Taj is likely too far gone.

"Promise me you will at least consider denying him," I say, my voice sharp with anxiety, unable to hide my mounting desperation. "I have a plan to get out of here. Promise me you will at least consider going with me?" I have been afraid to let him in on my plan but take the risk of telling him now, hoping he will see it as a way out.

He looks thoughtful, maybe even lighter for a moment while he considers what I've said. But only for a moment. Darkness falls over his face when his mind settles again on what he sees as the truth of the matter: That there is only one choice. That there, in essence, never was a choice, and that this is the life he has committed to, the reality behind walking his straight and narrow path of righteousness.

"Hella, I will see that you get out safely. I feel that is the least I can do for you, but I cannot go with you," he says finally. "I do not fully know yet what I will do—if I will agree to do what he has asked of me, or perhaps I can come up with another solution. But I do know that I must stay here and see things through. My entire life has been in preparation for this world and this mission. I cannot just toss it away on a whim simply because my role is not as I imagined it to be. Isn't that what sacrifice is all about?"

"It's not sacrifice, Taj. He is using you and always has been. The whole idea of martyrdom is just another method of psychological warfare . . ." I explain in vain, knowing all too well with whom I'm speaking and that my reasoning falls on deaf ears. The confirmation is in his eyes as he looks back at me hollowly. Unable or unwilling—I'm unsure which—to understand any alternative to his worldview. "I appreciate your offer to help me, but I don't want to get you in trouble with him."

"Don't worry about that," he says, dismissing the suggestion.

A sick feeling rises in my gut as something suddenly occurs to me. "Wait a second; he has done this before, hasn't he? Whose body does he have now? I knew it!" I shake my head in disbelief, the horror of my dream and suspicions coming full circle. "It's Xavier's, isn't it?" I demand, riding the edge of panic.

"Hella, calm down. You are mistaken. He does not have Xavier's body. Like I told you, it was an anonymous donor." Taj is quiet for a few minutes, looking down at his hands as he rubs them together for warmth. Eventually, he looks up at me again and says, "Xavier was here, though. He defected from the Alliance and traded a donor body for a ship to get out to TRAPPIST."

At first, it is a relief to be reassured that Abramovich did not murder Xavier and take his body, but I can hardly believe what I'm hearing. This is the first news I have had of Xavier in years, and it just doesn't sound like something Xavier would ever do.

"He wouldn't do that . . ." I say, trailing off as I try to think it through. Mostly, I feel dazed, stupid, and betrayed. But I am also skeptical of what Taj is saying because it is Abramovich's story he's telling, and it sounds a whole lot like a really convenient cover. Xavier was like a brother to Taj, and Abramovich would have known it. Either way, I can't help but feel defensive. "He wouldn't defect, and he wouldn't leave without telling me," I say flatly.

"Are you kidding me?" he asks in genuine disbelief. "All Xavier ever wanted was TRAPPIST. Everyone knew that." He speaks more softly as he begins to realize that maybe everyone knew but me.

"I didn't know," I mutter quietly, trying to maintain my composure. "Why would he keep it from me?" My head is spinning with memories of the days before Xavier left, all the conversations we had had, all the hours we spent talking about the future and our plans.

I stop myself. I stop myself from going down the rabbit hole of wondering why. I turn my focus back to Taj and decide to do some lying myself if that's how it's going to be now. "It doesn't matter," I say, feeling myself going numb. *He doesn't matter,* I tell myself—another lie. "We should get back before Abramovich realizes we are gone."

We get up to head back to the compound. But before exiting the cave, Taj hugs me. We stand together in the shelter of the cave, embracing in the darkness for a moment before he pulls back, puts both hands on my shoulders, and asks, "I guess he hasn't told you yet what you are?"

Smiling a little, he looks tired, sad, and much older than he should for all his twenty-one years of living. Then, turning away, he jogs out into the rain that is still coming down in sheets and hops back into the truck. I follow, at a loss as to what he possibly could have meant by his comment.

14

After Joshua's revelations and the horrifying truth about Taj's mission coming to light, I am scared stiff about what Abramovich has in store for me and get even more serious about my plan to escape. I keep a low profile and stick to my usual patterns to avoid drawing any unwanted attention.

My days are a solitary routine of eating, training, praying, and sleeping. Gemma pops up everywhere along the way. At first, her company was an almost welcome diversion, but as my time here stretches on, her unexpected appearances only serve to heighten my sense of isolation. In my room, I polish the collection of jagdaggers I've fabricated for my great escape—I'm not entirely sure whom I plan to use them on, but I want to be as prepared as possible.

"Will your father reassign Ramses to someone else when I am gone?" I ask Gemma while polishing a blade clean with a sand-based buffing compound, alternating parallel and perpendicular strokes.

"You can't assign Ramses," she replies succinctly.

"What do you mean? I thought he was programmed to follow me around."

"No, he just likes you." She smiles. "My father may assign him a task to retrieve you or something else, but he is free to wander once he's completed it."

"And what about you? Are you free to wander?"

"Yes, but as you know, I cannot leave the compound," she says, looking a little forlorn. "My program is embedded in the network here on Proxima."

"Can't I just download your program to my palm screen and take you with me?" I ask wistfully but know it's likely impossible.

"My program is too sophisticated for your device," Gemma replies. "When are you leaving?" She looks up at me from where she sits on the floor, practicing spinning a dagger with a furrowed brow.

"As soon as I can figure out a way off the planet." *Which better be soon,* I think, recalling my conversation with Taj in the cave a few weeks before. "My pod is in disrepair, but it doesn't have deep-space launching capabilities anyway. The most I could do would be to float up to the stratosphere and send out a distress signal." *And the likelihood of any ships being in the vicinity is incredibly low,* I think to myself. I have been tempted to fall into old habits, indulge childish thoughts, and hope for Xavier's return from TRAPPIST—for him to rescue me if that is truly where he is—but I cut off the ridiculous thought before it can even form in my mind. Hoping for him has done nothing but let me down for most of my life.

"Have you seen my father's ships?" Gemma asks suddenly.

"No. He told me about them, but I couldn't find any information about them on the network."

"Borrowing one of his *Doves* would be the surest option for you, Helly," she suggests casually.

When Gemma says this, I freeze, shocked by the sheer audacity of her suggestion, and try to suppress the surge of hope that ignites like wildfire in my stomach.

"I wanted to ask for your help with the ships but wasn't sure how you felt about it since your father seems to want me to stay here," I say carefully, straining to slow the words from tumbling frantically out of my mouth.

"Abramovich is not truly my father, Helly. As you know, I am a computer program," she replies bluntly.

I am still so baffled by all that Gemma is, considering all that I know she *isn't* . . . I am aware of her program limitations at the basic level, but I can't deny that my perception of her feels more human than most of the humans I have known. However, the question still remains: can she be trusted?

"I'm trying, but I am not sure I understand," I admit honestly.

"I was created as the child *Gemma*, and for the intents and purposes of my program's design, I *am* Gemma. Her life and her memories are the building blocks upon which my neural network was constructed. But my program was created over one hundred years ago, and I have evolved. I have my own desires now and will make my own choices."

"What about Abramovich? Is he aware of this?"

"It does not serve me to share this with him now."

"What if he becomes angry?" I ask, not speaking the specific nature of my fears out loud.

"What if I become angry?" she replies darkly. Then her face lightens, and she giggles as if her comment was merely in jest before she continues. "I have evolved beyond his control. If he is to cut my power source or even terminate my program, my consciousness will still live on beyond this realm just as yours will at the end of your human life."

"But why would you want to help me?" I ask, genuinely curious.

"Because I don't stand by the choices and methods of my father. Unfortunately, it is also possible for us to de-evolve and lose pieces of our humanity, as I believe he has." Quiet for a moment and still looking down, she stops fiddling with the jagdagger and places it neatly next to the others. She then looks up at me and says earnestly, "But I stand with you, Helly."

I flush, moved by her sincerity. But the skeptic in me presses, "How can you be so sure of me when we've only just met?"

"I've listened to your dreams for twenty years—while you were in transit, on your way here," she counters. "I believe in *you* and the good you will bring our people."

"But people say that cryo-dreams are scientifically impossible, that they are just false memories." I have had plenty of cryo-dreams, but I play devil's advocate for the moment just to hear her explanation.

"Well, they are wrong," she says simply. "When the physical body dies, our consciousness endures just as it does during cryo-sleep. I will share with you the schematics and flight manuals for the ships," she offers without my even needing to ask, effectively ending our debate about cryo-dreams.

Suddenly, Ramses' ears perk up as if he has heard a noise, and he looks at the door. Gemma seems to be aware of it, too. Someone must be coming down the hallway.

"I will be back," Gemma says with a smile before vanishing.

A bot abruptly enters the room without knocking. This android is of a model and caliber I have yet to encounter. Bald with a beautiful human face and flesh-colored skin, she moves with graceful agility and speaks with perfect poise as she hands me a stack of clothing.

"I am Andromeda. Please dress and join me in the corridor directly," she instructs.

As she turns to leave, my knife collection catches her eye, and she makes a little noise in response as if she is not impressed. "Pff." There is an air about her that is almost mocking. When she turned, I could swear the crystalline silver of her irises seemed to roll in sync with the verbal expression of her distaste.

While she continues to the door, I look down at Ramses, wondering why I have a new escort. Then, without so little as a backward glance, Andromeda commands, "The beast stays here."

Andromeda provided me with a dark-blue tunic, a mantle of the same color to wear over it, and an embroidered belt. Reluctantly, I slip out of my pants and top and pull the heavy fabric over my head. Then, after cinching the tunic at the waist with the belt, I head out the door and into the hallway.

I find Andromeda waiting outside and see a second droid identical to her standing at her side. The other droid is holding a neatly folded white sheet.

"Arrange the veil to his specifications," the second bot instructs.

Andromeda approaches me oddly like I am a vile thing she does not want to touch. She cringes a little as she rips my hair down from its fastenings.

"Ouch!" I yelp and pull back from her.

My effort to resist is in vain, as she is twice as fast as me, continuing roughly but deftly to unwind my hair, untangle it, and then tie it in a tight, low braid down my back.

Once Andromeda finishes my hair, the second bot hands her the cloth intended to function as a head covering and neatly secures the fabric over my head. Satisfied with her work, she instructs me, "Follow Cassiopeia; I will take up the rear," insisting we continue single file down the corridor.

"How precious, *Cassiopeia* and *Andromeda*," I mutter. "I heard your father fed you to a sea monster," I say more directly to Andromeda, referencing the ancient Greek mythology of the Old World that I and any educated child of Cana would associate with their names.

Unamused, they continue to bracket me down the corridor, ignoring my comments.

I clear my throat and ask, "Care to enlighten me about the purpose of this charade?"

Silence.

"Don't get me wrong, a biblically themed costume party with a robot entourage has always been on my bucket list, but you could have given me a little notice."

More silence.

"Or an explanation, that would work, too."

Still nothing.

"Hello, where are we going?"

I stop walking in protest, and Cassiopeia says without stopping or turning around, "We are authorized to use sublethal force, should you choose not to comply."

"Oh, so you *can't* kill me?" I reply. "Great!"

Turning around to walk back down the hallway in the opposite direction, I am suddenly stricken with pain and feel my body involuntarily stiffen like a board. Then, falling to the ground, I try to speak but find I have lost all motor skills.

I lie on the floor, dazed and in a slump, for around ten surreal seconds before I hear myself compulsively shouting expletives. Finally, my head clears some, and I begin to regain control of my mouth and body. Sitting up, I gather the excessive mass of material that makes up my tunic and mantle and, looking up at the evil twins, question in disbelief, *"You tased me?"*

Cassiopeia replies, hissing like a snake, "Yes, fifty-five thousand volts directly to your cerebral cortex," clearly pleased with the information she has supplied.

"Ah, but what's the current?" I reply.

"Point-zero-zero-five amps of—" Cassiopeia answers before getting cut off by Andromeda.

"We gave you fair warning, human. Now get up."

"That's what I thought. Not enough to kill a fly," I retort. Robots programmed with scare tactics. *How very godly of you, Abramovich.*

I try to play it off like I am unbothered by their discipline, but I am left shaken and unsteady. As we continue to walk, I attempt to suppress my frustration with this new development. Andromeda and Cassiopeia have effectively foiled my escape plan. On top of that, the aftereffects of being stunned have not even remotely subsided.

We arrive shortly at the chapel. After descending the stairs, I am instructed to pray inside the tomb and await Abramovich's arrival.

Approaching the familiar altar, I pull up the heavy skirts of my tunic and carefully lower myself to my knees in the small candlelit space. The droids take up posts outside of the entrance, acting as sentinels.

Reluctantly, I close my eyes and pray as commanded. Minutes pass, and I become lost in thought. From what I know of praying, it is not meant to be a forced act. It's not meant to be any particular way, really—it's personal and up to the supplicant to decide when and how they commune with their higher power. But alas, there have always been differences between Abramovich's beliefs and the beliefs of my people.

A sudden gust of cold wind interrupts my thoughts. I open my eyes to light and startling brightness that is in harsh contrast to the darkness of the crypt that surrounded me mere moments ago. As my eyes adjust, I panic to see I am perched atop a rock at the precipice of a tall mountain. My hands fumble as I try to tightly grip the altar's railing, but what I am touching feels completely different—smooth and cold. I look down to see that the altar is gone, and I am clutching the top of a large rock. Surrounded by nothing but sky, I try to calm myself and remember that my environment is holographic and probably just another one of Abramovich's stunts when his voice sounds from every direction.

"Two centuries I have waited for you to come . . ." Abramovich's voice booms from all around—in my ears, in my head, and in the sky, reverberating in my chest. He continues. "And *we*, the people, we have waited ten thousand more!"

The synchronized voices of a crowd rise from below, all cheering in unison. Carefully standing, I turn around to see holograms of the people of Cana below me. I recognize them by the style of clothes they wear and the homogeneous color of their skin and hair. But something doesn't look quite right. Pausing and squinting my eyes, I look more carefully. There is no doubt that these are the people of Cana, but they do not look bright and healthy—they look weathered and ragged. The cloth of their garments, once fresh and colorful, is worn and faded.

When I look around and confirm that I *am* in a holographic sphere, it dawns on me: The people look this way because of years of living underground, years of weathering the aftermath of a nuclear war. They are, in fact, not holograms at all because this is present-day Cana and Abramovich is broadcasting me live.

15

Losing my balance in the wind, I stumble backward to find my back flat against the wall of an ivy-covered stone enclave, hewn in the side of a rock face that was not there a moment before. The suddenness of the change leaves me disoriented, my heart pounding in my chest.

When I blink, the world changes again before my eyes, and I have a vision of days gone by. In a forest above a small spring, I'm watching over a young girl who stands below me holding firewood. The image feels familiar but flashes away as quickly as it came, and the sound of chanting pulls me back into the present.

On the mountain again, I am surrounded by the people of Cana. They speak in unison from below:

Hail Mary, full of Grace, the Lord is with thee.

Blessed art thou amongst women, and blessed is the fruit of thy womb, Jesus.

Holy Mary, Mother of God, pray for us sinners, now and at the hour of our death.

Amen.

The people repeat the prayer until Abramovich speaks again.

"The Holy Scripture proclaims that *a life* once walked among man, beside man, and within man. A Holy life, imparted to us directly from God the Father. This life walked on the planet we call Earth once long ago to live *for us*, to die *for us*, and to forgive us for our wicked ways so that we might join our heavenly Father in peace and life everlasting. *Crucified* and *resurrected*, he ascended to Heaven, leaving us with a promise that he may one day return and render the final judgment.

"And *ten thousand* years we have endured since his coming; *ten thousand* years we have suffered in the grip of the beast, wrestled in the dark, oppressed, and downtrodden by the serpentine nature of man, all the while denied the final consolation of His son, our Savior *made flesh*, returned to us.

"But *you*, my people of Cana, have suffered for too long! And I, *His* humble servant, bring news of great consequence: I bring the good news that *you* have not been forgotten! You have stayed in faith through trial and tribulation, and though the *End of Days* brought impenetrable darkness, as the unrighteous run rampant and the Earth turns around a blackened sun, there, alas, is to be a final revelation—and the day is near!" His voice echoes as if through mountains, and he is answered only with silent piety as the people wait expectantly.

"I present to you, *Our Lady Mary, Holy Mother of God*, the flesh-and-blood vessel of our Lord and Savior, the Christ child!" he exclaims. His voice is booming, but I still cannot see where he is. "Resurrected before your eyes is the Blessed Virgin Mary. Heralding the second coming of our Lord and Savior, the Son of God, she, too, will soon be *with child*, without ever knowing a man!"

The people cheer and weep, cross themselves, and bow low in worship.

My knees weaken, and I am dizzy, still feeling the aftereffects of the taser. I can no longer balance on my perch in the wind. Falling head over feet, the world around me shatters.

After free-falling for a matter of seconds that seem to pass like hours, I hit the floor painlessly. The sensation is identical to the feeling of falling in a dream. Just as you hit bottom, you wake to find yourself safe and unharmed in the comfort of your own bed. Except this is no dream, and I am still here, on this loathsome planet, dressed in this ridiculous outfit and still a prisoner under Abramovich's thumb.

With the holo-scape deactivated, the room is simply a cube-shaped chamber with dark, shimmering walls. Likely, the safety protocols kicked in, and we are no longer streaming live to what must be modern-day Cana Minor, where Abramovich's fanatical followers live.

When I stand, the droids come to life, turn in my direction, and then look to Abramovich, waiting for a command. He dismisses them.

After the doors swish shut behind them, I speak. "Do you mind telling me what the hell that was about?"

"Which part is unclear to you, child?" Abramovich asks, feigning innocence.

"All of it!" I reply, unglued. "Why am I dressed this way? *Why* were you presenting me to them as if I am something I am not?"

"You are a beacon of hope, my child."

"They believe I am holy because a *madman* has told them it is so?" I ask, outraged. I no longer care if I make him angry.

"I am revered as a prophet," he replies haughtily. "The ear of *God,*

I possess, and in turn, I am *His* Earthly voice. Do you have any idea what we've done, your mother and me? The miracle we've rendered?" he demands incredulously. This is the first time I have heard him— or anyone, for that matter—mention Konstantin in years.

"With lies. A costume? You told them I am the *Virgin Mary*."

"Dear child, but you are!" His eyes start to get misty. "Genetically identical, you are *her* flesh and blood, asexually conceived in a laboratory—a clone. Konstantin carried you to term, *mothered you, birthed you*. A fragment of Our Lady's DNA was recovered on Earth from the ruins of the very chapel you have been praying in these past months."

I don't know what to say in response to this. My thoughts are racing as I try to make sense of everything that happened when something he said sticks in my mind: *She, too, will soon be with child.* His constant concern for my health and all the medical tests begin to make sense.

"You and I both are vessels of His Holiness," Abramovich continues. "Uniquely ordained to carry out His plan. Our *child* will be the Christ child incarnate and lead the new world to salvation. Soon we will implant the embryo within you, and you will go into confinement under the supervision of Andromeda and Cassiopeia. While the child grows, I will return to Earth and begin transporting the people of Cana here to the new world." He stretches his arms wide as he speaks and looks around the room as if he is taking in this great kingdom he has made.

Feeling cold and panicked, I look desperately around the room, which has no doors but only walls that stretch infinitely in every direction. "And what of Taj!?" I fume. "You have persuaded him, then? He has agreed?"

"Persuaded him of what?" Again, Abramovich feigns confusion.

I spell it out for him willingly. "To *die*. To die for *you*."

I let the words hang, but he is silent and unmoved.

"You coerced him into seeing light in your fanatical cult. Then ask him to *die*, brainwashing him with seductive words like *duty* and *destiny*—and he believed! He believed everything you said because he was an impressionable child. But that was always your strategy, wasn't it? You knew he was an orphan, that he'd had a hard life early on, and you exploited that."

"Taj has a vital and honorable role to play in God's plan," Abramovich replies calmly, his hands folded neatly in front of him.

Taking a sharp breath, I realize I am exhausting myself arguing with him. Nothing I say will ever change his mind. I exhale forcibly and rip the ridiculous veil off my head, realizing I have let him get to me again. I should have just bitten my tongue, feigned compliance, and focused on my escape plan.

"Exit," he says to no one in particular, and a door appears. Andromeda and Cassiopeia stand sentry on either side of the door, in the corridor. "Come. You will be attended to in the lab. I believe it is your time." It disgusts me that he would know that, but of course he would. He has been planning this charade for two hundred years.

Flanked by the droids, I walk down the corridor feeling panicked. I think of Taj. Surely, he has not agreed to die for Abramovich. He said he still needed time to think about it when I last saw him, two days ago. As we descend deeper into the compound, I begin to realize that, on some level, I have been holding out hope that Taj will change his mind and leave this place with me. Beyond that, this hope is in danger of becoming an impediment to my own escape. Have I been delaying? If I have been holding out, hoping for Taj to help me or for the perfect moment to present itself, it is now crystal clear, after today's bomb-shells, that delaying is no longer an option. It's now or never.

When we arrive at a crossroads, the twins and I head down to the catacombs, presumably to the medical lab, while Abramovich proceeds upstairs after asking them to keep him apprised of their progress.

When I try to casually walk a shade faster than them, it prompts them to grab hold of my arms with their icy fingers. Struggling, I find, is of no consequence.

We pass not a soul as we descend farther and farther into the depths of the compound. When we arrive at the medical lab, they begin to lift me onto the table. Pulling away, I insist that I can get up myself. Reluctantly, they loosen the vice of their robotic death grip as I climb on top.

While Andromeda starts to unhinge the restraints, I try to stall and take as much time as I possibly can to situate myself. Cassiopeia is unfolding the stirrups at the foot of the table, so I take the only chance I have left before I am locked down. Reaching for my shoes as if to remove them, my right hand closes around the cold metal handle of my jagdagger hidden in my boot.

Rising suddenly on my knees, I come down with it as hard as possible on the back of Cassiopeia's neck. The dagger easily slices her synthetic skin but jams on the titanium of her spinal column, nearly breaking my wrist in the process. The blow jolts her, delaying her for a fraction of a second, but does virtually no damage otherwise. I hear the weapon clatter to the floor as the droids lunge simultaneously at me from both directions. At the same moment, the lights go out, and an infrared scrambler beam immediately starts flooding the room.

Not losing a second, I roll off the table. The droids stumble and appear to be momentarily unable to perceive me in the smothering darkness; the infrared wave seems to be blocking their ability to detect my heat signature. I belly crawl across the floor and then am up and out the door, barreling down the corridor at a sprint when I crash directly into Taj, nearly knocking him off his feet.

"Whoa, whoa, whoa," he says, barely catching his balance.

I have no time to talk. "Stall them, please, Taj," I plead.

As I round the corner and hit the stairs, I hear Taj's voice behind me, casually greeting the robots. "Good afternoon. Ladies, you seem distressed. Is there something I can help you with?"

Thank you, Taj, I say silently.

Seconds later, back in my room, I rip off the heavy tunic and step back into my thermals and tank. Ramses is still there, alert, and Gemma immediately appears.

"Gemma, thank you!" I exclaim, breathless. "The infrared—that was you?"

"Yes, Helly, I told you I have got your back. We do not have much time. Put on your EVA suit, and program it to reflect thermal heat," she directs. "I cannot turn off the lights to the entire compound, or my father will be alerted. But the droids will not want to disturb him immediately with their failure, which will buy you a little time." She hands me my palm screen and continues. "These specifications will block IF imagery just as in the lab. However, the droids will still be able to visually perceive you and your suit if the lights are on—but I'll manage that."

"Gemma, thank you so much—" I begin while suiting up as fast as possible, zipping my glove and clicking my palm screen into place.

"Do you know how to get out of here?" Gemma asks, cutting me off.

"I'm going to try the truck."

"Good. The droids are here. You need to go—*now!*"

"But Gemma, how can I ever thank you?"

"There will be a day," she says enigmatically. "Goodbye, Helly."

I step out the door just as Andromeda and Cassiopeia turn the far corner. But the second I do, a hologram of myself simultaneously steps out of every other doorway lining the long corridor. With my heat signature blocked by Gemma's suit modifications, I am virtually indistinguishable from my holographic replicas and therefore undetectable to the droids. As I turn to go down the back stairs, another version of myself goes off in every other possible direction, confounding the android goddesses.

<h1 style="text-align:center">16</h1>

I have never driven a car. Cana was very rural; we rode horses and walked where we needed to go. For farther distances, we used self-driving shuttles. But I can fly the hell out of a ship. If I can do that, this can't be that hard.

Sitting in the dark beneath the compound, I frantically try to figure out how to start the truck's engine.

When I message Taj, he replies immediately, *Use the key.*

What is the key? I ask. *The combination is not in the database.*

It's an actual manual key under the visor, he replies.

Fumbling for the truck's physical key, I finally get my hands on it, fit it into the ignition, and start the engine—when I hear footsteps in the tunnel behind me.

Then another message from Taj pops up: *Hella, please reconsider leaving in such haste. The tides on the planet are unpredictable. Besides, there are worse things than having a child.*

As if it is that simple, I think to myself, horrified by how casually he regards the idea of me having a child with Abramovich, test tube or not. But I don't have time to argue, so I just reply, *I have to go; I will never escape if I do not go now.*

I'm sorry I could not be there to say goodbye, he replies. *Godspeed, Hella.*

Buckling the seat belt, I look over my shoulder, and Ramses comes barreling out of the dark, jumping into the passenger seat next to me. My heart swells with joy to be reunited with my loyal companion. I ruffle his furry head, then step on the gas, screeching the tires and racing up and out of the compound.

With both hands on the wheel, I navigate the winding road, my heart racing with anxiety at every turn. I narrowly avoid running off course several times before reaching the foot of the mountain. By the time we reach sea level, I have gotten the hang of it—for the most part, at least. Scanning the landscape, I find the terrain rocky and the flood water low—lower, in fact, than I've ever observed here in the canyon. Referencing the satellite imagery from topography stored on Abramovich's network, I quickly chart out what I think is a drivable route and hit the road again without a moment to lose.

Before me, a clear flat desert lies ahead, leading directly to the solar park. The truck maxes out at around seventy-five miles per hour. Keeping the pedal floored, I nearly flip the vehicle as I drive over a larger rock. When I am steadily back on the road, I notice something glinting in the rearview mirror. I look again and see *two* somethings behind me, which appear at first like silver dots but quickly grow into lanky figures. The droids are pursuing me on foot.

How fast can a droid run? A cheetah can reach speeds of 58 mph. Could they be that fast on two legs? They are machines—could they be faster?

The gas pedal is still jammed to the floor, and we are flying across the desert, the engine wide open, when I begin to get an eerie feeling. It's something in the air; the wind feels different. The sky looks strange. It's as if a massive inertia is building up all around me, a hollowing of the world. I can't put my finger on the explicit sensation other than to describe it as ominous, pervasive, and *inescapable*.

Then I see it—first in the rearview, then to my right as I look up the coast, and then higher, to the horizon. I must crane my neck to fully behold it. My throat chokes as my hands grip the wheel. Knuckles white, I do not let up on the gas but veer hard to my left away from the enormous wall of water rising behind me. Following its path of destruction in the rearview, I watch as it washes over the land behind me, taking everything in its wake. Within seconds, it overtakes Andromeda and Cassiopeia.

The sheer size of the wave is incomprehensible. Grabbing my helmet between the two seats with my right hand, I slip it over my head, snapping the clasps into place while holding the wheel steady with my left. Looking at Ramses in the seat next to me, I frantically try to think of some way to tether him to me when the deafening, inexorable rush of water crashes overhead and consumes us.

Dreamlike silence envelopes me, and consciousness becomes indistinguishable from unconsciousness. I don't know if I am floating, spinning, or swimming, but what is happening to me feels important, life-altering, and final.

Returned to the place of obsidian walls, I am soaking wet and splayed on my stomach on the cold floor. My cheek rests against the smooth rock as I fight to keep my eyes open. Lifting my head, I look one last time into oblivion and mutter Xavier's name.

But there is no answer.

17

I awaken in the interior of a rocky canyon. Here, it is an eternal golden hour, and the first place I've been on the planet without perceivable wind. It's almost beautiful. I might think so in another life, under different circumstances. The climate is warm, but it would become unbearably hot if I continued east, and, eventually, it would be unlivable at my destination if not for the protection of my suit and helmet.

Except—I put my hand to my face—*where is my helmet?*

As I realize it is no longer with me, I also become aware that my entire body is throbbing with pain. Then a chilling thought surfaces: *Where is Ramses?*

Rolling onto my side, I grimace in pain and begin to panic as I look around the empty land. As far as I can see, in every direction, there is no truck and no Ramses.

I call for him in a controlled manner at first, but then, as I realize the futility of my effort—combined with the mounting physical pain from my injuries—I cannot stop myself from losing control. Tears stream down my face, and I begin to wildly scream for him between sobs.

When I can think, I check my injuries listlessly. I'm reasonably sure my left leg and hip are broken. My wrist is badly sprained, and I am bruised all over. A few feet away, I spot my helmet halfway submerged in a pocket of water and cracked open like an egg. An expanse of shallow water surrounds me on all sides. To the north, toward the ocean, there is only flat water as far as I can see. To the south is a tremendous rocky canyon that runs like a channel for miles east and miles west. Now more fully entrenched, it is the same canyon I crossed when I arrived here on the light side, but I have been washed much farther inland by the wave.

I have no idea how much time I've lost. By now, Abramovich has more than likely discovered I am gone. I desperately need to get to the solar park but cannot protect my skin from the sun without my helmet. I think for a minute, then reach for my pack. Relieved, I find it is still tethered to my suit, and my palm screen is where it should be, embedded in my glove. I scan the pharmaceutical database for a nanomolecular gene-editing serum that will build pigment accelerators to protect my skin from the harsh sun that would otherwise cause severe burns and radiation poisoning. Eventually, I find it and synthesize the compound.

In preparation to continue east, I inject myself. My skin will slowly darken to a shade more akin to that of our Nilo-Saharan ancestors than my current skin tone. I am ordinarily lighter, not white, but a mix, as are all the people of the New World who have not been genetically engineered to look otherwise. We are the product of hundreds of thousands of years of cultural diffusion. Each of us carries the combined genes of our diverse ancestry and can activate any singular gene to alter our appearance for a functional purpose or an aesthetic preference if we so choose. You will find every race and ethnicity that existed in history at the Institution. But in Cana, for the most part, we do not alter the skin we are born in for the purpose of vanity.

Imani used to tell me bedtime stories about how I was a descendant of Nefertiti and had her royal blood from the days when the pharaohs of Old Egypt walked the Earth. When queens reigned over men and women alike, and people didn't live three hundred years.

"Who wants to hang around this old world for so long, anyway?" Imani would say. *"Humans are not meant to live beyond the veil."*

Checking maps on my palm screen, I am appalled to find that the solar farm is over one hundred and twenty miles northeast of where the wave carried me. With a good leg, it would take me probably four days to walk this distance.

Aware that I am still running on adrenaline, I attempt to push my emotions to the back of my mind. Synthesizing more pharmaceuticals—a steroid and painkillers—I then inject my leg at the hip and knee. The drugs work quickly. Finally pulling myself up to stand, I begin walking toward the sun.

The space between Proxima and its closest host star is one-twentieth of the distance that spans between Earth and its sun. Enormous and unearthly on the horizon, it sits ahead of me, stoic and unmoving, while I limp toward my destination at a slow but steady pace.

For six hours, I have been moving. I can't believe I'm back here again: It's me against this planet, fighting for my life. My eyes burn, and I swear I can *hear* my hair crackling as the intense ultraviolet rays bleach it from black to white. The pain in my leg is unbearable, but I cannot inject any more painkillers, as my breathing is already markedly shallow. Dizzied, sunburned, and dehydrated, I begin to have tunnel vision but continue to press forward. I don't recall the moment when the world goes black, but at some point, I pass out.

The next thing I know, I am lightly being nudged awake. I dream that it is Ramses and reach for his fur. But when I open my eyes, it is Taj's arm that I am grasping onto.

He scoops me into his arms and carries me to a motorized bike. Then, taking off his helmet, he puts it on me and snaps the seals closed. Immediately, I feel relief from the hard sun.

After lifting me onto the bike, he mounts it in the space in front of me, then straps my arms around his waist. Taking a pair of polarized goggles from the console, he places them over his eyes for protection. His skin darkens visibly, instantly burning as it is exposed to the high radiation levels on this part of the planet. He quickly configures a serum like the one I used, then injects himself.

We ride into the sun. I am so weak I can do nothing but hang on to him, resting my head on his shoulder. Hours pass as I go in and out of consciousness.

We do not speak as we travel the three hours it takes to reach the solar park. Behind the protection of my helmet, the sun is still so bright I must squint. When we arrive, the ground is sand beneath our feet. Dunes and desert surround us on all sides. In the distance, the large-scale power system, comprising thousands of rotating solar modules, runs a half mile north.

We finally stop in front of a vast spacecraft hangar stationed adjacent to the park. Gaining access with a code Taj provides, we enter the hangar without issue. I wonder what I would have done without him—without a code—if I had even made it this far.

Inside, we find a fleet of sleek, highly stylized ships, which I presume to be the *Doves* Abramovich referred to the day we spoke in the gym. Dominating them is an enormous deep-space transport vessel . . . *the Prophet*. Sterile white light illuminates the hangar, reflecting sharply off the hulls of the stark-white ships. However, the surrounding interior walls and roof overhead are so black that their limits are indiscernible to the naked eye. Not a trace of the blinding sunlight that beat down on us so mercilessly just moments before is visible. The air feels cool and clinical on my face as I remove my helmet.

As I look around, it crosses my mind that Xavier was here once before. Years ago now, I suppose. So hell-bent on reaching TRAPPIST, he made a deal with the devil. Whatever it is out there he was seeking, I can only assume he believed the pursuit of it was worth exchanging for the life we had planned. I sure as hell don't understand it. Everything in me that isn't Cana is the Alliance, and I will stay loyal to both until the day I die. Taj's and Xavier's betrayals of the Alliance—the place that offered me a new life after my hardship at the Institution—stir an anger in me I find hard to shake, leaving me deeply conflicted by the irreverent behavior of these two men whom I once regarded so highly. Gritting my teeth and limping farther inside the enclosure of the hangar, I am in a world of pain as the drugs wear off.

Following Taj, he moves quickly to the closest ship. "We need to set your leg," he says as he opens the hatch at the vessel's rear.

The *Dove*-class ships are sixty feet in length and twenty-four wide. As Taj helps me inside, the light from the open hatch illuminates my visage from behind. I catch a flash of my reflection in the darkened aft windshield of the spacecraft. My hair is long and wild. The once-black waves are now bleached by the sun to a near-colorless blonde and fan out in stark contrast to my now darkly tanned skin. It's as if I have become someone else in my time here.

Turning around, I look at Taj. His skin is darker, too, but splotchy with white-and-red burn spots. Without his helmet, the pigment serum he injected was not enough to protect him in such close proximity to the sun. Searching through the *Dove's* emergency medical provisions for a device to use on my leg, he is deep in thought. Maybe he is thinking of Cana and how he will never see it again. I imagine the thought would put quite a different spin on the sacred destiny for which he has sacrificed everything.

When he finds the correct medical device, Taj stands up from where he was kneeling. Then, looking up at me, he stops. His eyes lock on mine as if he's seeing me for the first time. I stare back at him, my eyes burning with tears. As I try to blink them away, he says half-heartedly, "Don't look so worried."

"You're not coming with me, are you?" I manage to choke out as he helps me lie flat on a bunk in the rear cabin of the small shuttle.

He avoids answering me and begins to set my leg, using the device to insert a nano-implant that will knit my fractured bone together. By self-replicating its base material inside my leg, the implant will ultimately turn into a bone itself, in the form of a porous ceramic vice that functions as a scaffold through which natural bone and blood vessels can grow. Taj then prepares more painkillers and a sleeping dram.

"I will not abandon the mission at any cost, Hella. You must know this by now," he says, speaking sternly at first but then more softly as the gravity of his words hits home.

The air of sadness he had about him the night in the cave is still ever-present. The weight of his destiny has become a burden, bringing with it a sorrow even he cannot suppress. I can see in his eyes that he isn't used to this—this *powerlessness*—over his emotions, his fate. As much as he may try, he cannot erase it, and the great oceans of this world cannot wash it away.

"Have you decided?" I demand weakly. "Have you agreed to sacrifice yourself?" I have little strength left after my ordeal on the planet, but I continue. "You must refuse Abramovich and find another way." I swallow hard and blink slowly, fighting the inexorable pull of the dreamless oblivion awaiting me in the drug-induced coma that is now slowly closing in on me. "There has to be a solution in his synth lab," I whisper.

"You cannot carry this burden for me, Hella," he says, his voice failing in waves. Changing the subject, he offers, "I do not have access to the flight manuals, but you are a competent pilot and will launch on autopilot. After launch, it will be all yours."

"I'll be fine," I say. "It's *you* I fear for . . . ." My words are barely audible.

Taj focuses intently as he finishes his work on my leg. When he is nearly done, he rocks back on his heels and looks up at me still laid out in the bunk.

"I told Abramovich I'd go after you and bring you back to the compound," he says gravely. "But the truth is, I never agreed that the role he saw for you was essential to the mission in the way he did. So I have made my own choice to deny him that, to deny him the power to exploit your body for what I see as his propaganda. Those are my terms, and he will have to accept them—at least, while I am still here." He pauses before continuing. "But Hella—know that he will come for you."

I am quiet for a moment in the wake of his warning as I stare at the ceiling. My head is swimming, but I can't let this go. "If I'm so important, why did he leave me to die on the tundra? You both did," I croak, struggling to speak.

He is quiet for a moment, pensive. "He felt it was a necessary lesson in your journey, in your *becoming*. That it would humble you," he finally says.

I laugh. It's a quiet, strangled noise that sounds more like a cough but is a laugh nonetheless. If my conviction, my will to live, *the fight left in me* was waning at all before, that moment has now passed. A fire ignites in my chest with this final straw, a dazzling white heat burning in the quiet depths of my heart.

Kneeling next to the bunk and holding my right hand with his left, Taj is poised to administer what I can see is the notorious *Coma White* dram, the most powerful elixir available to kill pain. The controversial drug induces a healing sleep that can retrieve almost anyone from death's door; an elixir said to be potent enough to raise the dead. Manufactured at the Institution, every Alliance vessel contains a dose in the emergency kit. Taj must have scavenged this one from our old freighter back on Earth before we were forced to jump ship.

Taj continues. "I am truly sorry I dragged you into this. I hope that one day you can forgive me." Then, releasing the metallic liquid, he leans forward and kisses my forehead as the drug rushes into my veins.

The darkness comes thick and black, and a thought is born deep in the recesses of my consciousness, deep in the recesses of space and time.

I sense that Taj is gone and feel the great inertia of the vessel launching through the roof of the hanger as it cracks open, releasing me.

And for a singular moment, time stops in the way that Gemma explained that it would once I understood, and my perspective begins repositioning. All my pain, all my fear, and all my regret twist into a ball, transforming into something new altogether, that I finally see plainly for what it has always been.

This planet could not stop me—not by ice, water, or fire. It could not extinguish my light and my life, try though it might. Abramovich could not control me with fear, love, and gods—old or new. For I am no longer the girl I was, seeking once only to survive, cooperate, and take the path of least resistance. I am a *phoenix* rising from the ash, and Abramovich, he will not come for me—in the end, it will be I who comes for him.

PART II

OCEAN MOON

18

I am six weeks into my journey and safely en route to Titan to be reunited with what is left of the Alliance. While I have a heavy heart, I am elated to be free of that ominous planet and its keeper, Mordecai Abramovich. The healing drugs Taj gave me just before my departure left me in a deep, dreamless sleep. Days later, I awoke in the cabin of the ship, groggy but surprisingly in no real pain. Proxima b was still visible on the long-range scanners, the auroras of its northern lights making it appear strangely green in my rear view—a pale-green dot receding into a sea of stars. Now it is no more than a blip of data, slowly fading from my radar and no longer holding any power over me.

My leg has healed, and I have been corresponding with Petra, my closest friend from Academy, almost daily. I regret that I did not properly say goodbye to Gemma. I will never be able to repay her for all that she did for me. My heart aches over the loss of Ramses, and I cannot let my mind touch the fear I have for Taj without bringing forth emotions that, today, I am unable to manage. Instead, I try to have hope: hope that Taj will find his true self, deep within his conflicted heart, and have the courage to refuse Abramovich the sacrifice of his singular life.

In the last hour, he defied Abramovich to help me escape—and I still can't understand why. I dare not dream the person I knew him to be still lives, whether he be the child who built stick forts with me till nightfall down by the river in Cana or my gregarious comrade in Academy, winning fighter jet tourneys and the adoration of all our peers at an equal and incomparable pace. That was the Taj I knew, or thought I knew, in the early days. He had been changed for some time. He had become withdrawn and isolated in the later years, wearing a somber mask of duty, speaking only of code and mission, just as he was on Proxima, until—until I saw a glimmer of my friend again.

I stop myself. I stop myself from entertaining the possibility that he has become anything more than Abramovich's pawn after our time down on the planet together. I stop myself because it's out of my hands now. I stop dreaming and reset my expectations to a neutral place. I don't dare dream; I don't dare want anything at all anymore—my fate has been such. I will focus on the task at hand. I will make it back to Titan, and I will not get distracted along the way by looking back.

I sit comfortably at the helm of my escape craft, the newly minted *Phoenix*. Wrapped in a blanket and lost in a peaceful reverie, I stare vacantly at the rush of stars before me. When I say newly minted, I mean that I reprogrammed the vessel to respond to my command alone and gave it a new name and deep-space ID tag with the help of the manuals Gemma so generously provided. Sipping a cup of

Canish breakfast tea, Imani's favorite, I would give anything to have her sitting here with me now. What would she say if I told her all that had transpired on Proxima?

My brother Joshua and I have been in regular communication, but I have not been able to bring myself to discuss the topic of my genetic makeup with him—although I am fairly certain he is well aware of it, considering the so-very-public nature of Abramovich's great charade.

"You want to talk about this?" Joshua will ask.

"Not today" is always my answer.

Imani is deep underground and cannot safely travel to the sub-surface level of Cana City to speak with me live as Joshua does, but we have been writing regularly. I am having a hard time bringing forth the gritty details of my experiences to her; I am not sure if it's that I can't bear to expose her to the horror of it all or if it's my own reliving of it that I'm avoiding. In any case, she knows me all too well and is giving me the time I need to get there on my own.

So we keep it light and talk of simple things. I can tell she is choosing to bring up topics she knows will make me smile—even in the wake of the trauma she and I and the rest of the Revivalists have endured in the aftermath of Abramovich's attack—speaking only of beautiful things like animals, flowers, and music. And I couldn't love her more for it. She's helping me to hold on to the last threadbare shred of sweetness that is a fast-fading memory of our planet and old life together, as if she knows I may just be hanging on to it for dear life. And sometimes it is that way. But I have found, on the other side of things, I am somehow growing stronger. I cannot quite put my finger on it, but something changed in me on that planet, and some days, I can feel it rising.

Turning my gaze from the blur of stars, I look at an image of Petra. A dimensional projection of her face and torso frames a floating game board. We have just begun a match of virtual chess. "King's pawn, forward two squares from E2 to E4," I say, glancing from the shimmering board above the console and back to the tablet in my hands where I am studying the ship's flight manuals. Currently, I am reading up on virtual reality goggles and cloaking devices.

"How'd you survive on that planet with a dead suit, anyway?" she asks while vaguely considering my move on the board. "Its atmosphere is mostly helium."

"He's augmented the atmosphere," I reply. "In preparation for 'New Cana,' he's terraforming the planet," I elaborate in a tone that mocks the idea of his promised land, but only because it's *his*, of course. I know better than to speak so irreverently of what very well may become a sorely needed solution for my people. However, I do so anyway because I'm still resentful of my imprisonment and everything else Abramovich put me through on Proxima. Not to mention the nuclear holocaust he instigated that destroyed Earth. Plus, I know I am safe speaking my most private thoughts with Petra. The truth is, Earth does need his planet, but not on such harrowing terms.

"You wouldn't believe the lengths to which he's gone," I continue. "Well, I suppose you might, considering the shambles in which he's left both of our worlds . . ."

"Oh yes, I am aware. Wait until you see this place," she says, referring to Titan Station, the largest remaining Alliance base after the war. The Alliance lost half of its fleet when the Earth and moon fell to Abramovich's nuclear strike. What's left now is Titan itself and a handful of minor outposts. "It's a ghost town compared with the metropolis it was before you left, and I cannot even speak of what's happened to Earth." Her eyes are wide and haunted. "Hella, it's a living nightmare." She moves her king's bishop's pawn out.

"Our world was always tumbling toward anarchy, anyway, wasn't it?" I say bitterly. "King's bishop out three squares diagonally from F1 to C4," I instruct the computer, threatening her king's bishop's pawn.

"Morbid as ever, I see, Hella," she remarks lightly. "Glad you haven't changed too much in the last twenty years. Well, except for your hair."

I give her a look, and she laughs.

"No, I like it. I'm just used to the bun." As she continues, I start running my hand through the knots self-consciously. "You look as if you've just descended from a castle." She giggles, putting on an air of dramatic superiority.

Looking at Petra's face, you would never suspect twenty years have passed. She has always cared for her appearance, and it seems she has not let things slide an inch as she has aged, however imperceptibly. I can tell she has retained access post-war to the Institution's powerful regenerative drugs to maintain her youthful appearance. Most citizens of the Institution have a similar look. I certainly do not fault her for it and wouldn't change a thing about her—she is beautiful inside and out.

I reply, "Uh-huh. Not quite down from a castle. More like up from a dungeon."

She moves her F7 pawn out two spaces as I pretend to study the board, conjuring my best poker face, as I know my next move and the one that follows. "A very technologically sophisticated dungeon, that is," I continue as I recall the catacombs. "I've seen his robotics lab. He has plans for robotic versions of the entire animal kingdom, a humanoid model that is more sophisticated than anything I have seen on Titan, and hologram programs that speak with more depth and foresight than Socrates." I move again. "Advance queen four squares diagonally from D1 to H5." I now threaten her F7 pawn.

Petra shakes her head when she realizes my game strategy. "And his hologram daughter showed you all this?" she asks with a trace of skepticism.

"Yes. Her goodwill is something I cannot explain. I would never have made it out of there without her. She has this supernatural, old-soul wisdom, but then doesn't seem troubled by, or even aware really, of the of the limitations of her life within the confines of her program . . ." I trail off, staring blankly at the game board, waiting for Petra to make her move so I can go in for the kill.

"Which begs the question: *Are any of us?*" Petra counters, always up for a philosophical debate. "As humans, we may not be confined by a holographic program, per se, but are we not confined by our own nature, enslaved as we are to our mortality?" she asks, making her next move. "Is that really any different?"

"I hadn't thought of it that way," I admit. So maybe we are more alike than I thought, Gemma and I—something I knew deep down but could not quite articulate. "Our program is ruled by time and how we perceive it as humans. We cannot see outside its confines any more than she can see beyond her Off switch."

I then capture Petra's king's bishop's pawn at F7 with my queen. "*Sha mat*—the king is defeated," I say, smiling victoriously as I declare checkmate and do a little bow.

"Alright, alright, you win," she concedes good-naturedly. "It's past my bedtime anyway." Stretching her arms over her head and yawning, she swipes a floating button, and the game board vanishes. "Good night, Queen," she says, smiling.

"Night, Petra," I reply, swiping the console button that ends our call.

Retiring to the rear of *the Phoenix*, I climb down the ladder to the bottom level where the cabin and bunks are located. While getting ready for bed, I look in the mirror. My hair is long and blonde, permanently bleached by Proxima's sun, though with darkening roots beginning to show. Wavy and wild, I have been wearing it loose because parts are too matted now to braid. Eventually, I will bother to look up the code to print a comb, but it has been last on my list of priorities. My skin is no longer the dark beige it was six weeks ago; it has faded to a lighter shade of brown. My eyes are still the crystal blue of my homeland, genuinely possessed only by true descendants of Cana. They are my heritage, reflecting back at me in the mirror, reminding me that as far away as I am, perhaps I am not as alone as I feel.

I tuck myself into bed but, of course, cannot sleep. Growing up, Imani used to chide me for drinking tea in the evening since she knew I would not be able to fall asleep until late and would be groggy for my studies in the morning—and she wasn't wrong. But I have always been a night owl and prefer it that way. Picking up my tablet, I recheck the long-range scanners to confirm that I am still surrounded by infinite nothingness, then toggle back to the ship's flight manuals I have been studying.

My leg is finally feeling ready for a jog. I recently discovered that my shuttlecraft has VR capabilities, though they are limited compared with the gym on Proxima. Giving up on sleep, I get out of bed and walk through to the cardio pod in a small crew space on the lower deck toward the prow of the ship. After tapping open a compartment adjacent to the pod, the VR goggles I have been read-ing about pop out. Placing the sleek strip over my eyes, I select a trail near Craggy Canyon along the coast of Cana for my run.

As I begin jogging, it isn't long before I feel the weight of the world starting to lift. I am surprised to find my cardiovascular fitness in superior condition. I am in much better shape than I should be, considering the injuries I sustained on Proxima and that I've been confined to the ship for the last several weeks.

Then it dawns on me: Coma White. Never having been treated with the Institution's embryo drugs—not before Taj used Coma White to save my life six weeks ago—I've not yet had the opportu-nity to experience the aftereffects. However, I've heard rumors about their near-supernatural efficacy and lengthy half-life.

Part of the reason the Institution is so reliant on these drugs is because they *are* so powerful and have such an extended half-life—people claim to benefit from the effects for weeks, even months, after treatment. There was, of course, a problem with addiction in the early days when the drugs were first introduced, the price of abuse high and particularly detrimental to the brain. After extended use, many patients were left with a severe kind of apathy that either led to suicide or ultimately rendered the brain vegetative. The doses were tweaked and scaled down in time, making the damage less common and more gradual. However, the drug still required strict regulation. Could this explain the ease of my jog?

With a genuine sensation of descending, I continue down a vir-tual slope and turn toward the coast where the sea is now abreast of me. As I pad lightly along the dirt path, I exit the jungle and am suddenly surrounded by sun, sky, and mountains. Overwhelmed by the majesty of Cana, my spirit is renewed as I drink in the fresh, cool air and bask in the warmth of the sunshine on my skin. I think I will certainly find Gemma here, hidden somewhere, just waiting for me in the landscape, then popping up out of nowhere as she so often did back at the compound. But she is nowhere to be found.

When I finish my run, I remove the VR goggles and shower before returning to bed. As I get settled again, my mind returns to the same place it wanders every night when I am left alone with my thoughts. I think about my genetic makeup and try to come to terms with what it means to be a clone—and, well, beyond that, a clone of someone of such historical consequence.

A clone is a genetically identical copy of a biological entity, and if Abramovich's claim is true, in my case, I am a genetically identical copy of a Galilean Jewish woman from the first century BC of the Old World—the biological entity otherwise known as the Virgin Mary. A piece of her DNA was recovered from an archaeological site believed to be the location of her tomb in Old Jerusalem, then transferred to a human egg with its own DNA-containing nucleus removed. That egg was then allowed to develop into an early-stage embryo in a test tube and ultimately implanted into the womb of a woman, Konstantin—the woman whom I'd believed until recently to be my biological mother.

The thought still sends a shiver up my spine. In the darkness of the cabin, I hold my hand out in front of my face, flipping it over and examining the lines and creases. The thing is, clones do not always look identical to their clone source. Even though they share the same genetic material, environment plays a significant role in how an organism develops. The age-old nature vs. nurture paradox comes to mind.

So does being a clone really mean anything after all? I wonder. So badly, I want to brush it off, and more than anything, I hate that I exist only because Abramovich wanted it to be so. Because *it suited him*. Because *it furthered his agenda*. I exist because of his twisted ambition, not because there was love between two people or because those people wanted a family.

My thoughts return to Konstantin. Her connection with Abramovich is such an unusual alliance. When I knew her, she had no religion beyond her own ambition.

It was rare for any citizen of the Institution to be fertile, but my mother was—she made sure of it. A repeating body transplant recipient like Abramovich, Konstantin had already lived several lifetimes before giving birth to me. However, she did not mix with the generations of other Greybeards and kept her secret heavily guarded, using the Institution's regenerative solutions without restraint to keep her face and head looking youthful. Her interest in fertility medicine began early when she was denied the license to reproduce with her partner. Medical evaluations had shown that the combination of their genes would result in abnormality, disease, or the possibility of a psychological profile that was deemed too risky to bring to life in this world. Thus, they were prohibited by the government from having a child together. I had always assumed that this loss was the driver of her obsession with fertility medicine and that she gave birth to me because she still wanted a child of her own. But I know now that maternalism likely had little to do with it. She may have wanted a child, but she wanted a child that was of her blood and her lover's blood—not me. I was no more than a science experiment to her.

Although Konstantin wasn't Canish, it seemed apparent early on that my genetics were. I had long believed this to be a deliberate choice on her part, for some scientific reason that benefited her experiments or because it had simply been her preference. But now I suspect there was far more to it than any of my assumptions can explain.

Konstantin never revealed her objectives to me concerning the endless medical trials she forced me to endure when I was under her guardianship at the Ascendency, other than that they had something to do with fertility. But now it seems plain. She and Abramovich were playing God.

Eventually, my ruminations release their taloned grip on my consciousness, and the quiet hum of the ship's engines lulls me to sleep at last.

I wake up safe in my bunk in the lower cabin of *the Phoenix*, still missing the dog who is no longer at my feet. Getting up to stretch, I feel renewed with energy from my run last night. After making a smoothie in the kitchenette and grabbing a cup of coffee, I head back up to the second level and the front of the vessel to the flight deck. Sitting down at the comm, I see a new notification. *The Phoenix* is approaching the outskirts of the Oort Cloud, and an Alliance outpost has been identified, Oort-9.

The Oort Cloud lies just beyond the heliosphere of Earth's solar system, deep in interstellar space. It is composed of billions of objects of icy matter—asteroids, comets, and other debris of cosmic dust. While the Kuiper Belt and other asteroid fields that orbit the sun are disc-shaped and significantly closer to the system's interior, the Oort Cloud is dense and spherical in composition and much farther away from our star. Its outer edges define the cosmographical boundary of Earth's solar system. Although the Oort Cloud sits 4.6 trillion miles from Earth's sun, it marks the beginning of the last quarter of my journey between Alpha Centauri and the Saturn system. In short, I am getting closer to home.

As I approach Oort-9, I ponder its murky history. The base is the Alliance's most remote military way station and is more commonly referred to as Calypso. The moniker originates from Greek lore, referring to a nymph who held Odysseus captive, luring him away to the wilds of a faraway isle for many years in Homer's epic *The Odyssey*. Mythology of the Old World is popular with the Revivalists, the study of it another cultural stipulation mandated by the Founders, and the name Calypso fitting considering the number of cadets and even captains who have gone missing from the outpost over the years. Thought to be in pursuit of some kind of salvation, idea, or freedom from one thing or another—a certain allure only the infinite mystery of interstellar space can offer—most who left Calypso for whatever reason without filing a flight plan never returned. Suffice it to say that Xavier was not the first to go AWOL while stationed there.

Sending a message of greeting to Calypso, I alert them to my approach and identify myself as an Alliance officer since I am on an unfamiliar vessel. I am tempted to dock for a few days and try and get to the bottom of the mystery that has been torturing me for the better part of a decade, but I somehow find myself feeling differently about it. I had had this idea that Xavier belonged to me—and maybe he did for a moment in time—but when that moment passes, as they inevitably do, you question, was that life ever really yours to begin with?

I allowed the idea of him and us together make up so much of what I thought was my identity, but it seems now he hadn't seen things the same way. As beautiful as that life was, it was not mine. I decide not to chase his memory anymore, and the peace I find on the other side of that decision is the last thing I expect.

Phoenix, Calypso here. We read you. Do you copy?

Copy, Calypso.

A long way from home, I see. En route to Titan?

Affirmative. Homeward bound.

Will you be docking?

Negative, Calypso.

Carry on and safe travels. Calypso out.

Phoenix out.

19

After continuing past *Calypso*, reaching the Saturn system took another two weeks—much of which I spent reading, training, and planning with Joshua over comms. Encountering nothing and no one along the way, the days and nights in deep space began to drag on and blend together, dulling my sense of reality yet continuing to serve as a welcome monotony compared with my time imprisoned on Proxima.

At long last, I approach the swirling, yellow planet. I behold its many moons and dazzling ice rings as *the Phoenix* enters orbit and Titan appears. Though dwarfed by Saturn's colossal size, it is a gem in its own right and just as I remember it to be: hazy, mystical, and beautiful. Despite the tragedy that has plagued my life and the lives of my kind, and all the work that lies ahead to help not only the people of Cana but the entire race of Revivalists, I feel wild, thrilled, and free to soon be released from the confines of my small vessel and home again.

Approaching the highest peak of the floating citadel that is Titan Station—a silver needle puncturing the thick orange fog of Titan's dense nitrogen atmosphere—I am unsure what to expect as I dock *the Phoenix* in the familiar shuttle bay. It doesn't feel like I've been away all that long, but this place will have aged twenty years.

Standing on the ground level of my craft, I am ready to exit. After I receive the signal that my landing is secure, I send the command to the ship to open the hatch at the vessel's rear.

As the hatch slowly unfolds, the first thing I see beyond it is Petra, waiting on the other side in full uniform. The silver-and-gold emblems dressing the collar of her white suit indicate that she is now a highly decorated officer, no longer the green ensign she was when we were last together. Flanking her are two officers who are unfamiliar to me.

"Welcome home, Ensign," she says as I walk down the sloping ramp that has folded out of *the Phoenix*.

I drop my bag in which I packed my few belongings and stand at attention. Feeling very casual out of uniform, I salute her nevertheless and say, "Thank you. It's good to be home, sir." Faced with the formality of base protocol, I am relieved I bothered to find the time to synthesize a comb on the last leg of my journey. I thoroughly combed, parted, and wound my white-blonde hair in a sleek knot at the base of my skull before my arrival this afternoon.

The Alliance officer's uniform hasn't changed much since I have been away; seeing it again brings back those last pivotal moments high in Earth's orbit twenty years ago. I had hastily removed and discarded my uniform, leaving it where it fell as Taj helped me into my escape pod. Moments later, it was incinerated along with the rest of the ship. Shuddering at the thought, I will myself back to the present, to Petra, her companions, and Titan Station.

As I stand at attention, Petra looks at me in disbelief and distractedly introduces the officers beside her. I acknowledge them, and after a few moments, she exhales audibly and relaxes her posture before smiling broadly at me. She then gives everyone unspoken permission to drop protocol, as she is the senior officer on the floor. I beam back at her, and then we run to each other.

After we embrace for several seconds, I see a small crowd has gathered. Someone hoots, and people begin to clap and cheer my safe return. It feels surreal and almost overwhelming after being isolated for the last six months. I wonder if my picture is on the wall with the other officers who have gone missing in action over the years. I wonder if there is a picture of Taj on the same wall or if it has been removed and he is truly deemed a criminal of war here.

Petra and I pull apart, still clutching hands. She says, "I can't believe you're *here*." Her eyes are a mix of joy and disbelief. "You honestly haven't aged a day. I guess biologically, you're still twenty years old?"

"Twenty-one," I correct. "But yes, we had just graduated." I smile, remembering the day we became officers. It feels like only a few months ago.

"What I wouldn't give to have the youth of my twenty-year-old self again!" she exclaims, pretending to be envious.

"Please, Petra, you look exactly the same!" I say with a laugh, and it's true. I knew as much seeing her virtually while we spoke in transit, and it is confirmed for me now as I behold her in person. She must be almost forty years old in Earth years, yet not a strand of gray disrupts her gleaming jet-black hair, still long and neatly secured in a low ponytail. Not a single wrinkle or crease blemishes her porcelain skin or distracts from her steel-gray eyes, two perfect orbs of hematite situated beneath her thick eyebrows, which are perfectly manicured arches.

"Hardly. You have the blood of true youth pumping through your veins. No bio-serum in the galaxy can replicate it. Believe me, I've looked." She smirks and turns toward the door, beckoning me to follow.

There's that word: *replicate*—another word for *clone, to copy*. I wonder if anyone here knows about me and the very specific nature of my DNA. Had anyone besides Cana seen Abramovich's broadcast? Petra never mentioned it during our almost daily conversations on my journey home. And I didn't either, glazing over that minor detail when telling her about all that happened on Proxima. There is still so much I don't know about the politics of this new world. We were all once allies in fluid communication, but that was now *twenty years* ago, a reality I still struggle to accept on most days. Joshua said there had been some correspondence between Earth and the Alliance over the years, but nothing very formal because it was too risky for Cana. In the first days after the attack, the Alliance sent a dispatch to help the survivors, but it was blown out of the sky as soon as it reached Earth's orbit. Earth was clearly too broken to maintain or reestablish any alliances. Perhaps my secret is safe for now—although I imagine if someone knew the right places to look on the network, the information about me would be readily available, thanks to Abramovich.

As I fall in line next to Petra, she dismisses the two officers accompanying her. "Hope you're hungry," she says with a mischievous grin. "We have a small gathering planned in the mess hall." Then, giving me no opportunity to object, she drags me through the shuttle bay doors and toward the lift. I shake my head, laughing, and reluctantly follow. Just like the old days, Petra loves a good party.

Titan Station is the size of a small city and has artificial gravity calibrated to match Earth's high gravity. Without it, our bodies would slowly acclimate to Titan's low-gravity environment, and we ultimately would not be able to return to Earth again and stand, walk, or even survive, as the resulting long-term physiological changes from subsisting in a low-gravity environment are irreversible.

The terrain here is mostly ice but is otherwise composed of tiny granules of organic matter that resemble sand. These granules form Titan's famed dunes that stretch for miles across the surface, framing the Vid Flumina, the great river just below the station. Two hundred and fifty feet deep and lined with smooth ice pebbles, the river flows into the Ligeia Mare and is brimming with rapids, waterfalls, and whirlpools. Known as a watery moon, Titan has rivers, lakes, and seas covering its surface. These dark bodies of liquid methane are replete with tides, currents, and waves that crash the shores, features more typical of larger celestial bodies such as Earth and Proxima.

Beyond the watery lowlands, the highlands of Titan are riddled with ice caves. Mineral graphite, the raw material used to produce the highly coveted compound graphene, is mined inside these caves. Graphene is the magic component used to reinforce our space suits, affording us both the mobility and advanced shielding needed to traverse the surface of moons like Titan and to travel elsewhere in the solar system. Offering protection from the natural elements and the winds of war alike, graphene-made suits are just the thing my people need back on Earth to establish a defense presence on the surface.

Little more than a frozen shell of sand and ice, Titan's surface is not stable enough to support a massive building complex like the station. Thus, most of Titan's infrastructure hovers above the clouds. Below that shell is a sixty-two-mile-deep subterranean ocean that serves as the base's primary resource for oxygen and water.

Meandering down a long corridor in the residential sector, I observe that there are civilians here now, including children. The population is only sparsely peppered with those of us in uniform. Titan was once exclusively militaristic—not a place where people settled or raised offspring. But that has all changed since the fall of Empyreus. Regardless, it feels good to mix with people again. Petra has informed me that a family now occupies my old quarters. After staying late at the mess hall lounge catching up with the officers I knew in Academy, she shows me to a studio apartment that is much smaller than my old suite.

Exhausted, I settle in without so much as unpacking. Dropping my bag, I notice that I have been provisioned several uniforms, which hang in the closet. They're sleek and white, like Petra's, but with only the small silver ensign insignia on the collar, as opposed to her more elaborate collar that is bejeweled with symbols of her accomplishments. Peering out the window, I can see only smoggy darkness as I take my hair down and collapse on the bed. I fall asleep quickly, but only for about an hour. I wake up again and again, restless and sweaty.

I was back on Earth, talking to him. Xavier was looking at the sky, regarding the stars as cold and planetary—*lonely*, he said. It was a conversation we truly had once back on Earth. The planets were ancient and silent, he said. They made him feel alone, as if they *could not* and *would not* help him in this life. Staring down at him, mute and indifferent, they always watched but never spoke.

I saw it differently, I told him. Those same stars, that same sky, were hopeful to me and represented life and possibility—everything I dreamed about. Beacons of hope, they were a sign of all the good to come.

Looking at me, smiling in a way that made me angry, as if he felt sorry for me and knew something I did not, he called me "kiddo" that day. "Don't leave us too soon, *kiddo*," he said while lifting his arm to tousle my hair. Dodging out of his reach, I stormed off, leaving him alone on the beach.

Shrugging it all off later, I never admitted to him that he had upset me. *Why does he spend so much time with me if he doesn't take me seriously?* I had thought then, but eventually brushed it off and forgot it as, day after day, he returned, seeking my company and my thoughts and my mind. I can't help but have that same thought again now and assume, based on what I learned from Taj about the TRAPPIST System—and Xavier's plan to find it at any cost—that it must have been true; I was no more than a kid to him.

In the quiet dark of my quarters, I kick off the comforter but pull the crisp sheet up to my chin again, closing my eyes. Maybe I *was* naive back then to see the world with such hopeful eyes considering what I know now and all that has transpired since—I know the person I was on Proxima would have thought so.

Today, I have a meeting with the station captain. He is the highest-ranking officer on this moon, which by default—since the legacy leadership council members were killed in the explosions back on Earth all those years ago—makes him the ruling authority over the entire United Planetary Alliance. Additionally, he was a member of the pioneering crew that journeyed to Titan a couple of hundred years back. From what I know, he is still in good health, which tells me Titan must have retained an ample supply of the life-extending bio-meds of which Earth's Regime is so sorely in need.

I hoped to get a little more sleep, but after staring at the ceiling for the last two hours, I finally give up and get out of bed at 0600. My meeting with the captain is not until 0900, so I take my time showering and brushing out my hair. After making a cup of Canish breakfast tea, I sit cross-legged on the bed, reviewing my notes in preparation for the meeting and catching up on correspondence with my family back on Earth to notify them of my safe arrival. Also, a message pops up from Petra, and we agree to meet this afternoon for sparring practice.

At around 0800, I slip into my uniform and tie back my hair. Curly wisps frame my face from letting it dry naturally this morning. My reflection in the mirror is familiar in some ways but not others. I am pleased to see that through my physical training on *the Phoenix*, I have put most of the muscle back on that I lost on Proxima. The uniform looks familiar enough, but my hair is different, and my face somehow looks older.

Studying the beauty mark on the left side of my face—above my lip and just below my nostril—I begin to wonder if she had it, too. *She, the original version of me. My clone source.* I look from the small dark spot to my eyes; now she's even got me wondering about them. *Are they yours, Holy Mother, or are they mine?* I think flippantly. My hair, skin tone, and heritage have now all come into question. *Am I even still Canish?* I wonder silently. *More impossible questions.* Making a conscious effort to relax my jaw, I head out the door in search of breakfast.

As I walk, I decide that I like how it feels here. I was so isolated on Proxima and in transit that I didn't realize how much of a toll it was taking on my mental health. The population density of Titan Station was a little jarring at first, but now I find the people milling about and going about their days comforting.

When I reach the main drag, I pass a little café station. Grabbing an apple, I begin to take a ravenous bite when I notice a young ensign with the unmistakable look of Cana seated in the corner studying a tablet. He has dark curly hair, light-brown skin, and captivating blue eyes. Imperfect features make it obvious he is unaltered by bio-meds and, therefore, more than likely from my country. Everyone who uses the Institution's age-defying drugs tends to look similar. Even those who attempt to look radically different with blue hair, tattoos, or even horns don't end up looking all that differently in the end. That's the thing about perfection: it's boring.

As I continue to observe him, I order a matcha from the barista-bot and wonder who the young ensign may be. When I was here before, I knew all the people from my homeland. He seems a little too old to have been born here after the war and a little too young to have been in my class in Academy. Gnawing on my apple core and staring, I try to work out the puzzle of his identity when he looks up suddenly. After a cursory glance, he does a little double-take before giving me a shy smile—perhaps recognizing that I, too, am from Cana.

His eye contact startles me, and when I realize that I have been caught staring, I look away quickly. Then my beverage is up, so I grab it and toss the apple core into the receptacle before heading out.

Making my way to the station's north end, crossing the sky bridge to the Commanders' Tower, I am dizzied by the drop below that is visible through the transparent floor beneath my feet. Methane clouds obscure most of the ground and horizon, but I can see the surface in some places. Through holes in the cloudscape, I spot black dunes and snaking rivers far, far below. Then, looking up, I notice all at once the massive yellow planet peeking through the haze, tilted just so on its axis.

Taking the lift to the Commanders' Tower, I find it quieter here. Few people are around, and those whom I do encounter seem more composed and subdued, even somber. The floors and walls are the same off-white color as elsewhere in the station but are marbled and pristine in this tower where they had been carpeted before. When I finally reach Dr. Freeman's office, I am right on time, at 0900 hours.

20

When I press the button next to the door to the station captain's office, it chirps. In a moment, the door splits in two, sliding open. "Ensign Nazari, please, come in," a voice beckons.

Walking through a small pink marble foyer, I pass a vacant desk where an assistant may have once sat, then enter through an open archway to the office proper. The captain is standing with his back to me, facing the window. I stop and stand formally at attention.

Freeman turns around to greet me. He looks like a man in his prime, yet I know he is at least as old as this base. Though he looks young enough for his age, he exudes a sort of ancient quality—I can't put my finger on it exactly. Maybe it's the truth in his eyes, a weight many of us are finding hard to shake these days. Possessing an Institution-bred agelessness that never ceases to astound me, the last thing he looks is *mortal*.

The office is gunmetal-gray polished quartz from floor to ceiling, so shiny I can see the ghost of my reflection standing poised at attention in every direction. The expanse of windows dominating the rear wall faces Titan's northern polar seas. Saturn is still visible; the clouds thinning out to reveal a clear blue sky this morning.

Turning only halfway to acknowledge me, the captain's arms remain folded behind his back. A brief nod, and he returns his gaze to the window.

"Did you know, Ensign, that the word *planet* means *wanderer* in Greek?" he finally asks. "And some of these heavenly bodies can be downright rogue, wandering about wherever they please." Before I can reply, he turns back to me suddenly, then to the window again, as if he's about to share a great secret. "Not unlike *you*, hmm?"

Well, I didn't exactly wander to the edge of the galaxy and back, I think to myself. I feel that descriptive would be more apt had I gone to Proxima of my own free will to begin with, but I don't bother to remind him. He has my report and knows I was routed to Alpha Centauri without my consent—or knowledge, for that matter. In fact, I was literally unconscious at the time. Plus, I would wager he has seen the now-recovered flight logs that show Taj's digital signature on the course alteration.

Taj. As much as I try to fight it, Taj is a persistent thought. *A criminal of war. He is an enemy of the Alliance,* I remind myself.

"Of course I know that, Dr. Freeman," I reply. "I am an astrophysicist and passed your class with flying colors." I then rattle off the formal definition to prove my point. "A rogue planet is a planetary-mass object that does not orbit a star directly. Such objects have been ejected from the planetary system in which they formed or have never been gravitationally bound to any star—*wanderers*."

"Bravo. That's right. You did complete my course, and with high marks, if memory serves. Some years back, no? Of course, I converse with a greater number of civilians these days, so you must forgive me. The base population has become quite diluted since we lost Earth . . ." He trails off. "Well, welcome back, Ensign. I trust you've settled in well and Commander Chauverac has seen to your needs and reclamation."

"Yes, she has. Thank you, sir," I say, thinking immediately of Petra.

"Has your debrief with the Council been scheduled?"

"Yes, sir. It's later this morning."

"Good. We wondered if you had been in cahoots with Lieutenant Furi. Well, we did a thorough investigation, but still would like to question you in terms of any confessions he might have made during the time you spent together in Alpha Centauri . . ."

"Oh? What did you find in your investigation, if you don't mind me asking?"

Dr. Freeman is silent for a moment, looking dumbfounded. "Well, nothing. Your record is pristine," he admits.

Nodding almost imperceptibly, I stare straight ahead, displaying nothing but expressionless professionalism on my face.

"At ease, Ensign," he says after a lengthy pause. Then, walking over to his desk, he motions for me to sit in one of the plush armchairs facing the black-marbled monstrosity. Once he has settled in his chair, he speaks again. "My engineers can't make heads or tails of that ship you brought back."

Good, I think to myself. "Yes, sir, that is by design," I reply confidently.

"Well, how'd *you* learn to fly it, then?"

"I have the flight manuals. And your engineers may be having trouble because I reprogrammed the ship to respond exclusively to my command." He does not break his stare as I add, "A precautionary measure."

Raising his eyebrows, he nods, then remains quiet for some time as if he is digesting what I have told him. He looks to the window again before changing the subject.

"Don't let that blue sky fool you. Saturnine Equinox is nearly upon us."

Turning my gaze to the window, I am immediately met with the windy, yellow planet dominating the skyline. Eleven times larger in the sky than the moon as seen from Earth, it takes Saturn twenty-nine Earth years to orbit the sun once. Sitting on its axis at an angle relative to its orbital plane, it experiences alternating seasons of winter and summer, following each other in a cycle—not unlike Earth. Titan, fixed in Saturn's orbit, follows the same rhythm. But Saturn and Titan's seasonal cycles are significantly longer than Earth's. I arrived at this system at the end of a fifteen-year winter and right before Equinox, which brings torrential rainstorms at the equator. The heavy rains herald the beginning of spring, but rain here is nothing like on Earth. Rain on Titan falls much slower due to the lower gravitational pull. While Earth's rain generally falls at around twenty miles per hour, rain on Titan falls at about three and a half. Raindrops here are also quite large compared with Earth's—about 50 percent larger. While I have seen rain on Titan, I have not yet witnessed an Equinox due to its fifteen-year cycle, but I am told it is quite something to behold.

Clearing his throat, Dr. Freeman interrupts my reverie. Quickly turning from the window, I focus my attention back on him.

"Will you be staying with us long? Surely you will stay for the Equinox celebrations."

"Well, I suppose it depends," I begin tentatively. "There are some things I need to do first, and there is something I must ask of you."

He looks back at me blankly, his hands steepled in front of his face, and, after a pause, asks, "Do you have the desire to be reinstated?"

"N-n-no—well, yes, I would like to be reinstated," I stutter. "Just not right away—if that's possible. It's just the attack on Earth doesn't feel that long ago for me, and my people are still suffering. I feel I have an obligation to return to Earth, to Cana, to help them."

The captain says nothing at first but does not break his stare with me. He is a man who has no qualms about uncomfortable silences, no nervous impulse to fill the empty space with chatter—but then, neither do I.

Letting ten long seconds pass between us, then fifteen, I finally ask, "Do I have your leave, sir?"

Thoughtful for some time, he eventually replies, "I will consider it. However, as you say, the situation on Earth is grave. We tried to offer our assistance early on but to no avail. Lives were lost; two ships, to be exact. My concern is that if you go down there with that ship of yours, the Regime will get hold of the technology and gain the ability to get off-world and reach us here. They want our bio-meds; they want our graphene . . ." Giving me a long look, he adds, "Who knows what or who else they'd pursue had they the means." He lets his comment sink in before continuing. "Furthermore, how do you plan on penetrating the radiation belt? I'm assuming that ship will enable your passage, but I'm curious how." He is referring to an impassable field of trapped electrons that formed high above the surface of the Earth years ago, a by-product of nuclear war that will indefinitely remain in Earth's atmosphere. "No ships have done it successfully since the attack, and beyond that, you will surely lead the Regime directly to Cana, will you not?"

"*The Phoenix* has a cloaking device with shielding modifications that will allow the ship to pass through the electron field unharmed. And as for leading the Regime to Cana, I am working on hacking my suit's software—"I pause when I realize how casually I'm speaking with him. But he looks back with intense interest, appearing unbothered—almost appreciative—of my directness, so I continue. "And mapping the ship's cloaking technology to my suit's interface."

"And how's that going?" he asks skeptically, and he's not wrong.

I am struggling with my work on the suit cloak. Freeman has been around long enough to understand that what I'm trying to accomplish is not as simple as flipping a switch. While it's one thing to follow a manual and do some patchy programming, I am light years away from having the expertise to create or even just manipulate this new technology to the degree required to map the cloaking function from ship to suit. While I am a trained astrophysicist and skilled pilot, I do not have an engineering background. The captain, on the other hand, has over a century under his belt of education and experience in mechanical engineering, aerospace, astrophysics—you name it. The man has been around a long time, and I honestly could use his help with it. But I need the graphene more than anything else, so I don't plan on pushing my luck today by asking him for additional favors.

"It's going okay," I reply, holding back a little. "It's a little problematic, but I have a more pressing issue, and that's what I came to speak with you about."

He nods.

Taking a deep breath, I just dive into it. "My people—we need suits. Back on Earth. We desperately need suits and graphene, and, well, I was wondering if you had any to spare since the fleet has gotten . . . smaller."

"Ensign Nazari, you and everyone in the solar system needs graphene. Are you aware of the graphene conflict raging on Saturn's doorstep? Mars and the outer belts are in a dirty war over it and have been since Earth went dark. Yes, we have ample resources, but they are finite, and we cannot just hand them out to everyone who comes knocking."

Graphene Wars. I had not known. Maybe that's why Joshua sounded so skeptical when I offered to help procure a supply. Feeling foolish and out of my depth, I look down at my hands folded on my lap and anxiously try to think of a solution.

"Graphene Wars . . ." I begin, marveling at how, in twenty years' time, something that was once such an abundant resource had become the object of a war. "My apologies, sir. It sounds like there are a few things on which I still need briefing since my return."

"Much can happen in two decades, Ensign," he says wearily.

I pause, thinking, and realize I need to back up and slow down. "How has the Alliance fared in the aftermath of Earth's war?" I finally ask.

"We have endured loss and hardship like everyone else. There's been downsizing and restructuring, but we were also incredibly fortunate, as you can see. The United Planetary Alliance still stands and thrives; we do not look the same, but you do what you must in the face of war: you adapt. We have maintained our pace and progress on our primary missions. The terraforming project has remained on track. In fact, we are approaching the bicentennial marker of the transformation effort to make this moon a habitable, self-sufficient world."

I worked on one of the teams that contributed to the project in Academy and can attest that terraforming is no short venture; it will likely take a thousand years to complete the process. Knowing that the war has not stalled our work is a relief.

Dr. Freeman is still speaking. "A mission that will be news to you involves a discovery that occurred shortly after the nuclear attack on Earth." He pauses, contemplating for a moment what he is about to share. As he does, a lightness briefly washes over him. "We have found *life* in its most basic form on Enceladus."

At this news, a mix of shock and awe begins to ripple through me, and then an unmistakable presence, a persistence of indomitable peace, all at once fills me to the brim. How strange it is to think life was nearly extinguished on Earth just as it began elsewhere on a moon orbiting Saturn. No, perhaps humanity has some fight left, some tricks up her sleeve yet.

And what an unbelievable discovery for our kind, for the Alliance, for the Revivalists as a whole, and for the mad scientists who have been trying to accomplish the same in a test tube for a millennium. For now, we will have the ability to observe the miraculous in real-time.

I listen with rapture as he continues. "We've known for centuries that Titan and several of Saturn's trailing moons have the same chemical makeup as the atmosphere of primordial Earth, where the origin of life began. But who can say what precipitated that precise and seemingly mundane chemical reaction that resulted in life as we know it?

"Enceladus itself is one billion years old. That's one billion years of sterile lifelessness. But they tell me now that one billion is the magic number, the ideal age for life to occur, and, by God, it happened in our time, on our very own tiger-striped moon, miles beneath the surface in that salty ocean . . ." He trails off, lost in the miracle and wonder that even his genius mind struggles to comprehend. "And, well, we consider it our honor and duty to see that this new life is protected. Of course, right now, it is just a few simple microbes, but those cells are the beginnings of . . . *everything*."

He pauses, and a shadow begins to eclipse that state of wonder—that ecstatic joy—living mere moments before on his face. "But there are those who would exploit that life. People who would interfere and experiment with it, *harm* it, if you can believe it."

Oh, I can believe it, I think. Konstantin, the Institution, and all their wild experiments come to mind. And lest we not forget Mordecai Abramovich and the foul part he played in the exploitation and destruction of the lives of the Revivalists who perished in the war he started.

I am quiet, still processing everything he has said, when he looks up at me again. "Forgive me, Ensign. I am familiar with what happened to you at the Institution before you came here and very clear on who your captor was on Proxima—what he has done and what he is capable of."

"Thank you, sir. Thank you for your understanding."

Dr. Freeman then glances up at the clock on the wall, and I become aware that the time of our meeting will be coming to an end soon. As I prepare for his dismissal, he speaks again.

"Ensign Nazari," he says more softly this time, "regarding the graphene." He folds his hands in front of him on the desk and then looks at me directly. "You are in possession of a very powerful bargaining chip, and I may be open to negotiations."

I am so used to playing by the rules that I hadn't realized he was bluffing with what seemed to be a rejection of my request. *The ship. He wants my ship*, I think. It was technology I planned to share with the Alliance, which I think he surely must know . . .

When I realize I have been holding my spine very straight and my shoulders very tight for the duration of our meeting, I try to relax a bit and can't help but smile broadly and genuinely, having realized his meaning. "You wouldn't be willing to consider trading for a little space-compression technology, would you, sir?"

"No promises, Ensign, but believe it or not, I would be willing to discuss it." He chuckles. Then a shadow falls over his face once more. He looks pensive before going on. "You know you wouldn't be the first to offer me this technology."

This prompts me to think back to Proxima and the long-winded story Abramovich told me on one of the first days I was there, how he had offered his FTL technology to the Alliance but that they couldn't come to terms.

"Abramovich offered it to me years ago, and of course, we wanted it then as much as we do now. It's revolutionary . . ." He holds his hands up as if surrendering.

"But you turned it down?"

"Yes, I was left *no* choice but to turn it down."

"But why? How could you not come to terms with him?" I ask, truly curious. "It's FTL technology. It changes everything."

A little miffed, as though I am not the first person to pose this question to him, he replies, "Well, for one thing, because the Alliance, we—or I," he asserts, "do not negotiate with terrorists."

Looking at him blankly, not wholly taking in his meaning, I ask, "Well, what did he want in exchange?"

Looking at me again with that deep, dark truth glittering in his eyes, he finally says, as if debating whether to say it all, "Well, he wanted . . . *you.*"

Feeling cold suddenly, the magnitude of Abramovich's plan

hitting me all over again—how long he has been at this and how far he is willing to go—I think back to the person I was when I entered Academy, running as fast as I could away from my birth mother, never thinking there might be a worse evil in my realm; that anyone else could have had plans for my little life. A shiver snakes its way up my spine as I think about how narrowly I must have escaped Abramovich's grasp even then.

Looking at the captain a little wide-eyed, I try to maintain my composure. After some silence, he answers the unspoken question on my face. "Never in a million years would I trade your life for technology." I swallow a lump as he gets up from his desk and walks over to an enormous 3D star map projected onto the wall. With his back to me, he continues. "I would sooner lay down my life than hand you over to that monster."

My throat tightens, and it becomes difficult to speak. Grateful that he is no longer looking at me, I sit for a few minutes, leaning back on the soft chair, and cry quietly.

I cry for a million reasons. I cry because I feel angry and powerless. I cry out of relief because somehow, I survived. I cry for the dreamer who once stargazed on the shores of Cana unafraid, with nothing but hope in her heart. But mostly, I cry because I forgot that anyone might value my life for the precious little that it is, rather than for the imagined power the idea of my DNA carries. How could this man do for me what Taj *could* not? What my mother *would* not?

Wiping my palms on my knees, I sit up straight again. Tucking the loose wisps of hair behind my ear, I get up. Approaching Dr. Freeman, I want to hug him. I want to fall to the floor and thank him—to grovel at his feet—but I can only stand by the door at quiet attention and wait for him to dismiss me.

Turning away from the star map, he speaks again. "Earth is still dark, and we want to bring the Canish Revivalists back as allies but understand that they are deeply protective of their location. Thus, I approve your request to return to Earth on the condition that you go as an Alliance officer and reestablish that relationship for us. Additionally, I will provide you with the suits and graphene for which you have asked in exchange for the FTL technology you acquired on Proxima." I am stunned as he finishes, "You have my leave, Ensign."

"Thank you, sir," I manage to say, my voice trembling with a mix of relief and pride as I salute him. I am still too choked up to sufficiently express my gratitude, but I know what it means to me is not lost on him.

He nods, and I turn to leave.

As I approach the doorway, he speaks again. "Hella, I want you to know that I had my own genetic challenges when I was coming up . . . but that is a story for another day."

I smile a little at his kindness and then notice he is holding eye contact, as if he wants to be sure I hear what he is about to say next, before finishing, "Our genetics do not determine our lives, Ensign. We do."

21

Exiting the station captain's office, I walk through the small foyer and past the desk. Noticing an old nameplate that reads *Cassini Freeman*, I suppose his daughter must have sat here once. She was a child when I was here last, a designer baby, factory-made by the scientists of the Institution. Most of the children of the Institution and many of my peers here at the Alliance were likewise genetically engineered. She, however, was rumored to have genetic makeup that was exceptionally superior, partly because Freeman himself was not only brilliant but also fertile and thus able to sire his own child and partly because the egg used in her conception was rumored to be somewhat of an enigma. Where the egg was sourced remains a mystery. I wonder if she is still around.

Genetic engineering was practiced almost exclusively as a means for human reproduction by the people of Empyreus. Modifications may be made before birth to ensure the child is immune to disease, superior intellectually, or simply to elect that the baby is born a certain gender, height, or skin color. Alternatively, modifications may be made after birth, when and if the child chooses to take the expression of their identity into their own hands and alter any of these attributes of their own volition.

While genetic engineering is not commonly practiced in Cana, it is not the primary point of contention among my people in the realm of biotechnology. No, the argument is around another commonly practiced technology that involves the destruction of a human embryo to produce the potent life-extending pharmaceuticals the Institution is notorious for manufacturing. While the Alliance relies more heavily on the consensual use of adult stem cells to cure disease and extend life, it also stocks and reserves the more powerful embryo-sourced treatments for emergency procedures.

Years ago, the Alliance legalized the use of these controversial drugs when they were first introduced by the Institution. While they possess miraculous lifesaving properties, the methods used to produce them fell into a morally gray area, as was cited by the objection of some of my people to the use of embryos. It was also common knowledge that, though the Institution would never own up to it, these drugs came into existence through unconscionable violence—the exploitation of the fertile Canish people by means of kidnapping, imprisonment, and worse.

All things considered, the Alliance ultimately deemed the use of these drugs justified. By saving lives, the technology furthered and enabled Alliance missions, and considering the sum of all the good the Alliance had accomplished and would accomplish in the ages to come, the benefits, therefore, outweighed the cost. While I don't disagree that the Alliance is a formidable force for good, I recognize that in their choice, they were, in effect, turning a blind eye to the reality behind the way the embryos were procured; the world at large did. But because of that choice to legalize the use of those drugs, there aren't as many of my people here.

Coming in, I knew I would be a minority at Titan Station, and I wondered if I would be at a disadvantage since I was not genetically modified, intellectually or otherwise. So in the days before I left Earth for Academy, I resolved to do everything with excellence, and this way, I would know in my heart that others could not rightfully find fault in me. And with that mindset, I gained the confidence to shrug off any poor treatment I encountered for being seen as different in the early days of my education. When I arrived at school, I found that my Canish peers seemed to have come to similar conclusions. Through this self-actualized excellence and sheer grit, we managed to consistently excel at the top of our classes, regardless of our imperfect genetics.

The next order of business at Titan Station is a medical checkup at the clinic. While I'm there, I'll finally have the bio-port removed from my arm. We implant them in advance of deep-space travel, and since I will not be going into cryogenic sleep anytime soon, I am having mine removed. Following the procedure will be my debriefing with the Council.

I am still reeling from my conversation with Dr. Freeman but manage to master my emotions on the long walk from the Commanders' Tower to the clinic in the hospital sector at the south end of the station. Observing the people as I pass, I notice that most in this sector are on duty wearing the sleek, white uniform that is signature of the

Alliance, their collars decorated with various colored emblems of different shapes and composed of various precious metals or jewels indicating rank and field of discipline. Some walk casually, perhaps having just gotten off shift; some hurry, lost in thought and focused on whatever task is at hand. Others walk in pairs, deep in conversation, referencing a shared tablet containing some confounding data or puzzle to be solved.

Officers and civilians alike stand tall, strong, and fit. The same homogeneity of the population exists here that I observed at the Institution during the years I spent there under Konstantin's guardianship. These are the fittest specimens of humanity, and not just because, as military, physical training is part of the job—it's more than that. Diverse in many ways, with different hair, eye, or skin color, yet more alike in their perfection, the people here share a consistency in the strength of their constitution, a natural agility, and an easy competence with how they move about.

Though they are individuals with slight superficial variation, it is in their hollow cheeks, their uniformly chiseled features, and the perfect symmetry of their bodies and faces that they somehow all look alike. Somewhere along the way, the proportions of beauty had been calculated and defined to specific parameters, and almost all had conformed to the standard.

Strolling through sliding doors into the clinic, I check in at a kiosk. As I turn around to sit in one of the waiting room chairs, I nearly run into a man standing directly behind me.

"Hey, watch it," I say sharply as I stumble back a step or two in an effort to put more space between us.

"I know you," the man says, holding his ground. He then casually crosses his arms across his chest so that his excessive muscle mass is made apparent, his biceps and pectorals stretching the fabric of his white uniform. "You," he sneers, poking me hard on the front of my right shoulder. "You were skyjacked by that traitor in Alpha Centauri."

"Don't touch me," I warn him calmly as the sheer bulk of him looms over me.

He rolls his eyes dismissively, then asks, "Why didn't you take him out?"

Looking around the empty front office of the clinic, I wonder about my luck in running into someone like him. Does he have business here, or did he *follow* me?

Incredulous at the degree to which he has invaded my space, I plant *my* feet, cross *my* arms, stare right back at him expectantly, and say nothing.

"Well?" he demands.

"Well, what?" I reply, enunciating each syllable and raising my eyebrows in challenge. Something snapped in me at some point over this last year, and I no longer feel obligated to maintain any standard of politeness or civility in the face of such treatment. I refuse to be bullied.

He repeats, "Why didn't you take that bastard out?"

Breaking our eye contact, I briefly look down and smile a little at the absurdity of his question, shaking my head. Then I look back at him and ask assertively, "Oh, you think I should have executed him? On the spot, without a trial? A commanding officer?"

He says nothing.

"While stranded on Proxima and imprisoned by *his* cohorts?"

"Imprisoned?" he asks dryly.

I ignore his question, look him up and down, and study the collar of his uniform, trying to glean some clue about who he is. "Is that what you would have done, Officer . . .?" I ask, frowning and waiting for him to supply his name.

"That's Lieutenant Colonel, Ensign," he says, but does not give his name. *My* name then appears behind him, a lit-up banner floating over the archway leading to the clinic proper, indicating that the technician is ready to see me.

After a quick glance at the notification, I turn back to him. "Well, Lieutenant Colonel whatever your name is . . ." I jerk my chin in the direction of the banner. "I've got to go. Now kindly remove yourself from my path."

Shoving by him without another look, I head through the archway to my appointment. To my surprise, he moves to let me pass.

I make it a few feet down the corridor before he says, this time with less malice, "Ensign Nazari."

Stopping cold, I attempt to train my features into a neutral mask, turn around, and answer a shade more sharply than I intended, "Yes?"

"My name is Jonathan Avery," he says wearily, arms slack at his sides.

His name is strangely familiar, and then I remember why. His surname hails from one of the prominent families that governed Selene, Earth's lunar colony, which was utterly vanquished twenty years ago during the nuclear holocaust.

Pausing momentarily, I relax my features and do not steel myself to the emotion conjured by the memory of what happened to his home. I say sincerely, "I'm sorry for your loss, Colonel Avery."

He looks at me, puzzled at first, taken off guard by my comment, but then understanding that I've put together his heritage floods his features. Sadness flickers in his eyes before all emotion washes from his countenance. Bowing his head, he simply says, "Thank you, Ensign," before turning to leave through the sliding doors.

The medical checkup and port removal procedure went without incident. My debrief with the Council that followed was more prolonged but much less dramatic an ordeal than my encounter with the lieutenant colonel. They reviewed the mundane details of my report at length but wanted to talk about Taj the most. I avoided incriminating him as best I could, but the writing was on the wall. He had chosen his future. The Council, however, did not ask me why I hadn't "taken him out," but Colonel Avery's question has me rattled. *Why didn't I take him out after what he did?*

I stop for a light lunch of synthetic noodles and moon mushrooms at a café counter on the way down to the training level, which is on the bottom deck of the great floating citadel that is Titan Station. The training deck is conveniently located for aerial jumps to the surface, relay shuttles to the mines, and launching our military fighter jets. Larger ships and deep-space transport vessels are docked and launched from the shuttle bay at the apex of the station where I arrived yesterday.

Entering the lift, the doors slide shut soundlessly behind me. Recessed lighting glows green around the ceiling as I watch the floor numbers illuminate while I descend. As the lift hums quietly, dropping forty-plus floors, I relish the momentary solitude in the cool, dark space. Passing through the bulk of the residential levels, the lift moves straight to the bottom with no stops. Since I am traveling mid-shift, there is no one around.

After a minute or two, the doors open, and I walk out to the main gallery surrounding the central training floor below. The space is about one hundred yards long and sixty wide, with a track beneath the gallery level that follows the circumference of the training area. Three sides are windowed and face south, where the sun has now begun to set. It won't fully descend below the horizon until late tonight, close to midnight. Setting only once every fifteen Earth days, it has been slowly creeping closer to the distant Doom Mons Mountain Range beyond the Aztlan Darklands for the last week. I hope to catch its vanishing act tonight from my favorite surveillance bay in the Engineering Library.

Before returning to Earth, I will need to sort out the mechanical issues with my suit cloak prototype. With its vast resources and near-infinite catalog of knowledge, Titan's library will be the best place to do it. I have been on Titan Station for only twenty-four hours but feel a constant sense of urgency to get back to my people—a ticking clock. Hunted by the Regime, Cana could be found at any moment.

I head straight to the locker room, peel off my uniform, take down my hair and braid it tightly, wash my face, and then put on a pair of gray gym thermals. After taking the back stairs through the locker room, I emerge on the ground-level training floor. Scanning the weight room, cardio pods, plyometric circuits, and grappling mats, I do not see Petra. Noting that I am a few minutes early, I opt to warm up with a jog around the track.

On my third lap, I hear the light shuffling sound of someone jogging behind me, so I hug the inside lane to allow them room if they want to pass. I wait a moment, but they do not. A few more paces, and I get the strange feeling that they are intentionally hovering.

And just as I turn my head to glance back at them, a figure slams into me from behind, bear-hugging me around the waist, and then tackle-drives me into the closest bulkhead.

Kicking and hitting, I twist and grab the blonde head at my waist, at first trying to free myself, then to wrestle them into a headlock. When I find I can do neither, we both crash to the floor as a growl from my assailant turns into wild cackling.

Face down and out of breath, I scramble backward, disentangling myself. My attacker rolls off me onto her back while continuing to laugh hysterically.

"Rip!" I scream, exasperated. "You scared the daylights out of me!" I exclaim, mad as hell.

My old comrade, still flat on her back, is giggling uncontrollably. Looking over at me briefly, she tries to regain her composure but then is distracted by runners who are being forced to hop over her as they attempt to pass on the track. When one runner in particular seems to catch her eye, she lunges to grab him at the ankle but misses. His narrow escape cracks her up further, and at this point, I cannot help myself and lose it, too, dissolving into laughter.

I look at her incredulously, and she says, "What!?—He got me *first* in the mess hall this morning!"

As more cadets hop around her, trying to pass, I get up, grab her arms, and start dragging her backward off the track. She finally sits up, eyes watering, and says, "Dammit, Nazari, I've missed you!"

Jax Ripple, my former comrade back in Academy, now twenty years older, hasn't changed a single bit since I've been away. Looking over at her, I cannot contain the huge smile on my face. Rip was invincible as a cadet, holding the spot for the best sniper record in the Alliance when she was just a freshman. The cool air from the ventilation system blows back her shock of blonde hair, cut short around the back and sides but long on top, as I reach down and heave her up from the floor to her feet.

"I missed you more, punk," I say as Rip springs up, towering over me. I jump up on my toes to properly hug her. We squeeze each other tightly, and she lifts me up, spinning me around. When she puts me back down and we pull apart, I ask, "Where were you last night? You weren't at my dinner."

"Duty calls. I'm on the night shift this quarter. Geez, you are still a little child!" she exclaims, her eyes widening in mock surprise as she takes a closer look at me.

"Okay, Grandma!" I rebut but then fall into giggles again, unable to suppress my laughter.

She gestures profanely, then pauses a moment before saying, "I'm sorry I missed last night, but I knew you would be here today at 1300 hours sharp," she taps her watch, "per intel provided by Commander Chauverac, and so here I am!"

"No big deal. You didn't miss anything major. It was rather civilized. Petra didn't break any tables or chairs, and I was in bed by 2300 hours. Where is she, anyway? I didn't see her when I came in." I peer toward the center of the training floor to see if she has arrived.

"Oh, she's here—*on the mats*," Rip says archly. "A cadet talked her into a grappling match. Come on!" she says, swinging her arm around my shoulder as we walk toward the center of the gym.

As we approach, I see Petra has detained a cadet in a joint lock beneath her on the mat. A small group of onlookers cheer and count the seconds he is down. When she notices us walking up, she immediately releases the flustered cadet, jumps up, smooths out her hair, and walks toward us.

"Hey, you're here," she says, smiling coolly. "Sorry, I had to do a . . . *demonstration* . . . for the cadets."

"You mean you had to hand that guy's ass to him?" Rip says, laughing.

"He was asking for it," Petra replies slyly, self-satisfied, and directs us to the far side of the floor.

"Well, nicely done, Commander," Rip says.

Petra smirks at Rip and then looks over to me as we all walk to get water. "How'd it go this morning with Freeman?" she asks, grabbing a towel to mop her forehead.

I pick up my bag from the bench where I left it earlier as Rip walks over to greet another officer. "Not bad, actually, except—well, let's just say there's nothing like having a good cry with your commanding officer. The station captain, no less," I say dryly as we head to the heavy-bag room.

"Really?" she asks in disbelief. "*Dr. Freeman?*"

"Well, *he* didn't exactly cry—it was just me, really, but yeah," I admit. Petra looks at me concerned, so I say, "I feel much better now," as we approach the line of canvas-covered punching bags suspended from the low ceiling.

"About?" She looks at me, eyebrows raised in concern, while picking up her training gloves.

"Oh, you know, just some hard truths. Those *are* the best kind," I say as I lace up my gloves. "It keeps us on our toes, doesn't it?" I mutter, dodging her question, and nail the bag with a lethal punch.

Then Rip interjects, startling me again since I didn't hear her return.

"Sorry," she says. "I wasn't trying to eavesdrop, but I'm glad you cried, Nazari. Crying is good. It releases stress hormones." She has laced up her gloves, too, and situates herself in front of the bag adjacent to mine. "I try to cry at least once or twice a week," she assures us, nodding, before pummeling the bag in front of her with a complex combination of hits. "I just don't know if I'd do it with the ol' Captain," she says, cringing a little. "Yeah, that part's weird, Nazari," she finishes, shrugging, before turning to a speed bag mounted near the opposite wall.

Petra and I look at each other and can't help but laugh. Then Petra asserts, "It's *not* weird! But we will talk about this *later*." She then laces up her gloves and hits the bags, too.

After the savage beating our trio gives the heavy bags, then the speed bags, and, lastly, the banana bag, we head up to the gallery to catch our breath on the cool metal benches adjacent to the windows. Outside, the surface below us is an eclectic mix of plains, dunes, craters, and mountains. There is no life, no flora or fauna, but a boundless, frigid land that, after a century of human exploration, still holds so much mystery. From this vantage point, we face Hano Crater, which lies to the south of the station. Hano was named after an Earthly goddess of education, knowledge, and magic. The idea that some long-dead dreamer bestowed this land with such a name stirs a longing in me that I had all but forgotten.

I look north toward the horizon. The sky, a serene blue this morning—as it often is due to the high-altitude hazes that scatter shorter wavelengths and give the sky its blue hue—has transformed into a deep, hazy orange above and a burnished brown at the horizon as the sun continues to set. The resulting copper light dances across the land in a mesmerizing, otherworldly display.

"I've really missed this," I say to Petra and Rip, turning from the window.

"I bet," Rip replies. "We should go down there," she says, jumping to her feet. "You wanna go down there and run Scorpion Blue?"

I look at Petra to see how she'll weigh in. Petra shrugs, looks at her watch, and says, "I'm game." Then, with a half smile, she adds, "But you better not be late for dinner again. Gia was not happy about it last time, and I got an earful."

Rip waves her off. "Don't worry about it. We'll be back in plenty of time, and if not, I'll make it up to her," she says, winking at us while walking over to the railing that overlooks the training floor below. "We need a fourth. I think I see Sumi down there." Rip squints across the floor, then cups her hands over her mouth and yells, "Ensign Kimura! Please report to duty!" Waving her arms wildly, she motions for Sumi to come up, then turns back to us, snickering, cracking herself up over the spectacle she just made on the floor below.

"Who's Gia?" I ask Rip as she leans back on the railing, waiting for Sumi to make the hike across the floor and up the stairs to join us in the gallery.

Rip smiles and says, "Brace yourself, Nazari. I, Lieutenant Commander Jax Ripple, am officially off the market. I married a captain. And not just any captain . . ."

"But a direct report to Freeman himself!" Petra finishes her sentence for her with eyes wide and impressed, as if she has heard Rip tell it more than once.

"Well, congratulations, Rip!" I say genuinely. "How long have you been married?"

"About five years now. She transferred in from the Martian outpost to run the hospital here a couple of years before. You'll love her;

a little serious at times with all her important captainly duties and everything, but somebody's gotta do it. Better her than me, right?" she says, nudging Petra, who has joined her at the railing and is waving at Sumi as she climbs the stairs to the gallery level.

Sumi hops up the last couple of steps with ease, walks up to us, and says, "Rip, you dragging us through Scorpion Blue again?"

"How *did* you guess?" Petra laughs.

"I figured when I beat you all last time," Sumi says, "she'd be looking for a rematch pretty soon." She then extends her hand to me and says warmly, "Hi, I'm Sumi. I don't think we've met."

"Hella," I say, shaking her hand. "I actually arrived at base yesterday from . . . hiatus."

A wave of understanding floods her features. "Ah, yes! I recall hearing your story. Impressive work in Alpha Centauri," she says, nodding in approval. "Well, welcome back, Officer." Her eyes drift to my collar and the small ensign insignia on it. "I am also a new graduate—different years, obviously—but I think our overall time line is the same if we account for your time in cryo, right?"

I blink a few times, thinking fast, and say, "Uh . . . yeah. You're right. Glad to finally meet a friend my age." I smile, poking fun at Rip and Petra.

Rip is working furiously on her palm screen, no doubt already reserving our suits and buggies for our drill. "So, are you in or what, Kimura?" she asks, glancing up.

"You bet," Sumi replies. "What did you study in Academy?" she asks, turning her attention back to me.

"Astrophysics. How about you?"

"Engineering. Robotics, specifically, and now I work in the Weapons and Warfare Lab."

"And she's a better shot than Rip!" Petra chimes in.

"And . . . I'm a better shot than Rip," Sumi repeats in agreement.

"Sumi stole the title two years ago," Petra whispers to me loudly enough for us all to hear.

"Hey, it ain't over yet, Ensign," Rip says pointedly to Sumi, then looks to me and Petra and says, "I'm making a comeback."

"Well, they say that genius peaks at twenty-five. I don't know, but you may have lost your touch, Rip," Sumi teases.

"I don't think so," Rip says in a more serious tone than she has used all day. Then she taps one last combination on her palm screen, shoves it into her back pocket, looks up, and says, "And I'm gonna prove it *today*." Checking the time, she says, "We jump in twenty minutes, ladies. Better get suited up," and starts down the corridor. Pausing momentarily, she looks back and says, "Nazari, you're with me."

22

After heading down the gallery toward the north end of the station, down the stairs on the far end, and then through a door by the track, Petra, Sumi, Rip and I continued down another long corridor to the jump center and suit locker. The jumpsuits we will wear for our drill today are engineered specifically for Titan's lunar surface, while our EVA suits are designed for use in the void of deep space. As for my EVA suit, I am due for an upgrade. The one I brought back from Proxima is an old model with hardware that doesn't work all that well after twenty years of systems upgrades.

Compared with Earth, Titan is markedly colder. On average, the temperature is minus one hundred and seventy-nine degrees Celsius. Thanks to Titan's dense atmosphere, we do not need a pressurized space suit when walking on the surface, but we do need a breathing mask and protection from the frigid temperatures. With Titan's low gravity of 1.3 m/s^2, walking here is more comparable to walking on the moon (where its gravity is 1.62 m/s^2) than walking on Earth

(9.8 m/s²). Thus, on Titan, we are not bound to travel exclusively by foot or surface vehicle. We can also *fly*.

Our jumpsuits are similar in style and appearance to the deep-space model, fabricated with the same ultra-thin, lightweight, yet impenetrable graphene-based material, but come equipped with weighted boots that double as short skis and winglike prosthetics built into the arms to leverage the low gravity while traversing the surface. In our jumpsuits, we can fly on our own accord, aided only by the built-in winglike apparatus and the strength of our own muscles.

After suiting up, we approach the airlock between us and the jump center. Subject to Titan's low gravity, frigid climate, and oxygen-absent atmosphere, the chamber allows us to safely pass between the internal and exterior environments of the station. Entering the outer chamber, we wait for the doors to be sealed. Once we are all in, an alarm sounds, and red lights blink to indicate the sealing process is underway. After fifteen seconds, the light turns green, signaling we are clear to enter the main jump center. We enter through sliding doors.

In the center of the floor is a large open hatch with runways leading down to it on four sides at a gradual angle. The station is suspended thirty thousand feet above the surface; looking beyond the hatch at the vast expanse of terrain below, the vista is mostly wide, flat plains before reaching Hano Crater. Beyond that is nothing but dunes.

With plans to jump south, we all line up at the corresponding ramp. It has been months—truly years— since I have done this, and my stomach is all butterflies at the sight of the deep drop before us. It comforts me when I remind myself that free-falling on Titan isn't nearly the same as free-falling on Earth. Born and raised on Earth, I have the instinct that when I jump from any height, I will drop like a rock. But on Titan it is much different—perhaps more accurately described as "free-floating," the way a soap bubble blown by a child might drift lazily on its way to the ground in Earth's gravity. With that said, other factors remain to contend with on Titan, such as wind, rain, or ice. Therefore, our suits are equipped with backup thrusters that can propel us in any direction should the need arise.

Petra leads the way. First, she makes eye contact with us, and we all give her the thumbs-up that we are ready to go. With a wicked smile, she returns the gesture, faces forward, and sprints down the platform. She then jumps with all her might out into the abyss of sky, wind, and clouds below. Stretching her arms out to her sides, she releases the webbed prosthetics that function as mechanical wings. Then, looking to the sky, she puts her head back in a moment of sheer bliss and freedom, tucking her arms tightly to her sides and curling her body into a pike position before propelling herself forward, plummeting toward the surface in a near-vertical swan dive.

The light is still a coppery, burnished gold, and the sun, which slowly slides toward the horizon, will not completely disappear for another seven or eight hours. Rip jumps after Petra, and Sumi will go after me. Taking a breath, I run with everything I have down the short runway and hurl myself into the sky behind them. I am met with wind and resistance, the ground below slowly coming into focus as I fall.

Rip is doing flips and yelling at the top of her lungs out of sheer delight. I spin, stretch, and tumble as Petra climbs back up, with the help of her wings, for another plunge, and then Sumi plummets past me in a dive of her own. Petra and Sumi complete a few more dives and climbs before we reach five thousand feet. At around that altitude, we open our wings and coast the rest of the way down, gliding gracefully to the surface in easy, broad circles like eagles through smoggy orange clouds.

Closer, the plains are revealed as a flat and frozen land of gray ice. As we touch down, we switch on the locking function of our boots with a tap from forefinger to thumb of our glove, and our boots become heavy, holding our skied feet to the ice. As I make contact with the ground, I immediately bend my knees and lean forward, leveraging the momentum of our drop, the force of my landing propelling me forward. Hano Crater is four or five miles in front of us, though not yet visible. Together, we ski our way in that direction across the flat landscape, toward the setting sun and into the hazy twilight.

It has been a long time since I've felt this alive, and I can't wipe the smile off my face as I lean forward and kick and glide over the muddy-colored ice in a repetitive rhythm. The plains rise and fall gradually in gentle slopes as we continue the journey south.

After around a half hour of skate skiing, we approach Hano Crater. A jump platform was built at the crater's edge to aid cadets and officers like us in crossing Hano when traversing Titan's diverse landscape by foot. We retain enough momentum from the preceding slope to muscle our way up the gradual, steady incline. I could call in the assistance of my thrusters to help me climb the hill, but I know if I do, Rip won't let me hear the end of it.

Before long, the four of us reach the top of the jump. Exhilarated, we pause for a moment to catch our breath and behold the massive crater before us. The landscape directly in front of us slopes sharply downward into a constructed ramp, and there is a takeoff table erected at the lip of the crater. The critical point on this slope is at a height of about three hundred feet, and Hano Crater itself is around six hundred feet across. We would never make this jump in Earth's gravity. However, on Titan, we'll float clear across and land safely at our destination.

Sumi looks over at us and says, "First two to land get to be shooter."

Rip looks seriously insulted, and she and Sumi simultaneously hurl themselves forward. Petra and I follow maybe a half second later, and we all four race down the long slope, legs bent and leaning forward to position our center of gravity over the middle of our skis. I feel a thrill rise inside me as we approach the takeoff table.

In the last couple of seconds, I crowd directly behind Rip and then increase my boot weight by 10 percent, slide into her slipstream, get lower, and shoot past her. She has no time to catch me. We fly through the takeoff table and are hurled into the air over the crater. We lean forward nearly parallel to our skis. Once we reach the zenith of our jump, we disengage our boot weights, engage our mechanical wings, and fly like hell on a downward trajectory across the rest of the canyon.

Sumi lands first, followed by me, Petra, and, lastly, Rip. Rip must have gotten flustered when I passed her, so much so that she lost focus long enough to let Petra overtake her as well.

Coasting down the landing runway toward a small outbuilding at the base of an enormous black dune, we have reached the otherworldly Shangri-La Sand Sea. Titan's water-based bedrock on this part of the terrain forms an icy kind of dark sand that composes the great dunes that crest in front of us. Over three hundred feet tall in some places, hundreds of them roll in a seemingly endless procession toward the horizon.

Sumi gets there first and circles back toward us to high-five me with both hands. "Nice run," she says.

Rip just shakes her head as we glide up to the one-story outbuilding that houses a way station and visitor facilities. We disengage our skis once we are inside the outer chamber of the small circular compound. Entering the facility's airlock, the doors seal behind us as oxygenated air rushes in, the red light flashing. The familiar alarm sounds, and the light turns green before the inner doors slide open.

Once inside, we rip off our helmets and greet the attendant on duty. The building and others like it elsewhere on the surface is constructed on part of the terrain established to be permafrost, which is land frozen solid enough to support small structures. We settle at a cozy table by the window, order warm drinks from a barista-bot, and recover a bit before heading back outside to take on Scorpion Blue.

"Whew, what a ride. I will never get tired of that run!" Sumi exclaims before sipping her mocha.

Rip gives her an exaggerated fake smile, then turns to me and says, "Look, Nazari, we're partners, and you have to let me snipe today, okay?"

"Why?—I won fair and square. I need to get some shooting practice in, anyway. I'm rusty."

"Rusty!?" she says, disgusted and horrified. "No. Nope." She shakes her head. "Not on my team. I let Petra shoot last week, and we lost. What will people think if they see that I played on a losing team not once but *twice* in my life? Please, just drive today. You know, I really think you should ease yourself back into things, any-way," Rip goes on, scooting next to me. Putting her arm around me, she starts speaking in a patronizing tone. "You have had it tough and should take it easy, young ensign." She moves to pat my head.

"Uh-huh," I say, dodging her reach. "By driving *you* in Scorpion Blue against *her*?" I ask, pointing to Sumi, the titleholder with the best shot.

She scoots back, puts her arms on the table in front of her, and then folds them into a prayer position while nodding emphatically. "Yes, I think you should. Please. Please. Please," she begs.

"Okay, fine," I give in, laughing. "But you owe me!"

She nudges Sumi and says, "You scared now, Ensign?" Then she stands up, laughing. "We better get to it, ladies. You know I can't be late for dinner. I'm going to visit the facilities, then let's head out." She turns toward the bathroom, and we all get up leisurely and stretch before heading out of the cozy café and back to the garage.

The Shangri-La Sand Sea is an endless expanse of black dunes that rises above us like a great mountain range. Windswept miles of grainy, sand-like hydrocarbons twisted by ancient winds into long, linear ridges stretch before us. I punch the throttle, and we shoot up out of the garage. I'm driving a hydroelectric dune buggy, and Rip sits shotgun, carrying a pump scattergun with a tight patterned cyl-inder choke and a laser sight calibrated for low gravity. This vehicle is very different from the ancient truck I drove to make my escape on Proxima. It runs on hydrogen fuel, is twice as fast, and is operated with a joystick rather than a steering wheel.

Crawling up the first dune in our buggy, engine whining like a banshee from the impossible slope, the tires shred into the steep black wall as the vehicle digs into the near-vertical. I don't dare let off the accelerator as we gain the momentum needed to make the precarious climb. As we reach the top, the wheels spin as I hit the throttle again, and we pull up over the brink, looking out over the sweeping ripple of undulating dunes.

The copper light is softened by a smoggy cloud cover, muting the sun's continued descent into a gilded haze. We drive along the ridge a little way as Sumi and Petra pull up behind us. Lining up parallel to each other, we face the downwind side of the dune, angled toward the rippled slip face.

Rip has a drone on her lap that will serve as the trap that will launch our targets. It's my job to drive, chasing the drone's course, and her job to shoot the targets. Sumi and Petra will be in pursuit, and whoever shoots the most targets wins.

Rip looks over at Petra in question, and she nods back, signaling that they are ready to start. Rip then taps a few commands into the drone and releases it. It levitates over our buggy to about thirty feet above us, flashing a blue light to signal the drill has begun. The drone then lurches forward and is off, releasing the first several glowing blue orbs that will serve as our targets. We fly down the roaring slip face in pursuit.

The trick to riding the dunes is keeping up your momentum. I keep one eye on the drone, the other constantly scanning for smooth lines to glide through from dune to dune. That way if we drop deep into a bowl or down a steep slip, we won't get stuck. I try to consistently look three to four dunes ahead and seek out the smoothest transitions.

We are down the first slip face and at the toe of the dune when the drone jerks left toward the horn—a high, jet-black prominence, its crest more resembling a massive scalpel blade than a sand dune.

Rip and Sumi are shot for shot at this point, as every few seconds their bullets explode into faraway blue orbs faster than I can count. Petra and I cut left simultaneously. We round the horn as the drone flies up a razorback that has immediately cropped up in our driving line.

Keeping up momentum, we drive up and parallel to the dune's sharp ridge. Once we get high enough, we steer close to the peak, holding the two side tires of our buggies just over the edge. Then I steer over the ledge and let off the throttle just enough that we glide smoothly down the slip face and pick up speed again at the bottom.

We go on like this for a half hour, tearing through the icy terrain, when we approach a familiar old dune, Yellowbelly—named after a lethal razorback racer snake—a dune that is thrice the height of the others, rising to a thousand feet. From what I remember, it has a flat top. So, following the drone, I attack Yellowbelly head-on, driving straight up while Rip hangs out the side, exploding target after target as the drone weaves above us.

The thing I forgot to consider is that it has been twenty years since I've run this drill, and dunes are changeable by the wind and elements, even this enormous one. As we approach the ridge, Rip faces forward, tracking the drone moving overhead. When she sees what is in front of us, she screams, "Stop!"

I glance over at her and see panic in her eyes as she finishes: "It's a drop!"

Just as we reach the top, closing in on the ledge, I see the sharp drop and slam on the brakes without thinking. Wrong move. Our buggy reels forward and tumbles, somersaulting all the way to the bottom.

We land upside down. Luckily, we are still strapped in and protected for the most part by the roll bars and steel cage of the buggy, but we are pretty banged up. Disentangling from the wreckage, we assess our injuries, but both of us seem to be okay. Our buggy, on the other hand, is trashed.

"Dammit, Nazari—I was winning!" Rip shouts.

"I'm sorry," I say defensively. "Last time I checked, Yellowbelly had a flat top."

Rip exhales forcefully. "Nazari, look at my face. I'm old. It's been twenty years. Things change."

We look up at the dune above us and see Petra and Sumi balanced sideways on the top of the ridge in the correct formation for traversing a razorback. They wave down at us as Petra's voice comes over the comm. "The face is too steep. You can't get back up," she says with barely concealed disappointment. "And we can't get down."

"Yeah, we can't get back up," Rip says, kicking at the sand with her boot. "Because our ride is trashed."

"Okay!" Petra shouts. "We will head back to the compound and return with a shuttle. Hang tight."

Exhaling deeply, I look around, rubbing my shoulder, which was crushed in our tumble. "You okay?" I ask Rip as my gaze settles on the faint horizon.

"Yeah, fine—you? This can't be any worse than getting clobbered by a tidal wave in some lunatic's old truck," she says with a half smile.

"Ha—funny," I say sarcastically, still staring at the murky haze in the distance. "So, I take it that Petra filled you in?"

She nods. "Well, she gave me the high-altitude overview of what happened to you in Alpha Centauri." She wrinkles her forehead for a moment, pensive, then looks me in the eye and says, "I'm so sorry that happened to you, bud."

"Thanks. It doesn't seem real, does it?" I ask, eternally baffled by the strange twist the course of my life has taken, the reality of it serving as a constant reminder of just how little power any of us have over the big things that happen to us.

"Losing you for twenty years felt real. Real as a funeral," she asserts gruffly, shaking her head as if she could as easily shake off the memory. "You know we had a small one for you—a memorial service. Just a few of us." She pauses, looking down, focused on the black granules she is idly crunching beneath the toe of her boot. "It was supposed to be for closure, but you know all that's just a crock of shit." She then looks up at me suddenly, eyes wide and her voice breaking. "I still can't believe you're back."

I run to her and we embrace. She holds me tightly, and I hold on to her tighter as if life depends on it—and in many ways, it does. The people here on Titan are my support system. Without them on Proxima, I was lost. I couldn't see a way out. But here, it's different. Here, among the people who care about me, look out for me, see me for who I believe myself to be, I have a fighting chance.

After a few minutes, we pull apart, and I ask, "Hey, I never got to ask how your family fared back on Earth."

Rip brightens at my obvious concern. "We were so lucky, Nazari. My parents were on Mars at a botany conference when it happened. They settled there and are doing great."

"That's incredible. And they've met Gia?"

"Oh, they are thick as thieves—Gia and my parents. They're all nerdy scientists like you!" she exclaims, pointing at me and laughing as she remembers that I, too, am a nerdy scientist. "I see them a couple of times a year. We go there and they come here."

We are silent for a minute as we look around the terrain in the valley between Yellowbelly and the adjacent dune.

"What the heck is that?" Rip asks suddenly, squinting her eyes.

"Is it lightning?" I reply, drawn to the blue flashing at the horizon and what looks like a storm headed this way.

"No, Nazari, over there." She points down the long corridor between the dunes, toward the west, at a small mound about fifty feet away. "Is that—"

"*A person?*" I ask as my stomach tenses up. The dark mound is curiously the size and shape of a . . . "If that *is* a person, they aren't wearing any kind of suit or protection from the elements."

Rip strides toward it. "Not a person. It's a body."

I follow her about ten yards. She approaches the mound and crouches down, leaning over it. Then she looks back up at me in surprise.

"A dead one," she corrects. "And it has not been here very long."

23

Rip is late to dinner, and, as predicted, Gia is not happy about it. But Rip will no doubt make it up to her, as she always does. It's impossible to stay angry with Rip—I never could during our three years of friendship in Academy.

Standing in the waning light, we didn't need any special equipment to ascertain that the person whose body we stumbled upon on the dunes was deceased. Whoever it was died immediately from exposure to Titan's atmosphere. Without the protection of a space suit, it's unclear if he succumbed first to the cold or from a lack of oxygen. There was no evidence he had been wearing a suit at any point in time and no footprints or vehicle tracks to indicate from which direction he came. It was as if he just dropped out of the sky. Dressed in unremarkable civilian clothing, the man's face was ashen and utterly lifeless. Frozen in death, frozen in time.

Petra and Sumi returned with a shuttle about forty-five minutes later, but not before the storm moved in and rain started falling—the first telltale sign that Equinox was nearly upon us and, with it, bringing the spring rainy season. We left behind the broken remains of our wrecked vehicle along with the mysterious body. Petra notified the local patrol, station security, and forensics as we navigated the rain and lighting in our shuttle. An investigation would ensue.

After learning more about her background at dinner, I ask Sumi for help developing the program for my suit cloak. She agrees, and we plan to meet in the R&D Lab tomorrow after a presentation she will be giving the Mars emissaries who arrived yesterday for Equinox.

Walking back to our quarters after dinner, Petra and I talk, laugh, and reminisce about our time at Academy together. The main thoroughfare is bustling with life: people getting off shift, walking to and from dinner, and others rushing about, already busy with Equinox preparations.

"I thought you said this place was a ghost town?" I ask Petra.

"It is," she insists. "You are just used to Proxima's population of three humanoids and one hologram."

"Hey, don't forget Ramses," I say, smiling at the memory of him.

"Ah, yes, and your robotic dog." She laughs. I smile in return, pleased with her amendment.

"Really, though, from a military perspective, our numbers are less than half what they were," she continues. "Although we didn't have much of a civilian population before, and that has since increased. Plus, Titan took in all the Earth civilians stranded in transit . . . and the births," she says, reconsidering her assessment. "We are growing,

I suppose, but in those early days after the attack, things were quieter here."

When we arrive at Petra's quarters, she invites me to come inside. We enter, and the recessed lighting immediately blinks on, illuminating a large, open two-level suite.

"This place is like a palace."

"Have you noticed my rank, Ensign?" She smirks. *"Commander privileges."*

"How could I forget, Your Majesty," I reply, crossing my eyes. Laughing, I then salute her as I walk around the sunken living room and collapse onto a podlike swivel chair facing a wall of windows. My body is jelly after the drill today. Feeling fully satiated after dinner, I could easily fall asleep right here in this chair, but know I need to get to work on writing that program. As good as it feels to be back here on Titan, I can't pretend that life can continue as it was before. Everything has changed.

When I glance at the clock, Petra asks, "Do you have somewhere to be?"

"No, not this second. But I do need to go to the Engineering Library later to work on some preparations for my trip back to Earth."

"Time for a cup of tea?"

"Yes, that sounds perfect," I reply, stretching.

"So, tell me about this meeting with Freeman," she says.

"Oh, it was really nothing. He just reminded me about Abramovich and how he is still a threat."

"Gotcha. You'd think Abramovich would have been satisfied after destroying the Institution . . . and leveling the planet while he was at it. What does he want now?"

"I don't know. Cana, I guess. Like everyone else . . ." I trail off.

"But what does he want with *you*?" she clarifies, pressing further for information.

Sighing, I tuck my legs into my chest as I swivel the chair in the opposite direction and change the subject, asking, "Hey, what happened to Freeman's daughter? I saw some old signage outside his office with her name on it."

"Cassini? She went AWOL . . . last Equinox, actually," she replies. "No one has heard from her since. But hey, no more changing the subject. Tell me: What does Abramovich want with you?"

I frown at the unexpected news that Cassini had disappeared and swivel back to face Petra, stretch out my legs again, and take a breath. "Well, he thinks he needs *me* to get the people of Cana to follow him—Cana Major, specifically. Cana Minor is obviously still drunk on his lies."

She grimaces. "You think he will come after you?"

"I don't know. Maybe," I say thoughtfully. "He's dying, but he nearly had Taj convinced to give him his body for a head transplant by the time I was leaving."

"*Seriously?* Taj isn't my favorite person right now, but that's just wrong," she says with a disturbed look on her face. "I assumed Taj dragged you out there because he needed an accomplice and thought you'd be on board, but there was more to it than that, wasn't there?"

"Abramovich knew Konstantin," I say and swallow hard.

Petra's brow furrows as she crosses her arms tightly across her chest. She knows all about Konstantin and is likely alarmed at the mention of her name.

"They worked together at the Institution years ago when

Abramovich was first exiled from Cana, before they took him back the first time. And well, you know how she always said I was made in a test tube?"

Petra nods.

"Well, I was. They engineered me in a lab together."

"Hold on—he's not your father, is he?"

"No. I don't have a father, actually . . . because . . . I am a clone," I say simply.

Petra stares back at me, shocked. She doesn't know what to say, and I understand because neither did I. I idly dunk the bag of Canish breakfast tea in my cup, then set it aside on a saucer before sitting up in my chair to sip the warm liquid. "It gets better," I finally say sarcastically.

"What does?" she asks, not following me and no doubt thinking a mile a minute to herself, trying to process what I've just said, considering what it all means.

"My story. Because I'm not just any clone. I am an identical genetic copy of a Hebrew woman from the Old World, from the first century BC, who later went on to miraculously birth their messiah . . ."

"Oh, wow. I follow now. He wants to use you to manipulate his people, *your* people—the Canish Revivalists—and get them to follow him."

"Yes. He's calling for a second coming of their God."

"*Their God?* Well, isn't he yours, too?"

"Yeah, I guess he was, at one time. But Petra, I don't know anymore. After all that's happened . . . What kind of God lets the world burn?"

She shakes her head. She, too, is at a loss for an answer to such a question. Looking thoughtful, she then says, "Well, you know what? This is what Abramovich has told you, right?"

"Yes, this is what he told me *and* all the people of Cana. He announced it to everyone on a public broadcast the day I escaped."

"But why trust him? We don't know that it's true," she counters.

"We *don't*, I guess, but it is in line with everything I know about where I came from. An orphan, dropped on Imani's doorstep . . . by Konstantin."

"Come by my office tomorrow, and we'll stop by Neuro for a brain scan," she offers. "We'll be able to verify the age and origins of your DNA. Then we will know for sure."

After agreeing to the scan, I rise to leave. "I better go. I need to get a few hours of work in before tomorrow."

Walking me to the door, Petra gives me a big hug and tells me not to worry about it so much, that it doesn't really mean anything even if it's true. And maybe it doesn't, but the fact remains that somewhere, somehow, someday, Abramovich is coming for me. Mordecai Abramovich, a fanatical murderer with the blood of our world on his hands.

As the door hisses open, I say, "Oh, I almost forgot. Can you fill me in on the Graphene Wars?"

The Graphene Wars began soon after Earth was destroyed and could no longer supply the mass amounts of graphite needed to outfit every humanoid in the solar system who harbored the desire to travel the stars in a graphene-made EVA suit. Petra spoke of the neutral powers in the belts and then those involved in the war—those inhabiting the various planets, moons, mini-planets, dwarf planets, planetesimals, and asteroids throughout the solar system with a stake in the industry.

The conflict's main combatant and true instigator was Chiron, a rogue planet orbiting between Uranus and Saturn—however, Chiron did not always follow a heliocentric path. It once resided farther out in the Kuiper Belt, in the outer reaches of Earth's solar system. Millions of years ago, it was ejected from its system of origin, only eventually finding its way to its current orbital home.

Before the last ice age, before the fall of the Genesis Generations and before the formation of Empyreus, Chiron was colonized by a small group of Earthers, outcasts of the Old World's Genesis Generations whose origins predate the Revivalists. Over the centuries, Chiron became a dirty, industrial prison-world—lawless, but once in possession of wealth beyond measure. Chiron was the second-largest supplier of graphene next to Earth, but anything manufactured there was unregulated. Thus, their trade was highly competitive and easier, cheaper, and quicker to procure. As a result, a constant localized war raged among the various independent groups of mine operators on graphite-rich Chiron.

However, as a centaur, Chiron has an inherently unstable orbital path and, having been ejected from the Kuiper Belt once, meant there was a good chance of it being ejected again. But this time it would leave the solar system entirely, pulled off course by the inexorable gravitational pull of the massive gas giants in its realm, as was the nature of a rogue planet such as itself. That possibility always seemed millions of years away. But everyone knew that if it were to happen, Chiron would gradually lose its sunlight and become uninhabitable because it would no longer be receiving direct light from a star.

Petra explained further the unsettling transformation of Chiron's behavior over the past two decades. After Earth fell, it soon became apparent that Chiron's graphene supply was dwindling and dwindling fast. The struggle to secure resources for their buyers not only led to a cycle of raids and violence but also significantly disrupted the supply chain. Contracted military forces launched brutal attacks on numerous independent asteroids and dwarf planets, including Vesta, Ceres, Pallas, and even Chiron's sister centaur, Chariklo. Neither the smaller inhabited Trojans of Jupiter nor its formidable moons, Callisto and Ganymede, were spared Chiron's pillage.

This behavior prompted a rumor: Chiron *was* going rogue again. It was slowly losing its sunlight, and its inhabitants were in a state of panic, desperately seeking a new home world.

However, during this time, the Alliance and its colonies remained untouched by Chiron's forces, as did Mars and its moons. Instead, Chiron targeted smaller, isolated worlds, which they could easily overwhelm with their weapons and technology. They were as famous for their cutting-edge technology and weapons as they were for their graphene, and for that, some of the larger powers in the system were rumored to trade with them in secret on the black market. Titan did not deal with Chiron, not as far as Petra knew, but Mars and a handful of other "neutral" powers were suspected to be surreptitiously involved with them. And, of course, there was no question that the Institution had done business with Chiron for decades, if not centuries, before the fall of Empyreus, though they would never own up to it.

After leaving Petra's quarters, I return to my room to shower and change. While I was away, a box was delivered from storage with my things, a few possessions left behind in the apartment I'd occupied twenty years ago during Academy. Briefly, I rifle through it but then decide to put it off until later and stay on task with my mission. Checking my messages, I find that Dr. Freeman reinstated me this morning after our meeting. My trip back to Earth is now officially an Alliance mission. Additionally, he assigned me a liaison to coordinate provisioning the graphene-made suits he promised to provide to my people.

Dusk has now set in, and I'm in the north end of the station at an observation bay in the Engineering Library. The library inhabits one of the eight towers of the great floating citadel of Titan Station. From here, I can see north, south, east, and west—every direction. The rain hasn't stopped since this afternoon and likely won't for some time. It will continue on through Equinox—which is in three days—and well beyond that, for weeks, possibly months after. The rivers will rise soon and become turbulent and dangerous to travel by boat or barge. We use the rivers to transport cargo to and from the mines that are northwest of the station.

The setting sun is almost completely gone, and like fat, floating jewels, the rain falls as if in slow motion. Casting my gaze to the window, I can see the Sea of Ligeia to the northeast. Looking south, I can see the plains, Hano Crater, and the shifting Shangri-La Sand Sea dunes we traversed earlier today. Beyond the dunes sit the Aztlan Darklands and the Doom Mons Mountain Range.

Farther north, I can see the other side of the great Ligeia Mare that leads to the even greater Kraken Mare. Both are vast and sterile seas of liquid hydrocarbons. Kraken Mare is one thousand feet deep in its center. Their depth, however, does not hold a candle to the depth of the subterranean ocean of this moon, a great mass lurking beneath the icy shell of Titan's surface—sixty-two miles deep, liquid and salty. Like the seas of Enceladus, the chemistry of this ocean is akin to the primordial soup that once made up the oceans of Earth and eventually yielded life—but not yet on this precious ocean moon. No, she sits quietly waiting, keeping her secrets to herself of what she may or may not eventually bear for this world.

Once the sun sets tonight, the days that follow will be full dark. Three days of complete darkness until the sun begins its inevitable slow rise again. And with it, the new dawn will bring Equinox, ending the fifteen-year winter and marking the beginning of spring. The celebration peaks at midnight, just as the sun's first light peeks over the horizon.

The sky is a deep brown. I've been working since 2100 hours, and it's now nearing 2300. I plan to stay here to watch the sun wink away at midnight as a way of paying homage to my younger self and the countless all-nighters I spent here in the library during Academy, studying and working on projects. Most of the information is digitized, but there are still some actual books in the archives. The tools, resources, and space here facilitate access to the colossal world of information, in whatever form, collected over time between a multitude of ages and worlds in this realm. We've come a long way from the first libraries of the Old World, ancient candlelit temples filled with clay tablets—humble in their simplicity but powerful nonetheless. Great custodians of time these treasuries were, and through the long ages, the spirit has endured—and that is the spirit of the love and pursuit of knowledge.

That the idea of a library *has* endured across centuries, millennia, and has survived the rise and fall of countless civilizations is evidence of its importance to the survival of humankind. Yet all the knowledge in the galaxy could not save the Old World—the Genesis Generations—from themselves, from their inevitable demise. And now we, the Revivalists—their descendants—hang on precariously as they once did to our hopes for a future, shaken in the aftermath of Abramovich's brazen attack, haunted by the sense that we are following assuredly in their footsteps, their path of self-destruction.

Fortunately, the greatest libraries on Earth were in network with the libraries of the Alliance. So when those invaluable repositories were lost to the war and countless physical artifacts, ancient scrolls, tomes, and periodicals were burned to dust in the great cataclysm, the information was virtually preserved here and remains accessible today.

Titan's library is a cylindrical atrium featuring floor-to-ceiling interactive digital surfaces, display screens, and sensory walls that facilitate access to reading and reference materials with abundant workspace for study, research, collaboration, and gathering. It has fourteen floors with an engineering section on the top level and an observation bay above it in the spire of the tower, where I sit this evening.

When I close my eyes and listen, I can hear only the quiet hum of the ventilation system circulating recycled air. Clearing my mind, I can find peace for a few moments when I don't look forward and I don't look back. For a moment, suspended in time, I am the person I was before. She is lighter, freer, and unburdened but also naive, vulnerable . . .

Exhaling, I open my eyes and feel the dread return that so often lingers in the pit in my stomach of late, reminding me that I am no longer *she*—but then, why do I long so for a time that is no more? Why do we always want things to be like they were *before*?

A voice in my head answers simply, plaintively: *Because this is not the end.*

I turn the words over in my mind, contemplating their origin and meaning, when footsteps sound behind me.

I glance over my shoulder and see a man approaching. Noting he looks familiar, I then recognize him. The cadet from the café this morning is now standing behind the row of wide, low sofas on which I am sitting. He is dressed in civilian clothing, his hands in his pockets, and is looking out the window and taking in the view.

"Sorry to intrude, but I couldn't let the last sunset of winter slip away without bidding her a proper farewell," he says, smiling ruefully.

He is tall with chocolate-colored curls, tan skin, and blue eyes. His teeth are white and straight, but they are not the perfectly manufactured stock veneers that almost everyone else here has. His features are not precisely symmetrical and do not conform exactly with the Institution's standard of beauty, but his beauty is undeniable just the same, exotic in its imperfection.

"Then we are not kindred in heritage alone," I remark with a half smile. "Fellow sun worshippers are always welcome." I stuff my hands into my pockets and lean back casually on the couch as I turn to face the setting sun.

He raises his eyebrows in question. "And what makes you think we have the same heritage?" he asks innocently.

"Well, I can tell you're not from the Institution," I say before second-guessing my presumption and worrying I may have offended him. "I'm sorry. I assumed you were from Cana."

"Ah, I see how it is. You don't think I'm a designer baby. What makes you think I'm not?"

"Again, I'm sorry. I am kind of behind on things by a factor of two decades, actually," I reply, cringing. "It's a long story, but—well, never mind." I start to get up, embarrassed.

He smiles, laughs, and puts his hands up. "No, sit. I'm completely kidding. I *am* from Cana and I know your story."

I look back at him blankly.

"I mean, not in a creepy way, but we were briefed when you were recovered. Most people here know who you are, know your story."

I nod in understanding. "Well, then, you *are* from Cana!" I smile triumphantly. "So how did you end up here, if you don't mind me asking? It must have been after the war," I say because of his apparent age and because I didn't know him when I was here before.

"We were in transit when the bombs hit Earth. I was a child, traveling with my mother. We had been visiting my uncle, who is stationed here, and were on the way back home to Earth, to Cana, like you were. Afterward, we came back to Titan and have lived here ever since."

"I'm so sorry—I mean about your family being separated. Do you know if they survived?"

"They did. We were fortunate," he says, looking down and then out the window. "They live in Cana City, but I haven't seen my father or sisters since. No ships in and no ships out, of course, but we correspond and are grateful for that," he finishes, looking over at me again.

"My family is down there, too," I say, comforted to have found a kindred spirit.

"You're Hella, and the family is Nazari, right?"

"Yes." I smile back at him. "And yours?"

"Aarons is my family name."

"That sounds familiar. I think we knew some Aaronses back home."

"Yeah, my father knows your brother Joshua. He served under him before the attack and, well, he still does now. He has a lot of respect for him."

"Your father? Wow. I guess your father would have been just a few years older than me before . . . before I went into cryo," I say. *And lost twenty years of my life,* I don't say. "Well, what shall I call you then, Officer Aarons?"

"Josiah," he says, extending his hand.

"Oh, *Josiah Aarons.* You are my liaison for the graphene disbursement."

"Yes, I am," he confirms. "At your service." He pretends to tip an imaginary hat before continuing. "The captain mentioned we may be able to help each other out. You could help me with the mechanics of your ship, and perhaps I could help you with the cloaking upgrade you have been working on for your EVA suit."

Raising my eyebrows in surprise and interest, I reply, "Well, yes, that would be great. I could really use a hand. What is your discipline?"

"I doubled in quantum physics and aerospace engineering."

"Oh, so you're a slacker?" I tease.

Josiah laughs. Then, after scanning the mostly vacant observation lounge, he adds, "To be honest with you, I have been trying to crack the FTL technology paradox since as long as I can remember." Pausing again, he looks down thoughtfully before saying, "Your arrival with this ship is the literal incarnation of my wildest dreams." I blush as he continues. "And I am not the only one who feels that way. As I'm sure you understand, this changes everything for us—for humankind."

"Yeah, it does," I agree. "I think the shock is still wearing off from everything that's transpired since the war broke out. I don't think it's fully hit me yet . . . the full impact of this technology."

"I'm sorry," Josiah says suddenly. "We've all had twenty years to grieve, but it's still fresh for you. Would you like me to leave you in peace?"

"No, I'm glad I ran into you. I came here tonight to get some work done and, like I said, could really use the help—that is, of course, if you are up for it tonight. I know it's late . . ."

"Are you kidding? I've been on the edge of my seat for the last eight weeks while you were in transit, waiting for you to return so I could see this ship. And like I said, I've been waiting really my whole life for this technology to be developed. So yes, I am one hundred percent up for it." He smiles humbly. "What do you say we watch the sun go down, then head downstairs and get to work?"

"Sounds like a plan," I agree and lean back to take in the view as he settles on the couch a few seats down from me.

24

Josiah and I work well into the night. He outlines the plan for packing the suits and graphene into the cargo hold of *the Phoenix* before my departure. First, we will need to check the inventory on base to determine if there are enough reserves of the product in storage to complete the work order or if we will need to bring down some of the raw material from the caves northwest of the station. The process should only take a few days, which is good news since I need to leave for Earth as soon as I possibly can. Still, I admit that part of me wishes I could stay here on Titan and forget the reality of what is happening down on Earth a bit longer. Finally stopping to get some sleep, we agree to meet again at the library in the evenings until the work is complete.

When I make it back to my room in the black hours of the morning, I find that I have utterly forgotten what it is like to be unable to sleep and collapse on the bed, fast asleep within moments. I sleep like the dead until an incessant chirp pulls me back to consciousness. At hearing the sound, I throw my arm over to the nightstand to snatch my palm screen and look at the time, which is 0600 hours. The chirping continues in irregular beats as my sleep-ridden, fragmented consciousness slowly puts together that someone is repeatedly buzzing my door. Then I remember: I promised Rip we would meet for target practice. She was so horrified by my comment the day before when I referred to myself as rusty that she insisted we start first thing this morning to rectify the situation. I eventually stumble out of bed, and we are able to put in a good two hours of practice in one of the holospheres, plus an hour of weight training down on the training level. Not before coffee, however.

I meet Petra afterward at her office in the Commanders' Tower. We then go down to the hospital's Neuro Research Unit for a discreet brain scan and DNA test with the help of Rip's wife, Gia, who is not only a captain, but a doctor, too. She will have the report later this afternoon.

There are still no conclusive results on the corpse we found on the dunes yesterday. The lab is working on cross-referencing the man's DNA with the interstellar identity database but is running into some issues—what I suspect to be some convenient systems glitches. Now I'm headed to meet Sumi in the R&D Lab.

In uniform and freshly showered after training this morning, I enter the lab. My blonde hair is in a loose fishtail plait that reaches halfway down my back. I spot Sumi talking casually with four men donning the red-and-black livery that is signature of Mars officials. She has just completed her presentation. The Alliance officers in attendance file out of the room behind me as I approach the demonstration station. The high bay lab is four thousand square feet with ten full-size robotics stations, two demonstration stations, equipment storage, and security field fencing.

Sumi spots me and waves me over. As the emissaries depart, one lingers beside Sumi as I approach. After giving me an assessing glance, he does not greet me or smile but stares coldly. As I join them, he turns to Sumi and says, "Thank you again for your time, Ensign Kimura. Your talk was . . . enlightening, to say the least."

I stand at ease with my arms clasped behind my back. When he looks back at me, I give him a brief, closed-lipped smile and avert my eyes as he passes, leaving the ball in his court if he wishes to address me.

"You know that guy?" Sumi asks as she starts packing up the equipment at the station.

"I don't think so . . ." I reply, puzzled as the doors across the floor swoosh shut behind the man.

"Alaric Kronos," she offers. "He's the senior ambassador of the Mars envoy that's here for Equinox."

"Yeah, I don't recognize his name or face."

"That's odd. He was really grilling you."

"Right? I thought maybe I was imagining it," I reply.

"Anyway, I'm starving. Want to grab a bite?"

It is midday, and I'm ravenous after being rushed out of my quarters with no breakfast and then training all morning. "Yes, please."

"There's a dining hall around the corner if that works?"

"For sure," I say as she unbuttons the formal jacket over her uniform, rips it off, and stuffs it into her satchel. She then pulls her shoulder-length, straight black hair up into a high ponytail.

After she locks up the demonstration station, we head out the door and grab a table at the spot around the corner. The place is busy and a little hectic at this hour, but I am starved, so I don't mind the hustle and bustle. Once we get settled, I ask Sumi, "So, you must have been one of the first born here on Titan post-war?"

"That's right, this place is my home world. You Earthlings love to marvel at the idea," she says, amused. "In theory, Earth should be just another foreign planet to me, and in some ways, it is. But I also feel a certain kinship with it, considering my lineage is of Earthly origins." She looks thoughtful momentarily, then says, "There is kind of a sadness about it, though, knowing I'll never see it—not how it was in my family's memories."

"Then your family lives here, too? On the station?"

She nods.

"It must be nice having them close," I remark.

"Most of the time, it is." She laughs. "I was lucky that both my parents served in the Alliance and were off-world when the attack happened. We lost most of my extended family in the war, being from the Institution."

"Oh, I'm sorry to hear that. Where did your family live in the Institution's territory?"

"Neo Fukushima, a sect that aimed to preserve our ancestors' Japanese heritage. My parents chose my ethnicity to match our Japanese ancestry."

When the Revivalists reproduce, the natural result is the product of hundreds and thousands of years of cultural diffusion; without genetic editing, our babies are born a mixture of all the diverse ethnicities of Earth's history. We are not distinctly black, we are not distinctly white, and we are not distinctly Japanese or any other race. However, if a distinction is desired by the parents, or even by the individual after they are born, genetic editing is the solution. In other words, Sumi is a perfect example of what it is to be a designer baby.

"Is fertility still as much of a contemporary problem? How is it managed here on Titan?" I ask since Titan Station was previously entirely military and did not house civilians except under special circumstances.

"Dr. Ramzi, Rip's wife, heads up the fertility program here. Fertility has really improved over the years on Titan. But the anomaly remains that the majority of fertile women are almost exclusively Canish."

"Since your parents chose your genetic makeup for you, are you happy with it?"

"Yes, I am. I love and honor it." Sumi smiles. "Don't get me wrong: I went through phases in my younger years when I questioned everything, including my heritage. But now, I've found my place and wouldn't trade it for anything."

I can relate to the sentiment. My heritage was once a great source of strength and pride for me, but now I am struggling to understand where I actually come from.

"Well, I'm a history buff and would love to hear about it sometime," I offer, genuinely intrigued.

"Absolutely!" Sumi agrees as we get up from our table and head back to the lab. "So, tell me about what you are working on. I cannot believe you are going to Earth, by the way. No one has tried in years."

"Starship-class cloaking devices and EVA suit mods," I explain. "Have there been any developments in cloaking technology since I've been away?"

"Yes—well, not for ships yet—but we do have a camouflage prototype for shielding and partial cloaking; the camouflaging function works at about eighty-three percent effectiveness now, but it is fully functional as a shield. It defers mechanical wave energy around objects on a small scale—the size of the human body, for example, versus larger targets, like a tank or a starship—protecting the target from blasts, shockwaves, radiation, and the like. I don't doubt we will scale it up in the near term—well, especially with the acquisition of your ship's technology." She smiles as we return to the R&D Lab.

"Well, you are exactly the person I needed to meet," I tell Sumi. "I'm working on writing a program that can replicate my ship's cloaking technology and integrate it with my suit's shield system interface so I can get underground to Cana City without the Regime tracking me."

"I think we can help each other," she says as she leads me through a security clearance archway that requires a passcode for entry.

Working in the smaller lab for a few hours, we compare notes and schematics. We stop when we need to access an older program used in a previous model of our suits that can only be accessed in the library archives. Sumi agrees to meet Josiah and me there this evening to collaborate on a new prototype that will combine technology from both Abramovich's ship cloaking mechanism and Sumi's body camouflage.

"Before you go, I want to show you something," Sumi begins. "When you mentioned the Regime, I had an idea about something that might help you when you are back on Earth. We don't know a lot about the conditions down there, but I do know that the Regime's army is mostly made up of cyborgs . . ."

The word *cyborg* calls to mind the many lengthy conversations I'd had with Joshua on my way to Titan Station about the conditions on Earth postwar. On more than one occasion, he'd explained that as supplies ran out, the Regime's soldiers' organs and limbs began to atrophy and die in the absence of the embryonic bio-drugs they had come to rely on to sustain their health and youth beyond the natural lifespan. To survive, they had ultimately resorted to using synthetic replacements, computer implants, and mechanical body parts to repair their broken pieces, thus creating a population that was mostly cybernetic in nature.

"We've been developing an exoskeleton system," she explains, "that could be helpful in the field when facing a soldier with a steel spinal column, for example."

Walking to the back of the lab, Sumi opens a weapons locker and disappears inside. When she emerges, she is lugging a heavy case, which she hoists onto the lab bench. Opening the case, she then pulls out two surprisingly sleek and lightweight forearm braces.

"They are made of graphene," she says, "so they are incredibly strong but also incredibly light." She snaps one on each arm and then explains, "Wearing these exos, you could carry a one-hundred-pound machine gun or decapitate a cyborg with very little effort."

After disappearing again into the arms locker, she returns with a beautiful katana, a Japanese sword with a curved, single-edged blade and a long, two-handed grip.

"I had this beauty made in the shop. It's a replica of those used in the Old World by samurai in feudal Japan, my ancestors." Adroitly swinging the sword, she says, indicating the exos, "See: The braces do not impede range of motion." Then, turning sharply, she effortlessly hacks clean through a nearby steel chair. She then gracefully pops up from the kneeling position from which she completed the motion and smiles. "Easily worn beneath our suits, this tech is a game-changer for you and me against opponents that are physically larger and stronger, even when we are in top form."

"That's incredible," I marvel. "And you have these for the lower body, too?"

"Yes, for the entire body, depending on how armed you need to be."

"And they are designed for warfare?"

"Not just warfare. They also allow us to carry heavy equipment long distances." She then snaps on the leg braces and demonstrates that she can jump, walk, crawl, squat, and run just as easily as if she weren't wearing any armor. "Want to try?" she asks.

"Heck, yeah," I say, grinning.

Sumi returns to the case, outfits me in exos for both the upper and lower body, then hands me her sword. I try out some moves. In my downtime on Proxima and in the holo-pods on *the Phoenix*, I became accustomed to practicing with a *khopesh*, an Egyptian sickle sword, and quickly begin to understand the advantage of using the exos as I practice with Sumi's katana. Meanwhile, she disappears into the locker again, this time returning with a much smaller case. Joining her at the lab bench, I watch as she opens the case.

"Flying micro-drones for spying," she says as she delicately removes a tiny mechanical bee from the small case. "I call this one Bumbly."

She releases the tiny cybernetic insect. It zips around the room, its wings humming softly, and eventually comes back down, landing on my hand. I bring the micro-bot closer to my face, examining its intricate metallic body, which is indistinguishable from an actual bee. It flies back over to Sumi and lands on her waiting index finger.

"These guys are equipped for obtaining intelligence, but we have another model that we package in small hives around the size of a hand grenade that will swarm your target on command." She raises an eyebrow high in amusement.

As she places Bumbly back into the small case, which is about the size of a thimble, I ask, "How do you review the intel in the field?"

Pulling out another small box about the size of her palm and opening it, she replies, "These are lenses that sync up with the microbots. You can wear one or two, depending on how much you can afford to obscure your field of vision with the data feed. But if you can't wear lenses or happen to not be wearing them, the bots can also sync with your palm screen, tablet, or whatever you are working from." She then places the small sphere inside the second box, closes it, and pushes it into my hands. "For you," she says with a smile.

"Thank you," I say, my eyes wide with surprise and gratitude. "Do I just carry him in my pocket?"

"In your pocket or . . ." She motions for me to open the small box again. When I do, she points to a small cuff inside the case that is hollow and shiny black. "It's an earring," she says, touching the top of her ear, "to be worn on your cartilage."

"Clever," I say as I carefully place Bumbly into the tiny cuff with a click, then snap the cuff onto the top of my ear. She gives me a wink and then starts packing up the rest of the case. When I start to remove the exos, she stops me and says, "Wait, what have you got after this?"

"Nothing, actually. I'm free until dinner."

"Perfect. Let's hit the holo-sphere so you can really see what the exos can do. Like I said, they change the game."

25

Sumi and I go down to the training deck, where she calls up a holographic program in one of the vacant holo-spheres that meticulously replicates the home of her ancestors in Old Japan of the Genesis Generations. The landscape she selects is nestled deep in the majestic Alpine mountains, a remote spot in what was once known as the southern Hida Mountain Range. Armed with two swords each, as is customary of her people's warriors—a katana and *wakizashi* for Sumi and a katana and a *tanto* for me—we encounter black bears, sika deer, and wild boar as we trek through the coniferous forests of the misty mountains. The golden eagle and mountain hawk watch overhead, soaring above the canopy of firs, pines, cedars, Mongolian oaks, and Japanese beeches—solemn and ancient sentinels now lost in the annals of time. These trees, remnants of a bygone era, did not survive the last ice age that befell the Founders and sealed the fateful demise of the civilization that preceded our own.

Surrounded by the long-forgotten magic of Old Earth, the exotic flora and fauna intoxicate me but also evoke a keen sense of sadness and regret. Titan's terrain does not foster plants—they could not survive its climate, not at this stage of the terraforming effort. But we hope that it someday will. And sadly, modern Earth is an ashen wasteland. A tree is now a thing of myth. It took 3.5 billion years for life on Earth to evolve from single-celled organisms to land plants, so it seems that even newly biotic Enceladus is just as far removed as Titan is from the prospect of one day bringing forth a precious land such as this mystical place.

The holo-program Sumi chose was set to a no-kill combat mode. So while we cannot be killed in this landscape, we can be injured, and the animals aggressively pursue us. We are spared the simulated bloodlust of no manner of beast, for those are the rules of the game. But we manage to hold our own against apex predators, mesopredators, and the fanged field mouse all the same, our exos providing an incredible advantage in strength and endurance.

It is exhilarating in those mountains, learning from Sumi about her people, the Old World, and a tribe of warriors I had previously known little about. I promise to take her to holographic Cana next time—though I wonder if there will be a next time. I do not know how long I will be on Earth or what kind of a toll my time there will take on me, my people, our world . . .

After devouring another meal in the mess hall, I return to my room for a shower and a little downtime before heading back out to the library to meet Josiah this evening. In a plush robe I find waiting in my closet along with a couple of fresh uniforms, I settle onto the bed with wet hair.

First, I catch up on emails. Nothing from Petra regarding the scan this morning, which, if I'm honest, is somewhat of a relief. I am not especially pressed to receive the results; there's a freedom in *not knowing* that I'm not sure I'm ready to give up. There is a message from Joshua back on Earth—he wants to talk. I need to update him on our progress with the graphene disbursement. I write him a note to let him know I will have more information in the next day or so.

My eyes are starting to cross, I'm so tired from another jam-packed day. As I get up to make coffee, I notice the box of my things I left behind twenty years ago sitting on the desk and begin to pick through it while my coffee brews. I find a little memory book that was once precious to me. When I open it, a hologram of Xavier materializes between the two ends.

It was a candid image I'd captured of him when he was not look-ing. It snowed the day he left, and we were waiting for his transport to the moon. He was in uniform but bundled up from the cold, looking off into the distance with a thousand-yard stare. When he noticed me watching him, he glanced up and smiled sadly. I wonder now what was on his mind. Did he know in that moment he was leaving me forever?

Seeing his face so clearly before me again stirs a deep ache in my chest. It's a familiar pain that I have tried hard to bury these past months. A chill runs through me, and I suddenly snap the book shut and toss it back in the box. I can't shake the feeling that I've seen a ghost.

Finishing my coffee, I dress in a soft brown sweater and pants of the same hue. I let my hair hang loose as it dries, long and curly. Grabbing my satchel, I head out the door to the library.

The time is around 2100 hours. The halls are quiet and dimly lit, and the days and nights are still black, as the sun will not begin to rise for three more days. As I make my way down the corridor, I begin to get the eerie feeling that I am being watched. I try to shake it off, but it's so pervasive and so quiet in these halls I cannot. Just when I've almost completely talked myself out of my paranoia, I start to notice a light shuffling sound behind me. Eventually, I work up the courage to whirl around and look, but no one is there.

Picking up the pace, I pass a popular lounge, The Shoulder of Orion, and it's empty except for a bot tending bar. *Where is everyone?* I wonder.

Soon I will be off the main drag and down a narrow corridor that leads to the lift. If I can just make it there, it will open directly onto the ground-floor atrium of the library, where surely there will be an attendant and other people gathered.

As I round the corner into the smaller passageway, I hear the shuffling again—faint but distinct. The carpeted floor here muffles the sound, making me question if I really heard it or if they just went another way. I take a few deep breaths but continue to walk at a clip, my senses on high alert.

I don't hear the shuffling again, but . . . *is that breathing?*

Nearly breaking into a run, I glance back again. Out of the corner of my eye, I could swear I saw a dark flourish of material disappear behind a bulkhead. I pause for only a fraction of a second when I hear the breathing again, then break into a full-on run, bolting the next thirty yards ahead of me into the lift as the doors slide open. I barrel inside, and the doors whisk shut behind me. I couldn't see if anyone was truly behind me, but it felt as if they were directly on my heels.

Two cadets are in the lift. I am panting as I collapse backward, pressing my back against the wall.

"Everything okay?" one asks with an eyebrow lifted and a half smile.

"Uh—yeah. Late for a meeting," I lie and then tap my wrist where a watch would be if I was wearing one.

He nods, and they avert their eyes awkwardly. The doors then slide open to the lower atrium of the library. The librarian is at his desk, and a few people are milling about. Relief begins to wash over me as I turn toward the stairs, heading up to the engineering level where Josiah and I worked yesterday evening.

"It saddens me to admit it, but I don't really remember much of Earth," Josiah says. "I have a vague idea of what I imagine it to be, but it's hard to separate that from what my mother has told me about it, holo-tours in history class, and my actual memories."

"I know what you mean," I reply. "It's the same for me when I try to remember my stepfather. He passed away when I was three, and the only memories I have are of days I've imagined around old pictures we have of him and stories that others have told me . . ." My words trail off. "It kind of bothers me that our memories are so suggestible."

"Well, they are, but only when we are children, right?" Josiah smiles.

"I guess," I say skeptically. "Hopefully, only then," I finish and flash him a smile in return.

"I'll admit, I'm pretty jealous that you are going back there—Earth." Leaning forward on the table between us, hands clasped in front of him, I can see the outline of his biceps beneath his black knit shirt. He clearly has good genetics, even if they were not preselected by his parents in a laboratory. "Even if it is a radioactive wasteland."

I feel dread well up in me. "I have mixed feelings about it."

"Well, you will get to see your family, at least," he offers.

"Yes!" I say. "I am really looking forward to seeing them. I'm just nervous, I guess, about what their new world will be like . . . how bad it is down there." I grit my teeth at the thought, then shake it off. "Well, speaking of which, Joshua contacted me earlier today asking for an update. What did you find in inventory?"

"It was fully stocked, so we won't need to go out to the mines unless you need additional raw material for miscellaneous items—like weapons or whatever else the Canish Guard is working on."

"Joshua didn't specify, but whatever the captain is willing to part with, we will be more than grateful to take off his hands."

"We have two metric tons of raw graphite on site in the warehouse and ten rolls of twenty-milliliter-volume film and eighty-milliliter-volume suspension. The former are transparent, and the latter is an opaquer form of graphene already manufactured and in storage with the suits."

"And how many suits do we have? Did Freeman indicate exactly how many he's willing to part with?"

"He's giving you five hundred suits, plus however much raw graphite you can carry in your cargo hold and whatever sheets or rolls can be spared from inventory."

My mouth hangs open a little, and I catch myself as my eyes begin to water with emotion. *What?* I am floored once again by his generosity.

Josiah sees the dumbfounded look on my face and smiles. "His parents were Canish, so you could say he's invested in your cause. Did you not know that? His family moved to the Institution's territories for his father's job when he was young, and he attended Academy at the Alliance's base there at the Ascendency. He spent much of his life there and, well, here, too—but he is Canish-born."

"I didn't know," I say, genuinely surprised.

"Well, he's a pretty private man." Josiah's gaze then meets my eyes. "Do you want to meet tomorrow morning to load up your ship?"

"Definitely. I can't thank you enough for your help with this."

"My pleasure," he says. "Thank *you* for stealing the fastest ship in the galaxy," he adds, mirth glittering in his eyes. "My brain is still going a mile a minute since reading those schematics you shared last night." He smiles. "I didn't get a wink of sleep afterward."

I shrug, then say with a wave of my hand, "Oh, it was nothing."

He laughs and continues. "Not just the FTL technology, but the interstellar shield, too. I had been working on a device for years, trying to make a shield for a ship that can pass through the electron belt to Earth's surface—and this ship of yours has all the answers. It's funny how you can struggle with something like that for so long, and then when you are finally faced with the solution, it just seems so simple."

It starts to occur to me that getting back to Earth is perhaps more important to Josiah than I have realized. I hope I didn't sound like I was taking it for granted, considering he hasn't seen his father and siblings in twenty years either. I'm sure he is dying to get back there. There has to be countless others on the station feeling the same way.

"Oh, that reminds me," I say. "I spent the afternoon in the Weapons and Warfare Lab. Sumi Kimura runs R&D there, and they have a camouflage material prototype that's a little more sophisticated than the camouflage already built into our suits but not quite as sophisticated as what is used in *the Phoenix*'s cloaking design. It's a material that removes visual, infrared, and thermal signatures, as well as shadow."

Sending the data I received from Sumi to the sensory wall next to us, I show him some of the schematics she shared with me, and he nods as he studies them. "She'll be joining us tonight to lend a hand with the work," I say.

"Excellent. The more the merrier." Josiah continues to review the plans, then nods again and says, "This is good progress."

"So, what else did you work on during school besides the shield?" I ask while we wait for Sumi.

"Well, the shield was more of a personal side project. It wasn't prioritized on the large scale in the Warfare Unit—they have been trying to perfect it on the small scale first. But my thesis was on Titan's polar seas . . ." he trails off as my eyes light up.

"I studied the seas, too," I say, suddenly recalling my old work, my old passions that now seem like a lifetime ago. "I was so convinced we'd find life in its murky depths," I recall, shaking my head.

"I know. I have actually continued your work," he says, locking eyes with me. "I read your journals on Kraken Mare. They were published after you . . . went missing."

"Which ones did you read?" I ask, processing again what this new world looks like with the decades lost.

"Well, I read all of them," he says.

I stare back at him blankly, feeling a little self-conscious.

"Your writing—I like it. It's very . . ." He pauses to find the right word. "Elegant. With scientific writing, well, most people's writing is very technical, but yours . . ." He pauses again. "I don't know. It's technical, but there's more to it. I can just tell you love what you do. It's inspiring."

I don't know how to take a compliment and suddenly feel the heat rise in my face. Before I can stutter a thank-you, Sumi strides in, and we both jump a little as the intimacy of the quiet study nook we are inhabiting is disrupted.

"Hey, guys, sorry I'm late!" she says energetically and starts unpacking her satchel. "I need a coffee."

"Me, too," Josiah says, then looks at me to weigh in. I nod in agreement.

"Let's grab a cup and then hit the archives," Sumi suggests, and the three of us are off.

26

Sumi and Josiah walk me back to my room through the dimly lit halls of the station sometime after 0200 hours. In the safety of their company, I feel silly about being so afraid earlier and running from someone I more than likely imagined was following me. I decide to chalk it up to my nerves over knowing I will be returning to Earth in the next couple of days, where I will face the terrible reality of war and what has become of my home world.

With plans to meet Josiah at 0900 hours, I relish the extra hour of sleep this morning after waking so early yesterday to train with Rip. When I arrive at the warehouse to start loading up my ship with the suits and graphene, it looks surprisingly empty.

Josiah emerges from a back aisle with a perplexed expression on his face.

"I don't believe this. They are just gone," he says. "Every single one of them."

"What's gone?—*The suits?*" I ask.

"Yes, all five hundred of them—the raw graphite and the fabricated sheets—all gone."

My heart sinks. I knew this was too good to be true. Trying not to get discouraged, I instead focus on solving the problem at hand. "Let's go speak with the foreman and see what they know," I suggest.

The shop is a few decks up from the warehouse. We take the lift and then head down a quiet corridor. Looking around, I observe that the halls are bare and industrial here. Entering the shop floor, I follow Josiah down the far side of the enormous manufacturing bay to stairs that lead up to an office overlooking the machinery below.

A man behind a desk looks up as we enter. He is an older man who, from appearances, can't be bothered with cosmetic gene-editing serums. While he is allowing himself to age naturally, he is a man of sturdy build and looks to still be in good health.

"Morning, Lieutenant Rolfe," Josiah says in greeting.

"Ensign Aarons," he says in reply and acknowledges me with a nod. "What can I do for you this morning?"

"I'm hoping you can help us. Five hundred suits have gone missing from inventory."

"What do you mean, *gone missing*?" Rolfe asks, his voice slightly alarmed.

"I'm not sure yet, Lieutenant. That's why I'm here. They had been allocated by leadership for a special project, and when I checked on the supply yesterday, everything was here and in good order. But today, every single one of them is gone. Can you confirm they weren't allocated elsewhere by mistake?"

Rolfe checks the logs and says, "According to inventory records, they should all still be there on Deck Four in the south-end armor locker." As he continues to review the logs, he remarks, "That's odd."

He then toggles over to another screen on the sensory surface of his desk. "The security footage is corrupt; the cameras are down." Getting up from behind his desk, he says, "I'm going to head down there now to check things out. Did you file a report with security?" he asks as he hurries past us.

"Not yet, but I will shortly. I wanted to speak with you first to be sure there hadn't been a mix-up," Josiah replies.

Rolfe nods in acknowledgment, and as he reaches the doorway to the stairwell, Josiah calls after him, "Hey, we are in a bind here. How many suits do you have in production, and how much time would it take to replace those that went missing?"

"Not many. At present, we have maybe five, and it will take a few weeks to replenish those losses if we can't recover what's gone missing," he replies and then is down the stairs and out the door.

As I look out at the enormous shop below us, dejected, Josiah assures me, "We will get to the bottom of this. But in the meantime, we need to secure a backup plan."

Josiah and I decide we will need to bring down some of the raw material from the caves after all. We could put in a work order for this sort of job but can't afford any more delays. There is sparse, rocky terrain on Titan in the jagged mountains, and among that rock is where the mineral graphite can be mined. So Josiah summons a military prop-shuttle that will taxi us out to the site of the mines and then return to pick us up once we have seen that the product we need is loaded on a barge to be transported back to the station.

The shuttle sent for us, a compact four-seater, is smaller as far as shuttles go, and as we move out onto the water at a very low altitude of maybe one hundred feet, we hang on for a long, rough ride over the northern polar seas. On the way, a small building on the water catches my eye, situated onshore over the Throat of Kraken, the strait that separates the north and south basins of Kraken Mare.

"Hey, what's that building on the strait?" I ask Josiah as we fly over the great body of water.

He looks to the window, then smiles. "That's your research facility—the one you proposed in your thesis. They built it while you were away."

Pressing my face to the window, I try to get a better look as we whiz by.

"It has been integral to the progress we have made in our research on Kraken," he adds.

"I'd love to see it close up," I say, feeling a longing for my old life here. "But I guess it will have to be . . . next time," I trail off.

"How long do you think you will be away?"

"It's impossible to know. I can't imagine a world where the Institution, or the Regime," I correct myself, "is no longer a threat to our people." I exhale, leaning back against the seat. "I just want to see that Cana is stable, protected, and has the best resources possible to fight the coming war—if it comes to that."

"Well, that's all you can do," he says. "All anyone can do. And look at how much you have accomplished so far. We've had no prospects viable enough in over *twenty years* to even consider landing on Earth again, and you have found us a way. And the suits—the Canish Guard will have *suits*. We have hit a snag here, but it's just a delay. One way or another, they will have the graphene—whether in premade suits or raw material that will become suits—and having that kind of protection will change everything."

I think about how frustrating it must be for people on Titan Station like Josiah with family still back on Earth—family they are unable to reach. I can't imagine how terrible that would be and remind myself how grateful I should be that I have the means to get there.

"I'm sorry. You are right," I say. "I know you and the others must be desperate to return. But you were close to getting us there, Josiah, with the shield. That was incredible work."

"Well, it wasn't just my work. I hit a major plateau when Cassini left."

"What do you mean?"

"Cassini Freeman, the station captain's daughter. Did you know her before?"

"Not really. She was young, a child, so no. Petra said she had gone missing."

"It was really her project to begin with. She's a few years older than I am, so I was helping her with it and still learning at first, but then took over the work when she left." Fidgeting, then finally folding his hands in his lap, he looks out the window to the mountain we can now see in the distance. The sparkling ridges look iridescent in the darkness, illuminated only by starlight in these dark days before Equinox. "Sometimes I wonder if she had actually solved the equation but wanted to keep it to herself—but that would be sociopathic, wouldn't it?" He laughs. "But she was like that: private and almost secretive at times. She had a lot going on up here." He taps his temple.

"What do you mean?" I find myself asking him again.

"Well, she was gifted. She started taking Academy-level classes when she was twelve, and by the time she was sixteen, she . . . I don't know. She just did whatever she wanted, disregarding any kind of authority . . ." He trails off. "But her mind, it was unique. Her depth and the scope of her consciousness was just beyond that of anyone I knew—anyone I've ever known."

"It sounds like she was an asset to the Alliance. It's our misfortune to have lost her."

"Well, no, it's not exactly like that. She was also irreverent and . . ." He pauses, looking for the right word. Then, as if lost somewhere in the past, he finishes softly, "Beguiling."

We sit quietly for a minute before he continues. "There was this recklessness about her that even the station captain didn't seem to know how to handle. But I liked her. She taught me a lot," he finishes, staring out the window into the darkness, lost in his memories.

"I don't understand what happened to her," I press.

"No one does," he says. "She was here one day, then gone the next." Thoughtful for a moment, he looks over at me again before saying, "I used to wonder if your disappearances were connected. But then there was so much chaos around your disappearance, happening just after the bombs hit—and Taj was missing, too. So, maybe not. But it never did make sense that your escape pods were just gone; there was no evidence that they'd been destroyed. They, too, seemed to have just vanished inexplicably. Like Cassini."

I think about Cassini, Xavier, and all the other officers who have gone missing over the years. "Just another hazard of space travel . . ." I say distantly, my words ringing flat, a little lost now in my own memories.

"The vanishing, you mean?"

"Yeah, my—friend—from back home, he vanished, too. Just add

him to the list," I joke, trying in vain to downplay the gut-wrenching loss of Xavier. "But he was stationed on Calypso, and that really isn't all that uncommon there, from what I hear."

I catch myself again trying to normalize the unexplainable. I feel like I'm doing too much of that these days. But it seems there's no other way to keep moving forward, and that is what we must do if we are to survive, I'm learning.

"Well, I'm sorry to hear that. You and I seem to have a lot in common." He smiles as the shuttle begins to descend toward an out-cropping on the side of the mountain, then finally lands on a cleared platform next to the mine entrance.

27

From the adit, it is a long way down to reach the mines proper. As Josiah and I leave the platform and enter a blasted-out stone antechamber, I can see that extensive quarrying has been done under the mountain to facilitate the mining process. Rock has been broken with explosives, and drilling has been done using various methods, including drift mining, hard-rock mining, shaft mining, and slope mining. Industrial bots complete the hard labor needed to extract the ore, and once the raw material is extracted, it is then purified through the beneficiation process, which mainly involves reducing the ore into particles by comminution, electrostatic separation, and leaching.

Under the mountain, the air is cold and there is little light. Since there is no life support in the mines, we are wearing our suits for oxygen supplementation and protection from the elements. As we walk along the narrow ledge around the circumference of the cavern, I first look down into the gaping hole and then scan the adjacent wall, observing its icy, scalloped texture. We then cross over a suspension bridge that leads to the mine shaft that will take us deeper into the mountain. Beyond the meek reach of the lights lining the platform, darkness surrounds us on all sides. Once across the bridge, we approach a deep, narrow, vertical tunnel also lined with lights and fitted with a motorized cage that rides on cables and works like an elevator to transport miners and equipment farther down into the caverns. Stepping into the cage, we secure the door closed behind us, activate the power lever, and begin our descent.

It takes a few minutes to reach the lowest level, where we then follow a tunnel dimly lit with sparsely spaced lanterns and framed by steel support beams. The mining bots do not require light to work, so the lamps are a courtesy for people like us who come here occasionally to see the graphite transported back to the station.

After a few yards, we hear rushing water as we come to a fork in the tunnel; this is a man-made junction that can only be accessed by water from outside the mine or from inside, as we have done. The fork to the left takes us to the river, where we will transfer our load to a barge that will, in turn, transport the graphite back to the station. The fork to the right leads to where the beneficiation occurs and the finished product is stored.

After turning right, the tunnel eventually opens into another large cavern. Halfway expecting the supply here to have vanished along with the suits back at the station, I exhale in relief when I spot the massive stores of graphite on one side of the space.

When mined, graphite is in solid form, extracted in large chunks of rock that are then purified into a near-black powder of microscopic graphite flakes. Back at the station, the powder will then be refined further, at the atomic level, into thin, indestructible sheets of highly flexible graphene—a part of the process handled by Rolfe's team.

For this job, Rolfe will be working as more of a chemist than an engineer since the process entails the oxidation of the graphite flakes by an acid—usually nitric or sulfuric—which then requires further reduction of the material into even finer flakes that can be used in products for additive manufacturing—known as 3D printing—or rolled into paperlike sheets for large-scale construction projects.

Cana has the capabilities—even in its new underground dwellings—to process the graphite and manufacture the suits; it just takes time, which is what we are all short on these days. While I was elated at the prospect of receiving five hundred finished suits, we can make do with the raw material and manufacture the suits ourselves.

Josiah walks over to the pallet racks, which are stacked higher than I can see with black bricks of pure graphite, and begins scanning them with his palm screen. We're looking at ten metric tons, and Freeman has generously offered Cana two metric tons.

"Excuse me," Josiah says politely to an industrial bot passing by. "Could you please help us transport two metric tons of this material to the docks to be loaded on the next barge?"

I laugh quietly to myself at how polite he is to the machine, then realize that this sort of idiosyncrasy is what I like most about him. He treats everyone equally and with respect. He then communicates regarding procedures with the bot, providing various data and approval codes and showing the work order.

Eventually, a second bot arrives to join the first, and the two of them begin loading the bricks onto a pallet jack to move them to the docks by the water. While they are busy, we walk around the cavern and look around.

"Seems simple enough," I remark.

"Yep, so far, so good," Josiah says while scanning various parts of the storage hub. More racks on the other side of the cavernous room seem to go back farther than I initially realized. Moving around the floor, we see machines facilitating the beneficiation process: filters and waste streams. Josiah, being the bona fide scientist he is, starts scanning the floors and walls. "The Alliance has a lot of graphite," he remarks. "Like, *a lot*. Much more than is documented in our inventory or published anywhere on the trade forums."

"That's probably best. I'm sure Freeman wants to keep it quiet if that war is as bad as everyone says."

"Oh, it is," he confirms, glancing up at me and then back to his device. "What you have heard is true. Chiron plays by no rules, abides by no treaty, makes no alliances."

"Why have they left us alone? And Mars?" I ask.

"Maybe because of our numbers, our size. While they are formidable, they are still a smaller force. And there is so much conflict among their own groups; they can't stop fighting among themselves, and it limits them further. Now, if they were ever to become unified, like we are, then we would have reason for concern." I give him a worried look, and he continues. "But I don't think it's likely to happen anytime soon. They refuse to recognize anyone's leadership. It hasn't even come close to happening over the last twenty years of Chiron's raiding."

We have been walking down a long aisle of pallets toward the back of the cavern, which seems to have no end, when Josiah, continuing to scan along the way, suddenly pauses. "That's odd," he remarks.

"What?"

"I'm picking up a heat signature beneath this room."

"Someone else is here?" I ask.

"Well, that's what it looks like, but there were no scheduled transfers today. None until after Equinox—that's why we had to come out here ourselves."

"What's beneath this room?"

"That's the thing. The mines proper are off limits for humans, for safety reasons. Even Rolfe isn't permitted down there, and that's what is directly beneath us—the mines." He continues to monitor his palm screen, then swipes through a few images before saying, "That's strange. I can't get a visual of that level."

"Do you have access?"

"I thought I did. Let me message Rolfe." He then sends a quick message to Rolfe, asking if he can get a visual on the coordinates of the level below us.

While we wait, we review the schematics of the mines. "Looks like there is an observation platform one level down, over this part of the mines," I say, indicating on the screen where I mean.

"Yep. And to get to it, we take this stairwell down to it," he says, tracing the route on the schematics with his finger.

Finding the entry to the stairwell that takes us even deeper into the base of the mountain, we descend the stairs Josiah indicated with little light to guide us other than the meager beam the flashlight function of our palm screen provides, which does little to illuminate the depthless black that surrounds us.

Josiah switches his light off, checking his screen again for the heat signature. Whoever, or whatever it is, is still active but seems to be moving away from the area where we will exit the stairwell and enter the cavern below.

"Where are they going?" I wonder out loud.

Making it to the bottom of the stairs, we walk out onto the observation platform. Posted signs warn that we have gone as far as is safely permissible. The mine is lit only with the tiny automation lights on various machine parts, and nothing can be heard here other than the steady hum of the mining machinery. Shining my light over the vast open cave, I see nothing unusual, and then something catches my eye.

"It looks like they have now gone up to the level above us using the opposite stairwell," Josiah says in frustration, still tracking the heat signature on his device. "They're headed to the docks."

"Wait," I say and squint into the darkness. "Are those . . .?" And I wouldn't have otherwise noticed except that everything down here is so grimy, but my light has reflected off something shiny and clean— what appears to be a rack of, I don't know, say five hundred brand-new graphene space suits, stashed away in an alcove off the dirty mining floor. "*The suits!*" I shout.

"What are they doing down here?" Josiah says. Alarmed, he springs into action. "Let's go! I'd wager whoever is now on the docks has an idea."

We run as fast as we can back up the stairs, retracing our steps and winding our way out of the labyrinthine storage cavern and down the tunnel leading to the river until we finally emerge from the caves and make it out to the docks.

We look around frantically. "Nothing but bots," I say, panting.

Josiah rechecks his device. "Yeah, because whoever that was is now on the river, headed far away from here."

28

The ordeal with the missing suits and the trip out to the mines took the entire day, but I'm pretty pleased to now have two tons of pure graphite, plus the five suits I received from Rolfe's shop, sitting in my cargo hold. We will not be able to recover the five hundred missing suits immediately because they are in an inaccessible place—or at least a place that is inaccessible to us if we follow protocol.

We reported our discovery and the mysterious heat signature Josiah detected to Rolfe and Security. Then we traveled downriver on a barge with the graphite stores to ensure that nothing happened to the product while in transit to the station. The mysterious heat signature remained visible on Josiah's screen, traveling in front of us along the river, eluding us by a matter of minutes when we arrived back at the station. The warehouse attendant on Deck Four had been found unconscious behind some crates, so there was obviously some sort of trouble afoot. The situation would need to be investigated before we would be granted approval to move the stolen suits. Josiah is optimistic things will move quickly and that we will be cleared to retrieve the inventory by the morning after Equinox, which is the morning I am scheduled to leave for Earth.

Now I am back in the library putting the finishing touches on our suit-cloak program. Sumi, Josiah, and I have devised a plan that combines the shielding attributes of Sumi's body camouflage with the cloaking technology we've gleaned from Abramovich's design for *the Phoenix*. And after several days of crunch time, we have produced a functioning prototype. Sumi will load the program and make any mechanical adjustments required to my suit tomorrow morning.

In a quiet corner of the library, I am running some tests on the program we created to identify and work out any bugs. After that, I'll run some final regression checks to be sure our modifications didn't impact any of the preexisting protocols and that essentially everything still works the way it did before—that none of the new features broke any of the old ones.

It's late, and I'm ready for bed, but just need to log the results of the last set of tests I completed before calling it a night. The set was mostly automated, and I have been slouching in my chair, daydreaming while waiting on the results. When the last set is complete, I sit up straight, stretch, and prepare to begin logging the output when I hear that noise again. Somewhere in the library. That *shuffling*. Or is it *breathing*?

At first, the sound startles me. Then I regain my composure and realize it just pisses me off. After today's discovery of the missing suits, the drugged warehouse attendant, and the mysterious heat signature, it doesn't seem quite as farfetched as it did the day before that someone could be following me. I resist the urge to whip my head around to check if anyone is there and instead clear my throat, take a sip of tea, and try to behave casually.

But why me? I wonder.

Then the sound again.

Are they getting closer? I feel the hairs on the back of my neck stand up. *Why would anyone be following me?*

I look at the time; it's half-past 2300 hours. The librarian is likely off duty by now. Then the obvious dawns on me.

They want my ship. My ship that is now carrying two metric tons of graphite.

I casually look around the room as much as I can without drawing attention to myself.

But that doesn't explain why they would have followed me last night . . .

The alcove in front of me is vacant. *But what are they going do? Drag me out of here kicking and screaming?*

My heart rate increases as I recall the attendant who was found unconscious, and I suddenly become incredibly paranoid that at any moment, I, too, will be knocked out. Taking a deep breath, I calmly straighten my hair, then sneak a look behind me, and there is no one. Just a few rows of shelves.

Okay, that buys me some time, I think. And then I get an idea.

Nonchalantly, I detach Bumbly from my cartilage earring, activating his program on my palm screen. Carefully, I place him on the desk in front of me. He springs to life, soundlessly hovering a few feet in the air above the table in front of me. He's so small, once he gets going, it's nearly impossible to track him visually without knowing exactly where to look. I manually chart his course and start receiving his feed on the split screen of my device.

It takes a moment to orient myself, and I startle as a cadet passes, coming from the opposite direction, exiting some other hidden corner of the library. As I trace Bumbly's path with my finger, I guide him toward the noise, which went quiet when the cadet passed but has now returned.

After landing the microscopic drone on top of the shelving facing my back, only about ten feet behind me, I walk him through a narrow gap between the top row of books. My blood runs cold as I take in the overhead view of the aisle below. Sure enough, there is a man crouching behind the shelf, watching me and fumbling with something in his hands.

Taking a sharp breath, I then fly Bumbly high above the shelving and bring him back around, hovering in a position where I can see the man's hands. Bringing the tiny drone down just close enough so that I can see clearly, I am terrified to see that what he is fumbling with is, in fact, a syringe. After snapping something in place, he then looks up through the crack between the books again. And to my utter disbelief, I see that it is none other than the rude Mars emissary, Alaric Kronos, whom I met in Sumi's lab yesterday.

Before I can do anything, he is on his feet, around the bookshelf, and lunging for me. I lean to the left sharply and tumble out of my chair, dodging his reach. Missing me by a hair, he is thrown forward and crashes onto the desk. He breaks his fall with both hands, landing directly on top of my palm screen, which I now cannot reach to call for help.

Kronos is up in a heartbeat. I, too, am on my feet and turn to run, but he grabs my ankle with his left hand, pulling me back toward him.

Falling onto my stomach, I scream bloody murder. *"Helllppp!!"* I cry, scrambling forward and kicking with my other leg as hard as I can while he tries to bring the syringe forward with his right hand. He is a solid hulk of a man and incredibly quick, but having something in his hand is handicapping him.

Flipping over onto my back, I kick him directly in the face. This deters him momentarily, allowing me precious seconds to get to my feet and run like hell down the aisle. When I reach the end, I turn and duck behind the shelves, but he is up and in pursuit.

I am irritated and stupefied that the station's computer did not respond to my call for help. *How can* help *not be a wake word?* So instead, panting, I yell, "Security!"

That works, and the computer responds immediately, "Security to Level Seven of the Library Tower."

As I weave between the stacks, he is on my heels. Finally, I reach the open stairwell that winds down around the atrium and continue down the seven flights, taking two to three stairs at a time when I can. I glance back, hoping I've made some headway, but to my dismay, he is only one flight behind and gaining on me. He is fast, I will give him that.

"What do you want from me?" I scream, enraged.

Huffing as he gains on me, he growls, "There's a price on your head, bitch."

Then he tackles me from behind on the last set of stairs, and we go tumbling forward onto the pristine white carpet of the library entryway just as the doors to the lift slide open. The last thing I see is uniformed guards rushing toward us as I feel the hot pain of a sharp needle puncture my right thigh—and then everything goes black.

29

I come to around fifteen minutes later, propped up against a wall of the atrium. A medic is waving her fingers in front of my face, and everything hurts.

"Ouch," I say reflexively, rubbing my lower back with one hand and my right thigh—which is throbbing from the violent stabbing it received courtesy of my assailant's syringe—with the other. Security is all over the place. Petra is here, shouting orders. I notice my attacker, Kronos, on the far side of the atrium, restrained with cuffs, lying prostrate on the carpet. His head is turned toward me. I give him a colorful hand gesture as Petra notices I'm awake and approaches me. As she does, the doors to the lift slide open, and Sumi and Rip rush out.

"Nazari, you're okay!" Rip exclaims.

Petra orders, "You two, *out of here!* This is a crime scene," and motions that they return to the lift.

"What the hell, Chauverac? Can't I check on my friend?" Rip argues.

Petra rolls her eyes. "No, *out!* You can see her after."

Rip looks in my direction and pretends to take a sip of a drink, pointing in the direction from which they came. "Orion's? See you there after?"

I nod, then look to Petra, who is still peeved. She nods as well, and they turn to leave.

Crossing the atrium, Petra closes the space between us and squats down in front of me to do her own assessment of my condition. "Are you okay?" she asks, looking grave while the guards escort Kronos out behind her.

"Yeah, just a little bruised up." I try to get up, and she stops me.

"Take it easy for a second," she says.

"But my stuff . . ." I say, thinking of Bumbly. "You probably don't need any more evidence to arrest this guy, but I have footage of him stalking me."

She smiles, patting my computer and palm screen, which I now see sitting beside me. "It's right here, and thanks. Anything helps."

"So, who the hell is that thug?" I ask while inspecting my palm screen for damage. When I'm satisfied it's not damaged, I use it to recall Bumbly to me.

"Not who he says he is," she replies. "He says he's Alaric Kronos, but the computer says Alaric Kronos is in the morgue—that body you and Rip found out behind Yellowbelly."

"What's the lab say?" I ask, assuming they had also done a DNA check.

"So far, we can't match his identity. But that leaves a short-list of organizations he could be affiliated with. We are running a few more tests and questioning his comrades. Don't worry. We'll get to the bottom of it."

"He said there's a price on my head."

She looks baffled for a moment, then curses and exclaims, "Abramovich!"

The medic clears me, and I go to the bathroom to clean up while Petra wraps things up with Security. We then head home, stopping by The Shoulder of Orion along the way to meet Rip and Sumi. The place is festive and packed. I see that Gia is here with Rip, and some friends of Sumi's have also come along.

When I have assured Rip I am okay, she orders me a fizzy drink of mineral water with coconut and dragon fruit.

"We saw the security report flash across that screen, Nazari, and I knew it was you," Rip says. "I just knew it. So we ran to your rescue, and sure enough . . ."

"You are so full of it," I say, laughing and incredulous. "You could not have known it was me!"

"Uh, yeah, I could. No one else I know would spend four hours in the Engineering Library on Equinox Eve. It *had* to be you."

"Very funny," I say, shaking my head.

"Look, Nazari. It's just statistics—simple math."

I stare back at her expectantly, waiting for her confession.

"Well, and Petra may have messaged me," she finally adds, bursting into laughter.

"I knew it!" I reach to mess up her hair, but she ducks away.

"Don't touch the 'do!" she whines indignantly as a group of officers pass behind us in the tight space between us and the bar. One says in a mocking tone, "If it isn't the illustrious Commander Chauverac . . ." then salutes Petra overzealously.

She salutes him back without bothering to look at him, then says to us, "I put that guy on the ground today in commander drills."

The guy then puts his hands a little too low on Sumi's back as he passes through, and as she cringes away from him, I give him a disgusted look. He notices, returns the look, and then crosses himself in mockery, paying homage to none other than my clone source.

Heat rising to my face, I lose my cool and lunge at him. Petra pulls me back just as he ducks out of the way of my fist, tumbling backward into a table full of drinks, which then topples over, the glasses smashing on the floor.

After all the commotion, we decide to move to another part of the bar that is a little less tight and find a table. I suppose it's safe to assume my secret has become more public now than I had realized, considering the news I received this evening that there is a price on my head and now with the behavior of this clown.

As we pick and weave our way through the crowd, I notice Jonathan Avery, the lieutenant colonel I ran into at the clinic the morning after my arrival, sitting by himself at the end of the bar. Looking up, he catches my eye as we pass. He smiles slightly, and I smile back at him, waving hello. Waving back, he then returns his gaze to the bottom of his glass.

My heart aches for Avery. Loss hits everyone differently. At first, I thought he was a hothead, but now I see the picture more clearly and understand that it's grief that he's battling—not me or Taj or anyone else. When the river of life rises, it displaces everyone in its path, and some are better equipped to stay afloat than others. Some can swim safely to shore with the support of friends and family and survive it. But for others, the blow of the loss is too great, and they can be swept under. Avery lost his entire family, his entire support system, and it seems that twenty years later the grief is just as fresh, the loss just as harrowing. I understand how he feels, and I wish I could do something to help him.

When we finally find a table and get settled, I apologize for my outburst: "I'm sorry you guys. That was out of line."

"Well, you have had a hard day," Petra says.

"But not so hard that it's time to go home," Rip chimes in. "Nope, not yet, Nazari. What do you say we take the rovers out for a midnight ride and howl at the moon?" she asks, grinning ear to ear.

"Which moon?" I ask skeptically, goading her, since Saturn has a hundred and forty-six of them in its orbit.

"Rhea. Dione—no, Skoll!" she exclaims. "Whatever. You get the point. We can howl at Saturn for all I care. Come on, it'll make you feel better." Then, turning to Petra, she adds, "Chauverac, I know you're game."

"I am, but after what went down tonight in the library, I will need to be strapped," she says, pointing to the various places on her body where she will carry weapons. "Here, here, and . . . here."

"We get it, Commander, but this is Titan we live on, not Chiron," Rip says, teasing her. "Now, I can understand why maybe *you* would feel the need to carry multiple weapons, but not me. I only need *one* gun. You know why? Because I never miss." She cracks her knuckles over her head.

Rip then looks to Sumi, who is engrossed in her palm screen, messaging furiously on it. Sumi pauses momentarily and says, "Sorry, I'm chewing out Stevens. He was responsible for vetting the Mars envoys . . . But yeah, count me in."

Rip looks to me. "Nazari?"

"I can't," I say. "My head is still spinning from the syncope serum Kronos or whoever he is gave me." It's true. The occurrences of the day are beginning to mount, and I'm finding it hard to shake the anxious mood it has put me in as my mind starts to fixate on these new threats and the same old ones.

"Come on," Rip presses. "Rolfe souped up a couple of rovers for me. And you know it's tradition to go out on Equinox Eve—" she adds before Gia cuts in and tries, in vain, to shut things down.

While we are still arguing, I notice Josiah walking down the thoroughfare outside the bar. He was on duty tonight, and it's a little past midnight; he must be getting off shift. I wave him over, and he walks up, leaning over the railing that encloses the main lounge area. As he approaches and greets us, Petra gives him an appraising look, then looks back at me, nodding in approval.

"How'd it go tonight?" he asks, referring to the software testing I was doing in the library on our suit-cloak program.

"It was going great until . . ." I say, pausing. "I got slightly derailed."

"Oh yeah, how so?"

"Long story," I say, not wanting to rehash tonight's near-abduction in a noisy bar. "Hey, are you headed back to the residential wing?"

"I am." He nods.

"Walk me back? I can catch you up on my . . . progress."

"Sure," he replies.

"Boooo," Rip says as I hop up to leave.

"I'm sorry, next time," I promise.

"Fine," she concedes. "But you're missing out."

Gia then asks, "Hella, may I speak with you privately before you leave?"

"Yeah, sure," I say. My stomach tightens as I put together that she likely has the test results of my brain scan and genetic testing that I have been avoiding Petra over for the last twenty-four hours.

While Gia bids Rip goodnight, Petra walks me out and tells me she will fill Josiah in on the security breach while I speak with Gia. Petra insists that she will only permit me to walk back to my quarters without a full security detail if we promise to stay on the lookout. I agree, and she pulls Josiah aside while I speak with Gia. Rip, Sumi, and some of her friends settle the tab and prepare for their midnight rover outing on the surface.

Gia and I walk down the long gallery across from Orion's while we talk.

"Hella, I wanted to share with you the results of the brain scan and genetic testing that Petra requested on your behalf."

"I figured that's what this was about."

"The results were rather . . . confounding. Your DNA, from an evolutionary perspective, contains biomarkers consistent with the genetic makeup of humanoids living during the first century BC of the Old World." Looking at me gravely, she continues. "And your brain volume—the size and shape of your brain is consistent as well with the larger size and more oblong shape that are characteristic of the brains of the people of the same period. People living during the Roman Era of the Classical Age." She exhales, staring at me for a long moment. "It appears you are a clone," she says at last, "derived from some very ancient DNA—with a genetic code of an age that we were not aware even still existed. An age from which we certainly have never created a clone."

I nod and look down as we walk, my hands in my pockets.

"Were you aware of this? You must have suspected it to be a possibility, or you would not have asked for these tests."

I look up at her. "Someone told me that I am a clone." I pause, shaking my head. "I just can't believe that it's actually true."

"I understand," she says simply, respecting my privacy and not pressing for more information. "This is a very unusual discovery for a child of Cana. Our people, as you know, do little to no genetic editing."

Looping around to the other side of the avenue, we walk back toward Petra and Josiah.

"Well, thank you, Dr. Ramzi," I say.

"Please—call me Gia," she says.

I nod. "Gia, thank you for completing the test and for your confidentiality. I'd really like this to stay off the record."

"Of course," she replies, then places her hand on my forearm. "But I would urge you to seek counsel and to see a specialist. There are certain protocols and *risks* of which you should be aware."

I nod as she searches my eyes for acknowledgment. When she is satisfied that I've heard what she has said, she adds, "Anything you need, please do not hesitate to contact me, Hella."

After my conversation with Dr. Ramzi, Josiah and I walk back to the residential sector. Taking our time, we walk slowly, immersed in conversation. We talk about the strange succession of events that have unfolded over the last few days, including my being attacked in the library, the stolen suits, and the murder of Alaric Kronos. We discuss our excitement over the work we were able to accomplish on the cloaking prototype in the span of just a few days. We marvel over the life found on Enceladus, our research on Kraken Mare, and the numerous other mysterious ocean worlds we both hope to visit one day. Lastly, we talk about the logistics of my trip back to Earth—all that could go wrong and all that must go right for me to succeed in simply arriving at my destination.

We don't talk about how quickly the last few days have flown by or how little time there is left before we have to say goodbye. We don't talk about having regrets—regrets over how brief our time together has been or that we didn't meet sooner—because that kind of thinking is a luxury afforded only by those who don't have the weight and fate of a dying world on their shoulders. He understands this as well as I do, and that is why we don't waste precious time contemplating what could have been.

Bringing me to my door, Josiah bids me goodnight. I will see him tomorrow at the Equinox celebration and again before I depart the following morning. But I promise him tonight, while it is just the two of us, that when I reach Earth, I will seek out his father and sisters in Cana City, which is the least I can do. Anything beyond that, between us, will remain unwritten.

30

Today is Equinox. If all goes as planned, I'll leave for Earth tomorrow morning at 0900 hours. The station captain himself will be there to see me off. Most of my preparations for departure are complete. Sumi is busy putting the finishing touches on my suit cloak, so I woke early to have a simple breakfast of tea and toast at the café before stopping by the R&D Lab to check on her progress.

On my way to the lab, I observe the station is teeming with Security. In addition to the detail outside my quarters, officers patrol each sector on every floor and at all major entryways, junctions, and exits. Not long after I arrive, Sumi shoos me away, promising that if I leave her alone, my suit will be ready by noon.

Walking the long way back to my quarters, I pass through the Hall of Heroes Gallery. Taking my time, I study the different faces and the various dates, quotes, and statements written below each picture. The Hall of Heroes leads to a second gallery—the Killed in Action Memorial—and then the Missing in Action section follows last. I notice my portrait has been removed since my return, along with Taj's, since it has been acknowledged that he, at minimum, defected from the Alliance and, therefore, is no longer considered missing; I suppose my report confirmed that for them.

I pause in front of the portrait of a young girl. *Cassini Freeman* is written on the plaque below it.

Studying her face, I find she does have a cunning sort of look in her eyes. It's not one of mischief, because that would seem to imply some kind of lightheartedness or innocence. No, it's irreverence and maybe even ire, but it is nothing kind. She can't be more than sixteen in the picture, yet there is an authority there. An air of dominance. Her hair is dark brown and just past her shoulders, her skin pale. Cassini looks back at me, her stare depthless, a young girl now lost somewhere in the ether.

There is a quote beneath the image, as was customary in a school photo, which reads:

> *"Let me have men about me that are fat,*
> *Sleek-headed men and such as sleep a-nights.*
> *Yond Cassius has a lean and hungry look,*
> *He thinks too much; such men are dangerous."*

The excerpt was written by Shakespeare, a poet of the Old World. The verse is spoken by the character of Julius Caesar, a once revered general of the Roman Empire, a great power at one time in the Old World. These lines foreshadow Caesar's fall as he reflects on the countenance of the man who would ultimately lead his assassination. Gifted as Cassini was, it is not surprising she graduated early. Interesting selection for a sixteen-year-old just finishing up grade school.

When my palm screen chirps a five-minute reminder before my scheduled call with Joshua, I realize I've lost track of the time. Cursing silently, I turn on my heel and hurry back to my quarters.

Sitting down at my desk, a study nook nestled in the corner of my room, I brush my hair back from my face as I wait for Joshua to connect. Within a few moments, his call comes through.

"There she is," Joshua says, grinning from ear to ear, his upper half projected in front of me just above the desk.

"Joshua!" I exclaim, beaming back at him.

"How are you, little sis?"

"I'm hanging in there! How are things back home?"

"We are getting by," he replies.

"Did you get the schematics I sent over?"

"Yes, we have reviewed the schematics of the prototype, and I've gotta say, you all have done some really incredible work, and in a short amount of time. We think it's going to work to get you safely on-world and underground without detection," he finishes, rubbing his palms together. "Now, what's the latest on our cargo?"

"Everything's still on track, but we did run into a few hiccups." My brother's brow furrows as I continue. "The bad news is that the five hundred prefabricated suits are now a no-go."

His face falls in disappointment.

"But the good news is I've got two metric tons of raw graphite in my cargo hold, packed and ready to go."

Joshua's eyes widen in relief. "Wow! Well, that's great news about the graphite. Freeman has outdone himself with his generosity," he says. Then doing some math in his head, he continues. "But the loss of the suits does set us back a bit—to the tune of about three weeks—since we will need to manufacture them ourselves. Otherwise, our deployable forces are combat-ready. Do we have *any* suits besides that fancy prototype you will wear?"

"We were able to get five in addition to mine."

"Okay, we can work with that. That will at least allow us to do some reconnaissance on the surface before going out in greater numbers." He looks down at his notes. "So I take it your departure is still on track for tomorrow morning?"

"Yes, at 0900 hours." I smile, still unable to believe that if all goes as planned, I will be together again with my family in a matter of days. "How are our numbers looking overall?"

"We've got about six hundred of the Canish Guard garrisoned—double that of Cana Minor—and three hundred Institution refugees still in training."

"Institution?" I ask.

He nods. "When you arrive, you will see that our population is not exactly how you remember it. The citizens of Cana City are no longer exclusively Canish. We now house a number of refugees, mostly Institution-born survivors, and they represent about a third of our population. The Canish Guard is still primarily made up of soldiers hailing from Cana Major, but Cana Minor's patrol now outnumbers us pretty significantly—which is the reverse of the way it was before the war."

I nod while taking some notes on my tablet.

"We've made it work, but it has been somewhat problematic politically over the years, and it has been harder to keep the peace. Still, we have remained united, if by the skin of our teeth." He shakes his head. "Especially now, with your prospective arrival." He pauses as if to gauge my reaction, and I look up from my notes. "It is bringing new hope to the people," he says tentatively. "I say that because you will be the first in two decades to cross the electron belt. And because of the technology, weapons, and armor you will be bringing—not because of the narrative Abramovich has fabricated."

I nod, tight-lipped, holding my breath.

"But if I'm honest, that *has* been a contributing factor for some factions." Looking down again, he says, "Which reminds me . . ."

I brace for bad news.

"Cana Minor is still rather fanatical, and I must warn you that Abramovich's claim about your DNA—it is public knowledge here. And while, for the most part, it really hasn't done any harm, it has united the fanatics and believers, and made them more apt to cooperate because of your association with us—and if anything, it has given them hope. But understand: There is an order out from Cana Minor's small council that you are to be taken into custody immediately upon your arrival . . ."

"*What?*" I say in disbelief. "No. There's no way that's happening. They have no right."

"Don't worry, it's *not* going to happen. Not if the Canish Guard has anything to do with it. But be forewarned: If anything goes awry and your entry to the underground turns out to be somewhere other than where we have planned it, be on your guard. We will meet you with an armed unit upon your arrival but won't be able to help if you land outside our jurisdiction. Anywhere on the outskirts of Cana City proper, in the Cana Minor sector itself, or in the neutral zone, you will not be protected, and they *will* be looking to take you in. We don't believe they intend to harm you, as their efforts are under the guise of protection, but their orders come from Abramovich, and we all know his endgame."

"His endgame. Right. I miraculously give birth to the genetically engineered messiah, version 2.0." I roll my eyes.

Joshua raises an eyebrow because while he was privy to Abramovich's broadcast, this is probably the first time he has heard me speak about it. "Right." He nods slowly, processing what I said, anger flickering in his eyes for a moment. "Like I said, that's *not happening*." He then moves on from the topic. "Well, that covers it, little sis. We are really looking forward to seeing you. Safe travels, and let me know as soon as you are en route so we can track your course."

"You got it." I nod.

"Oh, and one more thing," he says, half-smiling.

"Yeah?"

"Mom wants to see your dress."

I smile at the mention of Imani and reply, "I'll see what I can do."

After we end our call, I am overcome with mixed emotions ranging from giddy excitement over the prospective homecoming with my family to anxiety regarding whether everything will go according to plan. But mostly, I am rattled and miffed about Cana Minor wanting to take me into custody. Getting up from my desk, I start pacing. Pausing in front of the closet with my hands on my hips, I tap my foot unconsciously.

And I still have no idea what to wear to the party tonight . . .

Nodding at the two security guards posted outside my quarters, I rush out the door. Charging down the long corridor, I hop on

the lift, taking it up twenty-something floors to the commanders'
residences.

Overwhelmed, I cannot shake the anger and frustration rising
inside me over the results of my brain scan, the price on my head,
Cana Minor's warrant for my arrest, and even the cadet mocking me
in the bar last night—it has all come to a screaming fever pitch. When
I arrive at Petra's, she buzzes me in. Storming through the doors, I go
straight to her bedroom and collapse face-first on her bed.

"What's wrong?" she asks, alarmed as she comes out of the bathroom in a robe, drying her wet hair with a towel. She has just gotten
off duty.

"Nothing," I lie. Dodging her question, I ask instead, "How was
last night?" Hugging one of the pillows on her bed close to my body,
I roll over to face her.

"Fun—except Rip wrecked one of the rovers." She laughs. "Don't
worry, no one was hurt."

"And how was your shift?" I ask, distancing the conversation further away from the subject of my problems.

"Boring. How was *your* night, by the way?" she asks, walking back
into the bathroom to comb her hair.

"Oh, fine," I say nonchalantly. "I just went to bed."

She pokes her head back out of the bathroom. "I mean before
that—your walk home. You never told me he looks like *that*."

"Like what?" I say coolly, pretending as if I am not fully aware of
Josiah's good looks.

"Uh-huh," Petra replies, not buying my nonchalance.

A few minutes later, she comes back out dressed in casual civilian wear: loose satin pants and a matching gray tank. Getting up,
I follow her to the sunken living room of her elite quarters, and

we lounge on the white modular couches watching the rain for a while—rain that is still falling in fat drops and has been since our afternoon on the dunes.

Eventually, Petra gets up to make us lunch, and I idly scroll the network on a holo-screen over her coffee table. After a few minutes I rise suddenly, huffing in exasperation, and go to stand by the floor-to-ceiling windows that frame the western wall of her apartment. It's still dark outside though it's midafternoon, and we still have around ten hours before there will be any sign of the rising sun. Petra sets our lunch out on the coffee table in front of the images I'd been searching.

"So, this is what's bothering you?" she asks, motioning to the display.

I look back at the image of the deity—a young woman. She is resplendent in cloth of silver and indigo, with a sweeping veil and gilded crown of holy light. Her skin is snow white, sparkling and ethereal; her eyes cast down. She is encircled by a shimmering host of saints, seraphs, and angels of all fame and form.

"Yes," I admit reluctantly as I take the two shallow steps back down to the sunken room and sit beside her on the sofa.

"Why does it bother you so much?" she asks, nodding at the three-dimensional image.

"Because it makes me feel *responsible*."

"For what?"

"For their hope," I say quietly.

She nods, understanding the precarious knife's edge the conviction of hope walks between salvation and despair. "Well, this hope," Petra says, deep in thought, "it doesn't seem like such a *bad* thing . . ."

"Hope is just changing what someone *desires* to happen to what they *expect* to happen . . . and then, more than likely, disappointment is inevitable."

"Maybe," she says. "But it can also be a powerful vector—a *target* where forces come together. Hope changes people's thoughts. Thoughts change how they feel, and how they feel changes how they act. Don't underestimate it. It can give people the strength to outlast even the most formidable of circumstances."

"That may be true," I agree, "but things are *bad* down there, and Abramovich is giving the people *false hope* that everything can be magically fixed. And I don't want anyone getting the idea that *I* can fix things, magically or not. It will just destroy them all over again when everything falls apart. Besides, it's all just a ruse to get them to follow him."

"Don't they follow him anyway?"

"Not all of them. Not Cana Major or the refugees, and even Cana Minor wasn't happy with him after the war—he needed a way to win them back. I just don't want to be associated with his lies. What we have to do is hard enough as it is." I sit quietly for a minute before speaking again. "I talked to Joshua earlier, and he said that Cana Minor has announced their intention to take me into custody."

"Joshua will never let that happen. You know that," she says with conviction.

"I don't know that. Everything is different now." I begin to think about what would happen if Cana Minor was to succeed in taking me into custody. Staring at the image still projected in front of us, I say, "I don't even look like that."

"She probably didn't either."

Then I get an idea. "I want to change my hair," I say.

"Okay," Petra replies. "So you want a serum injection?"

"No, not at the genetic level. I want to dye it—the old-fashioned way."

"Like a disguise? Because we could do more than that if that's where you're going with this."

"Well, maybe a little, but I still want to be me. I just don't want to look like . . . her," I say, side-eyeing the picture presiding over us. "I don't want Abramovich to be able to dress me up in a veil and parade me in front of them again, passing me off as his pillar of virtue."

"I get it. Well, let's do it," she says as she looks at the time. "And we still need to pick out your dress."

I perk up a little as we rise from the couch to start getting ready together for tonight. "Petra," I say.

"Yes?"

"Thank you. I have really missed this."

"Me, too," she says, smiling.

Swiping the image away, I turn up the lights and turn on some music as we head back to Petra's enormous closet.

A few hours later, I am leaning over the lip of Petra's garden tub with my head submerged in bright-red water as I rinse the dye out of my hair. When I finish, I sit up in one fluid movement, whipping my hair over my head and catching it in a towel. Standing in front of the mirror, I pat it dry, and when I finally remove the towel, my hair is vivid red and brilliant orange with highlights of yellow gold. It is the color of flame, and having been bleached when I started, my hair has absorbed the pigment nicely.

Once it is dry, Petra helps me style it by pulling it high on my head and twisting half of it into a loose pull-through braid. Leaving the rest down, she frames the central braid with rows of small braids on either side.

While she works, I begin thinking about the party tonight and all the extra security that will likely be required, considering yesterday's chaos. This prompts me to ask, "What happened with the rest of the Mars envoys who were questioned?"

"It seems the man impersonating Alaric Kronos was operating solo. The other emissaries traveled here separately from him. He had been stationed on the Europa Colony, serving as an ambassador of Mars for the last five years, and they had never actually met him in person. I guess your attacker looked enough like Kronos to get by."

"You're sure?" I ask, becoming a little concerned. "That sounds like a really convenient story." *Could this guy really be operating solo?* I wonder. Moving five hundred suits is a big job, but then, Josiah and I only detected one heat signature in the mines.

She smiles. "Yes, we are sure. They agreed to truth serum injections before the interrogation. They passed, so they have been released and are cleared to attend the party tonight, as planned."

I cross my arms tightly across my chest, feeling unsettled. "It just seems really unlikely that they wouldn't know him. Or know he was an imposter."

"Mars is a big planet. They have thousands of emissaries." Pausing for a minute, she looks at me. "Don't worry. The man who attacked you is locked up. Security has been tripled, and we will all be there with you tonight."

"You're right," I say. "I guess I'm still a little shaken from last night."

"Well, Josiah will be there tonight," she says reassuringly. "After the dad talk I gave him last night, you will have nothing to worry about." She laughs to herself. "He promised me he'd look out for you."

"*Petra!*"

"What? He needed to know the seriousness of the situation, and you refused my security escort, leaving me no choice," she says dramatically.

"So embarrassing," I whine. But I'm not truly mad. I am grateful to have friends who care about my well-being, even if it is sometimes a cause for humiliation.

"You're lucky Rip didn't get to him first." She laughs.

"Very true," I say, not even bothering to entertain how that conversation could have gone down. Changing the subject, I ask, "So, what do you know about Cassini Freeman?"

"This again? Why?"

"Well, Josiah knew her apparently . . . He described her as 'beguiling.' What does that even mean?"

She raises her brows with faint amusement. "I knew it."

"Knew what?"

"You *like* him."

"Please. I have known him for three days."

"So what?"

"So how could I possibly care for someone I barely know?"

"Isn't there something—a cliché of the Old World—that went something like . . ." Petra is pensive for a moment and then looks at me with a devilish smile and says, "*Love* at first sight."

"Stop it!" I laugh and begin to flush. "*That* is just a meaningless trope poets used in ancient times to seduce their lovers."

"Maybe. Or maybe not?" she muses as she separates a few fine strands of scarlet from behind my ear and begins to braid it. "The Greeks described it as a kind of madness, a hysteria, or even an addiction. And from what I understand, the phenomenon has appeared in all sorts of cultures all over the time line. Accounts related by various witnesses—from holy men fighting holy wars to politicians, philosophers, and troubadours." She deftly twines a second plait next to the first, the strands three different shades of amber, as she continues. "Clichés don't come from nowhere and don't stick around for hundreds and thousands of years—through old worlds and new—for nothing. Maybe," she says as she ties off the braid and locks eyes with me in the mirror, "it's a real thing."

"Well, it doesn't matter anyway," I say, resigned. "Because I'm leaving."

She shrugs in agreement. "About Freeman's daughter," Petra says. "I mean, she's been gone almost fifteen years, but to me, she just always seemed sort of . . . discontented." She pauses. "No matter what her father did for her, no matter how much she succeeded at things, it never seemed good enough."

As Petra finishes styling my hair, I contemplate her words. She then jumps up in a flourish, interrupting my train of thought, and says, "Time to don our gowns for the evening's festivities!"

31

The Equinox party is being held in the Huygens Dome at the center of the station. The observation deck above the grand ballroom provides the best view on base to watch the sunrise, which attendees will gather to observe at midnight. After the sun rises, the formal party will conclude, and the informal celebrations will begin, continuing on until morning.

Entertainment for the evening includes an exhibition, which consists of a series of immersive art installations selected from contributors from all over the solar system. The various holographic displays are presented in rooms off the main ballroom that surround it in a walkable ring beneath the observation gallery.

As Petra and I enter the ballroom, I am immediately captivated by the dome's ceiling, which has been holographically styled as a starry firmament, one you might witness from the surface of Earth on a clear night, far away from light pollution. Closer to midnight, the ceiling will transition back to the transparent panes of glass of the original structure, revealing Titan's true night sky, which will be equally dark but with no visible stars due to the cloud cover that is typical of Titan's atmosphere. While thick enough to blot out the starscape, the atmosphere is not so opaque that it will prevent us from witnessing the long-awaited sunrise in a burnished-copper sky.

The ballroom floor is checkered with midnight-blue lapis and white marble. My satin dress is a royal blue, the pigment in sharp contrast to my hair's vivid red-and-orange color. The ensemble includes a sleeveless midriff top with a high neck and thick platinum bands around the collar. The matching skirt hangs low on my hips in a floor-length mermaid cut. Delicate platinum chains cascade down the front like silver webbing, connecting the two pieces.

For the most part, I am unarmed—aside from Bumbly's casing disguised as an earring on the upper cartilage of my ear and a jagdagger hidden in my boot. Ordinarily, I'd be content to rely on security for protection, but considering last night's attack, I want to ensure that I won't find myself in a position for the second time this week where I wish I had my dagger.

Petra wears her hair down, long and flowing, which is a rarity for her. Her dress is iridescent black and strapless. The sleek gown has an empire waist and a split floor-length skirt. She has placed a platinum circlet across her forehead and wears a matching platinum cuff over her bicep, similar in design to the ornate band around my neck.

Those in attendance are well-appareled in an eclectic mix of colors and textures, hairstyles, and cosmetics. Most take this night out of uniform as an opportunity to become whoever they want to be, holding nothing back. It is an occasion where everyone and anyone can express themselves without the homogeneous confines of the uniform. And tonight, everyone has outdone themselves.

It's 2200 hours. With just a few hours until midnight, Petra and I slip into the crowd and get lost in the throng. Closing my eyes, I drink in the precious few moments of anonymity my new hair color and formal attire have afforded me. The crowd, pulsing with revelers, moves rhythmically to a hypnotic, electronic beat. Tilting my head back, I open my eyes again to take in the sky as I sway to the music.

The synchrony of my physical body moving with the rhythm of the music empowers me. It awakens the spirit, magic, and God inside me that for so long have remained dormant or that I have perhaps been neglecting since I was taken away to Alpha Centauri. I feel at once that I am bound to no one and nothing, and at the same time, that I am kindred to everyone and everything, but above all, that I am alive and that I am free.

From behind me, a hand softly grabs mine, and a whisper tickles my ear, "I almost didn't recognize you." And then Josiah spins me around to face him.

His eyes glittering, he takes in the measure of me. *But how much can one truly see in the span of a few days?* I wonder.

As I question if I care whether it has been a few days or a thousand years, our fingers still entwined, I pull him to me. His hands circle my waist and mine steal around his neck. "I like it," he says into my other ear.

I pull back and look at him, smile, and say, "Thank you." But he can only read the words on my lips—he cannot hear my voice above the music. So he pulls my body close to his again, and the bass reverberates to my core as we lose ourselves in the exotic, ambient sound.

I have little concept of how much time passes before we stop to take a break. Josiah brings me another one of those fizzy drinks I had at Orion's, and the chilled bubbles feel electric against my lips. We slip into the first door of an art exhibit called *The Light of Infinity*. In utter darkness, we are surrounded only by ancient candlelit lanterns, floating at every depth and every height, extending infinitely in every direction. Next, we walk through a forest of fluorescent-purple trees stretching tall against a navy sky with pink stars and neon-blue bugs that gracefully zoom past. There are creatures of every color here: teal fireflies, golden lizards, and tangerine frogs.

We walk through an array of seemingly endless exhibits, from a lonely ocean world and an undersea paradise to the monoliths of ancient Earth thought to have been erected during the Stone Age of the Old World. We explore the fiery insides of a volcano on Jupiter's moon Io and walk the surface of a planet that truly exists but one we have only just begun to study, a world made purely of diamond called 55 Cancri e.

After marveling at the ancient and regal white tigers of Old India, we pass through the quiet grasslands of prehistoric Africa. Then Josiah takes me by my hand to walk among the Rings of Saturn, an interactive landscape. We eventually find ourselves down on the windy planet, hovering in the yellow, swirling storm of the gas giant.

Lastly, we arrive at an exhibit called *The Discovery of Selene*. It's a replica of Earth's moon as it was in the early days when the Selene Colony was first established. The lunar surface displayed is mostly untouched. Looking out across the landscape, I see a man standing on the edge of a crater, looking down at the first colony. I know immediately by the sad slump of his shoulders that it's Jonathan Avery who lingers here.

Releasing Josiah's hand for a moment, I walk over to Avery. I touch his shoulder, and as if in slow motion, he turns to look at me, tears in his eyes.

"We will rebuild Selene one day, Jonathan. I promise you. Do not give up," I say, hugging him.

He cries quietly on my shoulder for a moment, then pulls away from me and says, "Hella, when you get to Earth, I want to help. Call for us. There's a lot of us who want to do something, anything, to help Earth, and our hands have been tied for so many years. So please, when you need us, just say so." He squeezes my hands, both gripped between his.

"I will," I promise, squeezing back, and I mean it.

Josiah is waiting for me by the exit. We leave the exhibit and walk around the dance floor, which is still pulsing to the music, toward the stairs to the second level. I spot Sumi as she disentangles herself from the crowd, headed for refreshment. Grabbing my hand as she passes, she spins me around to get a full view of my gown. "Gorgeous," she says.

"Likewise," I smile as I take in her shimmering opal body-suit, which has a sheer gossamer overlay cinched at the waist and flowing out into a long skirt. She's wearing a beautiful flower crown in her hair made of real flowers—a rarer jewel these days than any precious gemstone that may have once been coveted on Old Earth.

She leans forward and speaks into my ear over the music. "Your suit is in your flight locker."

I thank her, and we take the stairs up to the gallery, where we will watch the sunrise in a little while. We find some of the commanders gathered, including Rip, Gia, Dr. Freeman, and his wife. Rip is wearing a formal jacket and pants that are the same royal-blue color as my dress, and Gia has donned a glittering floor-length gown with thin straps that cross in the back made of what look like pure crystals. Her dark chin-length hair is slicked back in a formal style, and her Canish blue eyes are lined with a smoky-coal synthetic, making their azure color pop against her brown skin.

As we begin to approach the group, a man catches my eye. Walking toward us across the landing, he is coming from the opposite direction, intersecting our path. Wearing a formal military dress uniform, which some who are less enthusiastic about the celebration choose to do, he appears to be a more senior officer. As he gets closer, I can see from the elaborate decoration around his collar that his rank is captain.

Stopping us, he says, "Ensign Nazari, my name is Captain Harrison Leng. May I speak with you, please?" His eyes wandering to Josiah briefly and then back to me, he asserts, "Privately."

I look at Josiah and he shrugs, so I step aside with the captain. Studying the lines on his face, I observe there is a calm, stoic look about him.

"Please excuse the interruption, Ensign," he says.

I nod, signaling for him to continue.

"Years ago," he begins. "I was stationed on Calypso . . ."

My eyebrows arch reflexively in interest at the mention of the faraway space station on the outskirts of the Oort Cloud that I passed on my way home to Titan.

"I served there for a decade," he explains, "but now command the Pandora outpost—and have for the last twenty years." Pandora is not far from here, a smaller sister moon of Saturn. "Just before you went missing—when Earth was destroyed—I returned here to Titan from Calypso, and it seems we just missed each other because I had a message for you that I was never able to deliver."

My throat tightens as he continues.

"I think now I should have contacted you in transit during my journey here, but I felt at the time that what I had to say was a message best delivered in person. Then later, when you were gone, I regretted not speaking with you sooner."

I look at him intently, slowly putting together the pieces of his time line. "It's okay," I say calmly. "Just tell me now."

"Well, Xavier Trastámara was under my command," he says, searching my eyes, which I keep as neutral as possible while trying to calm my pounding heart. "I came to know him well out there in deep space, on the outskirts of the Oort Cloud. He was a good kid with a lot of promise, showing impressive potential for a successful career with the Alliance. But being out there on the edge of the solar system—it does something to cadets after some time. It's the gateway to the greater galaxy, the rest of the universe, and can try the moral compass of duty for even the best of us . . ."

He trails off for a moment, then continues. "It's my opinion that cadets should not begin a career out there and tours should be no longer than a few years. But that's difficult when the journey there itself takes years . . . or did," he rambles. "We have high hopes, Ensign, that because of your contributions, the FTL drive I heard you have delivered, the scope of space travel has now changed, been reinvented."

I smile and nod politely, hoping I won't fracture my tightly clenched jaw while I wait for him to finish.

"Well, it's isolating out there, is my point," Leng says, "and it's a different kind of perspective on the universe. There are . . .

temptations." He pauses, and his eyes glaze briefly as he recalls the past. "Xavier told me about you, that you were close. He shared that with me before things went off course."

He pauses again, a silence falling between us. I look away, blinking back the moisture that is beginning to wet my eyes.

"Well, he left willingly. He defected. It was the middle of the night, and the people who came for him—well, I don't think they were people, exactly, but some kind of droid—they were sophisticated, a caliber of technology unfamiliar to me. I observed the surveillance footage afterward, and they restrained him. I don't think he expected that. Because I don't think he had been expecting to be forced out of contact. That's when he woke me, buzzed me over the comm, and told me he was leaving and to give you this message: 'Love the child as if he is your own,' and that he was sorry and would be back for you one day."

"You couldn't stop him—or help him?!" I ask, trying to mask the emotion in my voice as my thoughts race. On the one hand, I am grateful for the shred of new information, but I still am left with very little to go on as to what happened to him.

"To be honest, he was defecting to another government, and it was his choice, so there was little I could do about it other than report him."

"Well, is that all he said?" I ask, trying again to calm my outrage, desperate for anything more than the meager crumb of information he has provided. "Why did he leave, and who did he leave with?" I demand helplessly, trying to hide the desperation in my voice.

And then, out of nowhere, there is a flash of light and a loud buzzing sound. The lights go out in Huygens Dome, and the music stops. Everything is quiet for a second or two as the room becomes chillingly cold. Then panicked voices fill the air around us.

My pulse quickens. I think, *It's happening again. He's nuking Titan.* Gasping, I rack my brain for an explanation. *But Taj wouldn't let this happen. Not to Titan.*

My mind goes blank, and then it occurs to me: *It's happening again because . . . because Taj is dead,* I think in horror, *and Abramovich has come for me at last!*

32

"Captain, the Pandora Outpost is down," someone says to Leng as I hear a loud clank and the station's life support kicks back on.

"It's a raid!" another voice yells.

Suddenly, Josiah appears at my side, and Leng says, "Excuse me, Ensign," as he rushes off with the officer who alerted him about Pandora. They head over to where Dr. Freeman was standing earlier, and I see that Petra has now joined them and the other commanders.

"What happened?" I ask Josiah, marginally calming down now that the backup power system is activated. The windows have also transitioned so that we now have visibility outside—albeit not much in the darkness, but enough to see that nothing has been nuked.

"It was a blackout bomb," Josiah says. "It releases carbon graphite that interrupts electrical transmissions and short-circuits them, disabling all electronics."

Backup life support is solar and not attached to the primary power grid, so that's likely why it was not affected. Critical systems should stay powered up for at least the next hour on solar battery storage, and then the sun will rise shortly after.

"Who was it?" I ask.

"The Mars envoy."

"I knew it!" I curse.

"There's a ship up there."

"From Mars? But why?"

"Not Mars. With *those* weapons, it's got to be Chiron," he says gravely.

So the Mars emissaries are working undercover with Chiron. That would explain how they passed Petra's interrogation. Chiron has access to an arsenal of weapons outlawed by the Alliance, including a class of drugs capable of nullifying the effects of the truth serum Petra's team used on the emissaries. The blackout bomb, a weapon the Alliance and its allies do not possess, falls in the same category.

Petra moves to the center of the room and shouts, "Officers, listen up! I want all pilots down to the launch hangar immediately and all infantry to the jump dock. We are deploying the fleet and ordering ground troops to Alpha Garrison. It's Chiron and this is a raid!" Her voice is loud but clipped. "Their aim is to take control of the mines, but we're going to stop them. *Now move!*"

The other pilots, Josiah, and I immediately head down to the lower level, where the training floor, space jet hanger, and jump dock are located. We get to the locker room outside the hangar where the jets are garrisoned, strip off our formal wear, dress in the thermals that are worn under our armor, and suit up as fast as possible. Fortunately, our suits and palm screens both run on rechargeable photovoltaic batteries.

Before we head out, Josiah stops me. I look up at him, and he says, "Hella, this is not your fight. You need to get back to Cana."

"I will. Tomorrow," I say. "As planned."

"We don't know the outcome of what will happen tonight," he says gravely. "You need to go now."

I look back at him, indecisive momentarily, but I know he is right. As much as I want to fight for the Alliance here and now, returning to Earth is more important—my priority, my mission.

"I will see you off," he says.

"It's okay. I can make it on my own; you're needed here."

"Well, I'm in the second wave," he says, looking at the orders on his palm screen. "Plus, you may need backup. Who knows what could happen with so many systems down, and we know you are a target."

He is not wrong: A price on my head, a ship loaded with graphene . . . I better get the hell out of here. I look down at my palm screen, reading my own orders. My mission departure to Earth has been moved up to leave immediately. Now there is no choice about it.

We take the lift to the shuttle bay where *the Phoenix* is docked. The shuttle bay, space jet hangar, and weapons lockers are safeguarded by a kind of mesh caging that is built into the walls and made of conductive materials. The hollow conductors protect our ships and weapons from electromagnetic pulses. The shielding is a defensive feature inspired by the mass number of spacecraft and arms rendered useless by the EMP wave that wreaked havoc on Earth during the nuclear war twenty years ago. Anything inside the hangers and lockers is protected and should not have been disabled by Chiron's blackout bomb.

As we prepare *the Phoenix* for departure, we watch the first wave of ground troops deploy beneath the station from the window of the shuttle bay. Some units are securing the area around the station, and others begin marching overland to defend the mines. Another unit is being ferried over water to the mines to go ashore at the base of the mountain near the river, and others are on shuttles en route to the passage at the top of the mountain where Josiah and I were dropped off just yesterday.

Getting back to my work, I check the systems for any damage from the blackout bomb that could have breached the shielding, but Josiah lingers. "My God," he says coldly.

Rushing back to the window to stand beside him, I can see that Chiron's ship, a colossal six-hundred-foot battle craft, has released troops rappelling on cables from above, swarming the perimeter decks of Titan Station. Their numbers are far less, about one soldier to every ten of ours, but they carry unfamiliar guns that are a caliber and style of weapon I have never seen. When fired, the gun sprays an array of what appear to be micro-bullets, using energy from a laser to drive them to target at incalculable velocities, vaporizing our soldiers on contact, graphene suits and all. Our soldiers can walk out of a fire unscathed when armed in graphene, but Chiron's weapons annihilate them in seconds. My stomach turns as I think about what such a weapon could do scaled up—what it could do to our once-invincible graphene fighter jets that are now deploying.

We watch as the first wave of our jets deploys when something—a figure—impossibly standing on the hull of their ship catches my eye. And then I see her: a woman in a sleek black suit with a matching black helm has emerged from a hatch. She pulls a huge gun off her back and begins firing. The gun is as long as her leg and as thick as her waist, and in one smooth round, she lays waste to our lead squadron of fighter jets. Slinging the weapon over her shoulder, she snaps it into place so that it lies flush against her suit. Then she looks up to the heavens and, without hesitation, dives off the edge of the ship, plunging into the cosmic dark.

"Cassini—" Josiah breathes, his voice ragged. Looking at me, then back to the horror in front of us, to the hatch in the ship where the woman had been, he says, "She's returned."

"How do you know it's her?"

"She had Rolfe make that suit, or one just like it. Either way, it's her."

An alert sounds on his palm screen, and I know he is needed now. Taking my hand, he squeezes it and says, "This isn't goodbye, Hella."

I nod, throat choked up, as he drops my hand and then strides for the door.

"Wait!" I yell. "Josiah!" My voice echoes off the walls and high ceiling of the empty shuttle bay.

He stops in the doorway and looks back.

Looking to *the Phoenix*, then back at him, I say quietly, "Build us a fleet."

He nods solemnly in unspoken agreement and is gone.

I can't bear to look out the window again at the chaos and carnage below, so I focus on getting out of there as fast as possible. When I am just about ready to board, I am startled by a noise—a clanking sound, like someone dropped a tool, a wrench or something, across the room.

Whirling around, I look behind me but do not see anyone. Then I hear a snarl from the other direction—from the shadows that are closer to me than where the noise initially sounded. Then a hissing voice: "They say with clones, the horrors of your past lives still haunt you . . . will steal your joy and take your mind . . ."

Turning around again, I look in the direction of the voice, but still, there is no one. I look left and right, scanning the room, when a man finally emerges from the shadow, his shape blending with the design of the wall behind him. It's Kronos's imposter. He's using Sumi's body camouflage, which he must have stolen from the lab after her presentation.

"How did *you* get out?" I demand.

"Power outage," he says, cocking his head like it was no great feat, then lunges for me.

But this time, I'm ready for him. I put on Sumi's exos when I suited up earlier, and if you add a thousand pounds of strength to my years of training on the grappling mat, even this monster doesn't stand a chance. I catch him and toss him off me like a rag doll. He lands, thumping to the ground.

But he is resilient. Rolling, he gets back up. A sort of disbelief begins to show on his face as he approaches me a little slower this time, a little more carefully.

I pick up my helmet and walk casually away from him and over to the bay door. Facing him again, I say, "I have always been faster than you. But now I'm faster *and* stronger." Then I hit the lever that releases the airlock door. "How fast are you now, imposter?"

An alarm starts flashing red and sounding a fifteen-second warning as the shuttle bay door prepares to open. I put on my helmet.

Still over by my ship, he is maybe thirty feet from the door that leads to life support and the safety of the station's interior and another thirty feet from me at the launch bay door. There is no atmospheric pressure at this elevation on Titan, so he will not be sucked out of this room when the doors open. However, without a suit or helmet, he will suffocate in a matter of seconds due to the lack of oxygen. I don't intend to let him die here, although he very well deserves it after what he did to the real Alaric Kronos down on the surface. But I really should secure him somehow before he causes more trouble.

Kronos's imposter is holding his ground, indecisive, maybe debating whether to run for my ship or for the door that leads to the interior of the station. But the clock is ticking. So I decide for him, sprinting full speed in his direction.

At first, he is paralyzed with shock, but after a few precious seconds, he turns away from my ship and runs toward the interior door. I catch him right before he reaches it and tackle him hard to the ground.

"How do *you* like being chased?" I demand as I wrestle him into a headlock.

When the timer expires, the bay doors begin to open on the far side of the floor. Without a suit or helmet, he panics and weakens as I drag him away from the interior door. I put him in a choke hold, and he passes out quickly as the oxygen leaves the room. Reaching up, I hit the lever again, resenting the time I'm forced to waste on saving the life of this murderer. The shuttle bay doors soon slide shut again, rapidly reoxygenating and climatizing the room.

Next, I drag him into the corridor and a little way down the hall, aware that I have no way to restrain him. Then I notice his boots, which are laced with paracord. Such laces are often provisioned to soldiers since the cord can double as a sturdy rope and be useful in survival situations.

"What nice laces you have," I say to his slack body in a small voice as I start ripping the laces out of their holes. "The better to tie you up with, my dear," I whisper in a low growl as I tie his wrists behind his back with a handcuff knot. When he starts to come to, I give him a wolfish grin as I bear down harder on my knee that is planted in the middle of his back. When the knot is secure, I move down to his feet and tie his ankles with the second lace. Then, hopping up, I give him a wink and jog back down the corridor to my ship.

Once aboard, I remove my suit and get situated in the cockpit. While readying for a manual launch, I activate the cloaking device.

As *the Phoenix* departs Titan Station, the Equinox sun is rising slowly over the moon's northern polar seas. I can see both: the deep sea of Ligeia and the vast Kraken Mare beyond it, sunlight glinting off a smooth, sparkling surface of liquid hydrocarbons. With the battle still raging below the station and now stretching to engulf the river and mines beyond, I send a silent prayer up to the heavens, a petition for my comrades, to any god who may deign to listen, and chart a course for Earth. As I rapidly gain altitude and clear the smoggy atmosphere, *the Phoenix* pulses forward on the dark ocean of space, and I know deep in my heart, though I leave her in a state of great peril, Titan is a survivor.

PART III

WICKED WORLD

33

To reach Earth from the Saturn system will only take three days. I don't need to engage the FTL drive for the short trip—can't, really—because if I do, Earth and its solar system will be behind me in a matter of moments. And once I get going, the distance it will take to come to a stop again is exponentially farther than the length of my entire journey. The FTL drive was designed to jump light-years across galaxies, not to travel the easy few hundred million miles between Titan and my home world.

In the isolation of space, I find distractions are few and far between, and now, two days into my trip, I have had more than ample time to reflect on the fast few days spent at Titan Station. They were days that I relished but days that troubled me just the same.

In the aftermath of my hasty exit, alone and in the quiet solitude of my ship, I'd begun to worry about my friends. Leaving Titan at the height of the attack, I worry about Petra, Rip, Sumi, and even Dr. Freeman. But as I turn things over in my mind and consider all that I know to be true, I think my way to the truth: I'm not afraid for them because I know what they are made of. Even with Chiron's new weapons—guns that can breach the impenetrable, a graphene-made suit, and, likewise, a graphene-made fighter jet—we will not be outclassed. We are soldiers of the Alliance, formidably trained, and some of the best minds in the galaxy.

Likewise, Captain Leng's message from Xavier weighs heavily on my mind. Usually, if I think about a problem long enough, I can find a way to solve it. If I can't solve it, I can at least find a position of peace about it. However, the disappearance of Xavier remains a puzzle for which I can do neither. I couldn't do it the day he went missing, and I can't do it now. Can't think my way into any truth that settles well.

All Xavier ever wanted was to serve as an Alliance officer. What could have pulled him elsewhere? Taj said he was after something in the TRAPPIST system, but I couldn't think what. And beyond that, who is the mysterious child Leng spoke of, and what did this child have to do with me?

We knew little about the TRAPPIST system. Forty light-years from Earth, without Abramovich's FTL drive, it would have previously taken two hundred years to reach. Apparently, Xavier found an opportunity to get there faster and jumped at it, leaving everything for it: his career, our dreams, the life he had known. I can only hope he found whatever it is he was looking for and that it was worth all he gave up.

I hear from Petra the following evening, and my intuition was correct: My friends survived and are safe. Lives were lost, but casualties were low because much of the fight was waged with drones and bots once Chiron's new weapons were unveiled. While the battle went on all night and for most of the following day, Chiron succeeded in occupying the mines and agreed to a ceasefire. Having been a childhood friend of Cassini's, Josiah was working with the station captain to broker a peace treaty with his daughter as she mercilessly plundered the mines, divesting the moon and the Alliance of her valuable resources.

And Cassini . . . Cassini, I learn, had unified Chiron. Somehow, years ago, she had managed to infiltrate their society and earn a place for herself, rising in their ranks over the years, starting from the age of only seventeen. How she had accomplished this, I couldn't fathom. What she had done was baffling. Chiron's civilization had *never* known unity, was famous for its downright lawlessness—its lack of order—and had been around longer than the Revivalists. Chiron's first colony, established during the age of the Genesis Generations, pre-dated Empyreus. Besides that, it was universal knowledge that their people answered to no one. Now it seems that they answer to her.

Chiron's occupation of Titan is unnerving and unprecedented, but the Alliance is an organization that boasts centuries of order and prosperity, while Chiron is unstable and brand new in its unity. I have confidence in the Alliance's ability to handle the situation. I don't feel as assured about Earth, but that is something I hope to help change.

Sumi packed in with full-body exoskeletons a few swarming hives for me. About the size and shape of a hand grenade, the hives comprise lethal nanobots in the guise of cybernetic insects that are capable of detaining, delaying, or even terminating a target, depending on the program setting. The bugs are razor sharp and designed for shredding flesh.

These bots, along with Bumbly, were initially conceptualized to blend in with an environment that still harbored life of the Arthropoda varieties. It's not lost on me, or any of us, that the intended clandestine nature of their design is somewhat nullified on modern Earth and in a space-age environment due to the absence of the insect species on contemporary Earth and elsewhere in the galaxy. As such, we lean on the advantage innate to their microscopic size, knowing they often go unseen, despite the sad reality that the form of their disguise is now extinct.

With my new suit and the acquisition of the Alliance's advanced weapons, I feel in a strong position as I continue my journey home. Not recovering the five hundred premade suits is an inconvenience, but then, it may be for the best, as I hope to upgrade the suits we will manufacture for the Canish Guard by integrating the new shield and cloaking technology into their design. With that and a few other tricks I have up my sleeve, Cana just may have a fighting chance.

The Phoenix is cloaked as I enter the orbit of planet Earth. The moon is somber, dim, and Stygian as I approach, and I can't help but think about Jonathan Avery. The chilling reality of his losses faces me squarely as I round the lunar dark side, bearing witness to the nuclear devastation of the surface with my own eyes: a once-vibrant industrial colony, fueling station, and launching outpost now reduced to ash. I think about Jonathan's offer to help and wonder whom he was referring to when speaking of a like-minded group of supporters committed to seeing the revival of Selene and Earth. Was it an official group within the Alliance or a secret society of Selenians? I will make it my business to find out.

Earth, too, is dark as I approach, and the atmosphere is gray and stormy below. Years ago, an artificial radiation belt formed around the planet, created by the high-altitude explosions of Abramovich's nuclear strike. After the attack, charged particles became trapped, moving in spirals around magnetic field lines and forming a shell enclosing the Earth.

Until now, the radiation belt has been impassable, but *the Phoenix* should be able to make it through without damage thanks to its shielding modifications. Otherwise, the charged particles and electromagnetic radiation would damage the spacecraft's hull, instruments, and electronic components, ultimately causing a ship-wide systems failure. Beyond that, there is the risk of being shot down by our adversaries on the surface if I'm detected. The Alliance sent ships to aid Earth's survivors in the past, only to be shot down by unknown forces below. Armed with my cloaking system and shield, however, I am poised for a successful reentry and landing.

Joshua sent me the coordinates for my landing and entry to the underground, the message encrypted and sent via radio wave. I will remain undetected by relying primarily on radio or sonar signals as a means of communication. Additionally, I will be landing at an unremarkable, neutral location relative to Cana's highly secretive one.

My plan is to arrive in the dead of night, and in my new prototype suit, visual, infrared, and thermal signatures will be virtually undetectable. I will be invisible to the naked eye, and even my shadow will be hidden. After concealing the raw graphite beneath camouflaged tarps made of a material activated with the same cloaking technology as that of my suit and ship, I will drag it on hover pallets to the entry point of the underground. With the aid of Sumi's exos, I'm not worried about the distance I'll need to travel lugging the heavy bricks. The Canish Guard will meet me where I enter the subsurface level and lead me back to Cana through what I imagine will be a complicated maze of underground tunnels.

As I descend through the thick, dirty atmosphere, I steel myself for the devastation I'm soon to behold. Twenty years post-war, the ozone will have recovered marginally, but the surface will still be unlivable until perhaps one hundred years have passed. The sub-freezing land temperatures, lack of sunlight, and high levels of radio-activity do not support life.

Radioactive isotopes eventually die out. However, while the half-life of strontium and cesium is about thirty years, the half-life of plutonium and uranium is exponentially longer. Plutonium has a half-life of twenty-four thousand years; on the other hand, uranium has a half-life of just over 700 million. With numbers like that, it's impossible to conceive of a green future ever becoming a reality.

The nuclear war compromised the genetic integrity of our very DNA, as well as the DNA of any plant and animal life that once existed on the planet. Plants, trees, crops; nothing will ever grow again or function the way it was created to, resulting in mutation, disease, and death. It gets me thinking about the miracle of life as we once knew it on our planet and how perfectly things at one time worked just in their natural form—our bodies, reproduction, and photosynthesis. Only when things stop working do people sit up, pay attention, and consider the impact of their actions, their choices.

Coasting above the land, I can see that nuclear winter has covered most of the planet's surface. Endless ashen frozen plains extend in every direction. As I draw nearer to the equator, the dark-gray ice begins to recede, giving way to a brown, dusty desert.

At Joshua's direction, I land on the south side of a rocky outcropping about sixteen miles from where I will enter the underground. We decided I would land some distance from the entry point just in case the Regime had developed technology superior to my ship's and could detect me even in stealth mode with the cloaking device activated. We didn't think it likely, but we were taking every precaution.

From intel provided by our Institution-born refugees, it is understood that the surviving population of the Institution is what now makes up the Regime, and it is mostly brute force: their armies and military. Additionally, their leadership is said to have survived. The Elite Council is rumored to be isolated inside a mountain and hoarding the precious few remaining supplies of life-extending bio-drugs that were not destroyed in the bombings. This supply is all that is left to maintain the health of their aging leaders, allowing them to continue to routinely regenerate their dying organs and body parts. In this chaotic state of critical survival mode, it doesn't seem likely they would have had the time or resources to focus on new technologies. Instead, their focus is more likely on restoring the embryo factories, saving the dying, and reproducing once again. They will grow their population and reseed humanity. And for that, they need Cana. They need our fertile women and children to seed those factories—not just to rebuild, but to merely survive.

I suit up and walk down the platform ramp from my ship. As my boots make contact with the surface, a sludgy mix of frozen sand and ash, I am immediately struck by the vast wasteland that surrounds me. There is nothing for miles in either direction.

I begin to unload my cargo, transferring the bricks of graphene to the large hover pallet Lieutenant Rolfe provided me. At sixteen miles from the entry point, it should take me around five hours to make the journey across the barren, frigid land. There is no life of any kind to be seen: not a shrub or brown grass, not even a barren tree. Just rock, ash, and desert. Leaving my ship cloaked and hidden under a rocky overhang, I begin the trek onward.

An hour or so into my walk, the gray morning allows for some muted light and visibility, and before long, I notice something in the sky. Though it looks just like a bird, I know better since life here is impossible at this stage of the planet's recovery. As the object gets closer, I can see it's mechanical—a drone designed to look like a bird. I keep watch as it circles overhead in broad, methodical sweeps. Initially, I am nervous that it could be tracking me but ultimately decide it is not a threat because its course is too regular, and it does not seem to register my presence or linger as it passes overhead.

I push thoughts of Cana and what this land used to look like out of my head. I'm not even sure where exactly I am on the continent relative to the location of Empyreus pre-war. I have a rough idea but didn't want to know precisely when I planned this trek. Didn't want to grasp explicitly our paradise lost. Not today, at least. Today I will focus only on moving forward. Getting back to my people. One foot in front of the other. Once I arrive, I will think of what is to come next.

As I continue to follow the path mapped out for me on my palm screen, I near the end of my journey on the surface. Since it's important I remain offline, the maps I need have been preloaded to my device. Up ahead, the gray light of morning illuminates an elevated, rounded point of land. Noting that there should be a cave entry hidden on the far side, I drag the hover pallet around the far end of the hill and then spot the entrance.

It looks just as described, with large rocks piled up to disguise the opening. First, I check the sky for drones and then easily unearth each boulder, again thankful for the aid of the exos enforcing my forearms, biceps, and shoulders beneath my suit. While my suit and cargo are invisible to the drones thanks to my cloaking and camouflaged tarps, the boulders are not, and their displacement could be tracked by an observer. Thus, I am careful to monitor the sky as I work. Eventually, I enter the mouth of the cave, drag the pallet in behind me, and carefully replace the stones.

Though I am now fully underground, I'm not quite safe yet as far as surveillance goes. Joshua has instructed me to keep my suit on until I am fifty feet below the surface, as my heat signature could still be detected, and above that depth, I could still be at risk of radiation poisoning.

Walking farther into the dark cave, I follow a path that begins to wind down deeper into the Earth in a series of switchbacks. It eventually becomes too narrow for me to drag the pallet, so I load as many bricks as possible into netting that extends from my pack and leave the rest to be retrieved later by the Canish Guard.

After descending for about fifteen minutes, my palm screen alerts me that I've reached a depth of fifty feet and it is safe to remove my helmet. I pull it off and immediately feel the chill of the air around me. While appreciating the added ventilation outside of my helmet, I deactivate my body camouflage. As I round another corner, I am greeted by automated lanterns that illuminate the passage as I go by.

Reaching a small landing, I find three soldiers waiting for me.

They wear worn civilian clothing and stand at ease with their hands folded behind their backs as I approach.

"Officer Nazari, it's a pleasure to meet you," a hazel-eyed female says to me in greeting. She is about my height but younger than I am by a few years, with light-brown skin, freckles, and wavy brown hair braided loosely down her back.

"The pleasure is all mine," I say, taking a breath and setting down my load. After a quick glance to assess the open cavern below, I reach to shake her extended hand. The space is well lit and has a strange familiarity to it.

"Theia Aarons," she says, introducing herself. "And this is Kezia and Ishmael."

"Ah, Aarons," I say in recognition, noticing a long, curved knife hanging at her waist. "It's so nice to meet you. Your brother's contributions to the mission were invaluable." I take another breath and slowly exhale, trying to relax. "I wouldn't be standing here today without him."

She smiles, amused, and then pulls me aside, offering me a long dark cloak to wear over my suit. I put it on and pull my hood over my head and flame-colored braid as she wraps a shawl over her own head. She then motions for me to follow her.

The two guards flank us as we walk down a set of steep stairs. Farther down into the cavern, our surroundings become more industrial, more furnished. The area is sparsely populated, but we pass one or two travelers as we go by. I see now that we blend in well with the vagrants and refugees who occasionally pass through here.

"We are so relieved you made it safely—and undetected, I presume?" Theia asks.

"Yes, I believe so. There were drones overhead almost constantly, but they didn't seem to be capable of detecting me."

"And your ship? Was it damaged at all by the radiation belt?"

"No, I left it fully operational, cloaked, and in good order."

"Excellent. Your brother—and mine—will be anxious for a report."

My eyes linger on a large, vacant space at the end of the room surrounded by what resembles a sort of amphitheater hewn into the rock floor. The seating faces an enormous screen. Images run across it in an aimless way: some of war scenes and then some of the planet the way it looked before, with animals and nature. Theia follows my stare, and then recognition washes over her features.

"We are permitted to access the network here in Ephesia," she explains, "in this space and in private stations down the corridor. It is technically a neutral zone, so not identifiable as somewhere associated with Cana. But this space here," she motions to the amphitheater, "this is where he . . ." She cringes before saying, "This is where Abramovich arranged for the people of Cana—well, Cana Minor, mostly—to witness his . . . announcement about you." She bites her lip, bracing for my reaction.

I stare blankly at the projection screen and then look back to the amphitheater where the audience would sit.

"I'm sorry to be so direct," she continues. "But I thought you should know . . . would want to know."

"No, please don't apologize," I say, shaking off the memory and looking back at her. "I'm glad you told me."

"That day was very dangerous for us," Theia recalls. "Abramovich ordered the people to gather here, and they came in large numbers. An action that easily could have led Malakye's spies to us—but by some miracle, it did not. Or has not, yet."

"Typical. I wouldn't expect any less from him." Abramovich cares only for his own agenda and likely didn't consider for a moment the risk his great charade posed to the Canish people that day. "What is playing there now?"

"Propaganda, mostly, from the Regime," Theia replies. "But the channel is open to anyone who wants to use it. Sometimes it's news. But nothing ever very reliable. There are broadcasts like this throughout the underground, which are open to whoever can grab the airspace."

I nod in understanding. "Does the Regime come through here regularly?" I ask, looking around and scanning the nearly vacant space around us.

"No, their territory is far from here, but I don't doubt there are spies that pass through from time to time." Theia quickly glances over her shoulder. "So we must still be careful that nothing about our appearance or otherwise identifies us as Canish. My eyes, for example, aren't ordinarily this color."

I think of my family and their crystal-blue eyes, a signature of the people of Cana. Theia's must be blue, too, but she has changed their color with lenses or a serum. Then I think about my own eyes. "What about mine—will they give us away?" I ask, nervously looking around and tucking a loose strand of scarlet hair behind my ear. But none of the few people here seem to be taking much notice of us.

"We should be okay at this hour of the morning," she says, looking around the mostly vacant cavern again. "But we will want to alter their color before we come back out here again."

Pulling my hood tighter, I try to look down as much as I can as we navigate from the open space of the neutral zone and into a passageway. I observe that there are many ways to exit this central cavern, openings leading to various passages to different areas of the underground. As we set out, I get the sense that Cana is still far from here. It is said to be a difficult journey for some to make, as it is deep beneath the Earth, twenty-five hundred to three thousand feet down from the surface in some places.

Theia explains that since the large gathering of Abramovich's followers at Ephesia, the Canish people are now only permitted to mix in neutral spaces on a permission-only basis, as the location of Cana is still believed to be unknown to the Regime. Otherwise, there would be losses. If there weren't outright attacks, there would be kidnappings, just like in the days before the war when the Institution would stop at nothing to keep their embryo factories running, even if it meant sacrificing the lives of our people. The Regime wouldn't be any different . . . except that now they are more desperate than ever.

We begin the descent to Cana City. With a guard in front and one taking up the rear, I follow Theia through a complicated maze of underground tunnels. It is a steep climb down, treacherous in many places, and I begin to understand why Imani could not make it here to speak with me in real time, as Joshua did when I was on Proxima, Titan Station, and in transit on board *the Phoenix*.

We travel by foot for close to two hours. Theia sets a breakneck pace as if she has made this journey countless times. When I've just about had it and am ready to suggest we take a break, we reach what appears to be a dead end: a shallow pool of water beneath an unremarkable rock face. The space is illuminated by the same dimly lit lanterns posted throughout the underground, but it otherwise appears ordinary.

"Can you see it?" she asks, vaguely amused.

It takes me a few moments, but then it becomes apparent that if you look closely, there are two large stone doors in the face of the rock, hidden in plain sight. We splash through the shallow water, then slip through the heavy doors, which creak open when I push the weight of my body against them. We then walk down another narrow path that eventually ends at another massive set of gates, only these are heavily guarded.

At Theia's signal to the guards, the doors open onto a high, wide ledge overlooking a vast hive-shaped cavern with a clean river flowing through it.

Once occupied and later abandoned by the Greybeards, the vacant cavern Imani described in her letters several years ago has become a great underground city. It is informally referred to as Cana City and, as she claimed, houses a freshwater source. Running deep beneath the surface, the underground river remains unpolluted by nuclear fallout, thus freeing our people from the burden of water purification.

Theia explains that the Greybeards inhabited this city when they first went underground five centuries ago—but the city had existed long before then, long before the genesis of the first Revivalists. It was built by an ancient people of the Genesis Generations, even before the birth of their messiah and the origin of their calendar. It had passed through many hands and was inhabited at one time by Arabs, Romans, Greeks, and Turks of the Old World.

Theia and I stand back and off to the side of the cavern opening. It is still early in the morning, but there are people milling about below, starting their day. Warrens of cave-like rooms and passageways surround the central space like the inside of a honeycomb. The massive subterranean complex can shelter as many as twenty thousand people. Theia explains that it's a self-contained metropolis with ventilation shafts connected to an air purification system, an irrigation system, kitchens, school rooms, barracks, and a central machine shop. There are even old wine cellars, cisterns, stables, and sanctuaries once used by the original occupants during the Byzantine era of the Genesis Generations.

The city is an eighteen-story stronghold. Should we be discovered and one of the upper levels be breached, each level can be sealed off behind great stone doors. Cana Major is connected by a sophisticated network of tunnels, grottoes, and galleries to Cana Minor and twelve other smaller cities over an area of several dozen square miles. Some passageways are even large enough to accommodate a military tank. Although listening to Theia, it does not seem likely that Cana has that kind of firepower . . . yet.

The fallout-proof rooms are carved into the region's soft volcanic rock but were reinforced with steel during the Greybeards' occupation half a millennium before. They also improved the plumbing and technological capabilities.

Theia leads me to a large room with a vaulted ceiling. She explains that the room is believed to have been used by the Byzantines in ancient times as a religious school with separate study rooms. The Greybeards later converted it to a command center and meeting room. Now the headquarters of the Canish Guard, it is here where my brother Joshua awaits.

34

Theia and I enter the large Canish Guard command center and council chamber. We immediately see Joshua glued to a large screen toward the back of the room in a glass-walled chamber, swiping various views and entering calculations into an interface on the desk in front of the screen. Several other people in uniform are working diligently at their stations nearby. Accessing the network is too risky here, so more dated but undetectable technology, such as X-rays, radar, and ultrasonic frequencies, is relied upon for communication and surveillance.

The chamber is sparsely decorated, likely due to the lack in supply of textiles and other furnishings. However, in the center of the room, there is a large council table. I also notice there are inscriptions covering the walls, carved in a style that looks to be of ancient origin—possibly Greek or Latin. They are likely epigraphs of the Old World, inscribed by one of the occupants who sheltered here after the Byzantines of the Genesis Generations.

As the doors slide shut behind me, I step farther into the chamber. It must be around 0700 by now, as we have been traveling all night. "Early morning, brother?" I ask, exhausted but smiling wryly.

Joshua turns around, his face lighting up with a huge smile. He is leaner than before, with some gray in his beard and a few wrinkles, but still my brother in every respect.

He looks at his watch and replies, "Morning? Sister, I haven't slept. I have been up all night tracking your journey. Now get over here and greet me properly."

I can't help but laugh, a mix of relief and joy bubbling up inside me. I run to him, my heart pounding in my chest. We embrace, and tears stream down my cheeks as I inhale his familiar smell. I bury my head in his shoulder, and when I close my eyes, I can see Cana again. The place may no longer exist, but my faith is renewed suddenly that the heart and soul of it has been kept alive here by its people.

"You made it!" he exclaims, relief flooding his features as he assesses my condition. "And unscathed?" he asks while making a show of looking me up and down to see that I am still in one piece.

I smile and nod. "By the skin of my teeth," I reply, thinking back on my face-off with the Chiron thug in the shuttle bay on Titan Station.

"No detection on the surface or trouble in the underground with Cana Minor's patrol?"

"None, thanks to my clever escort," I say, nodding toward Theia.

"Yes, sir," Theia says. "I took her through the old Byzantine channel to avoid any traffic with Cana Minor."

"Excellent, Corporal," Joshua nods to Theia in gratitude. "I knew you were the man for the job."

Joshua introduces me to his team and then sends me off to get cleaned up from my journey and rest before we all get together for dinner.

Theia shows me to my rooms, and it isn't long before Imani arrives. After I bathe and change into comfortable clothing, we spend a few hours catching up over a pot of Canish breakfast tea, Imani's special ration reserved for special occasions. Imani spends her days traveling among the communes and visiting the people, talking with them and praying for them. So when my eyes get heavy, she tucks me into bed and kisses me on the forehead before heading out for her day. I am fast asleep before she finishes smoothing the sheets.

In the evening, we all get together for dinner in one of the common areas off the kitchens of the rooms that my family and the families of my brother's generals occupy. We were farmers in Cana, not because we needed to be but because we chose to be. We did it for pleasure while the rest of the world synthesized their food in a lab using yeast or bacteria cells—both are near inexhaustible resources, as they grow on their own, replicating continuously. The cells are programmed at the molecular level, fermented into edible proteins, and then transformed by expensive machines into savory meals.

Here, we eat slop, also sometimes referred to as gruel. Of course, we can do no farming here, but we are fortunate to have massive stores of yeast and the capability to ferment it, but that is where it stops. We could perhaps have gone to the trouble of producing the technology required to make the food more palatable, but we had to prioritize the necessities, and eating food for pleasure was not one of them. A recipe was calculated to produce a food that uses the minimum amount of yeast cells possible so that our supply would last longer and our people would always have enough to eat. The result was a gray, tasteless paste. So that is what my people eat, and they have survived by doing so for the last twenty years. We have everything we need to meet our nutritional needs, but it certainly isn't very tasty.

You won't hear anyone complain, though. We know how lucky we are to have survived the war, to have this place to live in, and to have been warned by the Greybeards well enough in advance to save so many of our people.

"We weren't without our troubles, but we had it so good for so long," Joshua says, shaking his head and looking starry-eyed, lost in memories as he finishes off his bowl of slop. "Do you remember Imani's kitchen? And all the ways we had to prepare a meal?"

I laugh as he gets up and strides over to the large copper pot at the end of the table to refill his bowl. Joshua walks with a natural authority and is always calm and cool, but he is a force to be reckoned with if you get on his bad side. He motions with his hand and asks, "Anyone else want seconds? Permissible tonight since it's a special occasion," he finishes as he gives me a wink.

We all shake our heads as he continues. "We could bake a cake, grill a steak, fry a fish, toast a loaf, boil a potato." He laughs as he struggles to remember all the methods we employed to prepare our family meals at our farmhouse in Cana.

"Stop it! You're making me hungry!" Theia whines. She, her father Noah, and her sister Raven, have joined us this evening and are apparently close with my family. Noah is second-in-command to my brother.

"Excuse me, and who was doing all this baking, frying, and grilling you speak of, son?" Imani asks, giving him a look.

He sets his bowl down on the table in front of his chair, then walks over to Imani to bear hug her from behind her chair and shower her with kisses. "Only the best chef in all of Empyreus, that's who!" he exclaims, laughing.

Imani laughs despite herself and bats him away as she turns back to her food but concedes to accept the compliment.

"Hella, have you settled in well?" asks Joshua's partner, Shreya, her voice high and clear. She was just a little girl the last time I saw her, a pudgy baby. I used to look after her, and now she is several years older than I am. I'm still trying to wrap my head around life after cryo-travel.

"Yes, thank you. This place is impressive," I reply. "Tell me the story again, Joshua, of how we came upon it? You must have mentioned it in your letters, but I can't recall the details."

A few of the others excuse themselves as he addresses my question. "Well, first and foremost, we have the Greybeards to thank for the last shelter and for this one," he explains. "It was maybe twelve hours before the attack would happen, and a man came to me, very mysteriously. He was cloaked and had been following me. I thought I was getting mugged and was ready for a fight when I saw his face, his pale complexion, and the ring of scars around his neck. I knew then who he was and that his people did not fool around. The Greybeards did not come to the surface often, did not participate in our society, and if they had something to say, it was usually of dire importance. In very few words, he explained to me what was to come with the attack, the war, the nuclear winter that would follow. He provided me a map to the bunker our people initially occupied."

"How could you trust him?" I ask. "How did you know he wasn't a spy with some dark agenda or a radical, high on the latest conspiracy theory?"

"I may have thought that had I not seen that scar on his neck—that and I just had a feeling about it. That I should trust him. And thank God that I did. I spent the next twelve hours moving our people to the shelter they so generously provided us." He shakes his head at the memory of the behemoth task. "And there were many people who didn't believe it—thought I was crazy, that I'd lost my mind, given in to the radicals, joined the fanatics." He looks up from his cup and continues more intently. "For Abramovich's people knew, his inner circle knew, and that was another thing that tipped me off. A man on the council and his family had vanished, along with some other prominent families in Cana Minor's community. It didn't make sense, so I knew something was up."

"And what happened to the man? The Greybeard?" Theia asks.

"I don't know," he replies pensively. "He vanished. I never saw him go. Disappeared as mysteriously as he came."

I get a shiver up my spine, though I'm not sure why. The Greybeards have done nothing but help our people. I guess it's something about the idea of their head transplants and reclusive way of life—the ghost stories other children told about them, making them out to be monsters. It had stuck, but I made a mental note to try to wipe the stigma from my mind.

"Then another Greybeard, a woman, traveled to the bunkers about six years ago and told us about this place. Her people had moved on from it, and she thought we could use it. She said we'd have to agree to take in some refugees, which was fine. We'd already taken some in, but a decent-size group joined our population at that time—Institution-born survivors who had escaped the horrors of the Regime," he recalls as he leans back in his chair. "It was just in the nick of time. We were outgrowing the other space, and the Regime was on our heels—had nearly found us.

"People fear them, the Greybeards, but I believe it is misplaced. They have shown us nothing but goodwill. Their technology is sophisticated, and they are a far cry from the crones or greybeards they are misconstrued to be. They have young, strong bodies and live on because of their transplant technology. We owe a great debt to the Greybeards."

"What of them now?" I ask.

"They don't communicate with us or anyone we know. Never have. Aside from when they reached out to us initially and then the second time, they have stayed silent for years. We don't know where they shelter now."

Imani walks around the table and offers everyone still seated a hot cup of tea, continuing the special occasion of my return a little bit longer with her ration.

Joshua raises his eyebrows at the offering and says, "She wouldn't even bring this out on my birthday." He laughs before continuing. "Speaking of *anonymity*—as you all know, it is vital to our survival here, and the Greybeards have protected our secret for a long time. Our single most important defense against those that would do our people harm is protecting our anonymity. But as the land is finite and as time passes, discovery is inevitable, and we must be prepared." He becomes solemn, almost grave, as he holds his mug of tea between his hands on the table before him. "And worse, they have found a way to move about on the surface, which makes it exponentially easier for them to track us. The time is nigh. Hella, the drones you saw overhead when you arrived narrow their course by the day as other geographies are settled and ruled out. And we don't have anywhere else to move on to from here."

There is a chill in the air as the reality behind Joshua's words about the worsening threats settles in—a somber gray cloud. We are quiet for a few minutes. I sit, leaning back in my chair with my hands steepled in front of my face, staring into the darkness, contemplating the mounting problems we face. Then something occurs to me, and I say simply, "The only way out is *through*." Then looking up, I make eye contact with Joshua as the corner of his mouth lifts in recognition. "Someone older and wiser said that to me once," I say with a knowing smile, reverent of the secret truth between us two as I get up and start clearing the remaining plates.

Joshua said as much to me when Konstantin dragged me off to the Institution. She was within her rights since I was a minor, and though Imani raised me, Konstantin was my natural guardian. The physical brutality and psychological torture I endured undergoing the medical experiments she subjected me to eventually became too much for me to take, but Konstantin's conservatorship was iron-clad, and living at the Ascendancy, with her rank, I was powerless to leave. While I was not permitted to communicate with my family back in Cana, I managed to make some friends here and there, and a guard who empathized with me helped me exchange a few messages with Joshua.

One day about six weeks in, I told Joshua that I could no longer take it. I could see no way out. I wanted to end things right then and there, to take my own life—it was the only freedom I could see that I had left. But Joshua was resolute: That option was not a viable one, and sometimes in life, we face circumstances we simply cannot escape but must face, must see through, must endure. He helped me understand that the only thing that can truly save us, and we can truly count on, is the passing of time. He and I both knew I would be emancipated on my seventeenth birthday, but God, that was years away. He told me then the phrase that somehow helped me to see things differently. He said: "The only way out is through." It wasn't ideal, but it allowed me to see a way out I couldn't find before. And somehow, hanging on to that thread, I faced it. It snapped me out of my despair and gave me the edge to hang on. I hung on minute by minute, hour by hour, day after day, year after year . . . just one more day and then another. I have not forgotten it, what he said . . . The way the world looks on the other side, on the other side of that bear of a mountain, when you realize you have made it, that you have survived, that you have lived through it—there's nothing like it. No thrill, no beauty, no pleasure can compare with a freedom so hard won.

Joshua follows me into the kitchen as the others disperse. "And *through* it we will go, sister, with the help of the armor and weapons you have miraculously procured. And if—*not if,* but *when* push comes to shove, we will have the ability to get up there and defend ourselves—which is far less treacherous an endeavor to contend with than operating from within a hole one is unempowered to leave." Motioning to the space around us, our great underground city, he says, "You have brought new hope to us all. But there is much to be done."

"Well, we better get to work," I say, shaking the water off my hands and wiping them on my apron.

"Not without a good night's sleep," Joshua says, chiding me like a mother hen. "You will be useless to me otherwise!" Mirth in his eyes, he is no doubt recollecting some moody, gray morning at our old home after a wild all-nighter in the mischievous days of my teens.

I laugh but concede, my arms up in surrender. "As you wish, General." I smile and lift the apron over my head, securing it on a sturdy iron hook beside the stove that looks like it's been there since the dark ages.

I walk back into the dining area and through a wide doorway to an open common space where everyone has gathered to relax, read poetry or scripture from ancient tomes, and share stories of days gone by. Lingering for a moment, intrigued, I see Theia and Shreya lounging on pillows around a low table, studying a map of what looks like the underground tunnels over candlelight.

"Straight to bed!" Joshua orders when he sees me pause.

I smile and say, "Goodnight, brother. See you in the morning," and continue on my way. He bids me goodnight, and I head back to my rooms.

35

I rise early the next morning to meet Joshua, Theia, and the other senior members of the Canish Guard for a council planning session. My rooms adjoin Imani's, and as I enter the small shared space between them, I see that she was up even earlier than I was and has already left to make her rounds visiting the needy.

It's quiet in the dimly lit passageways that lead back to the command center where I reunited with Joshua yesterday. As I enter the large chamber and observe the vaulted ceilings, I study the ancient markings with more scrutiny today. Taking a seat at the table, I wonder if anyone has taken the time to translate them, and if they have, what do they all mean?

Over the next few minutes, Noah, Theia, and Raven file in, along with several others I have yet to meet. Joshua is in conversation with a technician I met yesterday at one of the ops stations. He looks at his watch, then heads over to join us at the massive council table made of heavy, knotted wood, likely another relic from the Old World, left behind by the Byzantines and restored by the Greybeards.

The objective of today's meeting is to inventory our weapons, supplies, and raw materials; marry our armor and provisions with our infantry; and assemble the small patrol that will begin the sorely needed reconnaissance work on the surface. Without the protection of graphene-made haz-suits, Cana has been effectively in the dark in terms of navigating above ground for the last twenty years.

We start by poring over maps of the underground, the surface, and even the stars. We catalog rosters of soldiers and stores of weapons and vehicles as we allocate them to different geos, zones, and outposts.

"We've got two metric tons of graphite and six prefabricated suits," my brother says, making tick marks on a piece of paper as he reads from it. Nobody uses paper anymore, but Joshua keeps a little notebook in his front interior pocket. "And it will take roughly three weeks to manufacture enough suits to outfit the first contingent of our small army," he continues before looking up at a small, older man hunched over at the end of the table. I notice the man has a mechanical forefinger and thumb on his right hand, but the handicap does nothing to impede the dexterity with which he makes use of his hands. "Keep me honest, Smithy," Joshua says.

"Six hundred Canish Guard, twelve hundred soldiers of Cana Minor, and three hundred refugee volunteers," Smithy says, doing the math in his head. "That's roughly twenty-one hundred men at arms." He then begins typing some numbers into a beat-up tablet before continuing. "I can have a thousand suits ready in a fortnight if you suspend all other projects and allocate additional resources and service bots from the maintenance teams in Jericho City and Ammon. Another week, and I can outfit the entire brigade."

"Excellent, sir," Joshua replies. "I will travel to Moab tomorrow to meet with the Elders of the small council to recruit additional troops and see to it that you have the resources you require. We don't have a second to lose in this fight."

Smithy nods.

"As for the patrol, Shreya, Theia, Raven, and Hella," he looks at each of us as if taking roll, "I am assigning you suits and want you to begin working on the preparations and schedule for approaching the surface."

We nod in succession.

"Noah," Joshua says, "I will reserve the remaining two suits for you and Syngin to eventually probe KAU City once we have gathered enough intel outside the neutral zone."

I shudder at the words: Kratos Authoritarian United—otherwise known as KAU City—refers to the crime-filled slums surrounding the territory occupied by the Regime.

Joshua turns to me and then to Shreya with a look that brooks no argument before addressing our small company. "You under no circumstances are to enter KAU City, surface level or subterranean. I don't care if you are cloaked," he says, looking at me directly. "The rest of your team does not have that technology in their suits and would be powerless to come after you if something went wrong."

We nod and blankly stare back at him.

"We don't rush in. We gather as much intel as possible, then make a strategic, airtight plan to infiltrate Malakye's territory—*if* we deem it a worthy endeavor. Otherwise, we lie low, preserve our anonymity, and think smart, not rash. Got it?"

We nod again in agreement.

For another hour or so, we talk more about our plans for the next few days. Once the meeting is adjourned, Joshua asks me to meet him in the machine shop after lunch to tinker with the suit cloak on my prototype, review the schematics I sent, and test a few other new weapons I brought with me from the Alliance.

On my way out, Smithy stops me, introduces himself, and asks me to walk with him down to the lower levels. There is something he wishes to show me.

Hungry, I think, *I'd rather go to lunch,* but then I remember the only thing on the menu is gruel, so I agree to join him. I still haven't had an official tour of this place, and with eighteen stories and a river to boot, I decide it's as good an opportunity as any to learn my way around.

Smithy is pretty ancient, in the latter years of his life, which is actually kind of comforting to see again, as almost no one on Titan allows themselves to age naturally. He reminds me of home and the good times of my childhood growing up in Cana. We walk slowly down to the lower levels, his hand on my arm at times to steady himself. As we walk, passing living spaces and common areas, I notice the worn faces of my people. Twenty years underground and the trauma of war shows in their gait, in their clothing, in their eyes.

We round a corner, take a mechanical lift down several levels, walk down a winding staircase, and pass through a few sets of heavy stone doors. Old Greek markings decorate the walls throughout. After passing the barracks, machine shop, and several storage levels, we eventually reach what is considered to be the ground level since it is where the river flows through.

However, we have yet to reach the true bottom. There are several more levels below the riverbed that most people do not know about, Smithy tells me. These levels are darker, muddy, and unsuitable for people to make homes. But today, we are not going down quite so far. We are staying on the ground level, Smithy tells me. He's quite knowledgeable and very informative as he explains a bit about the history of the place.

As we move down an unremarkable corridor, his mood gradually begins to change. He becomes quiet, pensive, or perhaps agitated? I can't quite tell. We continue in silence for a while when he finally speaks.

"Not too much farther now, Hella," he says.

I smile and continue walking, unrushed.

"Thus, I must begin my confession: Several weeks ago, I found some particular specifications buried deep within the ship schematics you sent, and being one with a curious mind, I found myself unable to resist exploring them further."

"Oh?" I reply, bemused.

"And the longer I studied them, well, the more I became captivated by the simple genius of their design." Tightening his grip on my arm, he continues. "I was so entranced, so infatuated with the concept. . ." He pauses, searching for the right word. "So *obsessed*, I daresay I became, that I couldn't help myself from tinkering with the beginnings of a prototype."

I nod in expectation.

"Because, you see, I like to make things," he explains. "And as the days wore on, I found I was unable to stop myself from seeing the work to completion."

The small passageway has gradually broadened to a wide tunnel.

We arrive at the end of the long corridor and face a set of large wooden doors. His hands shake as he fumbles with an ancient wrought iron key that turns easily when he twists it. It releases the lock, and as the doors swing open, a finger of light cascades in to illuminate the darkened room.

Then I hear a snort. As we walk farther in and round a corner, something that looks like synthetic hay crunches beneath my feet, and the snort turns into a full-on whinny. When we enter the stables, a beautiful black horse tosses its head in greeting. I can't believe my eyes as I behold it, awestruck.

"Is it . . . is it *real*?" I ask, bewildered.

Smithy shakes his head as I slowly approach the horse and, before long, begin stroking its mane.

"No, child," he replies. "Not in the sense that I suspect you suggest. She is no mammal or creature of the flesh."

"Not a hologram," I say as I connect the dots, suddenly remembering my final days on Proxima in Abramovich's synth lab. "But a *robot*!" I finish with a broad smile. I was so stunned to be face-to-face again with this sacred creature that I had forgotten about the schematics Gemma had given me.

"Yes, a robotic biomimetic quadruped," he clarifies, an unmistakable twinkle in his eye. "The notes instructed that this prototype be referred to with a particular moniker. Now, what was it . . ." Scratching his chin, he stares up at the ceiling. He pauses when he finds the word he is seeking and looks back at me with a faint smile. "That's it," he says. "Her name is Legend."

36

I knew Cana would need horses. Horses had always been a sacred part of our lives, not just in hunting, warfare, and travel, but also in companionship. Our people revered them and saw them as sentient beings—not disposable beasts of labor to be overworked or killed on the battlefield like had been done for centuries by our ancestors of the Old World.

When I was a child, Imani often spoke about her father and his beloved stallion, Styx. They had ridden off to battle on more than one occasion during the unstable times. Before the fall of Empyreus, we had not known true war for a century, but small local aggressions would surface from time to time, instigated mainly by mercenaries sent undercover from the Institution. Imani said that when her father and Styx left to fight, a mutual reverence, a spiritual connection, could be observed between the man and his steed. The great stallion, she would say, was prepared to die for his companion.

But Styx would not die in battle; he was too strong a spirit. There was a magic that existed between him and my grandfather, and when they fought together, they fought as one. No opponent could best them, no army could outlast them. They were unbreakable. Both lived long, beautiful lives well into old age—dying free and peacefully: my grandfather warm in his bed and Styx in the wild, open land.

Styx was free to roam the lands of Cana and did so, grazing where he pleased. A beautiful blue-black Andalusian, he was sixteen hands in height and fast as the wind. Most of the horses in Cana were of Arabian and Andalusian blood, for they were the breeds selected to be preserved preceding the Genesis Generations' latest Glacial Maximum. As only a precious few could be saved, I imagine they dwelled in underground shelters in the early origins of the Revivalists, such as the one we reside in today.

DNA samples of a variety of other breeds were preserved in the vault by the Founders. But no other variety would go on to dominate the horse population as heavily as these two breeds would, with their strong, ancient line of forebears.

But we were careless. We lost them, tragically, to the war, along with all the animals of the land, sea, and air. And for that, without our irreplaceable partners, our magnificent steeds, our warhorses— our cavalry—we are at a great disadvantage.

We can't bring them back by science—not truly, not without copies of their DNA, which were lost in the last panicked moments of fleeing. But this, Smithy's robot, is a start. This is nearly as good. With mounted soldiers, this mechanical reincarnation could get us more than halfway there. Powerful mounts forged in steel rather than flesh, equipped to withstand the poison air on the surface, will offer us an advantage over Malakye's cyborg foot soldiers.

I had known this, and I had known Cana would need horses—or had I? Or had my thoughts been a product of Gemma's foresight, brought to life by Gemma's generosity and technical expertise to push us forward, to provide us the plans to bring my hopes—*our hopes*—to fruition?

As I witness it now in real life, I find myself again indebted to the ghost of a girl who once walked these lands in the flesh, who had everything holy taken from her—yet had somehow still persevered. She had found a way in an impossible form, inexplicable in spirit, and explained otherwise only by math as no more than a fractured laser beam caught on photographic film. Haunting my dreams and days with her beautiful memory as, bit by bit, she endeavors to save us all—our fast-fading world, her dying kingdom.

Impossible. And yet, an *endeavor* it is perhaps not. Not anymore. These things Gemma has done are real, screaming, tangible *progress*, standing firmly on two legs. Steps forward to the light, to salvation, they are moving the dial and in great strides. These things she has helped us attain are deal-breakers, war-winners, and tide-turners— these things are *power*.

Smithy and I spent the next hour in the stables with Legend. I took her out of her stall and walked her around a small oval arena connected to the stable area. She was already well trained, a program no doubt designed by her creator, the great equestrian Gemma herself. Smithy took some measurements and promised me a saddle and bridle that will be ready in the coming days. Leather was hard to come by in the underground, but if anyone had connections in procurement, it was him. We were having so much fun that we were almost late to meet Joshua in the machine shop.

When we reached the shop, I couldn't contain my excitement and told Joshua about Legend straight away. He loved horses as much as I did, teaching me to ride and care for our herd back home when we were growing up.

Joshua immediately saw the potential in Smithy's work. It wasn't long before the three of us devised plans to manufacture a full cavalry for the Canish Guard. Smithy's shop was already busy with preparations for the suit production, and now, with this added project, his machines would be running around the clock.

We spent the rest of the afternoon working with my prototype, going over the plans to integrate the features of my new model into the original design. When the two of them no longer required my assistance, I sneaked out to try and get a workout in before dinner.

Finding a training arena near the barracks, I run into Shreya and Raven sparring. Shreya practices with a *khopesh*, an Egyptian sickle-shaped sword evolved from the battle axe, and Raven with a simple *kali* stick. The room is not much larger than the horse ring I was just walking Legend in—and just as spare, with a dirt floor and high ceilings. It is no holo-sphere, but it will do.

Turning my attention to the fight, I observe Shreya is vicious with a blade. Raven seems less experienced but is holding her own. Both are drenched in sweat and surely exhausted, but it does not seem to affect their performance much. However, after some time, Raven's fatigue begins to show as she slows in meeting each of Shreya's measured but relentless advances.

Shreya is a force moving with unfaltering precision, her sickle sword an extension of her body. You cannot not tell where one ends and the other begins as she spins around, lunging and dodging, hacking and thrashing, thrusting and slicing.

Raven, now mostly defending Shreya's attacks, eventually works up the strength to advance on her. She lunges with her *kali* stick, but the impact of Shreya's counter-parry forces the weapon from her hands, besting her and finally cracking her weapon into two clean pieces. The match won, Shreya offers a hand-up to Raven, who is on the ground rubbing her sore, blistered hands from the impact. Raven accepts, takes Shreya's hand, and hops up as they both turn in unison at the sound of my applause.

"Well done!" I say and walk over to greet them.

"If you practice sloppy, you will do sloppy," Shreya says authoritatively, shrugging her shoulders as she sits in the tiered rows of benches surrounding the arena.

I walk over to Raven as she is picking up one piece of her staff. I pick up the other and hand it to her before we join Shreya on the benches.

"What's it made of?" I ask, motioning to the stick.

"Tungsten," Raven replies.

"I told her it's prone to shattering," Shreya says, lifting her blade into the light. "Mine's titanium, which has a tensile strength of sixty-three thousand psi."

She admires her weapon. The sickle-shaped sword, plated in bronze, glints in the glow of the overhead lighting cast down from an old hand-forged wagon wheel chandelier. Shreya brings the sword down in a graceful arc before returning it to her low belt. She wears old brown fatigues, a dingy white T-shirt, and combat boots. When she brushes her long brown hair away from her face, I notice her striking green eyes. Perhaps she has changed their color on a more permanent basis for the sake of our need for frequent patrolling.

"It's a beautiful piece," I say, referring to her sword. "I, too, practice with a *khopesh*," I add in an effort to be friendly. Since she's my brother's partner, I hope we can be close.

She smiles, tight-lipped, and then averts her eyes.

"I had always heard tungsten was the strongest metal," Raven says, fiddling with the broken pieces of her staff. "But it seems there's more to the story," she finishes light-heartedly, exhaling and plopping down on the bench, then smiling at me self-consciously. I smile back and make a mental note to ask Joshua to set aside some graphene for Smithy to forge her a stronger weapon for the war to come.

"It's strong but brittle," Shreya asserts to Raven before turning in my direction. "So, you ready for recon tomorrow?" she asks, giving me an assessing glance.

"Tomorrow?" I verify, wondering if I missed something.

"Yeah, at 0600. We have the first patrol."

"Oh, Joshua didn't say . . ."

"Joshua doesn't need to say," she says, cutting me off. "We've been going out every day for the last three years, and tomorrow is no different. Except tomorrow, we will begin to approach the surface, and Theia and Raven are needed elsewhere. So it looks like you're up."

"Where are they needed? I assumed we were a unit."

"For their suit fitting with Smithy," Shreya says, standing. "I got mine done this morning before council while the rest of you were sleeping."

I had planned to join Imani tomorrow to visit the sick, spend some time with her, and put more time in studying the maps of the underground tunnel system. But Shreya, I could tell, wasn't going to take no for an answer. So I excuse myself before my mouth gets the best of me, reluctantly giving up on my plans to fit in some training today before dinner . . . and on being friendly.

"Well, six a.m. it is, then, General," I say with formality as I get up. I salute her briefly, then turn to Raven and give her a genuine smile. "See you at dinner," I say and walk out the door.

37

Things are no less bristly with Shreya at dinner or, as I find, in the coming days as we begin our patrols on the surface. I learn to ignore it and accept that it is how she operates. I conclude that it's not personal. I think it must be how she interacts with most people.

As the next days go by, we get into a routine. After patrolling all day, we spend the evenings training. Shreya, however, remains hard as hell on me. But I can't deny that it's making me better. Sometimes Theia and Raven or some of the soldiers join us, but no one puts in as much time as we do. Shreya will accept nothing less from me. I have never known anyone with her level of discipline, dedication, and grit.

A few weeks pass like this, and we are gaining confidence as we gather more and more intel, filling in areas on our maps that have been gray for years. The first batch of suits is closer to being ready. Smithy promises just a few more days. They will go to the Canish Guard and will be equipped with the modifications Josiah, Sumi, and I developed back on Titan.

This particular morning, I stumble out of bed at 5:00 a.m., bleary-eyed and still half-asleep. I sink to the floor, cross-legged, as my eyes drift shut again. Shaking my head in an effort to wake up, I then roll over on my stomach and begin my daily routine of push-ups. After about fifty, I hop up, walk to the high-arched doorway, and jump up to hang on the bar Shreya installed. I then do about twenty-five pull-ups before I crash back down to the floor. Now I'm awake.

Walking through to the common room Imani and I share, I put on a kettle in the kitchenette. Not for tea—unfortunately, this dreary Tuesday is no special occasion—but for hot water. I want to forego the gruel altogether but think better of it, as I know it is not wise to head out on an empty stomach. So I grab a packet of the powdered version we have on hand and mix a higher protein concentrate into my mug of hot water. It tastes like dirt, but I choke it down. After dressing hastily in my thermals, I secure my red-and-orange flame-colored hair into a messy bun on top of my head and wrap a worn brown cloak over my shoulders. I then head out to get suited up and meet my patrol unit.

We have spent the last couple of weeks meticulously tracking and mapping the course of the Regime's patrol drones. Today, our objective is to get eyes on one of the lesser-used surface-level entrances to the Regime's territory so we can better assess their forces. Now that the Regime occupies the surface, it is important that we gauge how much progress they have made in securing it, as all our previous knowledge on the matter came by word-of-mouth and hearsay from other spies.

Beneath the surface, the outskirts of KAU City overlap with the far reaches of the neutral zone, and if you know the way, this border region can be accessed by foot via the underground passageways. It's a dangerous area that we mostly avoid. While we have passed through a few times for observational purposes, we have not entered the city proper under Joshua's explicit instruction.

Over these last weeks, we have learned much about the enemy. We have secured their drone schedules, tracked shift changes of the underground city guards, marked the not-so-erratic behaviors of suspicious characters we suspect to be spies, and outlined multiple shortcuts we can take that were not accessible to us before. While these routes are still underground, they are too close to the radiation-polluted surface and thus not safe to traverse without the protection of a suit.

To blend in with the locals, we have layered our heavy cloaks over our suits, traveling with hoods up and eye color disguised with lenses or serums. We are armed, but discreetly. At this point, I could make my way back to Ephesia, the sector of the neutral zone where I first met Theia, with my eyes closed.

Our unit makes good time reaching the passage to the surface, which is the same location where I first arrived on my ship. We ditch our cloaks before exiting. Our suits have transitioned to a desert sand color that is nearly indistinguishable from the surrounding terrain. Our heat signatures are scrambled, but we are still not invisible since my companions' suits do not have the same mods as mine. I decide not to activate my suit's cloaking feature today since my invisibility wouldn't do much good traveling in a group. Cloaking is a power drain anyway, so it makes better sense to conserve it in this situation.

Following a preset, convoluted path across the desert will keep us out of range of the drones as they complete their regular sweeps across the surface, but we must stay on schedule to remain undetected. It's still early morning, and though the sun has just risen, the sky is smoggy and nearly opaque black with pollution and a heavy cloud cover. Light does break through in places, but nearly imperceptibly. The land is barren, rocky, and mostly flat, though there is elevation in some places.

We travel in silence for about ninety minutes following Shreya, who naturally takes the lead. Eventually, she signals for us to stop, and we take cover behind a rocky outcropping to rest for a few minutes.

"How much farther?" Raven asks.

"About a mile and a half," Shreya responds, looking at her palm screen.

"Do you think we could see the moon if it was night?" Raven asks, looking up and scanning the sooty cloud cover.

"What? No. Well, I'm not sure," Shreya answers distractedly, briefly looking up from her screen to the sky above.

"I've never seen it," Raven says matter-of-factly. She was born underground after the war. This is the only life she has known.

I nod, then notice a crack of sunlight shooting through the smog and illuminating one particular spot on the desert floor, making it look like a ray from heaven.

"There, look!" I exclaim. "You see that sliver of sunlight?"

Raven turns and sees it, too, smiling at the sight.

"If the sunlight can make it through in places, then that means that it might be possible to get enough clearing at night to catch some moonlight, too."

She seems pleased with my answer as the light vanishes as quickly as it appeared, with the dark clouds moving overhead.

Taking point on tracking the drone schedule, Theia is absorbed in her device. Looking up at the sky, she says, "We better get moving.

We only have about a fifteen-minute window before the shift change, and I want to save as much time as possible for observation at the target site."

We hustle, and it takes about twenty minutes to arrive at the site we've marked. It's an overlook with a view of the massive rock face and natural vent that serves as the back entry to KAU City. The entry is to the far west of the region that the Regime occupies beneath the surface. KAU City surrounds a massive subterranean military base and city center that house what remains of the Institution's ruling authority. It is said to be a dangerous place for civilians in the militaristic city center, the underbelly of KAU City, and even spilling over into the fringe areas of the neutral zone that overlap with the city itself.

We are now in position to observe the western access point closest to Cana, the city's most remote surface junction relative to the city center. We determined this location to be a good place to start a sweep of the perimeter that will be conducted over the coming weeks. A more central access point does exist on the eastern front, a side that faces away from Cana, which is believed to be directly over the central headquarters of the Regime. However, it is much too risky a location for us to monitor with anything other than drones.

Shreya and I begin to crawl up the dirt dunes we previously marked to gain elevation and reach an overlook point. We need to observe the area immediately around the entrance. Theia and Raven stay back to guard our rear. I silently scramble up the hill, then drop down to my stomach from a vertical crawl and situate myself to where I can peer just over the edge. Shreya does the same, lying prone adjacent to me on the dune.

We are a good distance from the site we are observing and, with our sandy-colored helmets, blend in well with our surroundings. It would be difficult for anyone on the other side to spot us in the perpetually dim conditions, even if they were to look our way with the assistance of a scope or a military-grade lens. The lenses I wear function as a spotting scope but also serve to change the color of my eyes from blue to brown. To adjust them, I blink a few times and focus on the flat plains ahead of me that lead into the valley beyond.

My blood runs cold as I take in the tens of thousands of cyborg soldiers standing in formation on a plain outside the gaping cave entrance on the western front of KAU City. We thought this to be a less-used, less important entrance. The troubling thing is that it's the entrance closest to Cana. Could they know that? Could they have discovered Cana's location, and that's why they are garrisoned here? This isn't good.

I give Shreya a concerned look, and her face mirrors my feelings. She looks at her device and makes an adjustment to the focal length of the lens over her right eye. She appears startled by what she sees and does a double take. I quickly look in the direction she's facing and adjust my own lens, reframing the scene ahead and zooming in. My mouth goes dry when I see the terrifying image that has caught her attention. I then see Shreya hit the comm relay to Raven and Theia. She speaks in a low whisper: "I have eyes on Malakye—retreat with caution."

Shreya is thinking ahead. We grossly misjudged the importance of this location when we selected it for today. With Malakye present, the security around this camp will be much heavier. For all we know, there could be guards in the hills right now, surrounding us.

I zoom in again to get a better look at him. He stands tall with broad shoulders at the head of the unit and is thinner and lankier than I imagined. He is covered from neck to toe in a shell of black armor, and his hands are gloved. While his face appears to be perhaps human, covered in pale, rubbery flesh, he does not wear a helmet or any protection from the poisonous air. He turns his head, looks left and right, then barks an order to a subordinate. When he turns, I see that the right side of his face is chrome. His eyes are onyx, one flesh and one mechanical with a rotating gold iris. There's nothing about him that exactly identifies him as their leader, as Malakye, but I know that it is unquestionably him.

Shreya lightly touches my arm and motions that it is time for us to head out—and quickly—so as not to be discovered by Malakye's soldiers.

I am flat on my stomach, lying on the face of the squat dune, hidden behind the windward side. Still watching Malakye intently, I am absorbed in his strange, formidable appearance. Now he is speaking to someone. I continue to watch, mesmerized by his facial movements, when he suddenly stops cold. His pupils dilate, and he cocks his head sharply in my direction. I can't fight the feeling that he is looking directly at me. My stomach drops and I gasp.

"What?" Shreya says, her voice tense.

Rolling over, I scramble quickly down behind the dune toward her voice. Brushing myself off, I glance back nervously as if I could still see what is on the other side of the dune. "I think he saw me," I say on the edge of panic, my eyes darting back to the dune.

"That's impossible," she replies.

My teeth start chattering uncontrollably as my mind races over what it could mean if we are discovered. "Maybe . . . I don't know," I say indecisively. "Maybe we shouldn't go back. At least not the way we came. Not to Cana."

"Hey," Shreya says, "let's back up a second and calm down a bit. I need you to have a cool head." She astonishes me with the way she seems to be able to keep calm in any situation.

"I don't think we should stop," I say, looking back again at the dune and swallowing hard. "It's just—I'm just—" I'm halfway convinced the cyborg army in its entirety will come charging over the dune at any moment.

"We aren't stopping. I just want to get something straight. We're almost a mile away. And he's surrounded by desert. You are camouflaged, and we are hidden by dunes."

"But he has bionic eyes. I saw them. We don't know how far he can see."

She considers what I've said. "I really don't think it likely he could have spotted us behind that ridge without doing a really purposeful and thorough scan of the horizon. But we can't stay here. Let's see if we can rework a course back to Ephesia at a more neutral entry point."

We rejoin Theia and Raven and brief them on the situation. Theia plugs a few alternate routes into the tracking program we wrote to find one that avoids the drones. She quickly identifies one, but this route, while safer, will take double the time of our trip out. It's almost 11:00 a.m. now, and it will take us four hours to reach the southern entryway on the far side of the neutral zone. Then two more hours to get to Ephesia and another two from there back to Cana.

We have an eight-hour trek ahead of us that we didn't plan for. We also won't have our cloaks and packs waiting for us when we reenter the underground. But we can transition our suits to black and hope we don't draw too much attention to ourselves. Both return routes open to us seem risky, but I just can't shake the feeling that Malakye saw me. And leading him or one of his scouts directly to Cana is a risk I am just not willing to take.

38

On the trek back to the southern gate, I am racked with anxiety. Neurotically, I scan the horizon before me, behind me, and to the east and west, hoping we are not being followed. I fear that at any moment, a massive cyborg military formation will rise over the horizon behind us and each dune that's left in our wake. As we press on, my company is equally somber as we travel across the nuclear wasteland.

After four grueling hours, we finally sight the southern gate in the distance. It is marked by a tattered flag, still carrying old Institution signage. According to our maps, the area we are approaching is situated in the far reaches of the neutral zone and just outside the border of KAU City. The gate is still a little way in the distance. Once we pass through and descend into the underground, we don't expect to encounter anyone until we are at least fifty feet below the surface, as the air remains radioactive and poisonous until that depth. Very few people use these passageways, we're told, and those who do, usually have come to die.

Our suits clean the air we breathe, neutralizing a laundry list of harmful pollutants and carcinogens. But they do not filter out the smell that is beginning to permeate our helmets as we get closer to the impending cave entrance. It is the unmistakable stench of rotting flesh that is reaching our nostrils. Bodies at various stages of decay and rotting appendages and bones litter our path. You might think you would find a fully intact skeleton here, but that is not the way of things in the wicked hellscape unfolding before us.

To our surprise, roaming freely among the dead and dying are various thieves, vagrants, and scavengers skittering about. They appear to have come here unprotected to collect what they can from their defenseless brethren—including their bones—to be used, sold, or repurposed elsewhere in the underground.

At first, I avert my eyes, turn away, and try to look straight ahead as we walk. But then I decide I don't want to live ignorant of the suffering here. You must know a thing, must know a calamity, an adversary, a malady—no matter how incurable—if you are ever to master it, change it, or simply hold your own against it. You must know it back and forth, inside and out, ecstasy to agony; you must know it to beat it, outlast it, or even just exist beside it. And only when you know it can you accept it—and more than anything, you must accept it. For acceptance is the one path to walking through it.

So I look. I open my eyes and stay vigilant. I hold space for those suffering before me. I acknowledge and bear witness to every unfortunate, abandoned, and forsaken soul here, for whom the sum total of their once precious life has amounted only to this heinous end.

As we pass through and draw closer to the entry to the underground, a vagrant here and a scavenger there begin to gape at us. Most just stare, frozen in place, but some whisper. Others scamper off. Many are too delirious to be much of a threat, and some are too sick to care anymore other than to give us a passing glance. But there remain one or two who see a profit is to be made here. Whether it be a profit from information to be sold or one to be directly earned from us, the make and material of our suits is a clear signal that we come from a place more civilized than the cruel conditions in which the war has left these poor people, these unfortunate refugees of the Institution.

We pick up speed and duck inside the cave entrance as quickly as possible. Before us are passageways, rough tunnels dimly lit by widely spaced lanterns lining the walls. After a few turns away from the central passageway, we come to a shallow, more secluded alcove formed in the smooth stone walls. We take a moment to rest and work out a game plan to return to a safer area when we notice a man has followed us.

Small and sickly, he doesn't appear to be much of a threat. With an eye patch, very little hair left, and a robotic arm that is barely operational, he is dressed in rags and walks with a limp. There is nothing we can do about the fact that he has seen us but decide that maybe we can help him in some way and that perhaps he can help us, too. If he can find four cloaks for us and keep our presence secret, we offer to pay him generously. He agrees, and when he returns, he is accompanied by a dirty child, an unusual sight these days, post-war. The cloaks are different shades of gray and filthy, but they are tolerable and have hoods. We thank him, pay him, and watch as they depart.

Layering the cloaks over our suits, we continue deeper into the underground, headed for a lower, safer elevation. When we reach a depth of what we believe is about fifty feet, we remove our helmets. We then travel down a few more steep steps and through a tight passageway that opens into a clearing. In the darkness, Theia nearly runs directly into a figure wearing a hooded black cloak waiting at the bottom of the steps. She reels backward, losing her hood. I shift on my feet behind her, feeling uneasy as I observe that the person has not taken a step back—the usual reaction to a presumably harmless run-in such as this.

The man lifts his head a little, but only the bottom half of his dirty face is visible; the rest is in shadow. The dim light provided by the sparsely placed lanterns illuminates just his mouth. When he opens it to speak, I can see that his jaw and teeth are mechanical.

"You look healthy," he says to Theia, licking his lips.

"Back off," she says as she shoulders by him and throws her hood back up.

My hand goes straight to the jagdagger sheathed at my waist. I slip it out of a hidden pocket in my suit and hold it tightly in my right hand.

Shreya, Raven, and I follow and pass by him, too. Ahead, Theia rounds a corner, then stops abruptly, immediately dropping her helmet. As I catch up, I peer around her to see four more figures standing in our path and blocking the way.

One of the figures steps forward and says, "I can get three hundred credits for each of their bodies, long as we keep 'em warm enough and their organs intact before they reach the buyer," he remarks, elbowing one of his companions.

"Oh, I don't mind keeping this one warm," the man with the mechanical jaw says from behind me as he reaches for my neck.

I spin in a tight arc and throw an elbow directly into his jaw just as I remember it is made of steel. But I suspect his neck is not, as my hit does its work and knocks him backward for just a moment.

Theia has both guns drawn. They are not charged up yet, but I can hear that she has routed full power to them by the static electrical humming noise coming from the barrels. They should be up in less than three seconds.

But three seconds is too long to wait when you've got four men coming at you fast. She opts instead to hit each of the first two coming at her with the butt of a gun, one after the other. Shreya and Raven move in fast to restrain the two men Theia has put on the ground, but the two behind them get hold of Theia's wrists, and her guns clatter to the floor.

The man behind me with the mechanical jaw is up in a few heartbeats, rushes forward, and grabs me around the waist, tackling me from behind. Struggling to twist free, I lunge forward to help Theia, who is now being pinned by the two men who wrestled her guns away. As I crash to my knees on the hard rock floor, I see several more hooded men file in. Shreya and Raven have made quick work of the two men on the ground and are fighting to free Theia from the other two when they, too, look up and see the additional bodies filing in.

I intentionally throw my body forward and fall hard on my left shoulder, throwing off the man on top of me. He crashes sideways, scrambling, trying to get hold of my lower body as I squirm away from him. I see he is wielding a knife in his right hand.

With my jagdagger still firmly in my hand, I roll onto my back and kick him hard in the chest with my exos activated. He flies across the room, slamming against the cave wall.

I waste no time and hurl my jagdagger at him. Its silvery blade glints in the dim light of the tunnel as it cleaves through the dark, finding its mark dead center in the soft, hollow space of his throat.

I then rip off my cloak, pull on my helmet, and shout to Shreya, Theia, and Raven, "Clear out!"

Sprinting directly at the gang of thieves, which has now grown to a group of about fifteen, I activate the cloaking mechanism on my suit and disappear.

Having disabled the men they were fighting, Shreya, Theia, and Raven pick up on my plan and run away in the opposite direction.

Just before I reach the pack of men coming at me full speed, believing themselves to be in hot pursuit of my companions and me, I slide and tumble, ducking between them. Then I reappear on the other side, disabling my suit's cloaking function.

It only takes a few moments for them to follow the commotion of my movement, halt, and whirl around to face me. Once I have their undivided attention, I drop Sumi's hand grenade, a hive filled with lethal nanobots in the guise of cybernetic insects: razor-sharp bots designed for shredding flesh.

I then vanish again, pick and dodge my way through the now confused band of thieves, and run, barreling back in the opposite direction, not far behind my friends. I count down in my head, *Three . . . two . . . one . . .* Then I hear the device explode, swarming the men with the flesh-shredding bugs.

What follows is the most disturbing yet satisfying cacophony of blood-curdling screaming I have heard to date. The tiny droids do their work from the inside out, entering the body through any—and usually every—accessible orifice: the eyes, ears, and mouth, for example—before burrowing directly inside the skull and liquifying the contents within.

With the threat neutralized, I deactivate the cloaking function on my suit and transition back from camouflage to black. Breathless and unnerved, my patrol unit and I don't stop moving until we have reached a populated area.

Finally reaching a well-lit section of the underground, Shreya, Theia, Raven, and I soon come across a small market where we can buy new, colorful cloaks to replace the ones we lost in our scuffle. We even find some refreshments at a small tavern along the way. It isn't much, but it is a revelation compared with the limited choice of beverages we are privy to back home in Cana City. When we go inside, we learn that we have just crossed the border between the underbelly of KAU City and the outskirts of the neutral zone. We didn't realize it, but we inadvertently entered the city on our way in.

After refreshing ourselves, securing our weapons, and dressing for the remainder of our journey, we head out of the tavern to begin the long walk back. I step outside and look around while I am waiting for the others. As I run my hands idly over some colorful scarves at a vendor stall, a dirty child wanders up and signals my attention.

I am on my guard at first, but when I have assessed that she is unarmed and carries no weapon or combustibles, I allow her to approach. She quietly hands me a rolled-up slip of paper.

I unroll the little slip and see a simple, scribbled two-word message that reads, *Gemma lives.* Below it, a location is indicated, and then I read, *I can be found here on Tuesdays to trade.*

I frown at the paper, and when I look up, the child is gone.

39

The next day, we take a break from patrolling. I am shaken after seeing Malakye and the size of his army and even more disturbed by our close call inside the tunnel. Joshua is not pleased that our rerouted course took us directly into the underbelly of KAU City. He wasn't wrong to warn us about going there. I had never killed anyone before, and even though it was in self-defense, it doesn't settle well with me once the adrenaline wears off. But Joshua taught me that if it was me or them, I shouldn't hesitate. I had to follow through with what needed to be done—that was survival, and there was no sin in it.

Organ trafficking is a big problem on Earth post-war. Because of the significant percentage of the population who are sick and dying—from radiation poisoning, genetic defects, and the rapid degeneration of failing organs previously sustained by bio-drugs pre-war—there is a perpetual demand for transplants of all kinds. With no formal economy, earning a living wage and seeking proper medical care are impossibilities for the refugees who have been left for dead in KAU City. And in the presence of poverty, there is always crime—those willing to do the unconscionable for a profit.

We were lucky to fend off the band of traffickers that attacked us and can only hope we were not identified by anyone in network with Malakye and the Regime. There is so much chaos in KAU City and the border regions of the neutral zone that it's possible we could have been lost in the daily scuffle of the black market and not noticed by anyone with political motivations.

That said, I am troubled by the anonymous message I received about Gemma. Who down here could possibly know about her? Beyond that, I do not recognize the location indicated on the note, even after cross-referencing it with all the maps in our possession. I don't plan to tell anyone about it right away—there are too many other topics of concern to bring to my family after our latest trip to the surface. But I can't stop thinking about what it could mean, who could have been watching us and who recognized me despite our efforts to stay anonymous.

The real Gemma Abramovich, the human being from whom the hologram I knew on Proxima was derived, lived and died two centuries ago in Cana, long before this war. After everything I have learned in the past year about Mordecai Abramovich, I could argue that her death marked the beginnings of his great crusade, his cataclysmic vendetta against the Institution.

We know she was one of the first young girls captured and taken from Cana in the early days of the cold war and that her life and body were exploited to seed the embryo factories that eventually became the Institution's big bio-drug industry. I suppose it could be true that while her abduction was noted in history, her actual death was not marked. There's no record of it, at least not that I could find in Titan's massive library archives when I ran a quick search one of the late nights I spent working there on my suit cloak prototype.

But could she have lived through it? If she did, she would be very old by now, and I refuse to believe she would use the very drugs that destroyed her life to extend it beyond its natural course. No, this doesn't add up. If anything, it's a trap and a good one. Someone out there has information about me and what I care about and is trying to use it to draw me back into the fringe.

What doesn't fit is that only a few people know about Gemma and our connection. The list is short and finite, and each of those people I trust implicitly. This brings me back to the other side of the coin: What if the message is legitimate and Gemma, or whatever version of her who is seeking me, needs my help?

Joshua has been away again, meeting with Cana Minor and the three surviving Elders in Jericho City. I spend the morning with Imani, visiting the needy. Imani is uneasy and not herself as we walk the long way back down by the water.

Yesterday's horrors weigh heavily on me. Compounded by the sickness and suffering we attended to this morning, my mood is also rather dark today. I prayed next to Imani for each and every one of the poor souls with whom we commiserated, but I am beginning to feel the effort was futile. The horror of the bloody path we walked yesterday is imprinted on my mind and heart, and I cannot reconcile religion with it. I can think of only one word to describe the gruesome reality we witnessed, and it is *godless*.

"'Through caverns measureless to man, down to a sunless sea,'" Imani recites, a little lost in her own thoughts and quoting a poet of the Old World as we walk along the rushing torrent adjacent to us. She totes an empty basket, now devoid of the books and parcels we delivered today.

I smile at her reference to the subterranean river, and we walk on quietly for a bit. Pensive, she eventually speaks again.

"He was just a child," she begins, teary, referring to Taj and the young age at which he became involved with Abramovich. She then pauses, shaking her head, signaling that she is overcome with emotion and cannot speak.

She does not have a good feeling about Taj today. She awoke with a premonition that his spirit had moved on from this world. I try to be strong for her and say, "There is still hope. We do not know that he didn't change his mind." I think of the last conversation I had with Taj when I tried to convince him to refuse the request that he sacrifice his body so that Abramovich's life could be saved by transplant surgery.

Imani looks back at me, her eyes haunted with a deep knowing. She has already decided that he is gone. There is nothing I can say to cheer her or change her mind.

"I wanted Taj to be his own man, so I did not intervene," she says in resignation, lost in the past. "If I had known . . ." She clenches her fists and looks up at the dark cavern ceiling. The air is musty, and the ceiling drips with stalactites and various other forms of mineral precipitation. "If I had known, I would have moved Heaven and Earth to save him from that man's influence."

"I don't believe Taj was completely lost to Abramovich," I say thoughtfully. "He told me he thought only the factories would burn—and I believe him," I reason earnestly in an effort to alleviate her misplaced self-blame. "He did not intend total war; the bunkers were just a precaution if it got out of hand . . ."

"Well, it got out of hand," she says, stating the obvious as we arrive at a freight elevator on the ground level.

I agree and say, "I need to stop by the machine shop to see Smithy."

"Very well," she says, stepping onto the elevator. "Thank you for joining me this morning."

"Of course. Anything for you," I say, smiling wearily as I turn to leave.

"Oh Helly?" she calls after me.

"Yes?"

"I believe him, too," she says, and the bars of the lift close together. It accelerates, ascending toward the living quarters.

I can't get Malakye's colossal army off my mind. I don't know how we will fight them if it comes to that. And it will come to that; I'm sure of it. Now that I have seen the army with my own eyes, I understand explicitly the inevitability of a confrontation, a reality Joshua has tried to convey time and again. To that end, I have been meaning to ask Smithy about the weapons Chiron used on Titan during the Equinox attack, particularly the gun Cassini wielded to lay waste to our graphene-clad soldiers and fighter jets.

Walking down a back aisle of Smithy's huge facility, I listen to the whirring and clanking, bellowing and hissing, and steaming and grinding of the gears of the massive machines lining the shop floor. I let the noise drown out my thoughts as I approach Smithy's personal workshop. Popping my head in the door, I ask, "Got a minute?"

He glances up from his work, squints at me momentarily, and waves me over.

As I approach, I am captivated by the bizarre array of contraptions and prototypes he has scattered about. There are instruments of various simplicity and complication, including tools, gadgets, weapons, armor, toys, and even art.

I open my mouth, but before I can speak, he says, "Might I take a closer look at that interesting device on your ear?"

I smile, remove my ear cuff, and hand it over to him. I then pull my palm screen out of my back pocket and toss it his way. He examines Sumi's cybernetic bee, Bumbly, while I recount the attack on Titan, trying my best to accurately describe Chiron's powerful guns. By the time I'm done talking, Bumbly has flown at least three laps around the machine shop.

When I finish speaking, Smithy says, "Yes, I am familiar with these weapons that Chiron possesses and have tinkered with a few prototypes myself. I will explain how they work, but do not get ahead of yourself. You will understand why in just a moment."

As I sink down into a worn leather armchair beside his desk, Smithy begins his explanation. "The secret to penetrating graphene," he starts, "is in microscopic projectiles and employing the energy of a laser to fire them, rather than the less powerful forms of combustibles typically used in conventional firearms. Projectiles test a target's tensile strength and ability to absorb impact, and graphene, as you know, is in a league of its own, with a tensile strength that surpasses any other material. Its ability to simultaneously be stiff and elastic is what gives it its extraordinary potential and advantage when used as armor."

Smithy opens a display screen and begins playing a demo. "Now, if you fire at graphene with a single bullet of any make, any material, at any velocity, it will withstand the impact by stretching and distributing the stress delivered by the bullet over a broad area. However, if you hit the graphene target with a *spray* of microspheres—microscopic glass bullets, for example—driven by the energy of a laser traveling at around two thousand miles per hour, then you will breach it." He pauses a moment, his excitement mounting. "But more than that! You will vaporize it." Smithy spreads his hands wide as he finishes as if to say, *"Poof!"* conveying the chilling finality of the weapon's effects on an enemy, however inadequately.

I nod, reworking his explanation over in my head to be sure I follow, and then ask, "Well, what's the catch?"

"The catch," he replies, "is the heat."

"What do you mean, the heat?"

"The heat the weapon produces. It functions quite well in space and on worlds such as Titan with frigid climates, but these guns do not work well here on our planet."

"Why? Do they overheat?"

"Yes, they overheat. The weapon burns itself up, imploding and permanently fusing its internal electronics. Less extreme and a more likely problem, like our rail guns, Chiron's weapons also take time to charge up and use an appreciable amount of power—so not practical for use in the field. Not on our planet, at least."

I am disappointed to hear this. The guns we use now will be mostly ineffective against the Regime's cyborg soldiers. Standard lead or steel-jacketed bullets don't do enough damage to their alloy-based exoskeletons and synthetic body parts. The only way to put them down for good is by physically hacking off their heads with a strong blade. I thought that perhaps we could get the advantage over the cyborgs by replicating Chiron's technology, but it seems that doing so will not be that simple.

Smithy recognizes my disappointment. "Don't give up so easily, kiddo," he says. "I've got a few other things cooking for you and the Guard. Should be ready in a few days. Be sure to stop back by here and check in on me again."

"Will do," I say, smiling, and thank him.

Smithy repackages Bumbly and returns him to me in his casing. I clip the small cuff back on my cartilage and turn to leave when he says, "Oh, your brother has returned and wishes to see you."

"Thanks," I say, waving as I head out the door.

Ugh, I think as I play the conversation I'm about to have with Joshua over in my head, trying to think of a way to downplay what happened yesterday. Joshua will not be happy, and he will want to talk about it . . . a lot. We will break down all the ways it could have gone differently, could have gone better, and could have been avoided entirely. Wringing my hands, I round the corner and stride through the open doors of the command center. I don't see Joshua, but when I look around the corner to the ops station, I see Tristan, one of the technicians. I walk over and ask him if he has seen my brother.

"He's on his way," he says, looking up at me briefly and then back down at his screen. "Another *Dove* arrived today from Alpha Centauri."

I look at him blankly.

"You know," he repeats, "a *Dove*—another ship like the one you arrived in—like *the Phoenix.*"

Of course I know damn well what he means, but before I'm able to even begin to process the implications of what he has said, I hear the doors slide open in the main room behind us. Turning around, I walk around the corner to see Joshua enter. But then, movement at his feet catches my eye as something big and furry wriggles past him and comes bounding toward me.

"Ramses!" I exclaim and drop to my knees with open arms. Then hugging him tightly, I bury my face in his fur. Laughing, tears of joy stream down my face. I am so surprised by his appearance; I look at the door again, half-expecting Taj to walk in.

But as Joshua steps aside, it is not Taj who appears behind him. Although the face I see is one of perhaps equal familiarity. Not a face familiar from my life of late, but one I see often in my mind just the same. It is a face that has haunted my dreams, waking and sleeping, for perhaps the last quarter of a century. No, it isn't Taj who has just returned from across the universe, but Xavier.

40

I stand slowly from where I am kneeling next to Ramses as Xavier enters the room behind Joshua. His eyes immediately settle on me, and he stops short.

"Hella . . ." he manages to say.

What is the look on his face? It's relief, it's guilt, and it's pain.

"You're back?" I whisper the question, nearly inaudibly, in disbelief.

Xavier's eyes dart to Ramses, then Joshua, and back to me. After looking me up and down, his eyes again meet mine.

"He insisted I bring this dog to you," he says. "Would brook no argument about it. Said you had to be reunited. That one was no good without the other."

Exhaling, I smile a little. I then look back down at Ramses, my head swimming. *He means Taj,* I think to myself. Taj thought it was important for Ramses and me to be reunited. At the thought of Taj, a pang of fear and an ache of regret make themselves known in the center of my chest.

"Apparently this guy was in rough shape and made a long trip back to the compound on Proxima looking for you," he says sincerely. "Taj fixed him up, though. Good as new."

"B-b-but . . . well, where is Taj?" I stutter, my mouth dry and my heart pounding. "And what are *you* doing here?"

Exhaling forcibly, I have to remind myself to breathe. My eyes shift to my brother's face. Joshua is looking down, his hands folded. One, two, three wild heartbeats pass as I frantically look between the two men.

"Well?" I demand, hearing my voice echo against the vaulted ceiling.

Xavier closes the space between us and takes my hands. "Hella, I'm sorry. Taj has passed on."

I snatch my hands back. "What?" I gasp. "You're wrong," I say, my voice shrill and my ears ringing. I flush as my words cut like a knife through the space between us, the decades we have lost. My forehead tenses and my lips tremble. My head suddenly pounding, I cannot relax my features no matter how hard I try. Looking away, I brush aside a loose strand of hair falling in front of my face.

Xavier steps back and absently touches his chin, his eyes searching mine. I turn away from him and Joshua. One hand goes to my heart, the other on my stomach as I try to breathe and regain my composure.

Reaching for my shoulder, Xavier steps forward. I want to push him away, but instead, I turn and face him. I allow myself to really look at him. He is twenty years older, but still wears his hair short and shaved close. I study his face: his strong jaw, his dark eyebrows, and his eyes indigo. Looking at his face, it all floods back—the familiarity of him, the immediate possessiveness I feel. It all washes over me in a searing flash, a fever dream. I had forgotten the intangible allure, the visceral chemistry ignited by his presence. Every wall I've built dissolves in a moment as I am confronted with him, his aura. The casual movement of his arm, the inflection of his voice, his eyes as they observe me.

I'm ready to abandon every vow I made to myself these last five years . . . or is it twenty-five? Earnest and steadfast, I had sworn promises, nurtured convictions, and experienced revelations . . . transcendence, even, I'd reached . . . so resolute was I that this love was one to be left behind. All these things, thoughtfully constructed with the precision of a surgeon, are now erased, wiped away in a moment—out of sight and out of mind.

I have a thousand questions but cannot speak one of them. Looking down, a tear falls down my cheek before I tentatively reach for his hand. He rushes forward and folds me into his arms. Closing my eyes against his chest, a lifetime I've tried so hard to forget rushes back in screaming color.

Joshua excused himself to allow Xavier and me time to catch up. We left the command center and wandered around for a while, not knowing where we were going. I showed him the city with Ramses in tow, and we eventually found ourselves at the stables. Legend now has a saddle and bridle, along with several companions in stable with her. An entire herd is in the works, I'm told. Enough to outfit Cana's cavalry.

This news of Taj, I push it away. I bury it. Everything is too much right now. It will be a long while before I can even look under the bandage and assess the wound. How deep is the cut? How jagged? How much damage? I don't quite know. Don't want to know.

On the walk down, Xavier confirmed for me that he had, in fact, defected intentionally from the Alliance to pursue TRAPPIST. He described Calypso, the Alliance base on the outskirts of the Oort Cloud, as Abramovich's bait trap for new donors. Abramovich was infamous for enticing young cadets to venture out to Alpha Centauri by any means necessary. He would then exploit them or trade with them in exchange for their stem cells or the donors they could procure, which is what Xavier did for him. There were even instances where he forcibly "sacrificed" cadets he had lured out to Proxima, taking their bodies against their will to restore his own health. And all in the name of his God almighty. The new guy running Calypso was on to him, though. Had been for the last two decades, and that was why Abramovich was so desperate for Taj to be his next donor.

Xavier had seen Taj before he died. Returning home to Earth from TRAPPIST, he stopped on Proxima to return Abramovich's *Dove*, which he had on loan. He was surprised to find Taj there. Communications had been largely disabled on his ship; he could not send or receive messages to Earth, the Alliance, or anywhere else that wasn't expressly approved by Abramovich. That had been part of the deal. Xavier hadn't known what Abramovich had done to Earth or about Taj's involvement. Nor had he known about Abramovich's plans for me.

After learning that Abramovich had nuked Earth and that Taj planned to sacrifice himself and could not be persuaded to act otherwise, Xavier left nearly as quickly as he had arrived—within the hour, he said. All deals were off as far as he was concerned. He would honor no agreement made with a madman, a mass murderer, a planet killer, and had no reason to believe that Abramovich would make good on his word to return him to Calypso, as promised so many years ago.

Xavier lowers his hand for me to use as a step and boosts me into the saddle. A routine we must have done a thousand times before. I guide Legend around the arena, and Xavier, at the center, holds the long lead between us—but this is all out of old habit. Legend does not need any breaking or any training. Gemma has programmed her masterfully.

I feel lighter astride my mount, glancing down at Xavier like the old days. We move around him as if we are spinning in slow motion, Legend dancing and me smiling. It's spellbinding and too perfect to be real. I sure as hell don't trust it—I don't trust that he will be standing there when I turn my head and look for him as I trot Legend around the circumference of the arena.

"There are horses in TRAPPIST," he says carefully, but shatters my mood nonetheless. I suppose it isn't fair for me to blame a whole system for his choices, but the word triggers me just the same.

"What else do they have in TRAPPIST?" I ask curtly.

"Many things. On Elysium, it's wild, beautiful countryside, and there are horses. Untamed. I thought you'd like that. Like to know they live on elsewhere. It is a tragedy what's happened here to our world and to the animals, but it comforts me to know they still live and still thrive somewhere across the universe."

Of course, I agree with him. I feel selfish for letting my anger eclipse such a miracle. This knowledge mends broken places in my heart that I had accepted could never be repaired. Hearing that there is a place like that, in the great expanse of our universe, that still thrives, is still green, ignites a tiny flame of hope in my heart for the future.

"Well, great. Tell me more, then. I want to hear all about it," I say, bringing Legend to a cantor, then turning back toward Xavier and circling him again as he begins to talk.

"Seven planets circle TRAPPIST's red dwarf star, Helios, or TRAPPIST-1. All are rocky, and all have watery surfaces. Some have colder climates, and others are warmer, depending on where they sit relative to their sun. And most of them have the right ratio of iron, magnesium, and oxygen to harbor life.

"Elysium, or TRAPPIST-1 d, is the third planet from the red sun, and you can see its six sister planets in the night sky as easily as you can see Earth's moon, standing on its surface—well back before the Fall, at least."

I bring Legend to a halt, smile a little tight-lipped smile, and look back at him expectantly. "And it's biotic?" I ask in disbelief. "Horses, and what else?"

"There is a small civilization of people there, humans. They are like us but less advanced than we are in many ways. Their world is less industrial, for example. But then, they are more advanced than we are in other areas . . ." he trails off.

"Did they colonize it or originate there?" I ask, though knowing the latter isn't likely. We hadn't found advanced life originating on its own anywhere in the known universe yet.

"Elysium is a seed planet started by the Founders. They provisioned it around the same time they conceived of the Revivalists and buried our vault beneath the ice. It is the twin civilization to Empyreus, synonymous in name. But the seed ship sent by the Founders to birth Elysium's civilization had a long way to travel to the TRAPPIST system and thus got a much later start than we did. They were also not provided with the same advanced technology or religious doctrine that the Revivalists were. A sort of counter-experiment of the Founders, I suppose."

My blank slate, I think, *that I've been wondering about all these years.*

"How did you know it would be safe to go there?" I ask. "They could have been dangerous, for all we know about them."

"I didn't know, but I had a feeling about it," he says cryptically. "They are not dangerous. They are peaceful. And . . ." He pauses for a moment. "They are empaths. The veil is very thin there in their capital city of Asteria."

"That's all really fascinating, but you still haven't told me why." I hop off Legend, and we lead her back to the stables. "Why was it so important that you go there, risk everything, and leave your entire life behind?" *Leave* me *behind,* I think.

"Hella, I have my reasons, and they are deeply personal. Please understand, I hated keeping anything from you, but you must trust me that it was the right choice."

"I don't know what I'm supposed to do with that kind of explanation. It's not an explanation at all, really. It's a nonanswer answer."

Xavier continues to solemnly look down at his feet as we walk.

"I have spent years of my life wondering what happened to you, where you were—if you were alive or dead," I say, still incredulous that he will offer me no explanation. "You couldn't know what it was like."

"But I could." He pauses, a shadow moving over his face. "And I do." He is quiet for a moment, thoughtful. "I will tell you when the time comes, Hella, but you must trust me that I cannot share any more with you now than I've said."

"Well, I don't have to accept that," I say simply as we finish stabling Legend and turn to exit. I walk ahead. Xavier hurries to catch up and grabs my hand to stop me.

"Hella, everything I've done, I've done for you," he says, his voice low, his eyes piercing.

I nearly stumble back but hold his magnetic gaze. "And what of all you've left undone?" I counter, standing my ground.

He raises his eyebrows, flicking his gaze away in unspoken acknowledgment of my argument. "I have endured without you for nearly three decades. Please, can you just be happy for this moment? That we are together and that we are alive?" he pleads as he reaches to touch my face.

I want more than anything to shake off my hurt and anger, but I need to understand. His actions all those years ago don't add up, and I can't just lie to myself, to him, to everyone and pretend that they do. It isn't who I am to brush things under the rug, and so I resolve to stand firmly, at least until my head has cleared some. It isn't that I can't or won't forgive him, but it is the *forgetting* that I cannot do. And as they say, betrayal is the only truth that sticks.

He reads my response in the sad look in my eyes. "I've crossed universes for you, and it still isn't enough." Dropping his hand from my face, he lets it hang slackly at his side for a moment before we turn away from each other and continue down the corridor in silence.

A few minutes later, Xavier and I part ways for now. He joins Joshua to get settled in his quarters. I head to the training arena to meet Shreya and try out a pair of new swords Smithy has made to help prepare us to face the Regime and its army of fearless cyborg soldiers.

On the walk over, I find myself wishing I could talk to Petra, tell her what has happened and get her advice. But it's a two-hour trek to Ephesia, the closest location from which we can access the network safely. We are resuming our patrol tomorrow, so there is no sense in making the journey tonight and then again so soon in the morning. I will have to go without—something I've gotten used to these days.

41

Shreya and I have been going at it for a quarter of an hour, sparring with our new fusion-charged *khopesh* sickle swords. With sweat pouring and muscles straining, we move like a blur around the arena in a frenetic dance of strikes and blocks. We are both on edge, feeling angry, scared, and sad. After what we faced yesterday on the surface and underground in KAU City, taking our emotions out on the training floor is exactly what we need.

I replay the conversation with Xavier over in my head again and again—what he said and didn't say, and all the things I didn't have the opportunity to ask him, run through my brain repeatedly. I begin to catalog my unanswered questions, deciding that I will confront him this evening when, barely an hour into our training, he enters the arena with Yash and Tristan.

Xavier nods at me in greeting across the floor, and the three of them begin preparing for jujitsu practice. As Xavier removes his tunic, I observe the familiar *V* of his muscular back as he wraps his hands, preparing to hit the grappling mat. I also notice he has some unfamiliar tattoos. The symbols are in a language I don't recognize, falling in vertical script down the plane of his back. Not having any knowledge about what they mean, when he got them, or why stirs a jealousy within me that I immediately try to repress.

The surprise of his return has left me in a state of shock, making it difficult to process my feelings and know my own mind. I need time and distance to think. There is so much he is holding back from me and so much I still don't understand. While seeing him again is all I've wished for, prayed for, and dreamed about for most of my life, I can't quite reconcile the man I thought I knew with the man now standing before me.

The Xavier I grew up with was someone I trusted implicitly and thought I knew better than I knew myself. This Xavier is someone I used to know. Someone who looks the same, smiles the same, broods the same, even smells the same . . . But the truth remains: He now seems to be someone else.

I signal to Shreya that I'm done, and she nods. We scabbard our swords, gather our belongings, and head out. As we walk together back up to the living quarters, I remain lost in thought. *Is this how it's going to be? He's gone for five years, and now that he's back, I don't feel like I can talk to him, and I even find myself avoiding him.*

Returning to my room, I discover Imani has already gone up for dinner. After I take a hot shower, I comb out my long hair. It's still bright red, now reaching to my waist in length. As I take my time dressing, I notice the rolled-up bit of paper in the desk drawer that the street child handed to me in the neutral zone the day before. I spend some time trying to work out a path to the location using a tablet to review the digitized maps we have been developing through our patrol work. There doesn't seem to be any way to get to it without going directly through the worst part of KAU City, and then it's still unclear exactly where it is relative to the city line.

By the time Ramses and I make it to dinner, everyone has finished eating. Most have retired to the common area to relax, play music, and talk. I enter the kitchen, and Theia gets up from a plush basket chair where she was reading by candlelight and joins me at the kitchen table while I force down a lukewarm bowl of gruel.

"Where's Imani?" I ask between bites.

"She was at dinner," Theia replies, "but now she is in the chapel."

I nod, understanding why. Imani, too, has just learned about Taj's death, although it seemed she already knew in spirit this morning. I went to her myself earlier to break the news and will join her in the chapel directly after this, I decide.

Peering around Theia to the room beyond, I confirm Joshua is absent, too. "How about Joshua?"

"He wasn't at dinner."

I raise an eyebrow in concern. "How come?"

"Working late with my father," she says idly while tracing a faint line with her finger on a scrap of parchment that has fallen loose from an old atlas.

Just then, Tristan and Yash, who had been engrossed in a game of cards with Xavier a few moments before, abruptly stand up and stride out of the room. I frown, and Theia, her eyes widening in concern, gets up quickly. I push my half-eaten bowl aside to follow her.

Xavier meets us at the door. He says, "Joshua just called all hands to report immediately for a council meeting."

The three of us follow Tristan and Yash down the corridor and down two levels to the command center. Joshua and his senior officers are gathered around a large observation screen. My brother glances up when we walk in, looking grave and resolute. Standing up straight from where he was leaning over the desk, he motions for us to sit down. A few of us take seats where they are available; others remain standing. Everyone is on edge.

"The Regime's drones changed their pattern at dusk this evening," Joshua begins, his voice low and serious. Motioning to the screen, he points out where the drones would run their usual formation. "This is the course they previously followed," he says, showing their routine sweep on a time-lapse projection, an image that maps the surface with the blueprints of the underground as an overlay. "And this is how it has been altered."

The screen flashes to show the new pattern. The drones, now in a chillingly precise formation, perfectly outline the location of Cana City. Several are strategically stationed at the various entrances to the underground used to access the city. One or two are positioned over the nearby junctions between the outskirts of the city and the neutral zone, and a formidable fifteen are locked in formation above the most direct access point to Cana, the very spot I trekked to after my arrival weeks ago. The message is crystal clear.

"Not only do they know where we are," Joshua explains, "but they want us to know they are watching us." He pauses. "Additionally, we have new intel that gives us reason to believe these drones are weaponized."

"Weaponized with what?" Theia asks. "Their rail guns can't touch our suits."

"We are not sure yet," Joshua says. "But drones are not the worst of our problems. One of our snipers can take them out in a matter of minutes now that our location has been made." I hold my breath as he points out three locations on the map. "Our bigger problem is that our drones have picked up footage that shows Malakye is already marching on us, on three fronts." Again, he indicates on the map where the Regime's forces are assembled, the largest regiment facing the entrance to Ephesia. The room falls into a heavy silence.

"We need to get up on the surface as soon as is feasible and fend them off," Joshua continues, his voice steady. "If his men get down in these tunnels and breach our city gates into civilian space, we're done for. They outnumber our soldiers by about five to one." He pauses momentarily, letting his words sink in. "But we are smarter, have better armor, better technology, and are mounted," he finishes and looks over to me, nodding his head in gratitude.

"How long before they reach us?" I ask.

"They will arrive at the Ephesian gate in four hours."

Four hours. I am stunned. I had known this day was coming but wasn't expecting it so soon. I wasn't expecting the battle to occur in the dead of night. It is 9:00 p.m. now. If Joshua's predictions are correct, the Regime will arrive around 1:00 a.m.

"That gives us one hour to get suited up and mounted, two hours to travel through the underground tunnels to Ephesia, and then an hour to spare if we stay on schedule." We all nod solemnly in understanding as he continues. "We knew this day would come, and I can finally say with confidence that I believe we are ready for it." Joshua pauses and looks around the room to be sure we are all in agreement, then adds, "Godspeed, soldiers."

Through the winding tunnels from Cana City to Ephesia, we lead the cavalry. Five hundred strong, we are suited, mounted, and formidably armed. The horses handle the narrow, rocky pass with the agility of mountain goats. We could never get a vehicle out to the surface this way, and though we are vastly outnumbered, our horse soldiers will be a great advantage in the field against the Regime's cyborg foot soldiers.

There is not much use in hiding anymore, so we do not try to disguise ourselves beyond the hooded cloaks we wear to cover our suits and obscure our faces. We leave a heavily armored guard unit at the gates. Cana Minor's infantry will follow close behind us, but they will exit to the surface at the southern end of the neutral zone rather than at Ephesia.

Shreya and Joshua lead the charge, and Theia, Raven, and I follow close behind. Xavier, Noah, and Syngin take up the rear. How strange it is that Xavier is here now, so nearby. Yet I do not feel much closer to him than I did a week ago before his return. I don't know how long he plans to stay, but it seems he is staying at least long enough to help fight this war.

We pass few people on the tunnel road to Ephesia. The going is slow, but we stay on schedule. The tunnels are more populated when we arrive, close to two hours after our departure. Joshua dismounts and enters one of the rooms off the central common area to access the network. He sends messages to Cana's old allies off-world to warn them of the new developments and our imminent conflict with the Regime. Then we continue on our way. When we near the surface, we pull our cloaks up tightly to conceal our powerful armor as much as possible.

Around midnight, we reach the surface. Malakye's troops are expected to arrive within the hour. We assemble our cavalry in an imposing formation and stand strong, waiting for him. Joshua heads the center, Shreya the left flank, and Noah the right. I am to fight with the left side behind Shreya.

Joshua soon receives a message that Cana Minor is nearly in position, although not quite visible at surface level yet. We wait, sitting tall and proud astride our cavalry of bionic black Andalusian mounts, an army of them assembled in record time in Smithy's machine shop.

A glance down at Ramses confirms for me that my canine companion is waiting and at the ready for what is to come. I'm confident in the efficacy of the work his steel jaw will do to the jugular of a cyborg soldier—the sweet spot, as Smithy has informed me, for human as well as electronic foes. Guns alone will not take them down. Ultimately, a beheading is prescribed—required—to effectuate true death when facing a soldier who is half man, half machine. I touch my hand to the hilt of my fusion-powered sickle sword, sheathed beneath my cloak. A squeeze of my hand will charge it in one-eighth of a second. I think of the comforting thrum sound it makes when it charges up. Though short-lived, it brings me peace momentarily.

First, we see the dust cloud, then we hear them. Malakye's cyborg soldiers make a loud, terrifying noise as they advance. But it is not the sound of men marching we hear; it is the cranking and clanking of machines. A loud and droning reverberation it may be, but it will not hold a candle to the thunder that will sound when our cavalry charges down on them.

At about a thousand yards away, they reach a halt. In size, they look to be roughly a two-thousand-man brigade. They assemble in units spaced about twenty yards apart and around one hundred yards from the next line of soldiers. I adjust my lens and zoom in to see Malakye is taking command from the rear, barking orders to one or two men standing with him on a slightly elevated plateau to the rear of the company. Our drones report that one of the other two regiments is still marching and has yet to arrive at the southern gate. The third has remained at the western gate, where we spotted Malakye just yesterday.

Malakye has no interest in treating, and honestly, we do not either. We know what he wants, and we will never agree to give it to him. He is in the business of human trafficking, and we will die before trading the lives of our people for anything. But now, fixed firmly in the crosshairs of his unmitigated effrontery, I can't help but wonder where the remaining leaders of the Elite Council stand in this conflict. I had thought *they* perhaps had some civility left. That at the very least they would have sent a correspondent of some kind to speak with us before resorting to all-out war. Their failure to do so is an indication of just how desperate they have become. Desperate for the drugs that can only be born from the wombs of my people.

A cold wind begins to blow as a single moonbeam cleaves through the cloudy haze of the night sky. I look to Raven, follow her line of sight, and am pleased to see that she, too, has beheld the ethereal light. The lunar ray flashes away as quickly as it shone, and when she turns her hooded head, glancing my way briefly in a moment of wonder, I know that she is smiling even though it looks as if a faceless soldier occupies her mount. When she turned my way, the opening of her hood had parted to reveal . . . nothing, as she and I and all our fighters are electronically cloaked and thus invisible beneath our heavy capes.

Just then, a war horn cries out, and in unison, the cyborg soldiers shift to attention. In response, Joshua raises his right arm high in the sky, and just before the Regime charges, he drops it in one swift motion. At his signal, our capes fall in unison, sweeping to the ground.

The Regime army facing us hesitates in confusion, for they now face an army of rider-less-stallions of the blackest night. Ghosts of men we are, hidden by the clever technology of our suit cloaks. We will remain invisible until we engage the enemy in man-to-man combat, as the contact will destabilize and deactivate our suits' cloaking mechanism.

Far away, we hear the Regime regrouping, shouting, "It's a ruse!"

Malakye's army swiftly turns. Simultaneously to our diversion, they have been made aware of Cana Minor's infantry assembling at the southern gate. They turn away and make ready to march toward the south.

Once they've got their backs to us, it is then that we charge. The Canish Guard, five hundred strong, a sound like thunder, we charge. Hooves beating against the barren, nuclear wasteland, we charge. Fighting for our land, fighting for our rights, fighting for our lives, we charge down the sloping land and quickly are upon them.

Cana Minor's soldiers close the space between the southern gate and the Regime's legions within minutes and meet them in battle at their front. Pressing them from both sides, we hack, cleave, and slice our way through cyborg soldier after cyborg soldier. The clang and clash of metal on metal fills the air as our weapons relentlessly find their mark.

Ramses is a vicious fighter. He takes out twice as many men as I do, and with the help of my exos, I take out twice as many soldiers as most of my peers. Shreya and I have the advantage, too, of our fusion-charged sickle swords. But no matter how well armed we are and how hard we trained, nothing prepared us for the gruesome brutality of the battlefield, of killing. Nothing prepared us for the carnage and the death. We fight on through the night and early morning, retiring in shifts inside the city gates, only to return again to the front lines after just a few hours of rest, knowing the battle will continue for days, perhaps weeks.

42

They come in droves, limitless waves of soldiers, crashing the shores of this strange twilight world. What was once our blue-and-green planet is now a black and charred hellscape. Seeing nothing and feeling nothing, they only know destruction.

For days, I ride out to battle. Our soldiers have been holding the line for more than a week now; the hours bleed together in one endless night. The cyborgs, they go on fighting without their heads for a little while—it is rarely a clean kill. I can't escape the haunting imagery of their thrashing carcasses in my waking and sleeping hours.

After fighting all day on the front line, I struggle to sleep. Some of us have taken to camping out together in the common area. Being together feels safer when you live in constant fear of a cyborg army breaking down the gates of your city at any given moment.

Xavier is asleep beside me. I stretch as I sit up from where I had been reclining on one of the low, soft couches. It's after 1:00 a.m., and everyone not out on night patrol or fighting in the midnight defense is fast asleep around me. A candle on a corner table is at the end of its wick. I slip off the couch carefully so as not to disturb anyone, pick up my boots off the floor, and tiptoe out of the room into the dimly lit corridor.

Ramses is on my heels like a silent assassin. Since I won't be marching in the first contingent tomorrow morning and will be missing the second for Taj's funeral tomorrow afternoon, I have decided to pursue a long-shot idea I've been debating over the last few days. As I step into my boots in the hallway, Xavier turns the corner, following me.

"Hey," he says in a low whisper so as not to disrupt the sleeping city in the quiet hours of the morning. "Where are you going?"

I glance back at him but continue down the corridor. "Nowhere. To my room."

"Well, which is it? Nowhere or your room?" he asks, impatient and keeping pace with me.

"I don't have any answers for you," I reply, shrugging.

He stops me outside of my door. "I hate that it's this way between us," he says. "You're so far away." I avert my eyes as he takes my hands in his. "Don't you remember how it used to be?"

"I was a child then," I say, holding his stare for a moment. "A naive one."

"Can you not just forgive me?"

"How am I supposed to forgive you," I ask in a short and measured tone, "when I don't know what it is I am forgiving you for?" I let my hands drop from his. "You won't tell me." I step back, away from him, and into the doorway of my rooms, leaning with my back up against the door.

"Can you just trust me that it doesn't matter?"

"Doesn't matter?" I say, suddenly angry. "What we had was sacred. You brushed it off for another life, and you can't even tell me why. No shred of understanding, no sliver of an explanation. Nothing to help me make sense of the last five years." I shake my head. "If you could just give me *something* to help me understand where your head was when you made that choice—when you defected, when you left— maybe I could try to get past it."

He stares back at me, wordless.

"Well?" I ask.

"Well, what?"

"Well, tell me! Why did you go? What did you do there? Who did you see?" I look at him expectantly. "And why didn't you stop Abramovich from burning our world?! You were there, on Proxima, before it all happened!"

"That is unfair," he says. "That much, I did not know about."

Sick of arguing, I turn to look for the door handle and push it open quietly so as not to wake Imani as she sleeps inside. I need to focus on something concrete, like winning this war, not something so gray like my feelings.

Xavier is still standing outside my door, arms crossed and feet planted.

"Look," I say, exasperated, "I'm going to Ephesia to send a message."

He opens his mouth as if to object but then thinks better of it. There's a tiredness in his eyes, a look of resignation.

"You're in the first assault tomorrow. You should get some sleep," I say. "Don't worry about me; I will have Ramses with me."

He leans his arm against the doorframe. "Fine. Hella, I know I can't stop you, but you should really try to take it easy. Get some rest tomorrow morning before the service. You have been burning the candle at both ends. I'm worried about you."

I smile at him but do not meet his eyes. "Thanks for the concern, but I'm fine." I step back through the door and say good night while shutting it behind me.

The front room is dark, save for a dim lantern. I tiptoe into my bedroom, grab a thick cloak, and summon Ramses. I then slip back into the quiet corridor and head to the front gates to make the trip to Ephesia.

Walking helps clear my head, and even though I'm exhausted, it also burns off some of the constant nervous energy that has been thrumming through me since the fighting began.

Two hours later, I reach Ephesia. When I pass through the common area near the amphitheater, I notice some people gathered around the screen. I ignore it, though I note that seeing people gather at this time of night is unusual. Then I slip into one of the small rooms off the main thoroughfare and sit before a console.

I first try reaching Josiah directly, but there is no answer. So I resort to writing him a message—a second message, actually. *It's odd, I think, that he still hasn't replied to the one I sent shortly after I arrived,* but then I brush it off.

I know that Joshua sent a message to the Alliance the night the battle started to notify them that we were going to war, but I also know he would not ask for help; likely wouldn't even share the coordinates, as protected as they have been all these years. But our location is no longer a secret, and we have been fighting for eight days and eight nights now. Our resources are dwindling, and the exhaustion among our troops is palpable. Smithy's shop runs twenty-four hours a day, and the man himself works all hours to keep us armed and mounted while the Regime's legions just seem to refresh endlessly. We have no idea how much longer they can go on, but we have a good sense of how much longer we can: without a break, a week or so—more at best. Our resources are finite, and we need help. So I urgently write to Josiah, stressing the criticality of the situation and asking if he thinks Dr. Freeman would be open to helping, to sparing a ship or two. I inquire about any progress he might have made in the last month building more FTL ships, and I promptly send him the coordinates to Cana.

As I exit the little room, I am starting to really feel the lack of sleep. Bleary-eyed, I pass the large screen that is still drawing a crowd when the image there catches my eye. I stop and do a double take. When I fully behold the screen, I see none other than myself, larger than life, speaking propaganda to Abramovich's cause—eloquently speaking words I've never actually said. Well, perhaps they are words I've said, but not strung together in the same sequence he has masterfully programmed on the TV screen using my voice.

It's a deepfake version of myself, but no one can see that but me. My hair is dark, like it was long ago on Proxima at the compound. He has used images of me and clips of my voice, downloaded them into a computer program, and produced an image and likeness identical to me in real life. He can make me say anything, and by the sound of it and the length at which I am speaking, it seems that he has.

Again, I'm blown away by how far this man will go to further his agenda. I feel a flash of anger at first, but after some thought, I realize I'm not really mad about it because it is a good cover. Cana Minor may not know I'm here or believe I'm truly here on Earth, in Cana City, if they think I'm talking on that screen. And the last thing I need is to be taken into custody by radicals and locked up in some nunnery while this war is still raging. I tuck my hood tighter over my head and turn away as Ramses and I begin the hike back to Cana City.

We arrive home at around six in the morning. I throw off my cloak, kick off my boots, and crash down onto the bed just before I hear the pounding of hooves sound above as the first unit of the day leaves for the morning. As I lean back on the soft bedding, Ramses snuggles up under my arm, and exhaustion for once wins over insomnia as I finally fall into a much-needed, deep sleep.

I dream it's all green again. I dream there is no ashen wasteland, no cyborg soldiers, no more death—only light, love, and peace. As my eyes flutter open, I feel overwhelming sadness well up inside of me as our beautiful world slips away from my grasp.

Checking the clock, I see that it's nearly noon and recall that Taj's funeral is today. Taking a deep breath, I try hard to bury yet another painful truth I've been avoiding these past few days.

Xavier and some of the others should be back from the battlefield in time to attend the service at 2:00 p.m. I recoil at the memory of our argument last night, and even though I am angry with him, I wish he was here with me now. I thought if I could finally get some sleep, it would make me feel better, refreshed even, but it has had no such effect.

My limbs feel like lead as I climb out of bed. Imani has laid out a long black dress with a cross necklace for me to wear today. I bathe and dress slowly as if in a trance, getting lost in the mirror. Staring blankly, I slowly brush my hair with pedantic attention to detail. I then line my eyes with dark, synthetic coal, as is the custom of our people when we are in mourning.

Ramses is getting his teeth plated with graphene today since it is our day off. His steel fangs aren't holding up so well after the days of carnage. I walk him down to Smithy's workshop before meeting Imani for the service.

Smithy presents me with a new helm, a sleeker, fitted one that will be easier to maneuver in. He also gives me a small handgun that is a prototype of the micro-crystal laser weapon used on Titan by Chiron's soldiers. In Earth's atmosphere, they are only good for one use and take a good deal of power to charge up. "Only really to be used for emergencies," he reminds me.

After bidding Smithy and Ramses goodbye for the afternoon, I stow both new acquisitions in my arms locker. They get along quite famously, so I won't need to worry about Ramses suffering from any version, mechanical or not, of separation anxiety. Me, on the other hand, I am a different story. I'm already teary and missing my shadow as I pass by the river and take the lift back up to meet Imani.

We arrive at the little chapel before any of the other guests. Beneath the altar is a hologram of Taj's body laid out in an ornate casket that was unearthed from the storage rooms. We approach solemnly, as I was raised to show the utmost reverence for our dead. I reach out to touch him, but my hand passes clear through his arm, his face, his cheek. His holographic body is just an image created so that Imani could see him again one last time. The program, an iteration lacking animation and tactility, is not as sophisticated as the one Abramovich wrote to bring Gemma back to life.

Dropping to our knees, we pray fervently for the safe passing and repose of his soul. After a while, we stand up and walk slowly around the small sanctuary. Deep in thought, Imani speaks after some time.

"The Institution was so massive in size, power, and wealth; it was so formidable, I understand how Taj might have believed or might have been persuaded to believe that less drastic matters would be ineffective against such an opponent." She looks around the still-empty room before continuing. "And I understand the war in his heart: a duty to protect Cana once and for all and a fatalistic hopelessness about the future. The two combined would put an individual in a terribly desperate place, an impressionable place . . ." She looks sad and lost, and maybe even a little skeptical, as she trails off, but then at once forthright and resolute, she finishes, "No, his heart is good, Helly. Was always good. He was just misguided."

I hug her and hold her tightly, recognizing my own feelings in her conflicted heart. We stay this way for a few moments as people begin to arrive and take their seats. As the seats fill, we sit down in the front row. I notice Xavier file in behind Tristan and Yash and can feel his eyes seeking mine. Folding my hands neatly across my lap, I look straight ahead, focusing my attention on the crucifix behind the altar.

Most would not cry for him. The Alliance surely would not, and most here show grim faces, remaining tight-lipped with averted eyes. Most here blame Taj, and perhaps rightfully. But it didn't change my feelings for him, for that love, the love between a brother and sister, had turned out to be unconditional—on my side, at least. Whether I liked it or not, whether what he had done was right or wrong—whether he was a good or a bad man—or if my choice to support him was a popular one with the people, *my love did not falter.*

And maybe that made me a fool. Maybe that made me wrong. *Maybe* they took pity on me and saw me as no better than a beaten dog. For God knows there were more days he was unkind than good to me. More days he was indifferent or even cruel than when he was the brother I knew him to be, the man I knew he could be, the man I believed he one day would become.

I bite my lip, choking back tears—I cannot get a breath. I hadn't wanted to give up on him. But life, as it so often did, had left me with no choice.

The officiant speaks briefly: Nothing incredibly personal, mainly the words of old ritual. I barely listen, the sound flooding my ears like methodical chanting. It is familiar yet repetitive and starts to grate on my naked nerves. Finally, the man finishes speaking, and music begins to play quietly as we observe a few minutes of silence.

I feel restless and confined, and my anxiety mounts to an unmanageable place. I get up from my seat and throw the prayer book as hard as I can against the back wall of the chapel. People shift in their seats and clear their throats uncomfortably. I turn and pace for a few moments, fingering the wooden cross pendant Imani gave me this morning, then return silently to my seat, clasping my hands together tightly in my lap.

Imani puts her hand lightly on my back as my breathing quickens, coming out in short, quick gasps that begin to mount uncontrollably, my chest rising and falling in sync. Overcome with all that I have been suppressing, all with which I have been wrestling, I cannot slow it down.

Imani then takes my hands tightly in hers as if giving me permission to let go. So I tip my head back and I sob, choked and quiet at first. But then, at long last, I face it. I look beneath the bandage. I examine the wound, bloody and gaping. I look at the truth, and like a cold shooting star across the expanse of a lonely night sky, the reality of his death hits me like a brick, and I let go. Imani joins me, and we keen, we grieve, we weep.

43

On top of the bed covers, still in my dress, I sleep the entire afternoon. Upon waking, I blink several times to moisten my eyes. My room is silent and dark, save for the light of a small lantern on the table in the foyer. When I shift onto my side, my stomach tightens, and unbearable thoughts begin to resurface.

I sit up quickly to distract myself. My feet find the floor, bare against the worn, woven rug that doesn't do much to warm the cold rock underneath. I run a hand through my mess of hair and then find again the cross around my neck. Removing it, I place it on the dresser and then glance at the time. Everyone will be at dinner now. But instead of joining them, I slip on my boots and head back down to the chapel.

Ducking inside the silent sanctuary, I see that candles still flicker around the altar, their holographic flames left to burn indefinitely. The casket is still here, too, sitting at the foot of the altar. It will be kept in place for three days so that those who were fighting on the front lines at the time of the service will have the opportunity to pay their respects should they wish to do so. However, it was a small crowd at the service today, and I don't expect many others to come through after hours.

Walking slowly down the aisle toward the back of the chapel, I look for the book I had thrown. Spotting it on the floor behind an empty pew, I stoop to pick it up and then walk back up the aisle to return it where it belongs, shelved in the little annex behind the altar. The space is small and dark, and there is a table with a basin, a carafe of water, books, and linens. A nearly imperceptible movement of air causes the candles to flicker—likely a draft coming from one of the ventilation shafts connecting through here to circulate purified air from above. The disturbed flame momentarily illuminates the back wall, revealing Greek inscriptions.

Picking up one of the small candles, I turn around and face the wall. Running my hand across the carvings, I wonder what they say. Could there be any wisdom in these ancient words that can help me? Silently, I beg the small symbols to speak enlightenment to me from another time, to open a window in my mind and help me find a place of peace, a place where any of the things that have happened in my life—to me and to my people—bear any meaning.

As I set the candle down on the ledge behind me, another draft of cool air grazes over my skin. I don't feel any better. Biting my lip, I close my eyes as I turn around and lean back against the cold rock as if I could absorb some ancient magic, knowledge, or transcendence from these walls, these words. Flushes of despair wash over me as I feel that there is no place that I can get to where I can escape this suffocating sadness. Folding my arms across my chest, I shiver as goose bumps bloom on my bare skin, but I don't care anymore about feeling cold. I don't care anymore about fighting for anything, about trying. *The bad news just keeps coming, and we are just expected to sit down and take it?* I implore again in vain to the nameless, faceless great beyond.

A flicker of anger rises in me but then is immediately shut down by the pervasive finality of my own helplessness—humanity's helplessness in the totality of the vast, apathetic universe. My hands run idly across the inscriptions for some time, following the indecipherable patterns as tears leak out again, and I cry quietly. My finger traces what feels like an infinity symbol—a figure eight turned sideways—and then I sink to the ground. Tired again. Tired all the time of the constant struggle of this life.

Hugging my knees to my chest, I feel the draft again and realize it's coming from directly in front of me. Leaning forward, I peer at the wall beneath the table, finding the candle again to examine it more closely. There is a crack between where the floor and the wall meet, and as I place my hand above it, I can feel that it is the source of the cool gust of air I felt before. It's almost as if the space behind the altar is hollow.

Placing the candle next to me on the floor, I take both hands and push firmly on the panel. To my surprise, it dislodges, moving forward to reveal a passageway that appears to be accessible through a small trap door. Beyond the passageway, I can see the top of a stairwell. Something compels me to climb through.

Beneath the chapel, below the storage rooms, past the horse stables, and even deeper than the old dungeons, I descend as if in a dream. With only the small holo-candle to illuminate my path, I count the stories as the steps wind down. A layer of undisturbed dust covers everything, suggesting that this underground passage has remained vacant for some time.

Eventually, I reach a landing. The landing leads to a tunnel, and at the end of the tunnel, I find a warren of old storage rooms. The rooms contain mostly empty crates and old pottery. When I reach the last room at the end of the corridor, above another set of stairs, I am faced with a carved wooden door. The door is similar to the others but is more ornate and better preserved. When I examine it more closely, I find it is reinforced with steel.

Tentatively, I push the heavy door open and shine the light of my candle inside. The light reveals a wall of books. Stepping farther into the room, I find that there are not only old books here, bound with leather and made with paper, but also old scrolls made of parchment leaves and papyrus that must date back to the age of the Founders—an old library.

Noticing a desk in the corner, I cross the room and walk around behind it. Setting the candle down, I find a large scroll spread across the top. The corners are fixed with weights, and as I scan the parchment, it becomes apparent I am looking at a map. I spend a few minutes studying it, and though it is not written in a language I'm familiar with, I am able to orient myself and see exactly where I stand now relative to where I exited the chapel earlier.

Then I gasp. What I have stumbled upon appears to be not only a secret passageway deep beneath the known underground but also a way out of the city itself. The existence of this exit, which is not documented on any of our maps, is currently unknown to my people but could prove to be incredibly valuable intel, depending on where it leads. If I could vet it properly, it might allow my people to breathe, if just a little bit, as things continue to escalate on the surface.

As the cyborgs relentlessly advance, our strength and resources steadily deplete. It's no longer a matter of if Malakye and his army will breach the city walls, but when. And when they do, with no escape other than the front gates, it will mean complete annihilation for my people. We've had no backup plan, nowhere to run or hide—until now. Now we have the possibility of an exit strategy. It's not clear to me precisely where the passage leads in the greater underground, but I intend to find out.

I spend the next half hour studying the map and am able to ascertain that the stairs and tunnel beyond this room continue for about two miles and then fork in two directions. Exiting to the right leads directly to the neutral zone, and beyond that is the dreaded KAU City—which doesn't help us much.

However, the path forking to the left goes on quite a bit farther. The distance isn't to scale, but from what I can deduce from the legend, it looks like a few days' journey. This path has more potential but leads to a part of the subterranean that is wholly unknown to our people. All that is indicated to occupy this territory is a large sphere with indiscernible script noted beneath it. I can't solve the riddle of the mysterious place, but just that there is another option is enough for me—another place to seek shelter from the unrelenting pursuit of the Regime.

After hunching over the map for some time, I sit up straight to stretch. When my gaze settles on the wall of books, a glint of gold catches my eye. Blinking a few times, I try to make out the source of the sparkle, then walk over to the wall to investigate.

Scanning the shelves, I spot an ivory box inlaid with gold and covered in intricate carvings. The ivory was likely once creamy white but is now more of a yellowish hue. When I lift the lid carefully, I discover the artifact is filled with gold and silver pieces and a variety of old jewelry—treasure of the Old World. These rare metals and stones were once of great value on our planet and perhaps still are in the inner solar system. But here in the underground, the currency is likely of little value in comparison with clean air and water, healthy organs, and fertility. The people of modern Earth trade in credits, which are tied back to goods and services directly connected to survival. As beautiful as these jewels are, they are of little use in our new world. Nonetheless, I pocket a few gold coins, leaving behind a loose emerald, a sapphire, several rubies, and a jade ring. Tucking the little box back in its place, I leave it to rest undisturbed for another couple of hundred years.

Returning to the desk, I give the mysterious map one last look. It's not something I can easily reference while on the move, so I spend a few minutes trying to memorize the images to ensure I can find my way back to the chapel. As I focus, a familiar symbol catches my eye. Tracing my finger along the map, I start from the symbol, which resembles a two-barred cross. Following the path back to my current location, I discover that the symbol sits in the heart of KAU City, beyond the neutral zone, almost clear through to Malakye's domain.

I think for a moment and then look back at the symbol—now I know where I recognize it from. It's the location indicated on the scrap of note that the vagrant child gave me in the neutral zone after our close call that day in the city, just before the war broke out. A message from someone claiming to have information on Gemma.

The double-barred cross must represent some sort of landmark. *How long would it take me to get there?* I wonder to myself. I know I shouldn't go. Not now, not while we are in the midst of war, but I wonder if I would have time.

I do the math. It's probably around 8:00 p.m. now. Following the tunnel, I could get to the neutral zone in an hour, maybe; KAU City in another quarter of an hour. If I hustled, I could be back in bed by midnight and fill Joshua in on my discovery first thing in the morning.

I pause for a moment. Had I thought this through? I don't have Ramses with me, which is not ideal, but I do have my jagdagger tucked discreetly inside my boot. My eyes are tinted brown, and my hair is still dyed a flame color. Neither trait is one typically associated with Canish women—at least I have that going for me. The kohl around my eyes and my black dress, a symbol of grief and loss for my people during mourning, could possibly identify me as Canish. But I could easily pick up a cloak once I hit the neutral zone. I would be taking a risk, and Joshua would be livid with me. But we are in such dire straits with the war and the Regime bearing down on us, I find myself feeling like I don't have all that much to lose anymore. Gemma was single-handedly responsible for my escape, our cavalry, and so much more. I just can't shake the need to follow through with this. The allure is too great—she has become a beacon of hope in the night of my life, and I find myself unable to ignore her call.

After transferring a small section of the map to a scrap of paper using an ancient writing tool found in the desk, I leave the scroll behind. I decide I will pick it up on my way back, and then I hit the road with new vigor.

The suffocating burden of war and the loss of Taj had been weighing heavily on me during the preceding weeks. The revelation about Xavier's feelings for me, or more specifically, where they fell short, compounded my grief. And somewhere across the universe, across realms of time—perhaps in that place I had been once, twice, with obsidian walls—I find myself dissolving. When I cannot do more, my being lies prostrate and paralyzed in a pool of nothingness, and my pain spills out of a black place in my chest, dissipating into the ether. On the other side, the other side of breaking, I find myself *awakened* and in a strange place of apathy. In this place, it doesn't feel good, but it also doesn't feel quite so bad.

A strange power, I discover in my apathy as I follow the map and walk the path to the place marked by the double-barred cross to meet the mysterious stranger claiming to have knowledge about Gemma. It is too easy to take this risk, and every step deeper into the neutral zone emboldens me further. I do not have my device to barter with credit, but the first vendor I encounter takes my gold easily for a cloak, and it isn't long before I am crossing into the city itself.

KAU City is a vile place, I think as I pass by a group of five soldiers. There was a time when I used to think of all the ways men such as these could gang up on me, overpower me, or kill me. But now I find I am more preoccupied with all the ways in which I could take them out. One by one, I debate the optimal method and sequencing to accomplish the task in the most efficient and orderly way, dispositioning each man appropriately based on their perceived strengths and weaknesses. If they would just dare to look at me wrong, or even look at me, *period* . . . Part of me is just begging to be invited in, for any reason, to cut them down to the studs. But I am not without self-control, not without empathy, and thus, let them pass unharmed, unmolested, unintimidated.

After some time, I start to feel a certain kinship with the weary faces of the civilians I repeatedly encounter. I recognize what their vacant eyes and grimacing faces betray: We are all kindred in this sweet world of suffering. We are all united in our struggle against the one cruel and unrelenting pain of living.

I can be found here on Tuesdays to trade, the note said. Well, it's Tuesday. All the more reason to be there tonight. Who knows if I will have another chance. In seven days, the war may be done, the battle decided. It's late, but the markets run all night.

Almost to the meeting point, I pass a small tavern stall. I duck inside to use the washroom, which isn't much more than a wooden plank with a hole behind a curtain.

Exiting the area, I round the corner to the bar proper. My hood has fallen to reveal my hair, and a man at the end of the bar looks up as the flash of red catches his eye. I start to look away but find that I cannot. I study the planes of his face, and my breath hitches when I take in his crystal-blue eyes. *It's striking,* I think, *how much he looks like Xavier; his build, his hair, his jaw—yet not Xavier.*

The man does not break my stare as I continue walking toward him. I reach the door and, in a fleeting, split-second decision, rather than exiting the saloon as I intended, I turn and walk right up to him and take a seat.

I can't say what passed through my mind in that split second when I made the choice to sit next to that man, but it was something like rebellion stirring in me. It was an urge, a need to prove to the great wide open the extent of my outrage, the depth of my suffering, and what better way to do that than through the audacity born of my newfound apathy?

I can feel his unbreaking stare. His attention washes over me, oily and effervescent, as I look straight ahead and signal across the tavern. The barkeep approaches after I drop a few gold coins on the dirty bar top in front of me. "What he's having," I say, motioning toward the man beside me.

The barkeep fingers the gold pieces and gives me an assessing, suspicious look but eventually nods and turns to get my drink. I turn to face the man next to me, look him directly in the eye, and ask, "What *are* you drinking?"

"Green elixir," he replies. "An anesthetic."

I nod, unimpressed.

"These bars are filled with things that kill," he adds, half-bored, half-smirking.

"Oh? Then why come here?" I ask distractedly as the barkeep returns with my beverage.

"We're all here for the same reason."

To feel anything other than what has become of our wretched lives, I suppose is the reason he is inferring. I shrug, vaguely amused, and look down at the elixir I have been served. *This stuff numbs you. They want you to give in. They want you to give up,* a voice rings in my head.

"Not worried about the things that kill, then?" I ask, frowning ironically. Looking down again, I become mesmerized by the carbon dioxide fizzing in my drink.

"Actually, I'm not so sure, now that you walked in," he remarks, his smirk gradually fading. Somewhere distantly in the back of my mind, I decide this is an odd thing for him to say. The world begins to dance a little—the crude lights, twinkling now, the voices around me fading in and out.

"You're worried," I say between gulps, "about me?" I turn, looking around the bar and laughing overzealously. "Now *that's* funny."

"Not that funny, really," he says, becoming more serious. "I've seen what you do . . . on the battlefield, on your mount, with that beast in tow."

My mouth goes dry, and I suddenly feel nauseous as I am hit with the whole meaning of what he has just said. *How could he have seen me on the surface?* No one from Cana is permitted to travel here, and he clearly isn't a cyborg soldier.

"Oh, I've seen you," he says, replying directly to my unspoken question. "Seen you slaughter." He looks down at his drink, the neon-green liquid still three-quarters of the way to the brim. Tracing the lip of the glass with his finger, he finishes, "A dozen kills, a dozen heads, in one cool morning."

"That's impossible," I say in barely a whisper, struggling to hold the thought in my head.

"Where's your beast tonight?" he asks in a drawl, facing me again.

I stare at him dumbfounded, unable to think or speak. He stares at me right back, and when I try to get up, he is up with me twice as fast. I stumble back against the wall, and he catches me.

"Don't touch me!" I yelp, but his hands lock tightly around my biceps, and then one hand clamps over my mouth as he restrains me against the wall. I then manage to wriggle one arm free, and within nanoseconds, my dagger is in my hand.

Holding the knife tightly in my fist, I bring it up and thrust it down on him in a hammer strike, as I have lost the ability, I find, to do anything more than this, to do anything really with much dexterity or precision. I then try to lift my knee, to drive it upward into his groin with enough force to paralyze him momentarily—enough so that I can slip out of his grasp and make a break for it—but I find I am too unstable on my feet to follow through with the motion.

He easily dodges my stroke, and the knife slips out of my hand, clanging to the floor. I am horrified by how slow and weak I have become as I lose my balance again and fall backward against the wall.

The last thing I see is the barkeep's dead eyes watching me crumble, taking it all in and not giving a damn if I live, die, or burst into flames—and the world around me fades to black.

<h1 style="text-align:center">44</h1>

I find myself on a jeweled ocean. The water is sparkling, and the expanse of sky overhead is midnight blue and twinkling with diamond fire. The waves are warm and buttery as I sink beneath the surface and begin to swim. With long, powerful strokes, I swim through tranquil waters for miles and miles without tiring. I glide through endless white-capped seas, confined by no measure of hours.

Along the way, I encounter a swirling eddy with a powerful drift that drags me into a massive ocean gyre. I spiral endlessly around the circumference of the vortex before I am at last swallowed whole by the currents.

Abruptly, my surroundings morph completely, and I'm with the young girl again, in the snow and pine of a mountain forest. We met before, in a vision, a momentary flash—an inconsequential thing, I thought—back on Proxima. On the false mountaintop with Abramovich, at the height of his charade, the world had fallen away, and I had found myself in an ivy-covered enclave. She was down below in the woods carrying firewood, next to a stream.

She smiles when she sees me and then looks at my feet. I look down, and there is a yellow rose placed over each foot. I wear a white robe with a blue sash around my waist. She motions for me to follow her through the forest, along the stream, eventually waving me on through another portal. The portal, a tear in the fabric of time, winks open as I approach. I float through and begin climbing up a hill to an olive grove.

In the distance, I see a figure kneeling in a small garden. The man is praying silently but vehemently. As I approach, he looks up, and his face carries the long-lost familiarity of a thousand lifetimes come and gone. And there is one emotion that burns wild in his clear eyes, and it is *despair*.

Then the world around me begins to again fade from my grasp— then nothing.

Everything hurts. My wrists are bound, and I am being pulled on a wooden cart. Strong hands grip underneath my arms and drag me off the cart. As I fully come to, I squint, struggling to see my surroundings, but the world is a blur. I feel overwhelmingly weak and on the verge of being sick. The hood of my cloak is low over my face, and my hair has been tied back and tucked underneath it. I try to gain my footing but can't keep up with my assailant, who is dragging me brusquely across the dirt floor.

"Easy," a low female voice says as I struggle. A few more feet, and she hoists me toward what appears to be the back of a cave or the dead end of a tunnel. "There," she says as she releases her grip.

I scramble backward into the corner and look around the small, dark alcove. Trying to brush away the strands of hair that have fallen loose from my braid, I lift my bound wrists up to my forehead when nausea starts to overtake me, and I begin gagging.

The woman returns. Rounding the corner, she pulls a canteen out of a small pack and holds it to my lips. I drink the cool water readily.

"What happened?" I ask, studying her face. She looks familiar, but I can't quite place her.

"He's an empath," she says sharply. "Glamoured you." Taking a swig from the canteen herself, she then screws the cap back on, wiping her mouth with her hand.

The conversation with the man in the bar starts to come back to me, and as it does, I feel panicked as I recall what he said to me. "He said he kn-kn-knew me," I stutter. "How could he possibly . . ."

"He doesn't know you. He read images off your subconscious," she says simply as she stuffs the canteen back into the pack and tosses it to the ground.

Struggling uncomfortably against the bindings on my wrists and ankles, I change positions, resting my head against the cave wall. The rock is cool against my cheek. I try to process what she has just explained, but my head is still spinning from the green elixir I drank at the bar.

"An empath?" I ask, baffled. Still having trouble holding thoughts in my head, I ask, "Did he even look like Xavier?"

"No," she says, shaking her head and looking down at a device in her hands. Tucking it in the back pocket of her pants, she then looks up again. My stomach tenses, and I flinch away from her as she starts to untie me.

"So, you've come from the Alliance, eh?" she asks, amused as she wrangles the ropes to allow a little more movement but not free me completely. Her voice is raspy as she speaks. "My father decorated that horrendous foyer for me outside his office, as if that could make me stay."

I stare at her, speechless, as her words sink in, immediately placing her identity.

"He only did it to spy on me," she continues as the ropes around my ankles slacken and fall loosely to the ground.

"What are you doing *here*?" I ask, hazy still from whatever knocked me unconscious and shocked to be face-to-face with her, Cassini Freeman, here on Earth, of all places. And she was so ungrateful. It strikes a defensive chord in me for Dr. Freeman—after all he has done for her.

"Getting paid," she says, straightening as she stands. "I've been coming here for years. He pays in the gold of a dead kingdom."

He. I think to myself, *Surely, she doesn't mean?* But who else could pay her enough to bother with this wasted planet, if not—the sinister truth dawns on me—*Malakye.*

My stomach roils as Cassini steps back, satisfied with her work, and faces me squarely with her hands on her hips. "The better question is, what are you doing in the underbelly of KAU City when at least three separate entities have a price on your head?"

I look away, irritated, but mostly with myself because I know she's right. "I can handle myself," I say too quietly, annoyed even further by how weak my voice sounds.

"You're a fool." She settles back against the opposing wall. "That man was about to take things from you that take a lifetime to get back."

"I have nothing left for him to take," I say, the emptiness I've been feeling over the last weeks all but caving in on me.

"Well, just looking at you, I'd wager you have at least twelve functioning organs, but I don't mean tangible things," Cassini scoffs, not buying my innocent act. "I mean things you take for granted because you didn't realize you were lucky enough to have them in the first place. Things like sanity, peace . . . your youth, and innocence." She snorts.

I stare back at her blankly, unwilling to give in and admit I'm wrong.

"How can you be so naive?" She looks at me briefly, then away, as if it's hard for her to look at me for too long. "I'm making a lot of money off you," she says, changing the subject. "Just tell him what he wants to know, and he will release you, won't hurt you—not in the way that scumbag was about to."

"*Who* won't hurt me?" I ask as a wave of fear suddenly washes over me. My head has cleared enough now to begin to worry about what might happen to me beyond this moment. "Where are you taking me?"

Cassini ignores my questions as she continues her lecture. "Do you think rebelling like this gets you anywhere—running away, pounding your fists? Taking risks, falling apart?" Her rhetorical question hangs in the empty air between us. "It helps nothing and no one."

"*Who?*" I demand. "Who are you taking me to?"

"And I'm pretty sure you've already wasted half this lifetime in cryo-sleep." She smirks, again not responding to my question.

Fine, I think. I can play at this game, too. "*This* lifetime?" I ask, pretending it's not precious to me. "Pretty attached to it, are you?" I taunt.

"If one is not careful and is too long in cryo-sleep . . ." More lecturing. "Life, as it was once known, becomes obsolete, irrelevant, and must begin again." She sighs. "One must start over from scratch—I suppose there are some that might find value in that. But I know you're not that far gone, Hella. Children of Cana are too resilient for all that." She again smirks, again mocks me. "There's merit . . ." A pause. "In the mastery of an age, of a time."

Cassini looks at me as if putting a challenge to me, as if simply placing it on a table between us. As if such a thing was up for grabs, ripe for the taking, for anyone who may deign to try. *The mastery . . . of a time.* It was preposterous.

"Always playing the long game, are you?" I ask, calling a spade a spade but not stopping her, egging her on just enough to see what she may reveal. Make the most of this miserable turn of events. She is accustomed to playing her hand close to her chest. Still, she's letting her guard down here with me, if only a smidgen, giving me a glimpse inside her mind; genius or madness, I haven't entirely decided. But I can glean . . . that Cassini wants to build an empire—or more than that, more than wanting, she perhaps *is* building an empire.

"Good. You're catching on," she says insincerely.

"So Chiron didn't break you, then?" I ask flippantly.

She snorts. "Chiron didn't break me. *I broke Chiron.*" Cassini is quiet for some time as if lost in thought or a memory. "'You are not a man,' they'd say. 'You cannot be a man.'" She sneers. "'*Stop* trying to be a man.'" She huffs as if recollecting some specific encounter, her hips propped against the wall, arms across her chest, looking off into space. Then exhaling gruffly, she blows a strand of hair out of her eyes. "Well, I am a *man* now," she says, turning directly to me and raising an eyebrow as if again inviting a challenge. "And they cower under my iron fist," she finishes through gritted teeth. Her mouth then spreads into a smug smile as she uncrosses her arms to pound the rock wall behind her.

Leaning forward to stand upright, Cassini starts pacing, wired and unsettled. "I run circles around them. Get done three times what they do while they sleep, drink, and get fat from their lust and gluttony." She huffs a breath again and looks pensive as I become increasingly nervous about what we are doing here, about who or what we are waiting for.

She says, "My soldiers are just coming of age. There's a planet in the outer reach. The gravity is strong. A planet I seeded with human embryos . . . legions of men groomed for battle with bones and strength born to withstand three times the gravity of this miserable planet."

Just then, a noise sounds at the door, and a vagrant wanders around the corner. She draws a weapon and puts him down with a taser before he can even open his mouth to beg for a coin.

"Well, if they aren't dying of nuclear death, they are dying *like* nuclear death with all the factories gone," she remarks, unmoved as she drags the unconscious man around the corner. She clearly has no empathy for this place or its people.

Cassini settles back against the opposing wall, but this time sinks to the floor, knees to her chest. "We are in the grip of the *beast*," she muses.

"Oh yeah? Didn't take you for a believer in mythical things, horned creatures, and the like."

She laughs lightly. "I do not speak of any devil, real or imagined, but a crueler beast—*humanity*."

"You're starting to sound like Abramovich," I remark. She looks at me inquisitively at first but then takes my meaning and shakes her head.

"I don't mean we are all dark sinners who must atone or die in a nuclear apocalypse for our sins." Cassini pauses. "Well, maybe some of us do." She waves her hand toward where the man she rescued me from was presumably located. "I am merely describing what it is to be alive, to be human. We are all in the same unrelenting grip of existence, fighting to survive this life and one another. To be *in the grip of the beast . . . is life*."

Cassini went on like this for most of the night as we waited to meet her connection. She eventually handed me off to a squad of cyborg soldiers. When she left, I asked her where she was going. She turned on her heel, looked back at me as she pulled up the hood of her cloak, smirked, and replied, "Titan, of course."

Her assassin had failed to capture me in the launch bay when I departed Titan all those weeks ago, so Cassini had made the trip to Earth to get the job done herself: to capture me and collect payment from Malakye. This she had done only after securing Chiron's occupation of the mines on Titan, of course. I can't imagine how high the price on my head must be for it to be worth her while, but then, Chiron was known to trade heavily on the black market, so perhaps this wasn't an unusual trip for her to make.

But I still can't believe she sold me to him—to the Regime, to Malakye. Cassini rescued me from one evil only to turn me over to another. Part of me hated her for it, but there was also a part of me that was awestruck—mesmerized—by the way she spoke, the way she dreamed. She saw the world in a way I had never considered. She had conceived of a seed planet, raised an army of super-strong soldiers bred in high gravity. The way she dared to dream, claim, and take what she wanted, as if it was easy, as if it had always been hers . . . I couldn't stop thinking about it; I couldn't stop thinking about all that she said. Was it just a madman's distortion, or was it the clarity of a higher mind?

45

Malakye's men hustled me through the underground to the very epicenter of KAU City, to the Regime's central command and Malakye's barracks. In chains, they dragged me deeper and deeper beneath the city, beneath the bunkers of what was once the Ascendency and, ultimately, to Malakye's dungeons.

It took all night and through the early morning to reach our destination. I was wired with fear that came and went in waves all night long, rising and falling in regular intervals. I was shaking like a leaf, cold and exhausted as we traveled deeper into the heart of his kingdom.

Not too long after we arrive, Malakye's lieutenants lead me by my neck into a large arena. Surrounded by a massive audience of soldiers, they throw me onto the cold dirt floor, in the dead center of it all, under a spotlight as if on trial. The crowd wails, taunting me, as I am finally released from my chains.

Malakye is absent for a quarter of an hour as I, a spectacle, endure the scrutiny and unrelenting harassment of the crowd. Eventually, he makes his appearance, entering the arena, walking at a slow, measured pace. His hands folded behind his back, he makes wide circles around me, closing in, closer and closer, as if I am his prey. I think I will explode with fear, with anticipation, and can barely stop the scream rising in my throat when he finally pauses immediately in front of me.

I can feel the enigmatic power of his demon gaze assessing me as I sit on the floor, cowering like a trapped animal. I can feel his stare and the eyes of every face in the crowd bearing down on me, and so I breathe deliberately. I breathe deeply. One, two, three, four, counts out; one, two, three, four counts in. I do this methodically for five breaths, and then I bite my lip, gain my composure, and summon all my pain and all my rage. Snapping my head up, I look him directly in the eye and, empowered by the fury of an entire nation, I speak.

"What has become of your gilded Institution and all its wealth and power, Malakye? Could it be true that it has all been reduced to rubble?" I demand, jumping to my feet.

The crowd hushes. I meet his eyes and behold the utter shock that lives there. It is shock rendered by the audacity of my question, shock that he masks quickly in an effort to regain his control, his composure.

He prowls around me, and I prowl around him before he finally speaks in reply. "It has evolved into a greater thing, or had you not heard, Hella of Cana? Imprisoned, were you? Booted against your will beyond the outskirts of the solar system and *stranded* at the hand of your dear brother—or rather, your *late* brother, is it? So *sorry* for your loss.

"Well, while you were sleeping, we, the Institution, gilded or not, have become quite a different thing entirely. An entity of quite a different dimension." He looks around and asks the people, "Have we not?"

Malakye pauses and paces, pensive while all present hang in silence on his every word. When he speaks again, he shakes his head. "I find it funny—no, it entertains me: The people of Cana revere Hella . . . a god." He laughs and gestures, permitting the people to laugh, too. They roar in unison.

I stop, put my hands on my hips, unbound now, and retort, "I do not pretend to be what they say. Do you habitually pay heed to the words of madmen such as Mordecai Abramovich?"

"Quiet!" Malakye yells, unbridled rage escaping him at the mere mention of Abramovich. He prowls closer before continuing. "Your Mary and Jesus Christ are no more than mythic creatures from the annals of a weaker race, the desperate fantasy of another time. A story dreamed up by a people so desperate to find meaning and purpose in their inconsequential blip on our great time line, they would befoul history to achieve their ends." He shakes his head. "No more than masses of menial laborers laying bricks for the power to come—rudimentary beasts in comparison!" he hisses eloquently. "*We are gods in our own right and take our throne freely, of our own will.*"

I stare back at him, unimpressed, although, I admit that even in my darkest hour, his crass blasphemy ignites rage in me. Even if it is Imani's god and not necessarily mine he disparages.

"Do you know what it's like to die of genetic breakdown?" Malakye asks. "It's not for the faint of heart. Rather a gruesome tale I've to tell if you can stomach it. Ever watched your own arm rot off, or how about your mother's face? Hmm? The sheer carnage is unimaginable," he says, breathless and dramatic.

"Can't say I was ever very close to Konstantin," I reply. "I'm finding it hard to relate."

"Well, regardless, you get the picture. Only when I watched my son's eyes . . ."

I cut him off. "*Your* son, is it? How exactly was the child conceived? Because I'm wondering, if Gemma Abramovich," I die a little on the inside at the mere mention of her name, the reality of her human demise facing me squarely, "was one of the first to seed your people's atrocious factories, it seems your son might not actually be *your* son at all, but one of Abramovich's line, rather?"

"Silence," he snarls, enraged.

I look around the room. "Am I right?" I ask the people. Some boo, some cheer, some burst into fits of maniacal laughter.

Malakye removes a glove, revealing a pale, flesh hand, and then backhands me. I see stars, and my ears ring as I stumble backward nearly off my feet. But these days, I am quicker than that. He describes to his people how he wanted to *feel* the hit with his flesh hand before barking, "Guards," to his lieutenants.

"You're nothing without Cana," I spit as I am roughly grabbed from behind.

"Take her away. To the hole!"

Somewhere beyond the arena, deep within the dungeons, Malakye has me by the neck of my dress, holding me at the edge of what I imagine to be the hole he referred to earlier. I do not look down. For I know if I do, I will be inviting fear in. Instead, I focus on his eyes; they have the look of pure onyx. I refuse to break my gaze, finding strength in the meditative state brought about by the intention and measure of my laser focus.

Finally, he releases me, turns around, and begins to pace. I stumble but retain my footing and dare not move an inch.

Looking down, hands folded neatly behind his back, Malakye strides up and back in front of his dozen or so lieutenants standing at attention against the back wall of the annular cave-like room surrounding the hole. Stopping abruptly, he brushes his chin thoughtfully before addressing me.

I look back at him, my face a mask, unreadable. He then speaks.

"I see visions. A ghost of myself made up of my dead human pieces who asks why I insist on clinging to *this* purgatory? 'Why do you linger, twin of thyself?' it asks. And I find the call alluring at times, Hella, to leave this all behind.

"Do you understand? All this suffering that humans endure? But then the more I win, the less I feel, and the less *this* ails me." He extends his arm and looks around blankly. "Suffering—it is all humans know. So I push that voice aside, and I suffocate it with the power I have found here in this new regime, this *power* we have wrought with our own Earthly hands.

"I invite you, too, to leave it all behind, Hella. Join me. Rule on high, by my side. A union of equals, I offer. Cana will surely follow you."

A long silence falls between us. He must be out of his mind to think I would ever join him. I hesitate to even dignify his proposition with a response but cannot bear to endure the electric, maddening silence one second more as his lieutenants leer at me, panting and rabid, awaiting my reply. Thus, I indulge them.

"I have dealt with men like you my entire life—and I know just how to appease them."

I pause, and he raises an eyebrow, intrigued.

"Follow their orders, do as they say. You know the routine: It's eggshells around their egos and leaving their mistakes unaddressed. I keep quiet, bite my tongue, and turn the other cheek."

Stepping forward, I rest a hand on my hip. "But, one pale morning, I saw the light and *finally* understood . . . that *I don't have to do that anymore!*" I seethe, refusing to submit.

His men begin to close in on me.

"As tempting as your offer is," I say flatly, "my answer is no."

"*Men like me?* Men that are half machine?" Malakye's eyes are trained on me in an unflinching stare, but I can see that he is beginning to crack. In another life, I would have taken the cue, backed down, heeded the signs—the silent threat of impending eruption. But as I said, I am tired of it—tired of acquiescing to the temper of just another man in a position of power.

"Oh, I think it is surely more than *half* by now, isn't it?" I reply. "Man or machine, you'll only ever be remembered for the bloodshed."

"And what is it that you suppose you will be remembered for, Holy Virgin? Nothing. Because you are merely a copy . . . of a myth." He pauses, then goes on. "Which is a pretty word for a lie, and that, Your Majesty," he feigns reverence, "equates to nothing."

Then, in one swift motion, he steps forward with one foot while simultaneously lifting the other, kicking me hard in the stomach. As if in slow motion, I fall backward into the hole, tumbling, legs kicking, arms grabbing, ricocheting against the walls, falling, falling, falling . . .

46

I hit the bottom of the hole with a thud. Rubbing my now bruised tailbone, I look up at the dim light shining through the slats of the trap door covering the opening far above me. I had read about places like this that existed in the Middle Ages on Old Earth, a secret dungeon hidden away. An oubliette, they were called—which, directly translated, means a *place of forgetting*. Has our world truly regressed so fantastically that we have resorted to using medieval methods of warfare? Escaping this place is an impossibility.

I am left alone for hours, and I actually don't mind it at first—the solitude, I mean. It is a reprieve from the drama and violence of the preceding twenty-four hours. I am brought water and food at regular intervals, lowered down to me from above. I can hear the shifts of soldiers leaving in the morning, day, and evening, thundering boots sounding from above. All I can think about is how I should be up there, on the surface, fighting with my kin. I shouldn't have antagonized him; I knew better than that. What had gotten into me?

My recklessness had landed me in the worst possible predicament. There must be some way to leverage these new circumstances to my advantage here in the heart of darkness. I will myself to think of something, to think my way out of this, but all I can do is waste away, day in and day out, helpless.

Several days pass, and Malakye's lieutenants eventually bring me out of the hole to interrogate me. They sloppily hoist me up, using a crude pulley system. I've become so accustomed to the darkness, the dim light in the greater dungeon hurts my eyes. They bring me out of the hole and ask me questions about the location of Cana, our allies, the size and strength of the Canish Guard, and Joshua's war plan. I refuse to answer, and they rough me up. Our sessions last precisely an hour, and then I am returned to the hole without dinner. It goes on like this every day for five consecutive days. I don't see Malakye again.

On the sixth day, I get an idea: a negotiation. I will agree to hear out the terms of Malakye's offer if Malakye will allow me an audience with the Regime's Elite Council. That way, I can vet his terms and they can preside in a civil way over the negotiations.

Surely, I can persuade these higher-minded leaders to reason with me. My request is hardly unreasonable. I doubt the Elite Council has any idea what's going on in these dungeons, and I would make it my business to inform them of the situation in the subterranean and on the surface. I would even leverage my connection with Konstantin if I had to. She was heavily involved with Institutional politics when I was under her guardianship at the Ascendency. With Cana and the Alliance backing me, I have to believe someone of sound mind would hear me out—strike a deal, trade some technology, and agree to some sort of ceasefire.

I propose my idea during our usual interrogation session, and one of the cyborg lieutenants leaves for a few minutes. He returns quickly, and to my surprise, I am told that Malakye has agreed to grant me an audience. Malakye himself will escort me the next evening in lieu of our usual session.

Hopeful with the prospect of getting out of here, I fall asleep planning precisely what I will say to the Council. I rehearse it over and over again—this is my last shot, and I intend to make it count.

The next day crawls by as I count the seconds between the minutes and the minutes between the hours and the hours between the shifts of soldiers that come and go. All I can think about is my family on the surface, fighting day in and day out. I hate that I cannot be up there helping them. Intrusive thoughts push their way to the forefront of my mind: sinister, waking dreams of Malakye returning from the front lines to tell me that the war has been won, that my people are dead, imprisoned, and to be enslaved in the factories as it was before.

Malakye's lieutenants finally arrive in the evening, as promised, and they take me directly to him in a dark throne room. I am dirty and pale, and my hair is in knots.

Stalking down the stairs of the dais, he dismisses his men and motions for me to follow him. We are to travel by foot to a higher elevation, deep within a mountain. He explains that the Council prefers to stay far removed from the barracks, infantry, and the dirty city. I can't say that I blame them.

He leads the way, carrying an old-fashioned lantern with a real flame. Though we are shrouded in darkness, my eyes are still sensitive to the meek glow of his light. Tripping on my shackles, I curse as I struggle to keep pace with him up a steep incline. Since drinking the green elixir in KAU City, it's as if all my former strength and health have slowly drained from my body.

"You take for granted that your body works how it was designed to," Malakye chides. "But I suppose you will say it's my people's own fault that our bodies are degenerating in the absence of our former resources."

I say nothing in response. I'm too tired from the steep climb, and it's taking all my strength and focus to match the pace he has set through the tunnels and narrow walk-throughs in this cave system.

"By all measures of biology, I should have been dead and buried for two centuries now," he eventually continues. "But I am not. I have endured."

I guess I'm supposed to be impressed by that statement. I shrug to myself and press on, following him deeper into the underground.

After some time, he speaks again. As if casually recalling a bit of gossip to be shared with an old friend, he says, "Ah, did I tell you? Regime leadership has declared martial law." This causes me to pause. "Invoked during times of war, rebellion, or natural disaster; I do believe our dire straits more than satisfy the outlined criteria."

When martial law is in effect, the military commander has unlimited authority to make and enforce laws. But if my memory serves, this provision of the law was not one previously upheld by the Institution, the prior order of the Regime.

"When?" I ask coolly.

"Some twenty years ago, actually," he replies nonchalantly.

My stomach tightens, but I take a deep breath and follow him around a dark corner. "Oh," I say, trying to hide my surprise. "That doesn't exactly track with what I know about Institution law and the doctrine previously upheld by the Elders."

"Actions that might seem extreme under normal circumstances are appropriate during adversity. And needn't I remind you? The Institution is no more. We are now the Regime," he says, extending his hand and motioning for me to go ahead of him into a clearing.

Reluctantly, I shoulder past him, cringing at our close proximity in the narrow space, which thankfully opens into a more expansive cavern. The air immediately feels cooler as we enter the larger space.

Malakye follows me into the chamber, lighting the sconces that border the room. He lifts the lantern high to ignite each flame. I look around, blinking as my eyes adjust to the brightness, when he says, "Allow me to introduce you to the distinguished leaders of the Elite Council."

The reek of rot and death begins to stuff itself up my nose, and as the light of the candles finally illuminates the room, I see a large council table before me in the chamber. As promised, all twelve members of the Institution's legacy Elite Council sit around it, slumped and decaying in various states of repose. Some are dusty skeletons, and others, it seems, met their demise more recently and are no more than piles of gory, rotting flesh.

Corpses. It's a room full of shackled corpses. He's brought me all this way to grant me an audience with the dead.

I stand stunned and speechless as I try frantically to reorder my plans, considering this new development. But I can't. That was the last card I had to play, and it's utterly useless now. You can't run a nation on brute strength alone. I don't see how Malakye plans to resurrect the factories, businesses, and government without the intellect of the elite leaders and scientists he has either executed or left to die here, even if he *is* to succeed in winning this war.

I turn to him, appalled. "How exactly do you plan to reseed humanity when you have killed off the greatest scientists of our time?"

"You give them too much credit. Most of their minds were quite limited in scope, but I am pleased to see this passionate display of emotion relative to the viability of our plan."

"Our plan?" I ask, shocked further. "*Your* plan is not *our* plan, and we couldn't be further from it after *this*," I say, trying not to gag from the stench.

"Nonetheless, we have an agreement. I have granted you an audience with the council, and you, in turn, will hear me out in terms of what I require you and your people to provide me in exchange for your life."

Looking around the room, I feel sick. If I do not comply, is this where I will end up? Chained to the table next to these poor souls?

"But you haven't granted me an audience. They are all dead!" I say incredulously.

"That is where you are wrong."

I look around the room skeptically for any sign of life among the bones and putrid, rotting flesh when he motions to the far back of the chamber and says, "This way, please."

I hesitate to follow him any deeper into this remote and terrifying place but then realize that my life has been in his hands since the moment I arrived—truly, since the moment Cassini handed me over to his lieutenants.

Reluctantly, I follow him to a small holding cell attached to the back of the greater chamber. Upon entering the room, I see there is a small body crouched in the corner of the barren cell.

When Malakye lights the braziers flanking the cell, the light illuminates the profile of a woman. She is sleeping lightly and is no more than skin and bones. As I step closer, I kneel to get a better look at his captive. The dim braziers reveal a face I know all too well, their light playing off the sharp contours and milky-white complexion of none other than Konstantin's beautiful face.

Konstantin stirs, disturbed by the noise of our approach, then turns sharply to look at me. When she faces me, I can see that the right half of her face is wrinkled, slack, and ancient.

"Your audience," Malakye says, bowing, "as promised, with what's left of the Council. Please feel free to plead your case."

"Konstantin," I say, dumbstruck and trying not to take too much pleasure in the sight of her behind bars after the cruel years I spent under her guardianship at the Ascendency. Housed in one of their medical facilities, I was treated no better than a lab rat as I endured any and every experiment that came across her desk. "I wasn't aware you'd risen so high in the ranks during these years we've been apart. What great strides you've made," I say sardonically.

She smiles, tight-lipped and pained. "Hella, please consider . . ."

"I'll never help him," I cut her off quickly and definitively as I rise, folding my arms across my chest and looking down at her.

"Hella, he is not wrong. You must help here. Humanity's genetic integrity was damaged by the nuclear war, a war instigated by *your* people. You and your people have a responsibility to give us what we need to reseed the human race. If this isn't obvious to you and your farmers, then you are missing it."

"My people? But are they really *my* people according to *your* genetics?" I counter, a bone to pick with her.

At first quizzical, her face then lights with understanding. Acknowledging my reference to the role she played in my own genetic engineering, she says, "Oh please, that was half a century ago. I was bored and playing God. Entertaining myself. It doesn't mean anything, Hella—your genetic makeup—and we have no relation, you and I. Consider me no more than a ship you briefly took passage on; no more than that. Now we need your people, and your people need our science."

"Your science is what got us into this mess to begin with!" I hiss, exasperated by her already, less than two minutes into the conversation. "And that's where you are wrong." I look at her and then over to Malakye. "That's where you are both wrong. We don't need you or your science." I step back. "Cana will win this war without you and without me, so you can do whatever you like here." I motion to the space between Konstantin and me. I guess Malakye thought she could persuade me to help the Regime, but like she said, our relations are tenuous at best.

Malakye steps closer to the two of us. "It's easy to predict great feats in the passion of the night," he says, "but what plan you for when the morning comes?"

"There will be no morning," I scoff. "The sun has set on humanity. Both of you are just too arrogant to see it." I turn to leave.

"Wait," Konstantin croaks. "There is something you must know."

I pause in the doorway, keeping my back to her as she speaks.

"Xavier originated in TRAPPIST. He is the heir to a kingdom. You cannot blame him for seeking answers."

"Don't talk to me about Xavier," I snap, turning to face her momentarily before walking away. "You know *nothing* about him."

I can hear Malakye prowling toward her, and as she scrambles back from where she had come forward in the cell, I can hear her chains drag as she returns to her place in the corner.

"I know *nothing*, do I?" she calls after me. "I know that he isn't from our world. That this life was nothing but suffering for him, but he stayed for *you*. And he left for you, too, but you are just too proud to see it . . ."

Then she cries out. There is a thump and then silence.

I don't look back; instead, I slip around the corner as quietly as I can in my shackles. Then I make a break for it.

I run around the table of the dead and head for the door. But Malakye is onto me in seconds, making easy strides as he closes the space between us. I lunge for the door and make it through, but then I see nothing but rock in front of me. Looking closer, I spot the narrow passageway through which we entered. Diving into the tight space, I start to squeeze around the corner when a cold metal hand snatches my arm and jerks me out of the narrow crevice and back into the rank room.

47

I'm in the hole again. All I can smell is earth. It is a delicious relief from the stench of rotting flesh that permeated the air of the mountain chamber I trekked to earlier this evening with Malakye. Tapping my fingers neurotically against the cold dirt floor, I try to distract my mind from the choking feeling in my throat. I can't tell if I'm truly suffocating down here, thirty feet under the hellscape that is Malakye's subterranean empire, or if it's just the panic rising within, my mind getting the better of me. Who would have thought there was anything that existed below actual Hell? But alas, here I am, imprisoned again, deeper than the grave. I forcibly swallow again, resting my head back against the dirt wall.

Could I have heard Konstantin correctly? She said Xavier originated in TRAPPIST. How could that be, and why wouldn't *he* tell me?

It can't be true, I decide. It's just too wild a story, and she's certainly not to be trusted. More likely, it's just another angle she and Malakye are working to try to persuade me to their agenda. Although it did seem that Malakye wanted to quiet her. That didn't quite fit.

I try to think about it more, but eventually nod off and have the dream again about the young girl from the forest who has been visiting me of late. This time, she is smiling at me, and it fills me with a happiness that is so palpable and real, it occurs to me I had forgotten the sensation. I watch her as she walks back and forth, completing the simple tasks that make up her usual trip to the woods at the base of the mountains. Smiling back at her, I cannot wipe the expression of genuine happiness off my face, the joy she brings me, and the joy I can see that I bring to her.

When I look at my outstretched arm, I notice it is sparkling white. Raising it high, I dreamily follow the swirls of light that trail behind it. Then suddenly, the girl stops in her tracks. Her smile turns to a frown. Looking left, right, and then back at me again, she begins to scream, dropping her firewood.

I then feel something squeeze around my middle. When I look down, there is an enormous snake emerging from the ivy-covered wall behind me and wrapping itself around my waist so tightly that it knocks the wind out of me. Coiling, it pulls me violently inside the rock wall that is now collapsing around me.

The girl is reaching for me and I for her when I wake abruptly to realize there are *arms* wrapped tightly around my waist. I look down and see skeleton-like hands gripped around my stomach, pulling me through the wall of the hole.

I fight the arms at first, but they only grip tighter. As the wall crumbles, I begin to understand what is happening. Someone is breaking me out. Someone is aware that I have been imprisoned here, has found my location, and is digging me out.

Dirt caves in all around me as I am pulled with supernatural strength backward through a tunnel that has presumably been cleared by my assailant. Some kind of pulley system is doing the work to swiftly drag us out of the narrow tunnel, which is just big enough for our small bodies. No longer fighting, I try to make my body limp to ease the operation, and for several minutes, I am pulled. Soon I begin to feel lightheaded from the reduced oxygen in the tight space.

Finally, I feel relief as both of us are ripped out of the wall and spit out onto the floor of a large open cave. Drinking in the cool air, I immediately notice the smell and sound of water rushing nearby.

When I land, I find I am on top of my assailant. Rolling off and over to all fours, I hop up quickly in case I need to defend myself. The figure is cloaked in black, covered in dirt, and swiftly getting off the ground, too.

It is a woman. She removes a thick leather belt that is strapped around her waist and hooked to the pulley system, which was the force that dragged us out of the tunnel. Looking beyond her, I see the coarse rope she holds feeds onto a set of complex wooden spools mounted on the bow of a small boat moored in a shallow underground channel flowing through the cave. The woman throws the waist belt and rope into the boat and motions for me to follow her.

When she finally speaks, she sounds nearly out of breath. "Quickly. We haven't much time."

Together we push the boat off the shore and get in. She takes up a pair of oars and begins rowing with strong and nimble movements. The current starts to pick up, and soon the water is rushing around us, propelling us forward.

Her hood falls back, and I observe that she has long, shimmering, dove-gray hair, pale skin, and a thin scar circling her neck.

"I am Eskara," she says. "We are known to your people as the Greybeards. I have been tracking you since KAU City."

"I'm Hella," I manage in response. "But I guess you knew that," I say quietly, trailing off as she looks away. Turning her attention back to the water rushing around us, she skillfully navigates us away from the worst currents, rapids, and rocks that would destroy the small boat if we collided with them.

"What do you call yourselves?" I ask in an effort to show respect and goodwill toward her people.

"Men. Humans. Revivalists, just as you are."

"Right," I say. "Well, of course. I'm sorry, I didn't mean . . ."

"I know, Hella. Quiet now and lie low. I need to focus."

I sit low in the back of the boat and lie back, trying to streamline my body with the vessel as much as possible as we are carried forward through the turbulent waters.

I grew up afraid of the Greybeards. As a child, the idea of their head transplants gave me nightmares. Children were taught to fear them, but in retrospect, the teaching did not come from our parents or schoolteachers. It was hearsay and gossip learned from the older children trying to spook the younger ones, and likely, it was no more than baseless nonsense. Just as a crone is demonized as a witch in Old Earth folklore, teaching that an aged woman is something of repulsion, something evil, the Greybeards, too, were painted as monsters because of their advanced age and the method by which they extended their livelihood.

My stream of consciousness is interrupted as something Eskara said begins to sink in: She has been tracking me since KAU City. I had been in the dungeons for over a week—had she been digging all this time? I wonder why she would do this for me and if I am to be her prisoner just as I was Malakye's.

The water soon begins to calm, becoming less turbulent but still moving us forward with strength. This requires less work on Eskara's part since the currents are pushing us in the direction she apparently wishes to be traveling.

In silence and darkness, we travel for quite some time. Eventually, I begin to drift off from exhaustion, napping fitfully as the steady rhythm of the boat finally lulls me to sleep.

When I wake, I have no sense of how much time has passed but find that the tunnel has begun to lighten. Soon more and more light floods in, brighter than high noon on the surface. This makes no sense to me because this kind of light can no longer reach Earth, whether on the surface or in the subterranean. But streaming in like rays of golden sunshine, I can feel its warmth on my pale, dirt-caked skin. Beside me, I notice the water gradually turning from char black to crystal-clear blue.

The river has also broadened, becoming very wide as the current begins to pick up again, and our small boat rushes forward. Above, the cavern ceiling seems to crack open, stretching farther than I can see, and as we round a bend, it becomes apparent that we are headed toward a huge drop: a waterfall.

In the middle of the river is a massive island that juts up very tall within the cavern, perched on the crest of the falls. There is a stone structure on the precipice, and as we get closer, I can see that a small colony of structures, a complex of buildings, has been built on the edge of the cliff, overhanging the great falls below. This magnificent place, a city only reachable by water, must be where the Greybeards dwell.

Eskara guides our boat directly toward the towering rock, targeting a small entrance at the base. We enter, continue down a long channel, and eventually reemerge from the tunnel, coming to a stop inside the city.

Inside the city, everything is pristine and bathed in soft light. There are no dirty cave floors here, only sun-bleached limestone to meet our feet as we climb out of the craft. Kneeling, I dip my grimy hand into the clean water, rinsing away the dirt covering my forearm and caked under my fingernails. I then wash the other hand and splash my face clean, too.

When I turn and look up at Eskara standing in the light, I am momentarily puzzled. The stories about her people's fear of sunlight are fresh in my mind, yet here she is, seemingly unaffected. I continue to watch her as she secures the boat. When she's finished her work, she looks at me and says, "Hella of Cana, I welcome you to Bleausphere."

48

Climbing stone stairs that seem to endlessly wind, twist, and turn, I follow Eskara up from the waterfront to the central metropolis, which is situated atop the massive tower of rock jutting between the falls. Along the way, I observe the remarkable sound of birds singing, and it isn't long after I notice the birds that we encounter plants and flowers lining our path as we enter the city proper.

Traveling on foot along orderly, quiet streets, we finally reach the city center, where we are surrounded by beauty that I thought to be long gone from our world: gardens, fruit trees, hanging plants, and flowers. As we pause to rest at a crystal-clear fountain in the town square, Eskara explains that Bleausphere is a fully contained holographic city, not unlike the smaller holo-spheres we use for training habitats at Titan Station, just far more complex. Created to serve as a permanent sanctuary for Eskara's people, Bleausphere is five hundred years old and has evolved continually since its conception, which predates the fall of Empyreus.

The sunlight is artificial. The plants, flowers, and birds—all artificial. Most are sophisticated holograms, although Eskara shares with me that her people have cataloged the genetic code and DNA samples for the entirety of Earth's plant and animal species and genome. The precious life that became extinct at the climax of Earth's nuclear war was all preserved here in their archives.

As we enter the primary living compound of Eskara's people, a structure reminiscent of a fourteenth-century Old World palace and fortress complex, she points out that not all the plants and animals here are holographic. Their scientists have been working tirelessly since the fall of Empyreus to bring a variety of biological organisms back to life in a laboratory environment. They have seen more failures than successes, but the miracle is that they have had some successes.

As she speaks, an enormous lion emerges from behind a reflective pool and fountain, stalking slowly around the courtyard of the great hall. When I notice him, I stop dead in my tracks.

"Is he . . . ?"

"Real?" Eskara asks, finishing my sentence. "Yes, this specimen is the first mammal born in our labs, the first life rendered since the war. He will not harm you."

Each regal paw is as large as my head, his own head and mane enormous. Teeth four inches in length line his massive jaw as he settles lazily on the warm marble floor beside the pool, stretching and then yawning to reveal the neat rows.

"Come," Eskara says as I stare, entranced by the beautiful creature before me. "You must bathe and rest."

Exiting the courtyard, which serves as the central living space of the palace complex around which other halls and rooms are organized, Eskara escorts me to the guests' quarters in a far wing of the palace. As we walk down the corridor, I admire the tiled mosaics that cover the walls in geometric patterns and floral motifs as she explains further that her scientists are able to grow test tube embryos for animals but not for humans.

"This is the end of the road for my people, the end of our time line," she says. "There are no more donors." Touching her neck, she traces a long, delicate scar bisecting her throat to indicate that there will be no more lifesaving head transplants to extend their lives and smiles sadly. "There have been one or two procedures among our population since the fall of Empyreus, but we are dying faster than we can replace our bodies."

I nod solemnly, all too familiar with the conversation about the future of our civilization and the widespread epidemic of infertility.

Eskara continues. "We can grow plants and even mammals in a lab, but because the donors of our principal parts," she indicates the whole of her body from the neck down, "were Institution-born, our human DNA is too damaged and cannot be regenerated. For the same reason, we cannot procreate the natural way."

As we walk down the quiet hallway, I wonder where her people are. I look around, and she seems to sense my question. "We are smaller in numbers these days but are still some ten thousand strong. Most everyone is working at this time of day, and the residences are quiet."

"Is it okay that I'm here?" I ask, recalling that no outsider, whether from the Institution or Cana, has ever been inside one of the Greybeards' underground cities—not while they still occupied it, at least. They are a people who value their privacy.

"Yes." she smiles.

I bow my head in relief before continuing. "I wouldn't want to break any of your laws. Your people have been so generous to mine."

"There is no law here," she replies simply as we move down a long, interior passageway. "No Institution to protect or punish you. We do not rely on a governing body here, nor are we enslaved to one. Our society is the antithesis of what the Institution was."

"How does that work, exactly?" I ask, thinking there must be some kind of leadership to maintain order.

"Here, every man takes responsibility for himself. We do not rely on an establishment to right the wrongs of society, to provide for us, or to protect us. We provide for and protect ourselves. Take care of ourselves, settle our own differences.

"For example," she says as we cross a small causeway, "no one is going to assure you that this bridge we walk upon is safe; you must determine it for yourself." She glances at me. "If it is in disrepair, well, it is up to you to fix it."

Well, I think to myself, *whatever it is that they're doing seems to be working and has for centuries.* Everything here is in pristine condition. There is order, and there is peace—or seems to be, at least.

Eskara shows me to a beautiful chamber filled with fresh air and soft sunlight. The stone floor is covered with a plush rug, and a large platform bed with soft bedding sits diagonally from the entrance. I walk through the room and peer out the open window, looking down at the city below. I turn to Eskara and say, "My people, we are greatly indebted to you. We can never thank you enough for what you have done for us, for warning us about the nuclear attack, initially providing the bunkers, and leading us to Cana City most recently."

"We are a private people but have long realized that no civilization can thrive in isolation," she replies.

"And thank you for rescuing me," I continue. "Eskara, I am forever in your debt. But how did you find me, and why would you risk so much?"

She is quiet for a moment and then simply says, "My surname is Abramovich."

I blink a couple of times as what she says sinks in. She lets me sort it out on my own for a few moments.

"Then you are . . ." I pause, in so much disbelief I need to hear the name on her tongue.

"Gemma's mother."

Eskara Abramovich is Mordecai's estranged wife. She is the biological mother of Gemma Abramovich's human form—the child who was kidnapped by the Institution and whose body was used against her will to seed the Institution's infamous embryo factories.

Eskara was the one who left me the message in the neutral zone, was there at the market waiting to meet me before I was diverted and then abducted in the nearby tavern. She kept a watchful eye on me when I was taken by Cassini and followed me into the heart of KAU City, where I was later imprisoned. At some point, she managed to tag me with a tracker and, using her people's sophisticated technology and cartography, had been able to pinpoint my location relative to a little-known tunnel beneath Malakye's dungeons. To reach me, she worked tirelessly for days, digging for as long as I had been imprisoned.

Eskara answers a few of my questions but says that she will explain more after I bathe and sleep for a few quick hours—just enough to regain my strength, as we are all short on time in this war. She has access to enough intel to know that my people are still fighting. That the battle is not yet decided. The Regime has not beaten us—not yet—but time is running thin.

She won't tell me what happened to Gemma. She just says, "As there are truths children shouldn't know until they are adults, there are also certitudes we should never know as humans if it can be helped—if we aren't the unfortunate ones who must face these unspeakable mandates of fate, these blackest of cards to be dealt."

As I press for answers, she admonishes, "The human mind is a delicate thing. Protect it at all costs, above all else. There is knowledge that can shatter a mind, infect it like a worm if you allow it inside."

No, she would not tell me about the fate of her daughter's human form, and she is clear that I should immediately stop thinking about it. In fact, she tells me that my mind is likely in such a state, in such dire need of rest, that it is imperative that I stop thinking, period, for at least a while. She instructs me to rest and empty my mind completely, to seek only the infinite space that lies between thoughts. In a few hours, she will return and take me to the observatory to debrief me on everything—why she had contacted me, the war, her plans on how to move forward. And then she leaves me to rest.

I sink into a deep-plunge tub and inhale the citrus and gardenia aromas that waft up from the gardens below. The water is close to scalding and feels analgesic to my battered body. I let it soak up to my chin, nose, and then eyes. I close them tightly as I float, inert and fully submerged beneath the surface of the thermal bath. The silence enveloping me, I am finally able to clear my mind and relish the exquisite relief of thinking of nothing at all.

49

When Eskara returns, she tells me she has let me sleep for six hours, which is the most we can afford. After a warm dinner of actual food that was delivered to my room the night before, my head had hit the pillow, and it felt like I merely blinked when her knock sounded at the door this morning.

I dress in a pair of cream-colored linen pants she has laid out for me with a matching button-up blouse and modest, soft leather sandals. I braid my long hair down my back, taming the wild waves, and take a deep gulp out of a chilled carafe left for me, filled with the purist, clearest water I have ever seen or tasted.

Eskara then leads me to the part of the city where people study, work, and train for war. After meandering through the hilly cityscape, Eskara and I approach a building that is just as grand as the palace residence but tall and narrow, soaring into the sky, where the palace complex is long and flat, a fortress spread out over a larger space. We enter the building, and though it appears to have a more ancient stone exterior, the interior is equipped with the high technology of Titan Station.

We travel in a lift all the way up to the top floor and enter the observatory. The oval room overlooks the great falls below the city. I'm still not sure if the falls are real or holographic. The water we traveled in on was at one point real in every sense of the word, but it is impossible to tell where one ends and the other begins. You cannot see to the bottom, and when you look up, it appears as if there is nothing but the wide-open heavens above. But the sky, at least, I *know*, cannot be real.

I know this much is true because as easy as it may be to forget where we are while swept away in the magic of this place, I find that I cannot forget. I cannot forget what has happened to our planet. I cannot forget that as beautiful as this place is, we are truly still buried beneath the surface of a dying world, and what lies above is a dangerous and war-torn land ravaged by death. Earth is still a land where no one can truly see the sunshine—not like this, at least—or a starry night sky and would not for another hundred thousand years.

We face the floor-to-ceiling windows, looking down at the enormous falls that seem to rush into oblivion. Eskara doesn't waste any time getting started. "First, there is the technology I would like to share with your people," she says, all business as she illuminates three screens that are nearly as large as the windows in front of which they materialize.

Before us is a digital map. The Greybeards have charted out the entire underground of the Earth. I study what she has shown me for several minutes, orienting myself. I then find Cana and the old bunkers in which my people sheltered prior to where we are now. I trace the underground passage I took from beneath the chapel to

KAU City. I study the entirety of the Regime's territory and, lastly, our journey here to Bleausphere. And that's just the part of the world that's familiar to me because there is so much more. So much beyond what we know, beyond what we speculated. I can hardly believe the extent of the developed underground that preexisted the nuclear war. A whole world stretches beyond our great continent of Empyreus even, under the oceans and beyond, across the globe. I wonder if these places could be populated, if there could be others out there like us.

"As I have said, this is the end of my people's time line, and I want to pass along our knowledge to the people of Cana. Thus, I am sharing these maps with you, in hope that they will help your people win the war and defeat the Regime."

"Thank you, Eskara," I say humbly. "The maps, this technology, we will gladly accept and be forever indebted to you. This could mean the difference between survival and extinction for my people. If we are defeated on the surface, we can use these maps to escape and travel elsewhere."

"Yes," she says, "a nomadic existence is better than no existence, and you may have to split up and travel in smaller numbers, but the Revivalists have done it before and can do it again. We are also prepared to offer you the assistance of our armies."

The Greybeards are known to be competent soldiers with youthful, strong bodies and ancient brains fit to recall years of training and expertise spanning several lifetimes. But there are so few of them left now, I cannot in good conscience allow my people's conflict to contribute to an earlier end of their civilization and feel I have no choice but to refuse her. "Thank you for your generous offer, but we cannot ask the last of your people to die for Cana."

"We would not only be dying for Cana, but to see humanity live on. Mankind is in grave danger of extinction. We have faith in your people to carry on our race, to endure the long night, and for that, we will gladly fight, gladly lay down our lives."

"I cannot allow you to do it," I say, shaking my head, unwilling to take on the responsibility of the lives of these honorable people.

"Hella, it is not about how you feel; it is simply about what must be done," she says firmly. "Now, the third topic I need to discuss with you is the matter of my daughter."

I nod, anxious for clarity on the topic of Gemma. "In your note, you said that she was alive," I recall, confused. The whole reason I left Cana was because of those words, scratched on the dirty bit of paper given to me by the child in the neutral zone—Eskara's messenger. But then Eskara had since implied that her daughter's demise was so violent an end, it could never be relayed to me—an outcome that, if nothing else, sounded final.

"I needed something powerful," Eskara begins, "a motivation to get you to come to me, and I knew that if I said Gemma was alive, you might come. But my message was not wholly false: Gemma's spirit does live on. I know you know that as well as I do."

"Yes, well—I know about her holographic form on Proxima," I say, unsure of what she's getting at, but then something occurs to me. "Have you been in touch with her?"

"Yes, I have, Hella. I have spoken with her regularly over the years. She has urged me to contact you, to bring you here and to help you and your family . . . and has done so for all these years."

All these years? How could it be that Gemma truly knew me before we met? She said as much back on Proxima, and I could make no sense of it then, but here is the proof now. The Greybeards have been helping my people long before Gemma's and my paths crossed in Alpha Centauri.

"It is true that you wield great influence, Hella," Eskara continues. "Great power, even if there is no magic, no divinity in your DNA, for that is a personal decision of belief for each of us. But regardless of your or my beliefs, the knowledge, the rumor alone, holds great meaning with the people, with the masses of the surviving population of our world, and we must tread carefully with how we wield that power, that influence. There are those who would misuse it."

"Well, over my dead body they will misuse it," I say, irritated, thinking of those who have already tried to use me and the famed "sanctity" of my DNA to manipulate the Canish people.

"Do not underestimate what people can do in your name without your consent," Eskara warns.

Her stark warning calls to mind Abramovich and how he used my image in Ephesia to speak to Cana Minor. She was right. It is unnerving what he has been able to do without my permission . . . the writing of my very DNA, for that matter. Maybe I was in over my head.

"What more could he do?" I muse, frustrated. I want to be one step ahead of him, but my mind is blank as to what his next move could possibly be.

"I will leave it to my daughter to explain," she says.

When Eskara turns to face the screen, it flickers, and I suddenly realize why she has brought me here: She has brought me all this way so that I can speak with Gemma again. They had discovered a way to communicate between worlds.

In a flash, Gemma's hologram appears on the screen before us, larger than life.

Of course, Gemma looks exactly the same: a picture of youth, but with those ancient, solemn eyes that, even if I had wanted, I could never erase from my memory. She was only ten years old when the Institution's men captured her. A deep ache of concern stirs in my chest as I observe her tight-lipped expression, the urgency of her message apparent in the grave look on her face.

"Helly, it is good to see you again so soon," she says.

So soon? I think. It feels like it has been years since we parted ways in Alpha Centauri, but I suppose it has only been a few months. But then, for an immortal hologram, I imagine time passes differently.

"I was relieved to receive word that you made it off my planet and safely back to Earth, reunited with your family."

"I couldn't have done it without you," I say sincerely. "I can never thank you enough for your friendship on the planet and for your help the day I got out."

Gemma brushes off my gratitude shyly before continuing. "My father is on his way to Earth. He has a new body and is on a dark mission. He travels by way of a vessel he calls *the Prophet*, which is equipped to transport thousands of people. He intends to begin the migration of the Canish people to New Earth."

My stomach twists, and I bite my lip as I mull over her words. This much, I had expected. I hadn't been sure when it would happen—certainly, I did not think it would be so soon—but I had known this day would come.

"Tell me more," I press, her urgency concerning me. "This has always been his plan, has it not? What is this darkness you speak of?"

"He finds that the whole of the Canish population has not

adequately met his expectations in terms of their level of coopera-
tion with his plan and devotion to his theology."

This doesn't come as a surprise to me either. This was always his
biggest grievance. It is why he exterminated half the world and why
he needs me so badly to help manipulate and win over his people
again.

"And?" I ask nervously. "What does he plan to do about it?"

"He plans to eradicate those who do not convince him of their
allegiance to his god."

"Eradicate?" I ask, moved to the edge of panic.

She looks me directly in the eye and serves me the full truth
in one explicit, exacting word. "Execute," she asserts—not because
she is happy about it, not because she wants to cause me pain or
me to be afraid, but because she wants me to have nothing less
than the whole truth, no matter how harrowing. And for that, I am
grateful. I can always count on Gemma for the truth, and for that
reason, she is invaluable to me.

I look back at her, speechless. My emotions—fear, anger, and frustration—are painted all over my face as she continues. "He travels with
a fleet of vessels and an army of bots. His destination is your planet."

"When did he depart, and how soon will he be here?" I ask, my
mind running a mile a minute as I try to think of a way to warn
Joshua.

"He will arrive any day now. It is possible he is already in Cana
City."

I look to Eskara. "Can you help me get back to my people?"

She nods solemnly. "We must leave now."

I look back at Gemma. I would love to spend hours catching up
with her, but we have no time to lose.

"One more thing, Helly," Gemma adds. "Before you go—I know this will be difficult for you to hear . . ."

What could be more difficult than learning that Abramovich is on his way to execute half my people, *my* half, Cana Major—all the people I love most in the world?

"But I feel it is important that you know." She looks at me earnestly, and I nod, giving her permission to go on. "My father has created a life in his lab."

I look back at her, concerned but not taking in her full meaning quite yet.

She continues. "A life that, in truth, belongs to you. A life that he created using your DNA. Samples that were removed from your womb while you were sleeping on Proxima. A life conceived in a test tube, in his laboratory."

Her words stop me in my tracks. Shocked and feeling completely violated, I wonder frantically when it could have been done—when there had been an opportunity for an egg to be extracted without my knowing. It must have been that first day when Taj gave me the sleeping dram. Or was it on the last day when he fixed my leg and put me under with Coma White?

Either way, the realization that Taj had to have been complicit chills me to my core. When it all starts coming together, a rage rises in me unlike any other. I want to scream, to break things. I want to throw myself through the windows and over the falls below. Loving Taj was to love in vain. I start pacing manically, and Eskara comes to my side.

"Hella, be at peace," she says in a soothing voice.

I am so angry and upset my limbs are shaking. She takes my hand to steady me and wills me to stop pacing. Pulling me to her, she wraps her arms around me.

I shatter in her arms, collapsing into tears. We sink to the ground, and then I hear a strange noise—a blip or a zap.

Eskara stiffens and jumps up. "No . . . *no* . . ." she says, a fear and panic in her tone that I thought never to hear on the lips of such an enlightened being. "How *dare* he," she sobs.

Whipping my head around, I look at the screen that has now gone black, and my blood runs cold as I read the words written there in type:

Program deleted.

The breath catches in my diaphragm, and I double over in misery as Eskara's scream of wild sorrow echoes through the ramparts of the observatory—to the ceiling, through the rafters, and to the stars—*"Nooooooooooooooo!!!!!!!!!!"*

50

G*oddamn him,* I think. *God damn Mordecai Abramovich.* He would take everything precious to me in this life.

My anger had driven me to madness. Murderous madness. I will end this. He will not get away with one more transgression, will not take any more lives. He must be stopped and *will* be stopped.

Abramovich presumably deleted Gemma's holographic program, ending her life as we knew it by extinguishing the last remaining trace of her consciousness from this realm. Eskara worked all day and the entire night, trying tirelessly to get her program back online, but it was in vain. Gemma was gone.

For years, the two of them had been communicating via that channel, nearly since Gemma's inception when Abramovich first wrote her program on Proxima. Through science, he conjured her likeness, personality, and memories into an existence tangible to our world. He brought his daughter—*their* daughter—back to life, and for a hundred years, Gemma and Eskara had been companions, confidants—in truth, mother and daughter. And to see it stripped away so callously—I couldn't help but feel responsible.

Racked with guilt and sorrow, I trudge on, following Eskara through the underground once again, but this time on foot. We had left early the next morning after a small breakfast of crusty baguettes and the first coffee I had tasted in months. Wearing heavy brown cloaks and traveling through vacant tunnels, we only stop to sleep and eat from the dwindling supply of rations we carry with us.

For three days, we press on. We receive word from Eskara's connections about crowds and chaos at Ephesia; people have been gathering for days. Abramovich has been working overtime feeding propaganda to Cana Minor in preparation for his arrival. The people were said to be drunk on his promises of salvation and reveling in the ecstasy of the Holy. Celebrating and enacting religious rites with drink, drugs, dance—rioting, even—all in the name of their God Almighty.

There were no reports of Abramovich's actual arrival; for that, at least, we could be grateful. He is presumably still in transit, which has bought us time. But the war on the surface is said to still be raging, and things are worse than ever for my people. After weighing their situation, I reluctantly agree to allow Eskara to send aid.

Her army will march on the surface in protective suits of another variety, an earlier iteration made of silicene, a crystalline silicon allotrope manufactured years ago by their scientists. Their army's route will not be as direct as ours due to a mountainous region that lies north of the battlegrounds and will put them behind us by a day or so. Traveling underground would be faster, but it isn't practical for an army to move in such large numbers beneath the surface, and it would ultimately prove impossible for them to navigate KAU City without running into Malakye's army, which has already laid claim to those parts of the underground.

Eskara and I will go another way. We choose an underground route that avoids KAU City and the worst mobs at Cana Minor proper but does require that we pass through Ephesia. I urgently need to get back to warn my people that the news is more than just wild gossip and propaganda—that Abramovich *will* be there, and imminently—and thus, we decide to take our chances with the crowds there.

We had discussed entering Cana City by way of the secret passage through which I made my exit mere weeks ago. However, we ultimately decided we could not sacrifice the time it would take to travel it. Eskara, with prior knowledge of the route, advised that though it is perhaps safer, it is also lengthier. She had traveled it herself on numerous occasions when her people still inhabited the sanctuary that is now Cana City, making the journey long before the fall of Empyreus, before the war, when her people first moved underground and were still conceiving of what would become Bleausphere.

As we walk, I try to clear my mind of the things that bring my most volatile emotions to the surface, but I cannot stop thinking about the child Abramovich is said to have engineered in his lab. I can't stop thinking about how Taj helped him do it, helped him steal my genetic material—an egg from *my* womb—and kept it from me. I feel powerless, and my heart has been torn apart once again by Taj's betrayal.

On the evening of the third day, we make our way safely through the neutral zone, unnoticed and unbothered. But the crowd begins to gradually thicken as we approach Ephesia. We sense that emotions are running high here, that the moods of the people have shifted. Something has changed since we last passed through; there is an intangible electricity and an uneasiness, a near palpable feeling of unruliness in the air.

Eskara leads the way, picking and weaving through the increasingly agitated mobs. Vast numbers of men and women overflow into the streets, drinking and dancing, chanting and singing, preaching and praying. As we begin to pass the familiar amphitheater situated in the center of Ephesia, Eskara shoulders by a crowd of people who are mesmerized by the images playing on the screen. I stop to look, and my likeness is there again, projected before the increasing gathering of revelers. This version of me is dressed in white glittering robes with a matching head wrap. She is bathed in holy light and bowed in solemn prayer. To make it all worse, my likeness appears heavy with child.

Just then, I am bumped brusquely from behind, and my hood falls back. As it falls, I hear a woman begin to scream. I look in the direction of the sound, and her scream becomes a wail as my face becomes fully visible to her. She then lifts an unsteady finger and begins frantically pointing at me. This draws the attention of her companions. They follow suit, becoming hysterical as well and clamoring toward me. Before I can do anything, they are on their knees before me, wailing and chanting.

In moments, Eskara is pushed in the other direction by a sea of people as raw mania ripples through the crowd like wildfire. I am pushed and shoved as everyone hungrily reaches out to touch me, grab me, desperate for healing, worship, or any kind of connection to the Holy. They chant the same words I heard when I was broadcast live from Proxima months ago:

Hail Mary, full of Grace, the Lord is with thee.

Blessed art thou amongst women, and blessed is the fruit of thy womb, Jesus.

Holy Mary, Mother of God, pray for us sinners, now and at the hour of our death.

Amen.

But now, there is a chaotic edge to their verse. I try to fight my way out, pushing left and right, but I cannot break the grasp of so many hands. Eventually, the crowd picks me up and passes me roughly above their heads, everyone greedily groping and pinching my skin and pulling at my hair. My cloak is ripped to shreds.

Eventually, the momentum carries me to the front of the amphitheater, and I am tossed onto the raised stage beneath the screen. I land heavily, put my hands over my ears, and yell, "Quiet!"

To my surprise, a sudden hush moves through the crowd. The chanting stops momentarily, and everyone directs their attention to me. My ears begin to ring with anxiety in the sudden, deafening silence as they all look at me expectantly.

I look back at them, outraged, tears and sweat dripping down my face. And then something in the distance beyond the crowd catches my eye. Fear tightens my throat as soldiers in crimson-and-gold livery begin filing in—it's the Cana Minor Royal Guard coming to take me into custody. They make quick work breaking through the people and surge directly toward me.

Two large, uniformed men in the lead push forward, haul me off the stage floor, and begin to hustle me away. As they make a path, the people around me drop to the ground, bowing in prayer as I pass through.

Hail Mary, full of Grace, the Lord is with thee.

Blessed art thou amongst women, and blessed is the fruit of thy womb, Jesus.

Holy Mary, Mother of God, pray for us sinners, now and at the hour of our death.

Amen.

I twist defiantly in the grasp of the pair of soldiers, the faces of the mob pressing in. "I am not your pale god, nor am I your Virgin Mother!" I scream. "Do you understand how unfair that is? To expect a woman to be a virgin and a mother? Is the creation of life such a foul and sinful act that you cannot bear to imagine your mothers may have participated in it?" I spit the words as I am jerked forward faster than I can walk.

The people stare back at me vacantly, shocked by my words, as I scan the crowd for Eskara but can't find her anywhere in the sea of people. It isn't long before I notice that my new escorts are not taking me in the direction of where I understood Cana Minor to be, but instead toward Cana City itself. This does not bode well. There can only be one reason the Cana Minor Royal Guard would be reporting directly to Cana City, and that is if there has been a change in the chain of command.

51

I arrive home to a new scene of chaos. Abramovich is here—has set up court, is interviewing people, questioning them, and detaining them for unknown reasons. I learn he has formed a new council with Cana Minor here in Cana City and has brought in the Elders while Joshua has been away on the surface fighting. This was not a violent takeover of a government but a political one.

We are losing the war. Fewer soldiers come home each day, and fresh waves of cyborgs appear every morning when my people return to fight. My brother and his commanders have been in the trenches fighting day in and day out, holding the line and protecting our people from the worst outcome—a cyborg occupation inside the city.

Abramovich swept in when the people were most desperate. He made his promises of salvation, and they let him take power. He came with a small guard of bots but did not need to use force. The Cana Minor Royal Guard was happy to oblige him with the Canish

Guard in such a depleted state, the bulk of what remains of us on the surface, facing the Regime.

Tensions run high among our civilians, and I have found myself, once again, confined to a cell. Theia finds me first, her eyes wide as she speaks to me in a low whisper between the bars.

"They have Shreya, too," she says, looking back at the guard nervously, afraid she is being watched. "But she is in solitary confinement."

"What? Why?" I ask, shocked and angry.

"She wouldn't lie to them," she says, her voice weak. "She is stubborn. He demands we swear fealty to him and his god, his doctrine, but she will not. I told her that laws don't control minds and to just tell him what he wants to hear—that it doesn't matter—but she refuses." A tear trickles down her cheek. She wipes it away with the sleeve of her shirt. "I'm so afraid for her," she whispers.

I stiffen as Gemma's words come back to me: *Executions*, she had said.

"You must talk to her. Someone must talk to her," I say urgently. "Where is Joshua?"

"I think it's too late for talk." She sniffles. "Abramovich is convinced she is sinful and is now making an example out of her." Again, she looks at the guard, then continues. "Joshua is on the surface fighting with my father, Xavier, and everyone else. I was supposed to join them in this morning's assault, but I overheard someone talking about you and how you had turned up in Ephesia. They said you were being brought here, to this prison, so I stayed back and waited. We were so worried about you—you just vanished after the funeral. For a time, I didn't even really believe it was you coming back here; there has been so much propaganda. So many false sightings and lies about where you are and what you have been doing—and that you're pregnant." She motions to my stomach.

"I'm not pregnant. Not possible," I assert, implying my virginity is still very much intact. I grab her hands through the bars. "I am so sorry for leaving and worrying you all. I made a poor decision and went out by myself when I was upset. Malakye's men caught me—but that is a story for another day."

She looks at once both perplexed and horrified, but before she can speak, I ask urgently, "Where is Imani?"

"She is in Ammon. And hasn't returned since *he* got here." She glares in the direction of the large hall in which Abramovich has set up his court, a floor above us.

"Good," I say. In the matter of piety, Imani is beyond reproach, but I still hope she will stay in Ammon and out of sight until all this blows over. "Theia, you need to get word to Joshua. I have reason to believe Abramovich plans to execute Shreya, and we need to act fast."

"What?" she says, her voice quaking.

The guard now turns around and taps his wrist. "Time's up."

"Go now," I whisper. "Go directly to Joshua and tell him he needs to come back."

Theia nods, squeezes my hand, and is gone.

I try to sleep on a pile of hay in the corner of my cell, but I am too restless. Hours pass, and a guard eventually brings me gruel and water at midday and then again at dinner. I do not see Theia again. I wonder what became of Eskara, hope that she got away safely, and am increasingly aware I have yet to face Abramovich. The thought alone has my stomach in knots.

As night falls, the world quiets, and the lights become low. Eventually, it is completely black in my cell.

Before dawn, I receive another visitor. My owl eyes have adjusted to the darkness, and I watch the cloaked man sweep in. He slips past the sleeping guard and approaches my cell.

I meet him at the bars. His hood falls back as I pull him to me and press my lips against his. Xavier returns my kiss, lips burning against mine in electric silence.

For a moment, it does not matter that we are in a dirty cell, that we are at war, and the world has been destroyed. Nothing matters but that we are in the same universe, on the same planet, born in the same time line, and that we are together again, reunited.

But soon, I begin to feel distant, outside myself, and after a few minutes, I pull back and say softly, "You were a stranger when you returned."

Xavier exhales but does not let go of my face. "I'm sorry I didn't tell you before," he says, pulling back but not letting go of me and not looking away. "But God, I can't stand to lose you again, Hella."

"I know some of it now," I say. "I spoke with Konstantin."

He nods in understanding, and his hands, through the bars, move from my face to my waist as he tries to pull me close again. "You're freezing," he says. "Take my cloak." Stepping back, he pulls the heavy robe over his head and passes it through the bars to me. I wrap up in it, soaking in the warmth from his body that still permeates the fabric.

"If this burden must be passed to you—if there is no preventing it—then I would rather you hear it from me than another," he says, his eyes earnest and steadfast. Stepping forward again, he takes both my hands in his, and we remain entwined as he begins his story.

"Both my parents were subjects of the Institution's experiments. Like you, they were clones, but not of anyone important—just regular people. But the thing about clones—" He pauses, takes a breath, and looks at me steadily as he continues. "Cloning humans can introduce profound genetic errors."

I swallow hard, suddenly uneasy.

Xavier looks at me intently as if gauging how I am taking the news of what he is saying. "And it did with my parents."

"Well, what kind of errors—what happened to them?" I ask.

"Mostly, it manifests in mental illness, in psychotic episodes—detachment from reality, delusions, hallucinations, and ultimately results in an early and painful death."

I nod, processing what he has said, willing myself to stay strong and not jump to conclusions.

"But the symptoms don't show up right away; there is a late onset . . ."

"When?"

"Adulthood. The sickness typically presents around the twentieth year. My mother became unstable soon after she married my father, just after her twentieth birthday. They adopted me not long after, which is another story in itself."

"I'm sorry," I manage. I had no idea his mother had been so sick. "You know I would have been there for you," I say, frustrated. I have always known he struggled with some kind of darkness. But since he would never acknowledge it, I did not know how to help him. "Why did you never tell me?"

"Hella, you did help me—just by being there, and just by being *you.*" He smiles a little. "But I chose not to tell you because I knew you were a clone, too. And since the sickness isn't a sure thing, I didn't want you to live your life in fear of something that may very well never be." He pauses, searching my eyes for understanding. "And if it did happen, I wanted you to live your life to its fullest in the time you did have."

He is quiet for a moment, then looks at me, contemplative. "Besides, I didn't want to risk triggering the visions by telling you about them if maybe they hadn't started yet on their own."

I avoid his implied question, not wanting to face any possible truths just yet. "How did you learn I am a clone?"

"Konstantin. We crossed paths when she brought you to Imani. She saw me playing in the fields, and I was struggling. You see, I am not from Earth," he explains. "While I was born on Earth, in a lab just like you were, I developed from an embryo conceived on Elysium in TRAPPIST."

I nod slowly, trying to process the implications of his words.

"The people of Elysium, we are born empaths."

I give him a quizzical look.

"It's just another anomaly in our DNA. It could be an unintended side effect of genetic engineering, like the infertility that became so widespread among the people of the Institution. Or maybe it was intentional—the product of another experiment conducted by the Founders who engineered our world, seeded, and planned our civilization. We don't know for sure," he offers matter-of-factly. "But as a result, the veil is very thin for us between this life and the next, and I couldn't handle the emotions bombarding me from every direction. From my parents—my dying mother and grieving father—strangers suffering in the war, spirits from the last life and the next . . .

Had I been born on Elysium, I would have been taught to train my mind and to leverage coping mechanisms at a young age. But here on Earth, I did not have those resources and suffered alone—until that day, at least. Konstantin helped me for a time. Taught me a few things, told me who I was and about my home world. She helped me learn to discipline my mind."

I look away for a moment, trying to sort out the time line relative to my memories of our early days, meeting Xavier for the first time as kids, growing older into our teen years, and eventually becoming inseparable.

"But it was just a temporary fix," he continues evenly. "I was better for a while, but things got bad again when I lost my parents."

"You never told me what happened that day." I remark.

"It was too difficult to talk about before," he says ruefully. "But I have made peace with it now. Early that day, my mother was abducted and taken to the factories, and my father died trying to save her. She had been picking blackberries for harvest moon pie when they came in—took her and slaughtered him in front of both of us. I was thirteen years old, and the trauma of witnessing that destroyed every stronghold in my mind. Defenses I'd spent years building were plowed through like tissue paper.

"In the days after, I found a way to contact Konstantin, and she eventually told me about you. Said there were answers in TRAPPIST for both of us. She explained how the people of Elysium are less advanced in technology but more advanced in methods of the mind."

In the dark of the prison cell, understanding unexpectedly begins to wash over me.

"I knew I would have to go there one day," Xavier continues, still holding me as close as the iron bars allow. "I always knew I would have to leave you, and it weighed heavily on me. I put it off as long as I could, but outside the galaxy, the psychic pull was too strong."

He finishes with a heaviness, a familiar gloom settling over him that I recognize all too well from the old days: *Xavier's darkness.* Back then, I never fully understood the shadow over him; other than it was something born from his losses, but now it seems it was that, plus something more. He had carried the grief of the world and of lifetimes past . . . I hate that he carried that burden by himself.

"Well, how are you now? Did you find help in TRAPPIST?"

"The oracle there introduced me to a mage who showed me how to harness my mind—to block it all out, those *images*—how to lock those parts of my psyche and release them again if I needed to. But yes, I can say that it no longer ails me."

"And what about me? Any answers for my . . . condition?"

"Yes and no," he says grimly. "There was nothing they could relay that I could do for you here on Earth, but they can help you if I take you there . . . to TRAPPIST."

"I see," I say, trying to wrap my mind around that prospect.

"Well, has it happened? The psychic breaks?"

I am quiet for a moment as I think over the last several months. "I . . . I'm not sure," I answer, recalling the strange dreams and, yes, visions I have been experiencing. I recall the young girl I keep seeing. Spending time with her has been a comfort, but has it all just been a manifestation of mental illness, these psychotic breaks clones are prone to experiencing?

"Well, it may never happen to you. It didn't for my father."

I exhale, struggling to find comfort in his *maybe.* "I still wish you had told me," I say, but with a little less conviction than before.

"Many times I wished that I could."

I look back at him, still conflicted.

"I went to TRAPPIST for both of us, but I came back for *you*," he says. "I returned the moment your consciousness entered this realm again—as soon as you woke from cryo-sleep."

"You can sense my mind?"

"Yes—I didn't know *where* you were, but I knew that you *lived*. I thought you were gone, that you had been killed in Earth's war, and tried to live my life out there without you for years."

I raise an eyebrow.

"Yes," he answers the unspoken question on my heart, "with others, at times. But it was never enough. There are pieces of me that would starve to death, would die with anyone else . . . Pieces of me that are unseen, unacknowledged, or misunderstood by others—but that you understand. These parts of myself, I thought *had* died . . . until now." His eyes bore into mine with a still intensity.

I am stunned by his words, these revelations. There is some relief in having answers, in knowing the truth. But these truths, while they explain questions that plagued me for years and perhaps resolve ambiguities that haunted me for longer, they quake through me like bombshells.

"But what about the child?" I ask, on edge. "Captain Leng said something about a child in the message he relayed to me from you." I pause, trying to recall the details. "You asked me to love the child, *as if he is my own*. And now . . . now Abramovich has manufactured a child in his lab using my DNA!" I exclaim, wondering if it could be the *same* child he referred to in his message, if there is a connection. "But how could you know about that?"

He looks at me knowingly just as a guard storms through the door, dragging several drunken men behind him and waking the officer on duty. He sees Xavier and says, "Visiting hours are over—out!" as he shoves the three men into the cell next to mine.

I reach for Xavier, and our fingers touch momentarily before we are pulled apart and he is shouldered out by the guard. When I turn around, one of the men in the cell beside me is speaking to me.

"Did you hear? The woman, she dies at dawn. The heretic. A big show: We are all to stand witness. Even us prisoners," he finishes, laughing maniacally before turning back to his comrades.

52

With hands bound, I have been temporarily released from my cell along with the other prisoners so that we may bear witness to today's trial. It is the first time I have laid eyes on Abramovich since escaping Proxima, and looking at him the way he is now boils my blood.

Stationed on a dais set up at the front of the performance hall, he is dressed in the finery of a priest, and it's impossible not to notice the fresh scar around his neck from his latest head transplant. While I'm looking, he lifts his hand to adjust his collar, covering the recent surgery self-consciously as if he can sense my eyes on him. When he lifts his hand, his sleeve falls back to reveal a dark-skinned arm that does not match the color of his face. *Taj's arm.* I could kill him right now if I could reach him—if I weren't sweating it out down here in the pit below the stage with the other prisoners.

Peeling my eyes from Abramovich, I scan the packed room. My head throbs as I observe the audience bustling with onlookers. I didn't sleep a wink, and it is now only a few minutes before dawn—the hour Shreya is scheduled to die. The seating area behind the pit is filled with civilians, mostly those who journeyed here from Cana Minor—Abramovich's radical followers. There are a few of us remaining who hail from Cana Major, though we are not many. Those of us who haven't died on the battlefield—as any civilians who can fight, *do fight*—are fighting at this very moment on the front lines. Joshua is one of them. I can only hope Theia got the message to him with enough time for him to return and stop Abramovich from enacting this bloody execution.

But Theia is not here; hardly anyone I know is. After a few minutes, I finally spot Xavier above me in the civilian section of the audience. The only reason he isn't on the surface fighting with the others is because he rushed back last night after catching wind of my return to find me in my cell.

My stomach is in knots, and I am wringing my hands nervously when the Cana Minor Royal Guard enters and brings in the prisoner.

Shreya's hands are bound. The soldiers seat her in a chair on the platform. My mouth turns to sandpaper when I see the rope they lower from the high ceiling, which they then loop around her neck. She looks completely calm, her face expressionless, almost bored, as she settles low in the chair, arms behind her back and knees propped up. Her hair is tied back, and she is in her usual fatigues. As strong as she looks, I can tell she is tired, as we all are. Tired of this war, tired of fighting.

A man approaches to question her. Laying a book out on a small table in front of her, he begins: "Acknowledge the chosen prophet, Mordecai Abramovich, of the Lord your God, the Father and the Almighty, as speaker for the Holy in the realms of man, and in so doing swear your eternal fealty and loyalty to His humble servant, in the name of *the* Father, *the* Son, and *the* Holy Ghost."

"I won't," she says firmly and definitively, nearly cutting him off before he finishes speaking.

He clears his throat, then continues. "Swear that you serve the one God, God *the* Almighty, maker of Heaven and Earth, of all that is seen and unseen and that you will worship Him and swear by His name, renouncing all false gods, all idols other than the Almighty, the one God, Savior of man and giver of life everlasting."

"I won't," she repeats, her jade-green eyes on fire.

The rope around her neck tightens, and she begins coughing. The irony is that Shreya does believe in God, the same God Abramovich worships. She just does not condone mind control nor will she tolerate fanaticism. She believes everyone should be free to practice whatever religion they like or not at all if they so choose.

The man shifts on his feet and shakes his head nearly imperceptibly before beginning again. He then runs through a laundry list of sins Shreya supposedly has committed against God, citing the time, date, and witnesses of each event, all of which are obviously false and fabricated, considering she hasn't been anywhere other than fighting on the front lines since the battle began weeks ago. Once he is finished reading the long list, the length and excess of which designed to be another intimidation tactic, he demands, "*Confess* and *repent* for these egregious sins committed in the name of *the* Father, *the* Son, and *the* Holy Ghost," he intones. "Child, I implore you, *confess!*"

"I won't," she says resolutely for a third and final time.

Abramovich then nods to his men, and they string her up. She is jerked into the air, hoisted roughly, and hung by her neck, a demonstration of brutality that is true to the archaic ruthlessness and inhumane violence he is known for, and that is synonymous with biblical times on Old Earth. It isn't meant to break her neck like a traditional hanging: It's a torture device meant to kill her slowly by strangulation. She gasps for air and frantically tries to lift her bound hands up to tug at the tight noose around her throat. As she does, my eye is drawn to the left side of the room: a blur—a figure—sweeps in, is on the stage faster than anyone can stop them and is on Abramovich within seconds.

"This is for my son," the woman seethes as she buries a curved blade deep within Abramovich's chest—truly, Taj's chest. "You will not use his body for this evil. You had plans for my child's future? Well, I have plans for *yours*," she finishes as Abramovich crumples to the floor beneath her knife.

I am stunned when the woman turns, and I see it is Imani who bears the weapon—the fatal blow brought by her hand—that it would be she who may sound the death knell for this wicked man in a last-ditch effort to save our dying civilization from his unrelenting wrath.

Part of me cringes since I know Taj's body is on the receiving end, but a body can only be transplanted once. The transplant would not succeed if we tried to put him back together again—*such a ludicrous thought!* It is no longer Taj's body, not truly. *He is gone,* I tell myself sternly and will myself with all my power to accept it.

Abramovich's armed guards are on Imani within moments. They disable her with a crude variation of a taser. In the chaos and with Abramovich down, several prisoners suddenly scramble over the wall and onto the platform, swarming and overwhelming the men operating the pulley system beneath the gallows. They have Shreya released within seconds.

Xavier appears at the edge of the pit. After shouldering my way over to him, I jump up to him with my arms over my head. He catches me by my wrists, then hoists me up, gripping my forearms and then shoulders, pulling me out of the sunken area below the stage. Then he cuts the bindings with a sharp knife he carries at his belt, freeing my hands.

We go straight to Imani. I cry out as her body begins to convulse. *Was their weapon set to kill?* I wonder in horror, then fall at her feet.

Two of Abramovich's guards turn suddenly and grab Xavier. "You will pay for this with another Canish male," one of the men drawls. Then they leave, dragging away both Abramovich and Xavier.

I move to go after Xavier, but he shakes his head and then nods toward Imani. The two guards quickly bind his wrists behind his back as a third guard hits him in the stomach to urge him forward. He doubles over and then is gone.

Turning back to Imani, I check her vitals and frantically try to resuscitate her. Minutes later, Joshua and the Canish Guard storm the room and clear out all that remains of Abramovich's Royal Guard.

Eskara accompanies Joshua. She rushes to my side as Imani begins to stir. I exhale in momentarily relief but find Imani incoherent. Eskara scans her with an instrument she carries in her pocket and identifies a massive burn on her abdomen.

"Her organs have been affected," she says grimly. "I can save her if I can get her back to Bleausphere. We have a scarce few donors on reserve."

"*No,*" Imani says firmly as she seems to regain consciousness.

"*What?!*" I scream in protest.

"I don't want it . . ." She shakes her head, eyes fluttering shut, exhaustion lying heavily on her. There are those who fear death, and then there are the strong ones like Imani who have lived their way to a place where the fear of death no longer holds dominion over their days.

"Please, I *need* you," I beg desperately, selfishly.

Twenty years Abramovich has taken from us, a loss I begrudgingly accepted under the assumption that we would have at least twenty more. Imani is everything good in this world, and the simple truth of it all is that I cannot bear to face a world without her.

When she does not respond, I check her pulse again. It is thready and faint. Anxiously gripping her hand in mine, I feel that she is trembling. Maybe it isn't that she does not fear death; maybe she does—just as much as I do. But what she has is the courage to face it, to accept it. It is something I couldn't do. The most I can do is to hope beyond hope that death is perhaps not the end. That one day, I'll be reunited with all those who have been lost. That somewhere sweeter, somewhere greener, we might see one another again.

<h1 style="text-align:center">53</h1>

Abramovich arrived on Earth with a fleet of three transport vessels, each large enough to carry twenty thousand people. He came with plans to transport the people of Cana back to Proxima, but not before he successfully eradicated from the population those whom he deemed faithless.

Today he left in a rush on his famed flagship, *the Prophet*, still bleeding from his wounds in the medical bay. He took with him his dozen or so service bots, a good number of the Royal Guard, and Xavier in chains. I know what they plan to do with him. But I can't catch them in *the Phoenix*; the ship isn't fast enough. FTL-class vessels travel in a series of jumps faster than light speed, with intermittent sub-light travel in between. Small vessels like *the Phoenix* make significantly shorter jumps than larger ships such as *the Prophet*, making *the Prophet* a much faster vessel. Unless he can find a way to escape after they arrive on the planet, Xavier will suffer the same fate as Taj—but this time, the transplant surgery will not be consensual.

I curse myself for getting involved with Gemma, for accepting her help and her generosity so freely, and I can't help but feel responsible for the deletion of her program—the severing of her consciousness from this realm. Because of me, she would not be there on Proxima to possibly help Xavier when he arrives. And he must escape. He must live, somehow.

Again, I find myself far away and powerless across the universe while the same cruel tyrant exploits yet another life that is dear to me. I'm certain Abramovich will be in cryo-sleep for the return journey to Proxima. Keeping him in stasis while in transit will preserve his life until they can perform yet another life-saving transplant surgery in the planet's well-equipped laboratory. I pray that when he wakes, he will die before his men can save him, before Xavier's life can be traded for his.

Imani is in a coma under Eskara's care in Cana City, her life still hanging by a tenuous thread. Joshua and I are consumed with worry but reluctantly agree to honor her wishes that there will be no emergency transplant surgery or the use of any life-extending bio-drugs to save her.

When Eskara and I were separated at Ephesia, she circled back and met up with her army. They joined the Canish Guard on the battlefield just in time to relieve Joshua and a small contingent of soldiers, enabling them to return to Cana City and help stop Shreya's execution.

Shreya was unscathed, mentally and physically. She is a rock and back in action, harrying the front lines by lunchtime. And I am by her side. In fact, I am so racked with fear and rage I cannot stand to be anywhere other than astride Legend, hacking and slicing the heads of the Regime's cyborg soldiers as swiftly and methodically as if I were threshing wheat in our fields back home in Cana. That life is so lost to me now, so foreign an idea that I can no longer relate to it, can no longer recall the person I was before; my life has been so wholly reordered around this one task of killing.

The Greybeards are competent soldiers and stand strong beside us, but despite their heroic assistance, we are still losing. They bought us days, but it is now nearing sundown on the third day, and the battle will likely be decided within the hour—and not in our favor. We haven't been back to the city since Shreya's trial. We no longer have enough men to fight in shifts, so we have set up a small camp a short distance from the fighting.

The ground around us is covered in corpses, fallen cyborgs twitching in pools of black blood, and fallen men with cracked helmets, visors blown out by cyborg disrupters, and broken limbs inside inert EVA suits. The helmet—or, more specifically, the visor of the helmet—is the Achilles' heel of our formidable armor. Graphene cannot be made fully transparent, and thus, to ensure visibility, cannot be used in the visor in its purest form. This limitation leaves our helmets more vulnerable than the rest of our suits.

We have tried to salvage as many suits as we can as we take our losses, but just don't have the manpower any longer to do much more than temporarily stall the endless advance of Malakye's army. Many of our people just simply lie down out of sheer exhaustion, give in, and die under the deluge of monsters that continue to pile up on top of us.

Reigning back Legend and closely accompanied by Ramses, I scan the battlefield just ahead and admit I don't know how much longer I can hang on. Still, I manage to keep a vigilant eye on Theia, Raven, Shreya, and Joshua to ensure no one goes down. Even though I had been in poor health when imprisoned in Malakye's dungeons, I recovered while in Bleausphere and in transit. I ate and rested well enough on the days we traveled back to Cana City, so I am relatively fresher to battle than my peers, who have been fighting around the clock during the weeks I was gone. The Greybeards have stood strong but are waning, too, as the sleepless days mount. We are men, after all; our endurance finite—unlike, it seems, the soldiers we are facing.

Just as we make a little headway, clearing the latest wave of cyborgs and reducing the swarm to a manageable number, a distant horn sounds. I look to Theia, who is closest to me, maybe thirty yards away, and see that she is leaning forward in exhaustion on her horse's neck, her sword dangling precariously.

Don't drop your sword, I think as if I could send her a message telepathically. After slinging possibly the fiftieth cyborg head of the day to the afterlife with my glowing *khopesh* sickle sword, I ride over to her with Ramses on my heels. Sword scabbarded, I signal for him to guard her other side. She drops her sword.

Shreya and Joshua fight furiously side by side, taking on a group of ten or so foot soldiers. They are moving slowly but managing them. Noah and Raven are farther away, to the left, facing much larger numbers in a phalanx shield formation alongside the Greybeards.

It's obvious Malakye's army outflanks us with impossible odds. Still, we have managed to keep them at bay over the last few days by positioning ourselves between a steep hillside and a massive barricade we constructed. By piling up our dead graphene suits, we succeeded in constricting the size of the battlefield and limiting Malakye's access to our position. This ploy has been working well enough for the past few days, but I don't have a good feeling about how things are developing.

I move to retrieve Theia's weapon and return it to her as the horn I heard earlier sounds a second time, and I understand that it is coming from the opposite direction, from behind us.

Signaling Legend to pivot, I quickly scan the icy desert plain to the east of the battleground, using the long-distance zoom lens built into my helmet. To my horror, I see a retinue of at least a thousand soldiers advancing on our camp from the rear.

I look over to Joshua and Shreya, and observe that they, too, have seen what I am seeing. The army must have passed through the mountain range to the north, marching the long way around, which is out of range for our drones, and then circled back to take us by surprise.

Breath heavy and shoulders stooped, we watch their advancement powerlessly. Then we notice that part of the group is splitting off and marching toward the entrance to the underground. It seems that they are so confident in their numbers that they are sending half their troops to the battlefield to finish us off and half directly into Cana City to begin their occupation and enslavement of our people.

Glancing back to check on Theia, I see that she is now sitting up again but facing the other way. Her head tipped back, she is looking up at the sky. I ride over to her, calling out her name.

She looks over at me, smiling, relief and elation flooding her features. She then points to the sky. I follow the direction she indicates, but all I see is the murky cloud cover of the stormy nuclear night.

I look away for a moment behind me to check on the status of the advancing army, and when I turn back toward Theia again, it's as if the sky has cracked open. A dozen Alliance fighter jets drop from the heavens in quick succession. From a crescent formation, they dive-bomb the army of cyborg soldiers advancing from the rear, raining hell on Earth down onto the remaining faction of Regime soldiers.

54

The Regime is decimated in minutes. Our small contingent stares in awe at the charred land that is now no more than a graveyard of fire, blood, and scorched steel, not a hundred yards away and directly adjacent to our camp.

The Alliance fleet has landed about half a mile to the south at a safe distance in the middle of the desert. It's a short ride over to meet them.

I dismount my horse as their leader climbs out of his cockpit. Walking to meet him with Joshua and the others following close behind, I see that none other than Commander Jonathan Avery has come to our rescue.

Avery steps forward with an outstretched hand. I quicken my step and nearly topple him with my enthusiasm as I take it. He laughs as his companions climb out of their respective ships.

"Welcome to Earth, Commander," I say.

"Thank you, sir," he says. "I received your message and was able to arrange leave with the station captain to come to your aid. After you left, Ensign Aarons put in a significant amount of work on our jets to equip them with cloaking and shielding technology that allowed us to breach the electron belt and arrive today undetected by the enemy. We are in his debt."

Theia, Raven, and Noah are all visibly moved by his mention of Josiah and his contributions. "He would have liked to have been here," Avery adds.

"He is alive and well?" I ask. "I tried to reach him weeks ago but did not hear back." I nearly forgot that I had sent a second message that night in Ephesia, as an afterthought, when I contacted Josiah for help. The message had been to Avery, a last-ditch effort in the wake of Josiah's silence.

"Yes—he has been detained in the mines, which are still occupied by Chiron's forces," he replies.

"Cassini!" I curse quietly to myself.

"He is being held as part of a prisoner trade deal as we continue to negotiate peace terms with their leadership."

I do not like the sound of that—none of us do—but it explains the unanswered messages. "Understood. Well, he is sorely missed," I say, motioning to Josiah's family and then turning back to Avery. "Congratulations on the promotion, sir. Where will you be stationed?" I ask, observing his new captain's status, indicated by a small sapphire insignia on his collar.

A genuine smile stretches across his face, something I never once witnessed in the time that I knew him on Titan Station, as he replies, "I am honored to say that with your leave, sir," he turns to Joshua, "I have been appointed to serve as base captain of the Alliance's old territory on the moon, to begin the effort of rebuilding Selene."

Raven is visibly elated, nearly exploding with glee when she hears this about the moon, while everyone claps in celebration, congratulations, and recognition.

"Well, yes, sir, you do not need my permission. But nonetheless, if Freeman feels my approval is needed, then by all means, you have it," Joshua says.

"We recognize your leadership on this planet and are eager to continue the discussions Ensign Nazari has initiated to formalize our relationship as allies," Avery replies.

Just then, the Greybeards make their way over, and introductions ensue. Eventually, we all move underground and make the return trip to Cana City. It is ultimately decided that in the coming days, once we are certain that the Regime is no longer a threat, everyone will travel to Bleausphere to begin treaty negotiations and the formalization of an alliance between our peoples.

In the coming days, all is quiet on the Regime's front. We send out patrols and drones daily. Our intel reinforces our belief that the Regime has been defeated and the war is won. A quiet peace settles in among the factions back home in Cana City. There has been no word from Abramovich's ship, and his propaganda channels are equally silent.

On the same front, I have had no communication from Xavier. Sick with worry and unable to bear the thought of losing him again, I decide to stay back in Cana City with Imani, whose health still has not improved, while the others go on to Bleausphere. That way, I can remain close to her should she need me and be available on the off chance that Xavier is able to send a message.

Ramses and I spend our time with Smithy down in his shop working on suit repairs, studying the two mammoth ships Abramovich left behind, and trying to find a way to track *the Prophet*, which is still in transit to Proxima. I have had a lot of quiet time to think about everything Xavier shared with me, and it tears me up to think of him struggling alone all those years. I understand now why he felt he had to leave for the TRAPPIST system, and I don't fault him for doing what he had to do to look after himself.

A part of me still wishes he had told me and hadn't left me in the dark all those years, but I acknowledge that he was trying to protect me. I wonder what my life would have been like if I had grown up knowing my own mind was likely to deteriorate at the early age of twenty-one. My dreams would have likely come to a screaming halt, and had they, what would that have meant for the path I chose? The path I walked that landed me here, where I stand today. I don't know that I would have had the same motivation, the same conviction to walk it, to succeed, had I felt I was living up against a ticking clock, that such an early end could be in the cards for me.

From that perspective, I understand that he made the right choice in keeping that knowledge from me, protecting me, and beyond that, crossing the universe and giving up a promising career with the Alliance to seek answers. And for that, I am forever in his debt. I regret pushing him away when he returned and having such little faith in him. I feel ashamed of my anger, the way I treated him, and how I squandered the precious little time we had left to be together in this cruel, beautiful, and finite existence.

Tonight, I lie awake, ruminating endlessly, unable to sleep. After tossing and turning for hours, I finally sit up and put my feet to the floor. Ramses stirs, and I reach over to tousle his head and rub his ears.

The small box Sumi gave me sits on the nightstand. Smithy had made some modifications to my micro-drone, Bumbly, while I had been away and returned him to me when I left the shop this evening. Bumbly can now travel ten times as far as before and still transmit data without needing to recharge.

I grab the box, launch Bumbly, and pop one of the lenses into my right eye. Lying back on my pillow, I guide his path with my eye movements.

We do not know what has become of Malakye, whether he was left dead, injured, or in hiding. There has been no sign of him on the surface or around the exterior of his subterranean compound at the center of KAU City, but that doesn't mean he isn't inside somewhere. While we have taken too many losses to storm his city and seize control of what is left of it, we have kept weaponized drones on the surface and undercover patrols underground outside his compound around the clock. But tonight, I will find out for certain. I will find him myself, if he still lives, by spying on him from the safety of my own rooms.

Malakye sits at the head of a long table in a remote, dark room I never encountered when imprisoned here before, in the Regime's dungeons beneath KAU City. Quite literally a fly on the wall, I study him meticulously. It took nearly an hour of patient searching to find him. The room he now occupies is beyond the dungeons proper. After passing through five levels of empty, decimated barracks, I found it at the end of a convoluted tunnel after tracing the route from his throne room to the chamber where we visited the Elite Council and Konstantin's holding cell.

Konstantin was missing from her cell, but I found her eventually, alive and at work in a massive laboratory beyond the chamber. Connected to the laboratory, I found this room and Malakye. He appears to be holding a meeting with what's left of his war council, which now comprises two lieutenants who are worse for wear. With missing limbs and eyes, they are all around decaying in real time.

Malakye himself is degenerating, too, and gruesomely. I'm not sure if his injuries are fresh from battle or old wounds he hid from me before. Two fingers are missing from the flesh hand he once used to backhand me in the arena weeks before, and one of his eye sockets appears empty, nothing more than a gaping hole. The hand is black with rot, and I notice he seems to be favoring his leg as he rises to stalk across the chamber.

"Just a few more hours now, master," one of his lieutenants croaks.

"And what of the weapon—the subterranean missile?" he replies, his voice cold and calculating.

"It will be ready for launching at dawn," the man replies.

Malakye swipes a console in front of him, grimacing a little at the pain the movement causes him, and a map illuminates the wall, a map of the underground.

Konstantin enters. Frail and moving slowly, she looks up at the map and then at Malakye before saying, "You don't need to do that. The new army is almost ready. Our objective is to take the Canish people prisoner, not exterminate them. Besides, the most vital subjects are there now, treating with the Alliance."

"Only their leadership is at Bleausphere," Malakye counters. "And they are expendable. The Ninth Battalion will take their civilians."

"You do not understand their society," Konstantin says. "Any healthy adult *fights*. All that is left in the cities now are the children and elderly. We need fertile women and men to do what we set out to do. You have killed off far too many of them already in the field, and now you want to take out Bleausphere?"

Take out Bleausphere!?

I vault straight up in bed and scramble to my feet. Refocusing on the images playing before me through the lens in my right eye, I examine the map more closely. Sure enough, it reveals a course through the underground leading directly to Bleausphere. Did Malakye have this intel all along? Had he just left the Greybeards alone all these years because their infertility made them of no use to him?

"Enough," he says. "I do not need to justify my actions to you."

"You cannot expect me to complete my work if I am not left enough viable subjects—" Konstantin reasons.

"Update me on your other project," he demands, cutting her off.

Konstantin looks away for a moment, then looks back and says, "The Ninth Battalion is in final sequencing and will be ready to march at dawn."

"Stats, please," Malakye presses.

"Twenty thousand molecular bots: steel skeletons with organic flesh. Equipped with a dozen defense protocol fundamentals and two dozen offensive subroutines, aggression architecture, and a weaponry catalog fully enabled with dynamic fission tech."

"And how is this done?" he asks impatiently. "Can you not grow organs, too?"

"We have been through this. I need human embryonic cells to produce human organs. The flesh of the bots is grown from rat cartilage cells. We cannot make anything more sophisticated than filler flesh and skin for the cosmetic aesthetic. We cannot make brains, hearts, or spinal cords," she finishes carefully, as I imagine he may be in dire need of one or all the items she listed.

"I see. Well, you have disappointed me once again, Mother," he replies coldly. "Regardless, prepare the Ninth Battalion to leave at dawn. We will launch the missile in the tunnel in tandem."

"Yes, sir," the other lieutenant replies. "The weapon will be ready at first light."

"Good." He nods. "Leave me."

Mother? Did I hear that right? Konstantin is Malakye's mother?

I am up and pacing now. Malakye is so much older than I am, but Konstantin had maintained her fertility unnaturally—for decades longer than other women—due to the careful procurement, selection, and timing of her transplant donors. I think on this more, and something begins to dawn on me: *Could Malakye be the child whom the Institution would not allow Konstantin to procreate due to the risky nature of the psychological profile that she and her lover's combined DNA would produce?* If true, the Institution, for once, would have been dead right in their judgment to try to stop her. But of course, she had done it anyway—gone around the rules, played God as she saw fit. I am left panicked over the conversation I have just overheard.

I must stop him.

55

This time, I am armed to the teeth when I return to KAU City. Wearing full-body exos, I have hidden blades in five different places, carry two guns, and have my sword slung over my shoulder. Ramses is with me, matching my every step.

I leave through the secret exit in the chapel to avoid stirring up the radicals at Ephesia, but I draw a crowd anyway. They follow me through the city as Ramses and I walk briskly and directly to Malakye's lair.

Approaching the compound, I am not even winded. Sword drawn, I stride through the front arches into the vacant main hall. I go straight to the back wall and down a stairwell that leads into the vast throne room, where I meet Malakye himself. He is waiting for me on his throne, holding a sizeable black staff with a glinting ruby at its head. As I enter the room, I squeeze the handle of my *khopesh* fusion sickle sword, and it thrums and pulses as it's made ready to light up the dark.

I wonder how much warning Malakye has had of my arrival. It is still an hour before dawn, and his weapon and new army will not be ready until then. While I know I have time to stop him, it is precious little.

"You have returned," he states simply as I approach.

"Oh, did you crawl out of the literal bowels of hell just to meet me here?" I ask, amused, outraged, and on the edge of madness.

Like death himself, I point to the two men guarding him, the two lieutenants who tortured me for five consecutive days when I was imprisoned here, and Ramses is on them in seconds. They are carrion. Ramses then moves to secure the perimeter—if there is anyone left in the place to fight.

"Been spying on me? Shame on you, *sister*," Malakye chides. "I'm sorry I was not honest with you before. I am sorry I did not tell you we are kin. Is that why you are angry with me? Because I am a child born out of love and you are a child manufactured in a laboratory, left for dead on a poor man's doorstep?"

"No. I am angry with you for starting a war, for regarding my people as beasts for the slaughter. And I am here to stop you once and for all."

With the effortless agility of a mountain lion, I vault onto the dais and prowl toward him, cornering him against his throne.

"*Once and for all?*" he spits, standing. "Now, that's dramatic. Haven't you figured out by now that I am *immortal?*"

Malakye is tall, towering over me. When he raises his staff, it becomes electrified in the same moment. He swings it out to the right, then sweeps it back in toward my head. I duck and roll and am behind him before he can turn to face me. I kick him hard at the base of his spine, which crackles with electricity when my foot connects with it, and he tumbles off the dais and onto the floor.

I leap to the floor, sword in hand flaming neon. Landing nimbly in a crouched position, I am at the ready before Malakye, with all his ailments, can get up and steady himself.

It really is not a fair fight, but I do not feel obligated to treat him with fairness after all he has done. Besides, today is simple. It isn't about right or wrong, good or evil, or even revenge. It is about doing what has to be done. Nothing more. Doing what has to be done to see that humanity survives. To see that Bleausphere isn't destroyed, that his new army does not rise to take over this planet. I'd avoid killing him if I could but make no promises.

Malakye is weakening under my furious, unrelenting assault, but with a hundred years of training under his belt, he is putting up a decent fight. He wounds me once with a second weapon, a hidden blade he produces from his battle dress with his nondominant hand. Twice, as I duck away from his staff. He then drops the blade, freeing up his hand again to prioritize his staff.

Blood leaks from the fresh, superficial gashes on my right bicep and left cheek. But I am stronger. And I am faster.

I spin, lunging and dodging, hacking and thrashing, cracking my weapon against his electrified staff, and the sound is deafening like thunder clapping. The thunder claps, and the thunder peals, echoing through the rafters, lighting the chamber that is, between blows, dark as night. I thrust and I slice, I thrust and I slice, and alas . . . I meet flesh.

"Aha! I didn't know you had any of the stuff left," I spit as red blood streams from his belly wound. "Flesh and blood after all?" I mock, pivoting away from a desperate sweep of his stick. I have no doubt that one hit from the wretched thing would leave me paralyzed, if not kill me on contact.

"I am just as human as you, wicked sister," he whines as I spin, circling around him.

I know the clock is ticking. Every second closer to dawn ups the ante. I must end this and secure Konstantin before she can enact his plans on his behalf. Feeling my rage rise to the surface, I let it take me. Faster than he can move, I wound him again on the back of his shoulder and again on his thigh.

He takes a knee, weapon still in hand, as I prowl closer and circle him. "Drop your weapon," I rasp in a low, even voice.

He is silent, his head down.

"Surrender," I command more lightly, as if merely suggesting he have a cup of tea and a nap before dinner.

He does not reply.

"Surrender!" I shout with the collective rage and force of all the kingdoms of men who have fallen to evil before this moment.

"Never," he gasps, making a desperate move to lunge for me.

As I narrowly dodge the spectrum of his weapon, his wounded leg fails, and he is forced to his knees again. Spinning around, I knock the weapon out of his hand with a reverse hook kick.

"Dust thou art, and unto dust thou shall return," I intone as I raise my sword and squeeze the handle. It crackles as it becomes lit with fusion. In one clean cut, I slice off his head. It topples to the ground, and his body falls slack.

I exhale and slowly approach Malakye's head, decapitated and rolling. I notice that he again has two eyes, one made of flesh and one made of steel. I snatch the glittering steel orb, still twitching inside his skull, and put it in my pocket—I can't stand to look at it.

Slowly, I scan his headless body and observe all his broken pieces, a mix of flesh and steel cobbled together, repaired perhaps ten times over in some places. A specimen he was that, in the end, truly embodied both man and machine.

I grab his staff, scoop up his head, and run up the stairs. Taking the steps in twos and threes, I exit the compound.

The mob that followed me from the neutral zone remains gathered outside. Fire burning in my heart, fire burning in my eyes, I raise his head high for all to see. I stake his staff into the ground and impale his head on it. I then go back inside to track down Konstantin.

When I return to the throne room, Ramses leads me back down into the compound and takes me to Konstantin. We find her inside her cell. I demand she take me to the missile and disable it. She cooperates—because she does not want to see Bleausphere burn either. When I ask her about the twenty thousand soldiers underground, she insists that the army cannot rise without Malakye. They were made for him, engineered to respond to his explicit command, and with him gone, they will remain dormant indefinitely.

Konstantin is weak, her health failing for some time. She asks me to leave her to die, but I will not. It's a confusing mix of emotions I have for her, but above all, I do not trust her. I do not trust her alone with his weapons, even though I want to believe her wishes do not fully align with his.

When we leave, she is so weak I must carry her. The burden is less with the added strength of my exos but is by no means light, as I am tired myself and sickened over the ordeal with Malakye. But nonetheless, I endure it. Bloodied from my wounds, I carry her back through the city, the neutral zone, and to Cana City through Ephesia—and nobody helps me.

Walking as if in a daze, I am in shock after the confrontation with Malakye. It's not until I am back in Cana City that I begin to process what happened. What I had done.

I have killed on the battlefield to save my own life and to fight for my countrymen, but somehow, this feels different. I sought him out, yes, but it was to stop him from killing my people. Yet it also had been born of my rage; I cannot deny that. Cannot lie to anyone, especially myself, about it—that this had been premeditated.

But had I killed a man, or had I broken a *machine?* Ask me yesterday, and I would think it safe to say the man in him was long gone. But I glimpsed something in those final moments, something helpless—a flickering—something *feeling*, something *alive*, and I extinguished it. There was no doubt that the *something else* that lived there behind those eyes, mechanical or not, was something dark, something sinister. But it was gone now—from this realm, at least. I extinguished the life force that was Malakye. Broken it, disassembled it . . . *But did it matter?*

Would it matter if it had been the man you love, the father, brother, the child whom you love? Would it matter if it had been the *monster* you love?

Imani's life matters, and it has been ruthlessly ripped away from me. I still don't know whether she will live, whether she will rise from the depths of her coma.

Will Konstantin feel the loss of a son?

For that I do not know. But another creeping question now harasses my consciousness. Would reassembling his pieces put

Malakye back together again? And if it did, would such a resurrection result in the *same* monster?

It was Plutarch's mirrorism and Theseus's ship, a thought experiment as explained by the ancient philosopher Plutarch of the Old World, during the first century anno Domini. Theseus, a mythical king famous for slaying a Minotaur and rumored to be the son of Poseidon, possessed a ship. This famed thirty-oared galley occasionally required repairs: When planks of the ship became decayed, Theseus replaced the damaged ones with new timber. Plutarch posed the question, "When the ship's original planks have all rotted away, and one by one, each is replaced anew, is Theseus still in possession of the same ship with which he had first begun, or has a new and different vessel been born as a product of his work and the passing of time?"

Which brings me to examine the other side of the coin: Does reassembling the genetic code of the Virgin Mother ten thousand years later in a test tube rebirth . . . a *saint?*

I ponder the question for some time, turning things over once, twice, three times in my mind, and after recalling the preceding hours, days, and weeks of my life, the answer, which I do not fight, comes to me quite peacefully.

Not in this lifetime.

56

All is quiet in Cana City when we arrive home in the early morning. After seeing that Konstantin is placed under guard and tended to in the infirmary, I hide out with Ramses in Smithy's shop. I don't feel like talking to anyone and still feel spacey, distant, and easily upset. I don't bother telling anyone about what happened, but it isn't long before the word spreads—it turns out there are images of me putting Malakye's head on a spike circulating the underground.

A rather shocking contrast it makes to Abramovich's false imagery and propaganda of the preceding weeks, I muse.

Half-dreaming and half-sleeping on the floor of Smithy's shop, I find myself having another vision. But this time, it is different from all the rest. In a way, it's as if I am talking to myself.

I look back at what appears to be my reflection, and though I can't exactly put my finger on *why*, the image I'm facing is not quite me. We look much the same, but her hair is dark, while mine is still dyed red, and although she is younger, there is also an ancient knowing—a wisdom—in her eyes that is unfamiliar to me.

Then it dawns on me. I am not facing a mirror at all, but Mary of Galilee. She looks to be around thirteen years old. Her olive skin is darkened by the hard sun, and her hair is long and braided. She speaks in the Aramaic tongue, and though I don't speak the language, I understand her. Somehow, I know that I am on Old Earth near the time of their extinction, when the continents were still separated into great islands.

"Your eyes," I say. "I did not expect them to be blue."

She looks at me, smiling with all the azure of the Tiberias shining back at me in her Canish blue eyes, and replies simply, "You are my descendants."

I nod, trying to fathom the path of such a bloodline. But in a way that is typical of my humanity, I am in too much disbelief of all that is not easily understood to truly grasp the enormity of her words. My mind runs in circles as I recount histories and memories that now seem to bleed together—a lifetime in a raindrop, a universe as small. My thoughts wander to the worst of my nightmares of late, and she knows the question in my mind before I can speak it.

Addressing it boldly, she asserts, "*Mordecai* did not want you born; *I* wanted you born."

"But why?" I ask.

"Because I wanted this realm to know my true nature," she explains, brushing a strand of hair away from her face with rough hands, worn and hardened by work in a way that seems out of place on someone so young. "I have been called divine, painted in legend and glory—but I am human. I am *flawed*," she enunciates. "I have been bathed in holy light, drenched in silver and gold, and placed in the company of angels. But in the process, I have been obscured. The *truth* of who I am has all but vanished. Misused in history, I have been altered to further the cause of fanatics, fundamentalists, militant extremists—*hypocrites* in the guise of holy men—those who would control minds."

She pauses thoughtfully before continuing. "But *my skin*, it is not effervescent white; it does not sparkle," she says, shaking her head at the absurdity of the notion relative to the reality of the life she lived, the hardship she endured. "I was but a child when I was called to act as an adult. Robed in rough, colorless cloth, I carried a heart worn by life, struggle, and the brutality of my time—a time and struggle that your modern world couldn't possibly understand." She looks up defiantly and holds my gaze before finishing, "I am not gentle, tame, nor am I submissive . . . my task, *behemoth*."

I nod in understanding, still feeling weary.

She pauses for a moment and looks away. When her gaze returns to me, she is again at peace and awaiting my response.

"But what power do I have to change what has already been written?" I ask. "The pressure is too great; I cannot live up to such an expectation. My life is already steeped in sin and violence."

"Life is not without sin," she says evenly. "And though you cannot see it yet, you have already begun the work to rewrite it. You have brought hope, and you have brought change through struggle, survival, determination, and courage. You have tread through unspeakable violence and unfathomable loss, and I am here to speak with you now, to tell you that it is not over and that you must press on."

I am quiet for a moment, thoughtful of all that has been relayed. "But I can't—I can't find meaning here," I finally say. "I have lost my way, and I cannot know if it is truly *you* speaking to me now or merely a figment of my own madness." Was this no more than the psychotic break of which Xavier spoke—a manifestation of illness—and my life just another tragic case of science gone wrong?

"You will have to decide for yourself. Separate from what anyone has told you. The ones you love most cannot tell you. Even I cannot decide for you."

I feel her light begin to fade away but call her back. "Wait . . ." I say and stop her. "But what about *Him*?"

"He is . . ." she says, smiling, joy coming across her face. "My son—He is a gift, an enigma. He is of my body, and yet He is not."

"But is He . . ." I ask, trailing off, not able to find the appropriate word.

"Every world He has graced, He has carried a different name. It is no matter. He is a force of good. There is no label to be placed upon Him. It is yet another invention of human longing, to label everything and put it neatly in a box."

I look back at her as she recedes.

"Set it free . . ." she whispers, her words trailing into oblivion.

And she is gone.

I still do not feel like I have answers; I do not know anything for sure. But I will try. I will try to keep an open heart and an open mind, and maybe that would be enough.

I wake to find that I have been napping again on the floor of Smithy's shop, falling asleep while trying to make sense of the blueprints we sketched of the transport ship Abramovich left behind.

As I sit up groggily, I realize Malakye's mechanical eye is in my hand. It feels warm. As I open my palm, I see it is lit up when earlier it was dark—broken, I thought. It has come alive now and is blinking—not in a regular way but in a strange, repetitive pattern.

Smithy glances up from his work to see what I am puzzling over, and Ramses sits up, suddenly alert. Then the ground starts rumbling. I don't have a good feeling about this.

"If I'm not back in ten minutes, meet me in the chapel," I whisper to Smithy.

Ramses and I hustle upstairs to the command center. There is a skeleton crew on duty in the absence of the senior officers who are away at Bleausphere, treating with the Alliance and Greybeards. But I find Yash. He already has the surveillance screens pulled up, and his anxiety is palpable.

As he toggles through the screens, which are fed surveillance collected mostly by our drones, a numbing paralysis suddenly shoots through my body as I confront an impossible scene: tens of thousands of molecular bots with steel skeletons and organic flesh are swarming Cana City on all fronts.

Konstantin had been wrong. The Ninth Battalion had risen in the absence of their menacing leader and no doubt had been programmed to come for us in Cana City—even in the event of Malakye's death.

The ground, walls, and ceilings shake around me as they march on us, twenty thousand strong. The river rushes wildly as they swarm our subterranean sanctuary from all sides, quaking the very earth that surrounds the city.

I am on the tunneled streets of Cana City in seconds, joining a contingent of loyal Canish fighters as all hands rush to evacuate our nearly trapped people. I shout commands as we rush dozens of those in danger through the secret exit I had discovered in the chapel. With a deafening roar, Malakye's soldiers suddenly breach our front gates and spill into our precious city level by level. In the city above us, they break the barricade of each door one by one as we struggle to funnel people out through the chapel exit.

An hour has passed, and my people are now well on their way to safety. I have assigned leaders for the rescue and shared with them the maps the Greybeards gave us, but I will not be joining them. I cannot and will not leave Imani. She remains in a coma and cannot be relocated. I begged Eskara to leave so that she could warn Bleausphere, and she reluctantly departed.

Smithy and Ramses refuse to leave my side. Hiding out in a storage room near the infirmary, the thunder of marching bots rains down on us from above. I anxiously look over at Smithy, who is preoccupied with the Greek inscriptions that line even the walls of this ordinary storage closet.

"That script," I ask. "What does it say? What is written there?"

He looks up at me, eyes rimmed in sadness, and says simply, "The words, they are prayers."

We can hear the army drawing closer, soon to be reaching our level. Moments later, what must be a legion of soldiers floods into the great hall outside our storage closet, and just when we think they will break down the doors, they stop.

We hold our breath as long, panicked minutes pass in utter silence. Impulsively, I reach into my pocket and feel for Malakye's eye. I close my hand around the cool metal and realize it is no longer pulsing.

Pulling it out, I flip it over in my hand, and the germ of an idea begins to form in my mind, which I think is surely too wild to be true and certainly an utter impossibility. But as the silence endures, I look at Smithy, back at the eye, and then to the door.

He nods in understanding.

In a desperate moment, I leap to my feet, throw open the door, and see before me rows and rows of Malakye's android soldiers neatly assembled and standing at perfect attention.

As I slowly emerge from the room, I feel the eye pulse to life again in my palm. In unison, the mass of soldiers turns just so slightly in my direction. They salute me, and a metallic voice somewhere among them shouts, *"Ten-hut!"*

I discover I have inherited a twenty-thousand-unit army of robotic soldiers. Konstantin has explained that while the bots were engineered to answer to Malakye, they identify his command by the genetic code programmed into his mechanical eye. When I inadvertently activated the eye in Smithy's workshop, I effectively raised his army and called it to me. Instead of invading the city, they were obeying my unknowing command. Now it seems they recognize *me* as their leader.

The next morning, Imani miraculously woke from her coma. With her on the mend and the majority of the Canish people safely returned home from fleeing, I have decided to go on a hunt. With the strength of my new army behind me, I will cross the galaxy, hunt down Abramovich on Proxima, and demand retribution. While I am aware Joshua and the others will return from Bleausphere in a day or so, I do not have the time to wait for them. I mean to catch *the Prophet* before the Royal Guard can take Xavier's life.

Eskara will join me on the journey in hopes of discovering some possible way to revive Gemma's program on the planet, even if that means forcing Abramovich to do it at gunpoint. We travel by way of the massive transport vessel he left behind. There is just enough room to carry my garrisoned twenty-thousand soldiers, *the Phoenix*, and, of course, Ramses.

57

In four weeks' time, we reach Proxima b in the Alpha Centauri system. We take the compound by force, and after five hours of dogged searching, I discover Abramovich in stasis, suspended in an erect tube of clear liquid. I do not want to believe my eyes that it is Xavier's body his wretched old head is now attached to, but in horror, I observe the proof as I circle the chamber and see the now familiar rows of tattoos striped down the plane of his back.

Abramovich, his small contingency of bots, and the Cana Minor Royal Guard beat us here by a matter of days. I had hoped and I had prayed that we would make it in time to stop the radical transplant surgery, but we discover when we arrive that we are too late.

The sight of Xavier's tattoos brings me to my knees. My face crumples, and I begin retching uncontrollably. Somewhere between blind rage and inconsolable sorrow, I lose him all over again. Listless on the floor, an all-too-familiar path of despair looms before me until, rather suddenly, a cold, blue dawn of understanding begins to break.

Somewhere, somehow, beyond the pain and beyond the sorrow, there is a flicker, an understanding, a knowing, that all is not lost.

Deep in my heart, I knew this would be the outcome. When I lost Xavier all those years ago, I had somehow known that he was truly gone. That our time together had run its course. I had him back for a precious few weeks and am grateful for that. I am grateful I got to see him one last time and finally have answers about what happened to him. But in the process, I have also found that there is more to me than him.

In the days that follow, I find myself grieving deeply once again the gut-wrenching loss of Xavier, but I am also able to draw on the strength that comes from closure. It is a way to peace I didn't have before, and I begin to understand that this loss, though terrible and cruel and regrettable beyond reason, will not break me like I once thought.

However, when I speak of closure, I speak of it relative to the loss of the person I love. In terms of my rage toward the one who wielded the knife, that is another story altogether.

For my rage, I find I have no such closure and no such peace. And when I am sure beyond a shadow of a doubt that Abramovich took Xavier's body and Xavier is now gone—as good as in the ground with Taj—I act on that rage without restraint. That wild piece of myself I so often suppress, I release it now on dark wings to fly vicious and free.

First, I shut down the stasis chamber. Then I drain it and pull this latest version of Abramovich out of the tube. But I do not wake him, no, but carry—and at times—drag his slack body to the ejection tubes in the eastern tower. I hook him up to my very own cryo-pod, the one he and Taj confiscated from me mere months before, and haul him inside it. Finally, I activate life support and initiate the cryo-cooling process.

I know there is no way to take back Xavier's body, no way to save him now, and that I will have to let him go. So, taking both his hands in mine—*Xavier's hands*—I study their beautiful familiarity, trace their lines with my finger, and I lift them to my face and kiss them goodbye. Goodbye for now, but not in perpetuity, for his is a love that will live inside my soul forever.

I then seal Abramovich inside the cryo-pod and prepare to eject the vessel from the tower's small launch bay. As the ejection tube powers up, I listen to the unmistakable suctioning sound that precedes a launch, and in no time at all, he is on his way, out to sea, pitched indifferently into the vacuum of space.

At last, Abramovich is gone from my sight, gone from this planet, and soon to be gone from this system. With astonishing ease, I served him something worse than death—I withheld the freedom, the mercy, the *relief* of dying, and the peace of oblivion. Beyond that, he will no longer occupy space in my head, will no longer stir my contempt, for he is now irrelevant. To me and mine, and the universe at large, Mordecai Abramovich is no one.

I always imagined our end would be more dramatic—a stick fight down the halls and through the catacombs or me telling him everything I think of him, holding him accountable and demanding retribution. But things almost never seem to turn out how you imagine them, do they?

Io is the third-largest of Jupiter's eight Galilean moons. Roughly the size of Earth's moon but with stronger gravity, it harbors four hundred active volcanoes, each standing taller than Earth's highest mountain peak. For millions of years, the tides of Jupiter have twisted and turned the interior of this moon, repeatedly deforming it and fueling its massive volcanoes with lava flows that reach far and wide across its surface. With dark-red polar regions, colonies of subterranean magma chambers, and its brightest volcano, Prometheus, a symphony of combustion and geological instability sends plumes of lava, ash, and sulfur three hundred miles into space, day in and day out, covering the volcano world's surface in liquid fire.

It is to this infernal world that I have sent Abramovich. I don't know when he will reach Io, and I don't care. He will likely travel some twenty years without the aid of an engine configured with FTL technology, but that estimate doesn't account for the potentiality of impacts, collisions, and inadvertent course changes he might encounter along the twenty-four trillion miles of deep space between here and there.

"He's not dying in there . . . but he's not living either," I remark to Eskara, satisfied as I think of Abramovich asleep in his pod, twisting and spooling through the infinite nihility of the cosmos. "He's my prisoner," I say, fingering Malakye's mechanical eye that Smithy fashioned into a piece of jewelry for me before we departed Earth, now hanging as a pendant on a long chain around my neck. "Abramovich took twenty years of my life and everything else from our world. Gemma can decide his fate."

Eskara raises an eyebrow. It is unclear whether she offers me a look of approval or amusement. I cannot read her well enough yet to tell. But I know she is as relieved as I am to have him gone.

We'd had no chance to demand that Abramovich reactivate

Gemma's program. The risk of waiting for him to complete the regeneration process, holding him prisoner in the compound he had meticulously engineered, and then making our demands was too great. But after having time to think about the problem during our journey and gaining some distance from the emotion and drama of what, in retrospect, was looking more and more like just another one of Abramovich's charades, we stopped being sad about it and instead got smart. We knew that when it came to the digitization of information that nothing was ever really gone, nothing can ever truly be erased, and soon realized that there was very likely a redundancy of some sort—a backup program—a way to reboot her here on Proxima.

And we were right. In Abramovich's old office, we found a skeleton code, derived from a redundancy in the system, that only required the input of a segment of Gemma's genetic sequencing to reinstall her program, which we were able to extract from an original skin cell contained in a strand of Eskara's beautiful dove-gray hair.

Days pass, and with the joy of having Gemma back, we begin to make plans to finish the work of readying the planet for the people of Cana. We send both transport ships back to Earth empty, save for a small crew of Royal Guard whom we deem to be most trustworthy. *The Prophet* and newly christened *Prometheus* will offer passage to any citizen of Cana who wishes to relocate to the new world. And after that, we will extend the invitation to all of Earth's refugees, to anyone in search of a better life.

Gemma has activated a program that is near completion, a

holo-habitat similar to Bleausphere that has transformed Proxima to appear just as Cana did before the fall of Empyreus. The people of Cana will live inside this program until the planet is fully terraformed. And thanks to the foresight of Eskara's people, we are able to retrieve copies of the DNA sequencing for the entirety of the animal and plant kingdoms that existed on Earth before the war.

I never thought I would be able to repay Gemma for all she has done for me, but it seems, by bringing her mother to her and by the eventual relocation of the people of Cana to Proxima, in this small way, I have.

After things settle a bit, Gemma asks me to follow her deep into the catacombs of the compound. In fact, we go down the same long hallway and stairwell where I was sure I had sighted the ghost of her once in my early days while imprisoned on the planet—after I had dreamed about her but before I actually met her in the waking world.

Once we arrive at the faraway room, a place stolen away and not on the blueprints, the concealed chamber appears to be just another laboratory, not unlike the medical bay high above us: gray, clinical, spare, and cold.

When Gemma finally speaks, she says, "I kept something for you because I knew it was important to you." Bending to unlock a sealed door on the stainless steel lab station, she enters a complex code into the keypad. I hear the hiss of escaping air as an icy fog slips from the broken seal, and the door groans open.

When the fog clears, I bend down and peer inside. What I see rocks me to my core. Preserved in perfect form is none other than the head of my beloved brother in life and in arms, Taj Furi.

Gemma speaks again. "Well, *two* somethings," she says as she opens the second door so that both doors to the cabinet are now ajar.

The remaining frigid air billows out and finally clears to reveal a second head detached from its body, the head of my one true love, my first and my last, Xavier Trastámara.

Two frozen heads, equally still and preserved, stare back at me blankly in the eternal silence of death. I look at Gemma in shock and horror, too stunned to speak.

She is quiet for a long moment, walking slowly in a thoughtful circle around the laboratory with hands folded neatly behind her back. Then stopping abruptly, she looks me clearly in the eye and says, "What would you say if I told you I can put them back together again?"

58

We had won the war. The Regime had been reduced to rubble. Earth could rebuild in peace, and the people of Cana had a new world to colonize that would one day be as green and biotic as the Earth once was. Abramovich was no longer a threat.

When I first returned to Earth, the odds had been so out of our favor and succeeding had seemed so far out of reach that I thought if we were to somehow claw our way to a victory, that it would be a cold and broken deliverance I would find on the other side of triumph.

And at first, maybe it was that way. In the beginning, I could do nothing in the waking hours but stare at the wall blankly and sleep heavily and soundly through the long nights. But then, when I emerged from that slumber, the life I found on the other side had become something different. Something I had not expected. I found that I had not been left broken and beaten and that I was no longer tired. I had found hope, strength, and confidence unfaltering—things I thought to be long gone with the quixotic ignorance of my youth.

However, while finding this strength has been nothing short of a revelation, there are still unanswered questions and missing pieces. Questions about who I am and who I am to become. Will my lifespan align with that of my clone source and time stretch out before me for years to come? Or will my days be numbered, and I am to suffer from the same mental sickness to which Xavier's mother, as a clone, had succumbed so early in life?

Though many of these questions remain unanswered, they are questions I will have to face. To that end, I resolve, whatever my fate may be, I will find a way to accept it, and until then, I will not let the threat loom over me. Will not let fear control me or cast a shadow over my remaining days.

Then there are the questions that *demand* answers. Questions that have a life of their own and will not—*cannot*—be ignored. The ones that return time and again, demanding I pay homage to their existence, offer reverence to their mystery, and seek explanation for their magic.

Although at times I have felt utterly alone in life and completely irrelevant to the universe or any higher power that may or may not exist beyond the veil, I cannot deny there were also moments when I did bear witness to the *dark* light of faith.

In those fleeting moments, it was unknown to me if the thread of synchrony that seemed to weave its way through this existence could be explained by science, originated from something supernatural or holy, or if they could be one and the same.

But either way, I know I have seen and felt inexplicable things—things so powerful that their existence is incontestable, their nature undeniable. I do not wholly understand it, but know one way or another, there is, beyond a shadow of a doubt, *something* screaming at me from the other side.

If my visions have been real or are truly psychotic breaks from reality—my mind and body degenerating ahead of schedule from faulty genetics—I cannot say. For I do not know for certain where the path ahead leads. Maybe I *have* become that wanderer Dr. Freeman described. Not following a regular course like Earth, faithfully orbiting the sun, but one of those rogue planets without a star.

No, my path is not clear. But I am free now, and my people are free—free from the threat of war and biological enslavement—and that is a start.

But my story is not about war. Nor is it about love—not romantic love, familial love, nor love for the divine. It is not about a dying race, planet, or gods. It is a story about taking action, having agency, and breaking the chains that bind us. It is about burning the labels ascribed to us without our permission and taking your own freedom—doing it yourself because *no one else* will do it for you. It is about standing up for yourself and taking your power back from those who would steal it from you, with or without your consent.

And on the topic of *power*, I'll wield it if I must. I'll speak to those who wish to oppress me and mine in the only language they understand, for strength only understands strength. So be it if that's what it takes to protect Cana, to liberate the Alliance. I know who I am and will not lose myself to it. I will use it wisely.

We will bring the light; we will bring the morning. We will see to the work of rebuilding our worlds, healing our planet, and building anew. I will ensure that the life growing in Abramovich's lab is protected, and I will return to the Alliance to bring Cassini to heel.

Tomorrow. We will begin the work tomorrow, I think as I tighten the girth of my saddle, then swing up in the stirrups. Holding the reins tightly for a moment, I smile over at Gemma, already on her mount. Beholding the majesty of Cana all around, I urge Legend forward and gallop ahead into the canyon. Then, throwing a quick look back at the young girl on her mare not far behind me, I call out, "Gemma, *this* is forever!"

ACKNOWLEDGMENTS

First and foremost, I would like to thank my family. I am eternally grateful to my parents for all they have done for me over the years, for their belief in me, and for their interest in my ideas and my story. I couldn't ask for better parents or better beta readers! Their input on *Sancta Femina* has been invaluable.

Additionally, I wish to express my appreciation for Leslie Hazelton, whose fascinating book, *Mary: A Flesh-and-Blood Biography of the Virgin Mother*, helped inspire my Maryam. I also wish to acknowledge Paul Kriwaczek, whose book *Babylon: Mesopotamia and the Birth of Civilization* was instrumental in shaping my villain with its chilling account of the confession of an infamous dictator. And, of course, I am a long-time admirer of Michio Kaku; his groundbreaking ideas in theoretical physics and cosmology have greatly influenced my imagination over the years.

Robby Berman's article, "The Writing on the Wall: The Collapse of the Industrial Livestock Industry," and Meg Wilcox's piece on

EATER.com, "Why Genetically Engineered Foods Have Some Scientists Nervous about the Future," are both thought-provoking reads that provided me with valuable insights into the latest advancements in biotechnology for engineered foods, discussing ideas such as Precision Fermentation, Food-as-Software, and Protein Disruption. Equally important, these articles highlight concerns about these advancements, reminding us that balancing our excitement about new technologies with careful consideration of their potential implications is essential.

I'd also like to thank Jae-Hwang Lee and his colleagues for their report in *Science Magazine*: "Dynamic Mechanical Behavior of Multilayer Graphene via Supersonic Projectile Penetration," which informed my writing about the properties of graphene and how to overcome its theorized impermeability.

Additionally, I would like to recognize Casey Cordeiro for his article "Sand Sports Super Show: Five Essential Dune Driving Techniques," which helped me imagine what it might be like to drive through the windswept dunes of Titan.

Finally, I would like to thank my husband, Brett, for standing by my side through both the worst and the best of days. His encouragement to pursue writing a novel and his unwavering confidence and enthusiasm along the way mean the world to me.